Lone Wolf

A Grayson Wolf Mystery

Jack ⚡ Kolbë

Cover & graphics by Mangled Wolfang

BadDogBooks

ISBN-13: 978-1976356216

ISBN-10: 1976356210

Family near and far, anxiously waiting with bated breath

Fans, loyal and sincere, eager to travel plot and ploy

Critics, as their wont, declare content but shallow shibboleth

This tome like others before, I offer for all to enjoy…

Or not.

CONTENTS

Chapter 1

A Novel Tangent

"Welcome back to Title Page Live streaming the inside scoop on the latest and greatest books, authors and trends produced by Objective Arts Media broadcast locally and globally via Sirius Radio. I'm Carolyn Mayor and you are listening to a rare and exclusive interview of the life and times of Grayson Wolf, author of over fifteen, indisputably controversial novels based upon the good, bad and often really ugly goings on behind people, events, business, higher education, social and political movements and the real people involved.

"Consistent with past novels, Grayson Wolf has not disappointed readers with his latest fictional non-fiction novel, The Impotence of Being You, that once again showers him with an emotional torrent ranging from harsh condemnation to profuse gratitude...."

"It's a good thing I'm not physically at your studio, Carolyn," Wolf said, "because you'd need to beef-up security at your doors."

"I'm happy to report that our straw poll suggests we'd need to protect you primarily from readers wanting to hug and kiss you." Carolyn laughed. "Of all the authors, you're hands down the most controversial of the hundreds I've interviewed over the years. For the benefit of any listener who is not familiar with your history, would you share what started you down this twisted and treacherous literary path?"

"It was a dark and stormy night," he joked, "when I decided I'd had enough listening to my peers in high school brag about their budding criminal careers and decided to write an account of their foolish decisions, behaviors and the consequences of their actions. I had written about ten thousand words when I lost interest and focused on a new interest: becoming a top ranked poker player. My goal was to participate in poker tournaments and raking in millions from my winnings."

"A goal which you did pursue after high school," Carolyn said. "What happened to make you put pen to paper once again? Playing poker not as rewarding as you thought?"

"The road to becoming a good—a great—poker player can be a rewarding experience: learning to read people, assessing risk, understanding strategy," Wolf explained. "Choosing to become a successful poker player means playing serious money, Carolyn. There came a point when I ran out of funds to continue my poker education."

"So, during your period of self-imposed poverty you turned in solace to writing once again?" she suggested.

"Not even close," Wolf replied. "One afternoon after summer vacation started my dad hustled me into his library and handed me a book called, The Goal. At first, I thought it was some kind of motivational tome but reading it turned out to be *the* pivotal point in my life, though I didn't know it at the time. The Goal is a true account of a factory manager written as a very compelling novel who has three months to get his plant profitable or the company would close it. The author changed the names of the company and all the characters and the book has sold millions of copies over the last thirty years."

"And thus, you discovered fictionalized non-fiction and the rest is history," Carolyn said.

"I wrote Lying and Cheating for Fun and Profit that summer," Wolf said. "Finished it before school started and it hit bookstores before Thanksgiving."

"And six months later you received a very lovely graduation present with many more royalties to follow."

"That first check was more than I needed to re-launch my foray into tournament poker, Carolyn." Wolf confirmed. "Between college and poker, my life was quite full the next few years."

"Including producing two more novels," Carolyn said. "The first about gambling, followed at the end of your college years by the novel that initiated the uproar over your works which continues to this day."

"My mom often reminds me that I've been a disruption in people's lives from the day I was born," he chuckled.

"You do have a *novel* way of really pissing some people off, Grayson." He heard Carolyn's smile through the transmission.

"A classic reaction anytime we pull back the bedcovers and discover the ugly little secrets and practices of hypocritical, malevolent people, Carolyn," Wolf replied. "Which is especially disappointing when the characters in question—elected representatives, CEOs, college professors and administrators—held up as paragons of culture and keepers of civilization's keys, reveal themselves to be mealy-mouthed, self-serving cowards and shysters."

"Which brings us to your bookend novel, Snowflakes to Brown Shirts, published last year about students, staff and the politics at many universities."

"I still get death threats about that book, Carolyn," Wolf said.

"I bet," Carolyn said. "I don't suppose you'd ever consider doing a college book tour?"

Wolf heard the host's chuckle in his earphones.

"Even if I were so inclined, Carolyn, you can be certain I'd be shouted down, spit upon and blocked by arm-linked students preventing my entrance to the podium in the first place. As much as it pains me to say this, I have more freedom to speak in China than at virtually any American university, having done so half-dozen times over the last four years without being verbally or physically assaulted."

"I suppose delving into the depths of the minds and motivations of these self-appointed justice warriors and exposing them as practitioners of intolerance, would cause these true believers to incur spells of rage and apoplexy," Carolyn said. "How dare anyone disagree with or challenge their politically correct narrative. The audacity, the outrage of it. Everyone in the country has witnessed mobs of unruly students shout down speakers, physically blocking writers from leaving their homes or entering public building, firebombing businesses who support an opposing candidate for office, pepper spraying someone being interviewed on the street."

"That, unfortunately, sums it up," Wolf agreed. "The entire collectivist cabal—the politicians who manipulate them, the professors who mislead and incite them for personal fame and the students themselves who choose to follow the herd—are intellectually bankrupt. They have no ideas, no principles, no future. All they have is rage at a reality that refuses to conform to their irrational dreams of that big, cozy nursery in the sky."

Carolyn took a breath and cleared her throat.

"Reading Snowflakes to Brown Shirts, like your other novels, you delve deeply into the minds of these *petits tyrans*, ferreting out their authoritarian ideas, elucidating their dark emotions and articulating their self-justification for actions and beliefs, which turn out to be even more disturbing than seeing these thugs rampaging on the news."

"One need only to spend some time watching the History Channel to see the parallel between our contemporary American Brown Shirts or Red Guards—there is no substantive difference—and their historical counterparts back in Nazi Germany, or Fascist Italy or Communist Russia," Wolf replied. "Like all true believers, they labored diligently to establish the totalitarian paradises that they so loved until death do parted them."

"Besides your novels exploring human motivation and actions through a fictionalized way," Carolyn said, switching direction, "you also founded the Center for Individual Rights. Would you tell us about that and why you created CIR?"

"I created the Center for Individual Rights as the non-fictional philosophical right arm to my fictional left arm," Wolf explained. "My novels record the words and deeds of real people. I explore the fundamental ideas and premises of the story's protagonists, record what they actually said and did and the impact of their actions. The central mission of the Center for Individual Rights is the protection of individual rights. Our website features individuals and organizations identifying each as either a protagonist or antagonist of individual rights based upon their *actions*, not just words."

"And by rights," Carolyn added, "you are referring to the rights enumerated in our Constitution, not invented group rights such as gay rights, women's rights, animal rights and all the other non-rights conjured out of the minds of the legal establishment."

"Absolutely," Wolf agreed. "And don't get me started about the endless assault on certain Constitutional rights by trial lawyers' associations for their fun and profit."

"You did a good job poking the legal bears writing your scathing Screw You, Suckers!" Carolyn said. "Are you and your Center still being sued or have our shining legal vultures finally given up?"

"Shining light on the collusion between legal firms, prosecutors and criminal elements means blowback," Wolf replied. "Corporate lawyers have deep pockets and lots of time on their hands so we still get the occasional suit. But unlike them, we have the law and the Constitution on our side and get the cases thrown out fifteen minutes into a hearing. What I find most disgusting about many of these law firms, Carolyn, is their lack of compunction to attack fundamental rights to make a buck."

"You're referring to the Legal Counsel Task Force's attempts to undermine the Second Amendment by suing gun manufactures and gun shops by claiming that these businesses should be held responsible for the actions people who have bought their guns or criminals who steal weapons or buy them off the street."

"Which is ridiculous, of course," Wolf said. "Weapon manufactures *are* held liable for a product that malfunctions like any other business that trades a product or service on the open market. That case and hundreds more against legitimate businesses is nothing more than an attempt to extort money. What's really sickening, Carolyn, is that these boiler-room law firms routinely represent criminals using illegal guns to threaten and harm citizens, while simultaneously attacking legitimate businesses who sell guns to citizens for protection against the thugs they routinely help to avoid justice. Quite a profitable racket."

"Visiting the Center for Individual Rights' webpage one is immediately captured by its most cheered and jeered feature. Tell us about that, Grayson."

"Often an individual or an organization does something so egregious we feel needs special attention. Then we feature them on our home page's Scum Bucket banner, starring the worst of the worst. Unfortunately, there is an inexhaustible supply of super nasties for that special distinction."

"And that brings us full circle back to your latest novel out this week, The Impotence of Being You," Carolyn said. "Critics point out that the book's title alone presents an existential challenge: am *I* an impotent actor in this world? Do I dare read this book and confront my worst fear: that I may be nothing more than flotsam or jetsam in the stream of life? I admit I was a bit hesitant to open your book."

"My novels function like mirrors," Wolf explained. "The reader cannot avoid encountering one or more of the story's characters reflecting back at him or her. The values, morals and principles exhibited and exercised by my characters are real people acting on ideas and premises they often do not fully understand, often totally unaware of, or work hard to evade. The mirror reflection back at the reader in The Impotence of Being You is much brighter due to the highly personal nature of the story and its characters. It's a compelling account of the evasions and consequences of the choices the characters make and what it says about who they really are and what they could become and might achieve."

"Which brings us back to the outpouring of emotion we see and hear about The Impotence of Being You as we close our show today," Carolyn said. "I believe it's very *encouraging* that a large majority of readers are applauding your books in general and expressing gratitude instead of vitriol as you take them on a journey elucidating the philosophical premises of the novel's protagonists and antagonists and the logical outcomes of the choices they make."

"That so many—tens of millions my publisher tells me—buy and many more read philosophical, psychological novels is itself very encouraging, Carolyn."

"Your books invite," the host paused, "*compels* readers to reflect upon their own premises and how they can liberate their potential to be the creator of their lives regardless of race, sex, age or social situation. You clearly elucidate the consequence of individuals evading these potent principles and how hidden premises can become one's jailers, imprisoning us in a humdrum, deadening existence... Thank you, Grayson Wolf, for the honor of interviewing you today, wherever in the world you are at this moment. I know I am speaking for all our listeners when I say that I'm very much looking forward to your next fictional, nonfiction novel."

"My pleasure, Carolyn," Wolf replied. "Thank you for inviting me."

"One last thing if you are willing to share," she said. "Is it true that a neighbor inspired you to write, The Impotence of Being You?"

"Indirectly," Wolf replied. "A spritely ninety-four-year-old was living alone in a large home with an extensive garden which she took care of. I'd see her working around the home virtually every day throughout the year. It made me worried, seeing her shaky frame and stiff gait, so one day I asked her if she planned to move to an assisted living arrangement in the future where she could live more safely. Her reply was the seed that eventually produced this book: I don't want to be dead before I die... Thank you, Carolyn and all who tuned in to the show today; wishing you and yours, best premises."

Wolf exchanged pleasantries with Carolyn, bid her goodbye, switched off the video link, removed his headset, and got up. The show's host was correct telling her listeners the interview with him was rare, because it was. Far rarer still was Wolf's face showing up on a television screen, or for that matter on any of his books' covers or on the Center for Individual Rights website. The last time his face made an appearance on a TV show or a book cover was when he left college fifteen years ago, deciding that less images meant more privacy, the latter especially important considering the type of novels he was writing.

Fictionalized nonfiction his novels may be, but the institutions and people populating his novels were real. Any reporter worth her salt could, and regularly did, rip away the thin veil of fiction and identify the names of individuals and institutions brining their non-fictional words and actions into public light and more often than not, legal scrutiny. Grayson Wolf and his Center for Individual Rights were popular among his legion of readers and supporters who cheered his unfailing defense of individual rights and the rule of law. Until, that is, they, too, found themselves placed under Wolf's powerful psycho-philosophical microscope and transported into one of his fictionalized, nonfiction exposes, their words and deeds spread worldwide.

A beeping from his phone alerted Wolf that he needed to shower and get ready for the "surprise" reading and book signing event in the Hotel's conference room, something he only did for a special friend, in this case the sister of his publisher. To minimize the chance of news vans, reporters, paparazzi and protestors, guests were not informed that Grayson Wolf would make an appearance, that his editor was doing the honors and signed copies of The Impotence of Being You, would be offered for sale.

The hostess had assured Wolf that guest would be informed moments prior to his appearance that all phones and cameras were to remain firmly tucked away in one's deepest pocket and that any that did appear would be confiscated. Anyone who did not wish to agree with that requirement would be asked to leave at once.

*   *   *   *

The event went smoothly, no one accosted Wolf with a phone or camera and he delighted the audience by offering several anecdotes not included in any of his previous books then answered questions for the next hour. The final segment was the book signing with dozens of excited guests queuing up with one of his books in hand.

Wolf looked up occasionally to check on the headway he was making reducing the line spotting a young woman hanging back near the exit. When she didn't join the queue after a while he assumed she was waiting for someone in line for their book to be signed, but as the queue evaporated and the crowd dissipated into the night, there she was still, hovering near the entrance. Peering directly at her, he noticed she appeared nervous, fidgeting with her purse, shooting him furtive glances.

Whatever she was about, Grayson Wolf sincerely hoped that her objective wasn't yet another demonstration against him. He had quite enough with mobs of self-appointed "freedom fighters" demonstrating for the right to express their opinions by hurling obscenities, bags of animal feces, urine or the occasional dousing of pig's blood at those who disagree with their views—or write scathing fictional exposes about them. There was a reason why Wolf lived and traveled exclusively in states permitting concealed carry and if it turned out this woman intended to execute some nefarious plan, he'd brandish his pistol to discourage any foolish act.

He thanked the beaming hostess for her invitation, collected his things and made for the door, keeping a keen eye on the young woman holding her position as he approached the exit. His free hand drifted toward the subtle bulge near the right hip under his jacket when he saw her take a few steps forward.

"Mr. Wolf…" She hesitated then looked away.

He was inclined to take advantage of the break to make a clean get-a-way but there was something in her expression that spoke of pain, not hostility. He turned to face her.

"Did you want to ask me something?"

"Um … I don't want to bother you," she began, "but I don't really know where else to turn."

Could be a ruse. His hand rested on his side, very near the bulge inside his belt. He was about to ask her how she knew he was here then changed his mind.

"Are you in trouble?"

Her eyes met his. She was young, perhaps twenty.

"Not in trouble." Her voice became more confident. "Troubled. I think I caused a friend to, ah, to commit suicide."

Wolf wasn't sure what to say to that, so he said what had been on his mind when the event ended.

"There's a restaurant a few blocks from here. Join me for some refreshment?"

A wan smile and nod conveyed her acceptance and the pair made their way to the restaurant. Stepping through the entrance Wolf was surprised to find most tables occupied even though it was approaching ten pm. A pleasant attendant led them to a cozy corner table and bid them to enjoy their stay.

A waiter appeared on the heels of the departing attendant. Wolf ordered a beer and an appetizer to share, his companion settled on water. Looking at her troubled expression, Wolf guessed she might not have bothered to eat dinner and insisted she order something more substantial than a garden salad.

Wolf took a draft of his beer. "Perhaps we can begin by telling me your name?"

"Sarah Lewis," she said. "I'm a senior, was a senior, at Overland College east of Castle Rock."

Wolf grinned knowingly. "I've had some experiences at Overland."

Sarah acknowledged his comment with a low snort. "It's what happened to me at the College I need to talk to you about … I'm hoping you might be able to help in some way or suggest someone who might."

The appetizer arrived. They picked at the food.

"At the end of last term..." Sarah kept her eyes on the table, "I was raped... I have no memory of, um, anything."

Wolf said nothing. He knew better than most that keeping silent encouraged others to talk; asking questions, especially under emotionally charged situation, resulted in mouths closing and staying shut. The script unwound as expected.

"I was drugged," Lewis continued. "Rohypnol, they said. The rape kit confirmed that I had been raped. There was semen."

At this point, Wolf felt he could venture a question or two.

"Did the authorities find and arrest the culprit?"

"The police had no trouble finding and arresting him," she replied. Wolf thought he spotted a measure of doubt in her expression. "I knew who it was...he was lying next to me on the bed, asleep, naked. I was, too."

"May I ask you a delicate question?" he said. "I'll understand if you don't want to answer."

A suggestion of a smile touched her lips. "No, I was not partying. No, I was not having sex with the boy. And no, I had absolutely no reason to um do anything to James. That's his name—was his name. James Collins. I called the police and they arrested him fifteen minutes later. Police found the drug in his pocket ... case closed, justice served."

"And yet here you are," Wolf said. "Why?"

Sarah reached into her purse and produced a paper that she unfolded and slid across the table.

"This was delivered to me last week. It was written by James shortly before he killed himself... it was addressed to me and the prison sent it. I've haven't slept much since and um..."

Her words faded and Wolf read the note. It was hand written, the script surprisingly graceful, artistic even. It was short and to the point. James offered a most sincere apology and though he claimed he had no memory of what he had done, accepted responsibility. The note ended with a plea for Sarah to forgive him.

Wolf looked up from the paper. "I would think this note should offer a sense of closure. James admitted his guilt and feeling remorse for his heinous act decided that he could not live with what he had done…" He didn't finish the comment.

Sarah shook her head. "I … there's too much uncertainty about everything. He says he doesn't remember: did they test his blood for drugs? I don't know. He was asleep when the police entered the room and seemed dazed when they took him out. I was directed to visit the clinic where they took my blood, did the rape kit and discharged me. Later I heard that James pled guilty; all the evidence pointed to him. Mr. Wolf, there are too many holes, too many questions with no answers and James commits suicide…" She got up. "You must think I'm crazy… I'm sorry to have bothered you."

"Please sit," Wolf said. "Dinner is coming any second and I don't think you're crazy at all, Sarah. You've raised good questions and my inner writer is telling me there's a bigger story lurking underneath the cover page than meets the eye."

Sarah slipped back into her chair, Wolf figuring the girl's hunger as powerful an incentive as the hope conveyed by his comment, his assumption confirmed when the food arrived and she wasted no time working steadily to consume every scrap of her meal along with the extra rolls provided.

"Now that we've had a chance to refuel," Wolf said, moving his empty plate aside and placing an iPad on the table, "tell me everything you know. Names, contact information, location of anyone connected to you and James in any way, then go over the events again, this time leaving no detail out…"

Chapter 2

Puzzle Pieces

It was a surprisingly mild March morning when Wolf ventured out on his 9th floor balcony of the Colorado Springs Regency Hotel. He took a deep breath taking in the sweet, spring-tinged air, admiring the golden glow of the morning sun reflecting off the peaks of the mountain range looming above him only a few miles away.

He came back inside and headed for the exit, finding the expected collection of newspapers neatly stacked against the wall adjacent to the door. Wolf had access to several papers online but enjoyed the feel of newsprint in his hands, opening its large pages and spreading them across the spacious kitchenette counter to peruse whatever caught his eye first while sipping a hot cup of freshly brewed coffee.

The unplanned encounter with Sarah Lewis last evening had thrown a wrench into his plans to drive up Pike's Peak followed by a visit to Cripple Creek enjoying the sights, sounds and aroma of the old mining town and perhaps even descending into the bowels of the earth and view a gold mine or two. He did indulge in perusing one newspaper this morning after which he packed an overnight bag for his trip north to Castle Rock to begin his inquiry about James Collins at the city's municipal building, housing the county's courts, the police and the prosecutor's office. Coffee being critical for maintaining peak brain function, he filled a large container with the dark liquid at the serving cart in the hotel's lobby and made for his car.

Cruising north on I-25 at a steady eighty, the forty miles from Colorado Springs to Castle Rock was a thirty-minute ride and Wolf pulled into the town's municipal building's parking lot a few minutes past ten thirty. He reached for the attaché containing his case notes from Sarah Lewis and an I-pad, stepped out of the rental and placed the brown cowboy hat on his head. When in Rome, do as the Roman's do and Wolf couldn't resist slipping into classical Western motif complete with boots, jeans and ranch shirt covered by a fawn brown suede coat. The only thing missing was a six-shooter hanging from his hip, though he did pack a Kimber that he locked in the glove compartment before setting out.

Wolf couldn't help grinning at the looks he got walking through the lobby making his way to the police department located in the west wing of the building. He especially enjoyed the humorous expressions of the women, tipping his hat as he passed by, topping off his performance with a wink.

"Well howdy Sherriff Longmire," the police sergeant behind the reception desk said, giving Wolf a most droll expression. "What brings you all the way from Wyoming to our neck of the woods?"

"Rape, pillage and suicide, officer Hernandez," Wolf retorted.

Hernandez became instantly alert. "Who, where, when?"

"Sarah Lewis and James Collins, Overland College, last December."

Hernandez gave a knowing look and nodded. "Got a lot of attention, that's for sure. We don't have much serious crime around these parts, but there's always something foolish going on at the college. Too much money and too much time on their hands; always a recipe for trouble. Sorry to hear about the Collins boy. How may I help you, Mr.—"

"Gray," he replied. "I'm a mystery writer and this case might provide an interesting plot for a future novel. News reports don't provide the detail needed to give me deeper insight into police procedure, full account of the testimony or the motivation of wrongdoers to write a believable story."

"Unfortunately, case files are restricted," Hernandez said. "I can get you copies of the case summary which gives more information than what the media typically reports. To get access to the complete file you'd have to seek a court order and for that you'd need to convince a judge that you have a compelling reason to review the file."

Wolf happily accepted the officer's offer for the case summary and Hernandez produced a form, which he told him to fill out. The task completed, Hernandez led him to a small conference room.

"I'll have one of the clerks bring you the summary; take a couple minutes."

Wolf thanked the officer and took a seat and as promised a young woman entered in short order handing him a thin sheaf of stapled papers.

"This is a copy; you are welcome to keep it."

Wolf thanked her and began to read. He didn't expect to learn anything new and was not disappointed, Sarah having provided more detail than the document in his hands. The only benefit gained from the case summary was a more accurate record of times, something that *might* be important if and when he discovered new information whereby a particular recorded time brought forth an inconsistency or contradiction leading to a new suspect. Wolf did not plan to hold his breath about that happening any time soon. He placed the summary into his attaché and made for the main desk, thanking Hernandez for his assistance, bidding him to stay safe out there on the mean streets. He liked the man, sensing that the officer was okay about him, too.

"You take it easy now, Sherriff Longmire," Hernandez grinned, "and be especially mindful watching your back traipsing around Overland; the she wolves have sharp teeth and I'm not talking about the students."

"You'll be the first call I make if any bare their fangs," Wolf joked, "but first a visit upstairs to meet with the District Attorney and get her perspective about this case."

Hernandez's grin expanded. "She's got impressive fangs, too, so you best tread carefully. Good hunting, but I think you're going to be disappointed finding some dark mystery to write a book about. We investigate a dozen date rape cases annually and the college handles dozens more sex related complaints in-house."

"What's the outcome of your investigations?" Wolf had a good idea.

"Only a few ever make it to trial," Hernandez replied. "Most are resolved behind closed doors by lawyers. As they say, money talks, bullshit walks."

"Which was it for Collins?" Wolf asked, keeping the officer talking. "Cash poor or piss-poor lawyer?"

"Ironclad case, I'm afraid," he replied. "You read the summary: arrested in delicto in the victim's presence, positive rape kit, Rohypnol in his pocket...open and shut. Even if he had tons of money the evidence was stacked against him. Best deal was to plead guilty and he did."

"His family have money?" Wolf already knew that answer, too.

Hernandez looked thoughtful. "Not sure... I had to guess, I'd say no."

"Thanks again for your help, Sergeant Hernandez," Wolf said, extending his hand.

"Always like to help out a fellow lawman," he teased shaking Wolf's hand. "And for the record, you didn't keep me talking."

"Never thought I did," Wolf said. "But I appreciate it nonetheless." He tipped his hat to the officer and made for the staircase.

The door to the prosecutor's offices faced him stepping on the second-floor landing and he walked through the entrance. A receptionist desk occupied by a pleasant looking middle-aged woman guarded the inner sanctum, looked up from her computer as he approached. Judging from the woman's hard gaze, Wolf concluded that guardian wasn't so far off. He imagined her slipping out a sawed-off shotgun from underneath the desk at the first sign of trouble.

"Good morning, ma'am," he said, removing his hat. Gentlemen cowboys do that. "My name is—" he almost said Longmire, "Grayson Wolf. I'm here to speak to District Attorney Sylvia Catelli. I don't have an appointment; I was downstairs meeting with Sergeant Hernandez and thought I'd come up and see if she was available."

Wolf rarely used his real name when out in public, but the name Grayson Wolf did work wonders opening doors; if not for the honor of his visit, then most likely fear of failing to meet with the author of incendiary exposes that have laid low dozens of national figures ranging from CEOs of international corporations to college presidents.

"Grayson Wolf."

She said it as one might say, piece-of-shit. Or maybe he instinctively interpreted her tone in that manner having so often encountered such sentiment in government agencies, corporate

Board rooms, the halls of academia and activist groups everywhere. Millions may love him as the radio host claimed during the interview yesterday, but in the higher echelons of public and private officialdom, Grayson Wolf was as welcome as the plague.

Seeing her hand move, an image of her reaching for a real shotgun nestled under the desk flashed through his mind, but only a phone appeared in her hand. She announced his name and listened for a moment; her lips pressed into a pucker that Wolf imagined to be a smile and hung up the phone.

"Ms. Catelli will see you, Mr. Wolf. Door on your left."

Wolf gave her a warm smile and made for the door.

"Come in Mr. Wolf." The DA stood behind her desk; she was as tall as he. Straight, shoulder length dark hair, dark eyes. "Please sit… how may I help you?"

All business. Someone not to mess with, much like the receptionist out in the entry. He liked her—so far.

"Thank you for seeing me." Wolf took a second to decide what to say next. His ruse with Hernandez about doing research for a mystery novel wasn't going to fly with the prosecutor who handled the Collins case. "New questions about James Collins have been raised and as a favor to a friend I promised to look into the matter."

Catelli's eyes narrowed. "What kind of questions?"

"I understand when Collins was arrested, he seemed dazed and confused." Speak and act like you're in the know and people assume that you are. "Why wasn't he tested for drugs in his system—specifically Rohypnol?"

"Why would the police test him for a date rape drug?" she said, looking skeptical. "He's not the one who was raped; Sarah Lewis was."

Wolf took another leap into the dark. "I would bet that a person under the lingering effects of Rohypnol, a drug that clouds judgment, induces confusion and impairs memory, when confronted with evidence of an assumed crime while under interrogation by the police, might very well believe that he committed a certain crime. Collins never asked for legal representation during his interrogation, did he?"

Catelli looked steadily at Wolf. "Can you produce any evidence that James Collins was drugged? No? Doing research for your next work of fiction perhaps? A tale of corruption and intrigue in small town America?"

"No." Wolf's lips twisted into a grin. "But I'll be happy to autograph your copy of The Impotence of Being You sitting on the shelf behind you."

It did the trick and she smiled, albeit involuntarily. She reached back, retrieved the book and placed it on the desk in front of him.

"Knock yourself out."

He picked up the book and a nearby pen, peered at the prosecutor for a moment then proceeded to write an inscription. He signed it, his bold 'Wolf'—he only used his last name—most certainly visible to Catelli four feet away. He handed the book back to her.

She read the inscription, her eyes growing wider. "You believe me to be a woman of integrity and honesty from knowing me for only five minutes?"

"Ms. Catelli," Wolf began, "I've been immersed in human cesspools for over a dozen years. I knew you were a reasonably upstanding public servant within ten seconds of meeting you." She didn't say anything, but her expression softened slightly. Wolf continued. "I've found most people who work in policing and legal services to be honest and hardworking public servants, as I know you are, too. I assure you I'm not working on a new novel, just asking some questions about the Collins-Lewis case for a friend. If I do find new evidence or uncover some evil conspiracy, you can be sure I'll share that with you."

"Thank you—for the autograph," she said. "Unless you have further questions, I do have pressing business to attend to."

Wolf stood up. "Lunch?" Catelli held up her left hand, a diamond glinting on her ring finger. "It's just lunch, not a proposition."

"You do know that being seen with you outside this office is the kiss of death." She barked a laugh. "Whether my clothes where on or off would not make an iota of difference."

"I was wondering why I keep striking out with women," he said.

Catelli shot him a droll glance. "You're full of it, Mr. Wolf."

His big grin lit up the room. "Like I said: honest. Thank you for your time."

He waved at the office attendant on his way out and made for his car, standing by its open door thinking. Too early for lunch and a change of clothing would be necessary before heading out to the college. Looking like a character out of a western novel was not conducive to blending in on a college campus, even if it was located in a western state. Wolf hopped into the driver's seat, started the motor and headed for the Castle Rock Inn.

His room was ready and thirty minutes later so was he. Looking at the mirror, Wolf guessed that he could pass for some hip college instructor, his outfit a good balance between edgy and fashionably restrained as it should be if he was to blend into the milieu of flowing bodies on campus. His immediate destination, however, was the classic diner on the north side of town to grab some lunch, but more importantly, gather gossip because the waitresses at eateries such as the Rockface Diner tended to be older locals who knew all the juicy stories.

Wolf wasn't disappointed. Juanita was a fountain of news and willingly gave and gave, Wolf's easy smile and occasional wink playing a main role in his effort to gather information. Gossip by its very nature is often unreliable, its content distorted by hearsay, bias, prejudice, spite and sometimes malice, which when stripped away can produce kernels of truth and insight. Kernels such as college men engaging in sex with underage locals and the elixir of money making it all go away. Or the fact that there was a rising animosity toward the "spoiled brats infesting Overland College." Truth be told, the former wasn't news to Wolf though the rising animosity piqued his interest.

Too often people's feelings about the rich are thinly disguised envy, but in this case Wolf gathered it really was disgust for the disrespecting attitudes and disregard for the community so overtly and routinely displayed by many of the college's student body and certain members of the Faculty. Juanita supported her strong opinion by claiming that a majority wished the college would just disappear and screw the money it generated. A big tip resulted in a solid kiss on his cheek by a very happy Juanita and his extended gossip-gathering luncheon done, off to college he went.

Overland College, located six miles east of town, was situated in a broad, shallow valley nestled between low, rolling hills. Founded in 1936 by Franklin C. Overland, the region's mining baron, the college admitted only men from the most noteworthy and successful families, all of whom paid handsomely into the school's endowment fund. The college became coed in 1976 after a protracted battle of its Executive Board resulting in the resignation of every Board member of the losing minority, their prophetic warning about the demise of standards resulting in a rise of complacency, compromise and disorder coming true almost immediately.

Wolf slowed the car as he crested the hill overlooking the college and subsequent commercial and residential development spread along the main thoroughfare skirting the school's southern edge. This was not his first nor second visit to the "Yale of the West," the school having played a significant role in two novels, Universal Deceit and Appeasement, Compromise & Cowardice published four and three years ago respectively. The first explored the self-serving and cynical views of activist Faculty in universities across the nation teaching and promoting ideas contrary to free exchange of ideas and freedom of expression. The second novel a searing indictment of complicity and fecklessness of college administrators and department heads folding at the first sign of pressure exerted by activist students and faculty demanding an ever-increasing list of politically correct policies and actions.

Policies such as the Star Chamber-like committees investigating accusation of sexual misconduct, whereby a student's fundamental rights such as the presence of legal counsel was abrogated. A finding of guilt was based upon minimal, often uncorroborated evidence and the sole testimony of the accuser, often not even present at the hearing and not subject to cross-examination by the accused.

Rolling down the slope into the valley, he entered an oasis of green crowded with trees and vegetation thanks to the genius of forgotten engineers that delivered water from near and far. Wolf wondered if this novel investigation might bring to fruition yet another book about the growing level of distrust (and disgust) aimed at American universities, a rising sentiment solely of their own making.

Overland was conceived as an intimate configuration of classical and graceful architectural structures embraced by the stark beauty of its semi-arid natural host and designed to radiate outward from its central cluster as it grew in size and student body. Had the traditionalists of the Executive Board managed to maintain architectural control over subsequent construction, Overland would today be the stunning architectural jewel its designers envisioned. Instead, what one saw from looking at the college from the tops of surrounding hills was a spacious core dotted with elegant structures surrounded by a hodge-podge cluster of multi-hued boxes randomly positioned much like the bits of food found in vomit splatted on sidewalks by drunken freshmen.

Drivers could reach every corner of the campus via two main arteries encircling the college. The Inner Ring skirted the older central core, the Outer Ring bisecting the more modern construction including most of the dorms, which were clustered in the western and northern sectors. Though small compared to typical state universities, Overland housed over seven thousand students and the campus sprawled across the shallow valley it inhabited.

Wolf breezed past the student sentinels stationed in the dorm's lobby, heads bowed in obeisance to the electronic masters resting in their hands. So much for security, though he did spot cameras aimed at the entrance when he walked in. A quick jaunt up the stairs, Wolf snaked his way through a corridor littered with groups of students making his way to Room 205 and knocked. No one answered so he knocked again, louder this time, but the door remained shut.

"Jennifer is in class," a female voice said behind him. "Should be back by three."

He glanced at his watch: thirty-minute wait. "Thank you."

"There's a common room end of the hall," she volunteered. "Games, refreshments and comfortable seats."

"Thanks again," Wolf said.

A sweet smile appeared. "I'm going that way, too."

Wolf followed her to the common room, which was much more than promised. Pool table, TV alcove complete with comfortable looking recliners facing the screen, mini-kitchen complete with a microwave, oven and fridge, fully stocked snack bar, game tables and more. He took a seat in the far corner facing the entrance hoping that Ms. Park would not be delayed on her way back from class.

Wolf waited extra five minutes then made for room 205. He knocked loudly and waited. Nothing.

"May I help you?"

Wolf stepped back from the door. A young woman holding a key in her hand waited expectantly.

"You must be Jennifer Park. Sarah sent me to talk with you."

Park held his eyes. "Mr. Wolf?" He nodded. "Come in…"

She opened the door and held it wide. Wolf followed her in.

"May I see some identification please?"

"Of course." Wolf produced his driver's license. "You're the first person to challenge me since I stepped on campus."

Park looked at the license; her eyes grew big. "Grayson Wolf?"

He made an exaggerated worried face. "Are you going to call campus security on me?"

"No." Park issued a low laugh, shut the door and handed back his license. "It's an honor to meet you, sir. I've read three of your books last semester; they're required for Sociology 451."

Wolf's grin lit up the dorm room. "Was there a communal book burning at the end of the term? Roasting the author along with Marshmallows?"

Park made an ironic face. "Your books were the highlight of the course and quite popular with the class. The professor, too." His face must have shown his surprise because she added, "Not every student liked what you had to say about unthinking useful idiots, of course, but the class agreed that we've got plenty of them lounging around college year after year taking a couple courses every semester and graduating in six, seven years; just like you wrote about in Universal Deceit. Overland is a good school, some of the best professors in the country, but I'm glad to be graduating in two months."

"My grandmother used to say that idle hands were the Devil's workshop," Wolf said. "Add easy money, free rides and lacking a sense of purpose and we have people easily led into all kinds of mischief and evil… Which brings me to why I am here."

"This may sound weird considering what happened, but Sarah was far angrier about being drugged than the sex," Park said, shaking her head in disgust. "It's ridiculous; date rape drugs, I mean. There are maybe a couple virgins per dorm on this campus. No guy needs to drug a girl to have sex, Mr. Wolf. I could walk you down the hall opening doors along the way and guarantee that there'd be students having sex in at least every third room right this minute."

"Rape is about power not sex; something I'm sure you know, Jennifer," Wolf said.

"Yeah, but that type of rape tends to be violent and committed while the victim is conscious at the time," Park replied, "otherwise the perpetrator doesn't gain that sense of power over his hapless victim."

"True." Wolf nodded. "However, though we may very well find a dozen students getting it on in rooms down the hall, that possibility doesn't preclude that some guys might be too, ah, shy or intimidated to jump into bed with a girl and drugging them frees them from whatever inhibitions they have…. Or the opposite scenario: the girl drugs the boy for some nefarious reason; jealousy or getting even for being dumped for example."

Park's expression turned angry. "Not in a million years! No way would Sarah *ever* do something so vile. James and she knew each other, took classes together every so often, but that was as far as it goes. I know that James liked her—lots of guys did. Sarah is pretty, smart and a nice person. Smart enough to stay out of the meat market, though she dated occasionally."

"By meat market, you're referring to—"

"Ho's of both sexes racking up frequent humping miles," Park ejaculated.

Wolf laughed. He wasn't averse to enjoying variety, but the idea of mindless sex had always struck him as an empty, soulless activity.

"Tell me about James; he did confess," Wolf said. "Maybe the only way he could get Sarah was by drugging her."

Park looked mystified. "I don't understand any of it. James dated a few girls and I know that a couple had sex with him. I've never heard anyone say that he was weird or kinky. If anything, James was one of the more serious guys around, focused on his studies. He didn't go drinkin' or druggin' like lots of other guys. I just can't imagine him drugging and raping Sarah or any girl for that matter. Makes no sense… but apparently, he did." She shrugged adding, "I guess you never really know a person."

"Jennifer," Wolf said, looking at his notes on the iPad, "Sarah and James were found in some building off campus. Do you know anything about that place?"

"Sure," she replied, puckering her mouth. "There's a collection of abandoned buildings, old stores and such. Make convenient hang outs for partying, though not for college boys—way too downscale; mostly it's local teens. I can take you to the one where Sarah was, ah, where it happened if you like me to show you."

Wolf definitely wanted to see where the rape had occurred; never know what bit of information one could glean from the site of a crime that others may have missed because of complacency or sloppiness.

Or missed because the place was a total mess with trash littering the exterior of the building and conditions deteriorating with each step inside.

Wolf marveled at the collection of discarded bottles, drug paraphernalia, food containers, used rubbers and sundry bit of clothing strewn about helter-skelter.

"I would definitely want to bring a date to this fine establishment," Wolf said, sarcastically. "Who could ever forget the ambiance, the sights, the smells and disease one would pick up?"

Park walked past him into a narrow hallway on the right calling him to join her. He found her inside what he guessed was once a storage closet. A mattress was shoved against the far corner.

Park was standing at its foot pointing down. "This is it. Dirty, ugly, revolting; appropriate for worthless girls screwing worthless boys—or for a rape."

Wolf peered at the mattress for a long moment, concluding there was nothing new to discover. He walked back to the front room looking at the disheveled furniture, the boarded-up windows. The piles of trash everywhere.

He heard Park coming up behind him and turned to face her. "This appears to be a popular place, judging from the sizable collection of human trash."

"Lots of teens hang out here frequently—so I've been told."

Wolf nodded, taking in her response. "How frequently? Every night? Mostly on weekends?"

"Weekends absolutely," Park confirmed. "I'd imagine a few times during the week, too."

Wolf held her gaze. Park's eyes grew wide.

"There'd most likely be no witnesses…"

"Last thing Sarah remembered was coming to town to visit someplace that Wednesday night," Wolf said. "Next thing she remembers was waking up in that closet back there. How did James know no one would be hanging out in this lovely vacation spot on a Wednesday night?" Wolf added rhetorically.

"And did he just walk Sarah in here?" Park wondered. "From what I know about these date rape drugs, they're quite powerful. The guy has to know enough not to overdose or under dose his victim or she'll either pass out before he can hustle her into a car or be sufficiently conscious to resist and call for help."

"So, either James was, one, the luckiest date rapist ever, or two, a professional date rapists... or three..."

"He had help," Park said, ending his sentence.

"Or four," Wolf continued, "he was set up."

"Or five," Park added, "Sarah was set up and James was just collateral damage."

"You have a sharp mind, Jennifer," Wolf said. "Might want to consider a career in law enforcement."

"I'll take the compliment," she replied, "but a sharp mind is not necessary. The bitch click's been hassling Sarah and just about anyone not floating in their cesspool since day one."

"Bitch click?" Wolf repeated.

Park made a nauseated face. "Think Mean Girls squared and armed with social media accounts."

Wolf made for the exit and to his car. "Sarah gave me some names..."

"Karla Grisham for certain," Park said. Wolf nodded and she continued, "our reigning queen bitch. Bitch doesn't get even close to what she is. Frankly I'm surprised that no one has put her out of her misery yet—I've been temped several times over the last two years."

Seeing the look on Park's face, Wolf had no doubt that she was capable of putting the queen out of her misery. A thought struck him.

"Considering all the hate this girl is generating, I'm surprised that someone hasn't gotten even or found a way to harass the hell outta her."

"Mostly we avoid her and her gang like the plague," Park replied. "Most students I know want to get through and get out. We all just do our best to ignore her, her worker bitches and her bitch boys."

"I assume there is a king bitch boy?" Wolf grinned.

"Oh yeah," she replied, her words dripping with distain. "Kerry Bellamy, her evil twin."

"Bellamy, as in Justin Bellamy, CEO of New World Hedge Fund?" Wolf said.

"Yes, and apparently a chip off the old block," Park confirmed. "Professor Richards claimed that Bellamy is featured in Screw You, Suckers!"

Wolf looked out the car window surveying the area. "Maybe I did…maybe I didn't…but your comment sounds very much like our fearless hedge fund leader."

Park must have noticed Wolf peering distractedly out of the window. "What are you looking for?"

"Just thinking that this place is quite isolated; away from other buildings along the road."

"One of the reasons why it's a popular party joint," Park said.

"As is the fact that one can cruise up this way at night and not be spotted," Wolf added, "especially if one turns off the lights. Once behind the building any car is out of sight. Easy to enter and leave without being seen day or night."

"Could we leave now?" Park said. "This place gives me the creeps."

Wolf nodded. "Me too."

He started the car and pulled away from the structure. Fifteen minutes later he was back in her dorm room.

"Jennifer, is there some way for me to get photos of the bitch, er, photos of the students who've been making everyone's life miserable around here?"

"Easily." Park stepped over to a computer resting on a desk, negotiated the tracking pad and pulled up the school's website. Entering her password, she accessed the student roster producing a color photo of the students in question, printing each image and name on a color printer.

"This will do nicely," Wolf said, looking at the collection of photos in his hand.

Park continued her work on the computer, now accessing data about the students, printing a copy of the results. She made some notations on the printout then handed them to Wolf.

"That's a copy of each student's academic schedule and local address," she said. "The bitch click all live on campus; the bitch boys live in private housing off campus. My notes indicate where they typically hang out between and after class. The reason I know that is so that I can avoid them. Is there anything else you need, Mr. Wolf?"

"I think I have everything I need," he said, placing the papers into his attaché. "Thank you for all your help, Jennifer. Too late to hunt any down today, but I'll be back in the morning."

"Don't hesitate to call me if you need anything," Park said. "Maybe you'll find something the police missed."

"I'll do my best, Jennifer…have a restful night."

Wolf was pretty good at uncovering secrets, discovering information and exposing the ugly side of human behavior, but nothing he saw or heard about today was out of the ordinary that he'd seen and heard many times before. He didn't feel particularly encouraged as he walked to his car and drove back to the Castle Rock Inn.

Chapter 3

No Smoke, No Fire

Wolf had no trouble spotting the queen bitch and her entourage when he entered the Overland Student Union lounge. Karla Grisham was holding court ensconced in the far corner sipping on what Wolf guessed was an extra-large cappuccino. The group was loud and he had no trouble overhearing their banter sitting several tables away, his gaze on the iPad in his hands pointed in their direction, its camera focused on his target.

For twenty minutes Wolf listened to an endless stream of superficial prattle fueled by the women's incessant texting, tweeting or snapping while studying the faces of Grisham and those of her inner circle on his screen. If any were involved in the Lewis rape case, he was hard pressed to see any signs of concern, worry, nagging doubt or other manifestations of guilt on their faces, though having dealt with sociopaths over the years negated any initial impressions of innocence. What was communicated loud and clear were endless expressions of scorn, mockery, disapproval or derision of anyone who did not meet or share their dissolute values. Talk of sex and sexual exploits were mixed throughout with descriptions often exceeding the level of crudeness Wolf heard in locker rooms and in the company of previously mentioned sociopaths.

Checking Grisham's schedule, he was trying to decide where to intercept her when he felt a presence behind him. Looking over his shoulder stood the object of his surveillance. He rose from his chair

"Karla Grisham... just the person I want to talk with."

A suggestive smile creased her face. "That's disappointing."

"I'm flattered." Wolf had no trouble resisting the Siren's call, but understood how younger and eager males hopped into her lair to be "milked," a term heard often repeated by her and her entourage.

"You've been eyeing me the entire time you've been sitting here," she said. "So, what's the deal?"

Wolf gestured at a seat. "Please join me."

Grisham pulled the chair closer to his and sat. She leaned toward him, reducing the space between them to a foot, her open blouse revealing generous cleavage. Wolf gazed at her, the smile playing on his lips having nothing to do with anything related to arousal. Truth be told, he was pressing his lips together to keep from laughing.

"You know my name," she said, or more accurately, breathed. "What's yours?"

"Gray... I'm a freelance writer doing research on the sexual mores of today's college students." Wolf had over a decade's practice improvising and felt that the subject of sex would yield the biggest bang for his buck. "I've been told that you might be able to speak to that topic quite effectively."

She leaned closer. "I'm far better at show than tell."

Wolf's grin held, preventing any hint of distaste to manifest itself on his face. The last thing he'd be tempted to do was to sample the potpourri of toxins sure to be simmering within her depths.

"Being a writer, I'm more interested in the telling than the doing." He leaned in whispering in her ear, "Though I admit to being very tempted."

It was a lie delivered with unreserved believability, eyes sparkling, smile twisting in a suggestive manner, tone slightly hoarse. Wolf had learned quite a lot immersed in human cesspools over the years.

"Well..." Grisham took a breath. "The first thing you need to know is that anything goes and it's going on all the time in every dorm room. One of the best things about college: free to be you and me as often as we want to be. And believe me, Mr. Gray, it's hot 'n heavy at Overland."

"Okay," Wolf replied. "Sex, sex everywhere...but not a love in sight?"

"Love the one you're with, baby." She bit her lower lip. "I need lots of variety. I bet you do, too... Sure you're not interested?"

"If I were," he said, slowly steering the conversation "where would we, ah, go? Your room? My car? Stairwell?"

"Any and all work for me."

"I've heard there are convenient buildings beyond the campus where locals like to crash and party."

She didn't blink or miss a beat. "Ugh, no way I'd ever be caught dead in those dumps. They're hangouts for high schoolers and pimply-faced freshmen." Her face brightened. "What kind of a girl do you think I am?"

One that indiscriminately screws anything with a dick was what he wanted to say.

"Not just high school kids," he replied. "College kids like to crash there too... in fact, wasn't a coed raped in one of those dumps back in November or December last year?" He spotted a faint tightening around her eyes and pressed on. "I just can't understand that, especially drugging the girl. You're telling me about college being sex nirvana with everybody doing it everywhere all the time—and I believe you—what boy would want to bother raping a woman? Too much trouble, don't you think?"

Grisham's expression changed. Wolf was hoping for worry or even fear, but she just appeared to look thoughtful. After a moment, she spoke.

"Rape isn't about the sex. It's about having power over a woman. I'm happy to have sex with any boy that strikes my fancy, as are most of us, but I guess some guys only get off by raping us. They're sick."

"Yeah, but a guy that gets off raping women wants them to *feel* powerless, right?" Wolf said. "Drugging a girl means she's out of it. From everything I've read about rapists, they want their prey awake and struggling so that they can get off by forcing them, which is why the large percentage of rapes involve some degree of physical violence. Did you know the people involved in the rape?"

"No," Grisham said. "I mean I know who the girl was and the guy who raped her. She wasn't in my circle of BFFs, not the party type, if you know what I mean."

Wolf suspected that Sarah Lewis wasn't even in the same universe as Grisham. "What about the guy...what was his name...ah, James something I think."

"I saw him around."

"Ever hit on you?" Wolf said. "You're sexy; he ever try anything with you or any of your BFFs? You know, pushy, acting weird?"

She shook her head. "Not that I can remember. But I always got a creepy feeling the few times he was around—social mixers, the occasional party I'd see him at. Definitely nerdy; never in my pants, for sure!" She got up and placed a hand on his shoulder. "If you want to continue interviewing me you'll have to come to my room and show me what you got. It's hard to find any real men around here who know what to do with a woman."

Wolf was quite certain that real men included any number of the male faculty and most likely a few female members, too. He rose.

"You are quite a woman Ms. Grisham," he said, taking her hand and holding it. "Thank you for your time and company. You can be sure I will not fail to think of you and if conditions permit it, might come by for another chat."

She leaned close and whispered, "You can visit me anytime and enjoy my company as often as you wish, Mr. Gray."

She placed a kiss on his cheek and walked away. Wolf couldn't help but admire the sway of her hips as she made her way—slowly—through the lounge. He was after all, a man, and enjoyed looking at women, even the ones he'd never want to physically touch.

A movement near the doorway caught his attention as Grisham walked through; a man wearing a dark outfit fell in behind the exiting coed. The man's purposeful movements suggested some type of muscle…bodyguard perhaps or something less savory? Wolf stored the iPad in his attaché and hurried after the departing Grisham and her shadow. He watched as she crossed the campus green making for one of the instructional buildings with her tail not too far behind. Curious to discover the man's purpose, Wolf hustled after them, figuring that even if the man had some evil intent he'd not take any foolish action with a hundred students milling around.

He caught up to them as they entered the building, walked briskly up to the man and stepped in front of him, preventing further progress. Their eyes locked.

"Hi," Wolf said, his tone upbeat. "You in the same class as Karla?"

"You're a funny man, Mr. Wolf." He looked past Wolf assumingly to keep an eye on his charge.

"You know who I am," Wolf said. "Who are you and why are you stalking Karla Grisham."

The man shot him a wearied look then retrieved a wallet from his pocket, allowing one part to flop open revealing private security identification. He pressed the ID close to Wolf's face. It was the name of the security firm printed in gold across the bottom, however, that piqued his interest: Silverstone Security & Investigative Services.

"Sam Becknell," Wolf said, reading the name. "Based on what her peers have told me about Ms. Grisham, I understand completely why she'd need a bodyguard."

"Like I said," Becknell deadpanned, "you're a funny man. Excuse me…" He slipped past Wolf to go after his charge.

He watched Becknell disappear around the corner, his thoughts occupied by the discovery that Silverstone Security & Investigative Services was providing security for Grisham, one more name—an alarming one—added to his inquiry into the rape of Sarah Lewis and death of James Collins.

Wolf exited the building, stepped out of the line of traffic and slipped his phone from his inner pocket.

"Good morning RJ; I've got a task for you … no, I'm still in Colorado. I need you to dig up any connection of significance you can on a young woman, Karla Grisham … what? That was fast. Are you sure? … You're the best; Google's got nothing on you … no, just a diversion, I think—*no,* not that kind of diversion I assure you. Might wind up to be something more, but not book material; I'll keep you informed, say hi to the gang for me."

He tapped an App opening a file containing names, schedules and brief details of everyone connected with the Lewis rape case, scrolled rapidly to Grisham's name typing into her notes what Reginald Jano, Head of Media & Communications for the Center for Individual Rights had conveyed to him. The fact the Karla Grisham was the daughter of Terrence K. Grisham, Senator from Illinois only added more weight to Wolf's negative view of Karla, years of experience with the offspring of the rich, famous and powerful supporting his assessment. He closed her notes and scrolled to the next name on his list to visit, checked the professor's schedule and made for the Humanities Building.

Carl Richards, Sociology professor, was not in his office the receptionist directing Wolf to the faculty lounge at the end of the corridor. Half dozen people were busy lounging on an assortment of comfortable looking sofas and recliners, a drink or snack at their elbows. Though a photograph may not necessarily be an accurate representation of a person, Wolf was certain that none of the faces looked remotely like that of Professor Richards, four being female and of the two males one was Black and the other bald.

He heard his name called from a side vestibule. A young, shaven face with a full head of hair Wolf recognized as the face he was looking for walked toward him, his hand extended.

"Carl Richards, Mr. Wolf. It is an honor to meet you."

"Professor—"

"Carl, please," Richards interjected.

"Wolf?" one of the women said, getting up from her seat, "as in Grayson Wolf?"

"Yes, Sandy," Richards replied.

The woman strode up to Wolf. "You bastard!" Facing Richards, she continued, her expression hard. "You had better get him out of my sight before I do something reckless."

"Mr. Wolf is my guest," Richards replied, his tone frosty. "He has every right to be here."

"It's fine," Wolf said. "Perhaps we could go to your office, I would rather speak with you in private."

The two professors glared at each other for a long moment. Richards made a dismissive noise and gestured toward the exit, arriving at his office a minute later, shutting the door behind him.

"I'm very sorry about that, Mr. Wolf."

"Don't be, ah, Carl," Wolf said, an amused expression on his face. "I'd be disappointed if I didn't get such a welcome when entering a faculty lounge. And please call me Wolf."

Richards smiled. "I can't say that you are everyone's favorite person, but I can't think of a reason why Sandy would react *that* strongly to you. I've read all of your books and there is no character I recall representing Sandy—specifically."

"Some hate me because a character in one of my novels is them," Wolf explained. "Others despise me for what I stand for or stand against; many are academics as I'm sure you know. Sometimes I get the evil eye because the person is in the same industry whose dirty laundry I exposed or are friends with, or related to, a person that is a character in my novels that did not, justifiable, fare so well in the story. Any or all of these reasons puts me on many people's permanent shit list."

"Well, you're not on my naughty list," Richards said, chuckling, "and I can relate since I'm not the most popular person with the faculty either."

Wolf held his hands out in a helpless gesture. "Having your students read my books and saying positive things about them might account for that."

"It's one factor," he replied. "There are other, more pressing reasons, not the least being that my politics are not aligned with the herd. But you're here to ask me about Sarah Lewis and James Collins." Seeing mild surprise on Wolf's face he added, "Jennifer gave me a head's up."

"Sarah is concerned that she is somehow responsible for James's death," Wolf began, "and she is haunted by the possibility that James is innocent even though he pleaded guilty. She feels strongly that there is more going on."

Richards grinned good-naturedly. "Well she certainly has recruited the master of ferreting out conspiracies and cover-ups."

"To be honest, Carl," Wolf said, "so far, I've found no evidence to contradict the facts about this case, just typical human behavior: gratitude, kindness, spite, insecurity, nastiness… you know, same old, same old. Nothing even remotely resembling conspiracy or cover-up. Is there anything you can tell me about Sarah or James that might throw new light on the matter? Might Sarah be lying about what happened? Could James have drugged Sarah and raped her?"

"Both Sarah and James have taken my classes since freshman year," Richardson replied, "and though one never really knows a person, I feel that I know both of them well enough to say that I very much doubt, not just doubt, but am quite certain that neither would be involved in anything like this; not voluntarily. Students do foolish—stupid—things and some engage in criminal activity, but Sarah would not entice a boy for a lark and James would never drug a girl, let alone rape one. I can't imagine it."

"Can you think of any girl or boy that could?" Wolf asked.

"I can think of quite a number of students who are cruel and nasty," Richards said, "but not any who would drug and rape a girl. You already know some of their names since you've spoken with

Jennifer yesterday. I'm not comfortable naming names considering the gravity of the crime. I hope you understand."

"Of course," Wolf replied. "I'm not making any accusations either. Just trying to find out the truth or confirm the truth of this sad situation for Sarah in hopes of giving her some peace of mind. Thanks for your help; it's a pleasure to have met an academic who doesn't want to beat me up. If you think of anything, any small or insignificant thing, please don't hesitate to call me." Wolf handed Richards a card and shook hands. "Good luck with professor Sandy and the rest of the herd, Carl. Watch your back; nothing more dangerous than zealots, which are what any herd of true believers is."

Wolf was thinking about his next objective, Kerry Bellamy, the king of the bitch boys that Jennifer had named as being among the dregs of Overland College's student body, when he was intercepted by two members of the campus police as he exited the Humanities building.

"Good morning officers," Wolf chimed. "I was wondering how long the administration dallied before designating me as a VIP and provide a security detail."

The officers appeared to look embarrassed, or perhaps confused. The taller one spoke.

"We're not... um, we've been sent by the Dean of Students to escort you to her office, Mr. Wolf."

Wolf looked pointedly at the officer. "And if I refuse her kind offer of being escorted to her office?"

"Then we are instructed to escort you off campus," the shorter officer replied.

Wolf weighed his options. Have a chat with some nice, grey-haired dean or a coarse and offensive bitch boy brat. He chose the former and soon found himself gazing at a grim, pinched-faced Dean of Students, wishing he'd picked the bitch boy instead.

"Why are you prowling around my campus, Mr. Wolf?" She did not ask him to sit.

"What wolves do best." His eyes scanned her name plate. "Dean McMillan. Prowl."

Wolf's never give an inch approach was guaranteed to provoke further escalation, a useful strategy often eliciting responses not intended to be uttered. McMillan took the bait.

"You are persona non-grata on this campus as you well know," the dean spit back. "Fishing for more material about Overland to add to your collection of lies, distortions and misrepresentations about universities, are we?"

Wolf had an offhanded quip ready to let fly, but said instead, "That's exactly what I'm here for, Dean McMillan: uncovering lies, distortions and misrepresentations. Perhaps you would be willing to speak to one or more? About certain male students having sex with local underage teenyboppers and it's all swept under the rug? Or about the ruling bitch click of bad little girls and boys tweeting, posting, Instagraming lies, distortions and misrepresentations about anyone they deem too clean, too nice, too smart, too considerate, too respectful? I'm sure you have a pile of juicy stories locked up in the wall safe behind that fake Okreno Bavarian landscape painting."

"I'm warning you, Mr. Wolf," the irate dean retorted, "you are not welcome here and banned from setting foot on my campus. I will have you escorted off the grounds and have you arrested for trespassing if you dare return. Do you understand me, Mr. Wolf?"

"I do," Wolf said, trying, but failing, to not raise the corner of his lip exposing an incisor. "There is one little problem with your demand: I was invited on campus by one of your students. According to the college's rules and regulations, you cannot ban me from entering the grounds if invited by any faculty member, administrator or student. To ban me officially requires a majority vote of the college community, so until then, I will come and go as I damn well please… and now, I'll leave." Wolf stopped at the door and looked back. "And you better tell your officers not to lay a hand on me or I'll sue you and your precious college back into the Stone Age. Do you understand *me*, Dean McMillan?" He walked out of her office leaving the door standing open.

Don't tread on Wolf or he'll rip your throat out.

Wolf was tired of the fake outrage displayed by spineless, complicit and enabling bureaucrats, politicians and academics wailing about the injustice of his novels while turning a blind eye to the real injustices and nonsense being committed under their watch.

Back in his car, Wolf was intending to visit Kerry Bellamy as he was going to do before being derailed by Dean McMillan, but changed his mind deciding that he was too riled up to conduct an intelligent investigation. Confronting a loose cannon like Bellamy who has gotten away with god-knows-what all his life while angry would not end well.

Best thing was get the hell outta Dodge for now and visit the remaining candidates on his list, Silverstone Security & Investigative Services and Centennial State Prison. Silverstone was in Aurora, a Denver suburb east of the city, a thirty-minute ride north. The state prison lay an hour east at Arriba, but the fastest way would be along interstate roads, so north to Aurora it was then south on I-70 to Arriba.

Aurora, a Denver suburb, was a sprawling community composed of residential, business, industrial sections and even an air force base resting in its southern region. According to his GPS, Silverstone Security & Investigative Services was a mile east on 6th Avenue and Wolf took the exit ramp off I-295 and merged on the road rolling happily through a string of green traffic signals. Turning south on Norfolk he soon came to rest in a parking lot located thirty yards from the building and cordoned off by a string of impressive car-height boulders preventing anyone from driving up to the facility with malevolent intent.

Wolf thought about leaving his gun in the car, deciding that most likely he'd be required to surrender the piece before allowed entry anyway. He never liked leaving a weapon in a car because a thief could easily bust windows and locks in seconds and steal it so he took it with him.

If he thought that entry into the building would simply be a matter of surrendering his weapon and passing through a metal detector he was seriously mistaken, his journey most closely resembling a passage through several circles of Dante's Inferno.

First stop was the recessed entrance, it's door constructed of reinforced steel and blast-proof glass. After giving his name, pressing his ID on the view screen and notifying the voice on the intercom that he was armed, he was instructed to place the weapon in a tray that slid out from the wall in front of him. Next came a series of questions inquiring why he had come, if he had any intent to do harm and other questions of that type. Apparently, the voice was satisfied with his responses because the door slid open far enough to permit Wolf to enter and shut silently behind him. He was instructed to place his jacket, shoes, belt, wallet, keys and any other lose object in a tray and place it on the adjacent conveyer belt then walk forward into the body X-ray scanner and follow directions.

"Just like the airport," he said, to no one in particular.

At this point Wolf assumed he had been sufficiently examined and would be allowed access. He was mistaken. He walked forward into a narrow cubical, it's door closing behind him. Nothing seemed to be happening, but he did feel air blowing past him, the direction of the breeze changing every few seconds. There was a ding, a door opened in front of him and he walked forward into a reception area where he was met by a grim-faced, armed man.

"I suppose an anal probe is next," Wolf quipped.

"I can arrange that if you wish," the man deadpanned, "though I can assure you that nothing hidden in or on your body was missed by the body scans."

"What's with the air tube?" Wolf said.

"Sniffer," the man replied. "It can tell what you had for lunch three days back, the type of deodorant you used, if you're attempting to bring in a pathogen, radioactive material, poison gas, or invisible to the X-ray explosives. Of course, if you were, you'd not be standing here."

"Next time I come I'm taking the back door." Wolf thought he spotted a slight hitch of the man's lips.

He pointed to the tray resting on a counter. "Your things are over there and your weapon will be returned to you when you leave. Please follow me when ready."

Wolf collected his belongings and followed the man down a narrow corridor, which opened into a comfortable reception area. He was surprised when his escort continued onward through yet another corridor coming to halt at a closed door at the far end. The escort stepped in front of what appeared to be an intercom with a camera to the right of the doorway and waited. A moment later Wolf heard a buzz and the door opened. Layers within layers of security, much like a Russian nesting doll, Wolf mused.

He entered a smaller reception area; his escort gestured at the woman sitting behind a counter.

"Ms. Jones will assist you," he said, then aimed for a corner seat and sat down.

Wolf realized that the man was his personal escort while in the facility: one more security nesting doll, apparently.

He smiled at Ms. Jones. "I'm—"

"Grayson Wolf." He turned his head toward the voice. "Let me guess: you're here to gather sights, sounds and smells to write a smear novel on private security and investigation firms."

The woman glared steadily at Wolf; he held her gaze. "Ms. Silverstone. Good morning."

"It was a good morning." Her tone was dripping with sarcasm. "What do you want?"

"I was hoping to invite you to lunch." Wolf said this with utter sincerity. Silverstone's hard expression softened just a bit, most likely from incredulity rather than amusement.

"I see." She came closer. "Having transformed my father and his law firm into a money-grubbing, corporate-looting scumbag in your uplifting novel, Screw You, Suckers! you thought that asking his daughter to lunch was the perfect icing on your toxic cake."

"I was joking ... occupational hazard I'm afraid," Wolf replied. "To be fair, I did not transform your father's law firm into a money-grubbing, corporate-looting scumbag. He did that all by himself."

For a second Wolf thought that Silverstone was going to strike him, but the moment passed and he continue to stand unscathed.

"Why have you come?"

"To ask you about one of your agents providing security for Karla Grisham at Overland College." Silverstone said nothing. "Karla Grisham, the daughter of Senator Grisham."

"We do not discuss our clients."

"I'm not interested in discussing Karla's private life, what little there is of it, having had the pleasure of being propositioned by the Senator's little darling," Wolf said. "I only want to know where she was for a couple days back in December and I know your agent, Sam, won't talk without your permission."

"You came here to ask me for a favor?" This time she did smile. It was not a happy one. "Let me put it this way: you have a far greater chance of me joining you for lunch and that possibility is absolute zero. Anything else?"

"I believe in negative numbers."

"Get out."

*   *   *   *

It was worth the visit, Wolf mused driving north on Chambers Road toward I-70. He was swinging past Silverstone's company on his way to Centennial State Prison anyway so nothing ventured, nothing gained. And he did gain something of value including that Colleen Silverstone allowed him to enter her fortress, that she didn't deck him for the remark about her dad and most importantly, planting a question in her mind about her security detail for Karla Grisham. He may not be Silverstone's favorite person, quite the opposite in fact, but no one in his or her right mind would ignore a comment dropped by Grayson Wolf, not if they didn't want to wake up one morning to a world turned upside down.

If the reception by Silverstone was frosty, the one he experienced at Centennial State Prison was glacial. A string of stone-faced, hostile administrators mouthed identical responses to Wolf's questions about James Collins and his suicide. He was refused any information about guards on duty during the time of Collin's death, any signs by Collins that he was despondent during the days leading up to his suicide, if he had any conflicts with other inmates or guards or what he ate for breakfast that fateful morning. Prison officials only provided confirmation that James Collins was an inmate and that he committed suicide on March 4th.

Sitting in his car reflecting on the reaction of the institute's administrators afterward, Wolf was tempted to consider the fear and loathing he experienced as evidence of a cover up, except that being the recipient of fear and loathing was a routine experience. Whereas Silverstone might have been tempted to clobber him, Wolf definitely got the impression from at least one prison official that they'd be delighted to lock him up in one of their most remote solitary cells.

He was debating his next move, the rumbling in his stomach making the decision for him when he realized it was past two and he hadn't eaten lunch. He pulled out of the prison lot and made for Arriba a few miles back the way he had come selecting a Wendy's as the safest bet for a hot, quick and tasty meal.

Wolf had planned to drive to Lewis's home to meet with Sarah and her parents with what he hoped would be some positive news about her assault and James Collins's death, but sadly had not found any tangible evidence of some dark conspiracy or cover-up to report. It was pushing three o'clock and Castle Rock was over an hour's drive west on Rt. 24, so he decided to call it a day and make for his hotel instead. Tomorrow was Saturday and he'd visit the Lewis's in the morning and... that would be that.

He had done all he could and after meeting with the family he'd visit Cripple Creek and resume his mini-vacation before heading back to Virginia and becoming immersed in the hustle and bustle of his brainchild, the Center for Individual Rights.

Chapter 4

Near Miss

He drew the curtains wide and sighed. It was an overcast and gloomy Saturday morning; appropriate for reporting to Sarah and her family that Grayson Wolf had failed to sniff out any remote scent of hope from which to re-open the Lewis-Collins case. To be fair, though Wolf was an effective investigative novelist, switching to criminal investigator didn't just happen in a day or two. At worst, his efforts confirmed the known—to the public—facts of the case. At best, his poking around seemed to rile a bunch of people up and maybe some new bit of information might pop up because of it. Either way, he called Sarah Lewis informing her he'd drop by around ten.

Woodland Park is a scenic twenty-minute drive northwest up Rt. 24 and Wolf arrived at Lewis's home shortly before ten as promised. The front door opened as he stepped on the porch.

"Good morning Mr. Wolf," Sarah said, greeting him, as did two muscular boxer dogs who quietly eyed him as he approached. "Please come in."

"Thank you, Sarah." Wolf extended two fists toward the dogs flanking the entrance. They performed their inspection and he walked in. "Beautiful dogs."

She pointed to the one with a white blaze on top of his head. "That's John, and," looking down at the second boxer, "this one's Galt."

"I guess now we know who John Galt is." Wolf carefully extended his hands caressing the dogs under their chins. "Intelligent creatures, boxers."

"Yes," Sarah agreed, "but not long-lived, unfortunately. Mom and dad had several over the years."

Wolf followed Sarah to a sunroom at the rear of the home, John and Galt trotting a short distance behind. There was no sunlight pouring through the windows this morning but the indoor plants and bright décor lit up the room quite nicely. Her parents appeared to have finished a late morning breakfast, the father rising from his chair as Wolf entered the room.

"Good morning Mr. Wolf; I'm Reed Lewis," he said, shaking his hand. Gesturing toward the woman he added, "this is Brenda, Sarah's mom... would you like coffee? Something to eat?"

Wolf raised a hand. "I'm good, thank you; it's a pleasure to meet you both..."

"Please sit."

"From the look on your face, Mr. Wolf," the mother said, "I'm guessing you haven't found any new information or a smoking gun, as they say."

"I'm afraid that's so," Wolf replied, looking contrite. "Nothing new, no leads and no smoking gun."

Sarah leaned toward him. "I'm sorry to have wasted your time, Mr. Wolf. You're a very busy man and it was very generous of you to do this... Thank you."

"Hold your horses, Sarah." Wolf couldn't resist making classic western remarks while visiting a western state, though he chose not to dress in his cowboy outfit today; not proper attire for the business at hand. "I have the time—no other pressing engagements currently. Besides, I'm always up for an opportunity to explore mysteries, question people and probe behind curtains to see what's hiding there. Never know what I'll find."

"Then I guess James really was guilty of, um, assaulting me and committed suicide," Sarah replied, "because if anyone could find out if there was a conspiracy it would be you."

Wolf smiled at the girl. "Thank you for your confidence in me, Sarah. I am sorry that I haven't uncovered any nefarious activity associated with your case, but if my work over the last fifteen years has taught me anything it's the probability that money and political pull can work wonders to cover up nasty or stupid actions and behavior... especially such acts by their children."

"Did you find anything like that, Mr. Wolf?" Brenda asked. "Sarah's been harassed by that Karla Grisham girl since her first year. Her father is a US Senator; Sarah had told us about that girl and her friends' dubious behaviors."

"Dubious and overt behavior I might add having spoken with

Karla yesterday on campus," Wolf replied.

"She came on to you, didn't she?" Sarah said. "She hops into the sack with every Tom, Dick and Harry."

"Thanks for destroying my illusion that she thought I was special." It took a second, but they all laughed.

"The only special males on campus are those she has not slept with," Sarah retorted.

"Was James one of those special males?" Wolf asked, "or was he one of the common ones?"

Sarah shrugged. "James was a nice boy. We had classes together over the years, I know he liked me but we never dated. I don't think he hooked up with Karla since she trashes geeks, though Karla is the definitive skank."

"We've gone over this for months," Mr. Lewis said, "and it always comes back to the facts: that Justin drugged and ra—assaulted you. Maybe Justin's not the nice kid you believed him to be and the note suggesting innocence is his way of assaulting you once more by torturing you with doubt. I think it's best that you let this go and get on with your life. Just let it go, honey."

Sarah looked like she might agree with her father when Wolf spoke.

"Tell you what, Sarah. I've been asking questions far and wide and I'm sure me doing so will shake something loose sooner or later if there is anything to shake loose. If something viable pops up, I promise you'll be the first person I'll call."

Wolf wasn't hopeful that anything of consequence would appear but it seemed to make Sarah feel better and that was as good as it was going to get on this March Saturday. After some minutes of inconsequential chitchat and an offer to autograph several of his books that the Lewis's had purchased Wolf made his escape, deciding that he would visit Cripple Creek as planned.

He rolled west on 24 turning south on 67 ten minutes later. Rt. 67 swings west of Pike's Peak winding through scenic mountainous terrain, with steep drop-offs near the edge of roadbeds that required drivers to be attentive to the task. Distracted drivers living in rugged areas tend to have shorter life spans than their counterparts living in the Great Plains.

Wolf had been a national-ranked gambler back in the day and when it came to driving he never played the odds, always keeping both hands on the wheel, head up and eyes continuously scanning ahead and behind. No phone call, runny nose or hot date next to him would entice him to take his eyes off the road, hands off the wheel.

Not all distractions are physical, however. Wolf was driving leisurely—he wasn't in a rush—thinking about the last two days going over the interviews at Overland and visits to Silverstone and Centennial Prison hoping to spot something he'd missed the first five times he had gone over the details in his mind. Wolf was like a dog with a bone, his incessant review of notes, comments, documents and the contents of his memory often producing breakthroughs that culminated in completing chapters and entire novels.

He was approaching a sweeping left turn thinking that he would go back to Overland and have a chat with the bitch boy Kerry Bellamy before his travels took him elsewhere when there was a loud thud and his car careened off the roadway. He slammed on the brakes, the anti-lock braking system doing its best to slow the car, which bucked and reared much like a rodeo bronco over the bumpy ground skidding inexorably down the incline toward a steep precipice shortly ahead.

In one swift move, Wolf unbuckled his seatbelt, shoved the car door open and jumped clear of the doomed vehicle. He rolled— sort of—then extended his arms and legs allowing his body to slide to a halt close to the edge of the cliff. He didn't see the car go over the cliff, but he heard the sounds of repeated crashes as the vehicle smashed into whatever unyielding objects barred its way.

Wolf was gathering his wits, glad to be alive when he became aware of pain far down his lower back, right shoulder and various other parts of his body. He guessed the car was traveling well under twenty when he bailed, but jumping out of a moving vehicle is dangerous at any speed.

After several failed attempts, he finally got to his feet and ever so slowly made his way up the incline to the road. He wondered, briefly, why no cars had stopped as people often do at accident sites, remembering that he'd seen few cars on the road today so none were around when the crash happed. Then it hit him: why was there no car stopped? The driver that ran him off the road had kept going.

Son of a bitch!

He tried to recall what happened but the rising pain in his rear end and shoulder trumped his efforts. Padding his coat, he was relived to feel his phone in the inside pocket and he called Sarah, her being closest to his location. Several cars stopped, offering assistance during the twenty minutes until his rescue team arrived; Wolf thanking each for their kindness and assuring the Samaritans that help was on the way.

A black SUV came to a halt in front of him. Sarah hopped out of the passenger seat and came up to Wolf.

"What happened? Are you alright?"

"Someone ran me off the road and I managed to jump out before the car went over the edge." He pointed toward the drop-off. "I'm alive but banged up."

"Have you called the police?" she said, helping him to the car. "No."

"I'll do that," her father said.

Sarah helped Wolf into the seat then walked up the road where she could look over the side. Couple minutes later she returned and got in.

"I saw the car... you're very lucky, Mr. Wolf. It's near the bottom of a deep ravine, couple hundred feet down all smashed up."

"The police are sending a cruiser," her father said. "I told them we're taking you to the clinic and to meet you there."

"Thank you for coming so quickly, Mr. Lewis" Wolf said. "I suppose it's pretty obvious I need a doc to check me over."

"Let's just say you moved a lot faster when I saw you back at the house," Lewis joked. "I am glad you're up here and not down below with your car." He checked the road and made a U-turn back to Woodland Park. "Did you catch a look at the idiot that ran you off the road?"

"It happened real fast," Wolf replied. "There was a bang and then I was bouncing off the road making for a cliff. Have no clue who hit me, but I'm pissed they never stopped to help me."

Lewis shot him a quick glance. "Little early for drinkers to be out and about. The driver was probably passing you and got distracted by a phone or something. Sideswiping your car would easily knock you off the road. Shame it didn't happen another thirty yards up the road 'cause you'd have hit the guardrail keeping you on the road."

It being noon on a Saturday the bulk of Friday night's emergencies at the Woodland Park clinic had been treated and released and Wolf was seen by a doctor within ten minutes of arrival. Based on his patient's story about leaping out of a moving car the medic insisted on an MRI to determine any internal damage.

"Well, now we know why you're in so much pain, Mr. Wolf," the doctor said, looking at the image of the MRI. "You have a micro-fracture in the left Ischium. Nothing to do about that but take it easy for a week; no leaping out of moving cars, jumping from heights, no contact sports or skating." When Wolf looked puzzled, he added, "The Ischium are the lower arches of the hip…it's the bones we sit on."

Wolf shot the doctor a droll look. "You're saying I busted my ass."

"Yup, that's what you did," the doctor grinned. "There's no evidence of internal injury to organs and the shoulder, nothing serious: ice for next day or so then heat. The rest are bumps and bruises. All things considered, you're lucky, Mr. Wolf."

The doctor gave him a prescription for pain pills and reminded him to see a doctor immediately if he experienced new symptoms such as dizziness or unidentified pain and sent him on his way. Wolf was self-insured, paying the bill before leaving the clinic after first yielding to the Sarah's insistence he stay with them for a few days until his pain receded and got back on his feet.

The police never arrived at the clinic, but did show up at the Lewis home before dinner asking Wolf questions that he had no answers for.

"No, I didn't see the vehicle that struck me… No, I didn't look after I got hit, I was busy trying not to get killed… No, I was not drinking… No, I have no clue who ran me off the road… No, I was not taking any drugs… No, I was not on the phone or texting or watching U-Tube or driving while distracted."

The last statement wasn't totally accurate—he *had* been distracted, thinking about the people he'd spoken to over the past two days, looking for any clue in their remarks. Which is why he didn't see anyone come up from behind, didn't notice the vehicle pass him and never saw the car that ran him off the road.

The police promised to investigate but Wolf knew that they wouldn't find anything that would point to the culprit. The car was sitting at the bottom of a two-hundred-foot ravine, smashed beyond recognition of its former self. The most the police might find is a sample of paint from the offending vehicle scraped against the crumbled driver's side, but beyond that, what more evidence would there be?

The Lewis's took good care of him, providing meals, company and conversation. Sarah especially was very attentive, bringing Wolf snacks and drinks, accompanying him on short walks, telling him stories about the history of Woodland Park and driving him around town and nearby attractions that he could look at from his seat in the car.

Wolf was on one of these excursions Tuesday afternoon when a thought struck him and he asked Sarah to drive him to the scene of the accident. They arrived at the site half hour later, Wolf asking her to pull over on the shoulder. He slid out of the car and stood gazing at the road ahead. His fracture was healing as promised and he could venture out on longer walks, so he started to walk up the road toward the guardrail located a good forty yards ahead, Sarah coming up next to him.

"What are you looking for?"

"Not sure," Wolf replied. "Just remembered the guardrail up ahead and your dad saying how it was a shame I didn't get run off the road next to it since it would have stopped me from nearly doing a swan dive over the cliff."

"And you'd have at least seen the car that hit you," Sarah said.

They reached the guardrail and stopped. Looking ahead, the road made a sweeping left turn, the guardrail running the entire length of the curve. Looking down into the gully he spotted his destroyed sedan, its sleek lines smashed and twisted. He would have never survived that crash.

Sarah stood silently next to him. "You would have been killed."

"My thoughts exactly." After a long moment, his gaze drifted up the cliff's face and back along the incline his car had bounced and skidded, its angle becoming less acute the further from the precipice becoming horizontal with the roadbed where the car rested on the shoulder down the road.

"Why there?" Wolf said to no one in particular.

"Excuse me?" Sarah said.

Wolf gazed down into the ravine then back toward the parked car. "I was just thinking: why did I get run off the road where the car's parked and not further down the road or couple seconds later when I reached the guardrail? Why at that particular spot?"

Sarah peered back toward her car, looking thoughtful. "Why did James plead guilty then send me a note suggesting he was innocent?"

"Quite a non-sequitur," Wolf said, "but it makes perfect sense... running me off the road at that spot virtually guarantees a terminal ending to my journey and had I not bailed when I did, terminal it would have been."

"Perhaps there is something rotten in Colorado after all, Mr. Wolf," Sarah suggested.

"Or perhaps they're just coincidences," Wolf replied.

Sarah cleared her throat and said, intoning, "A disconnected incident is a coincidence, two connections is a pattern, three and more a conspiracy might make."

"Bold move quoting Grayson Wolf." He laughed. "Still, it's just one incident and one note and no further connections by which we can pull them all together." Sarah appeared to look troubled and he added, "Did you find a string to pull on?"

"No..." She looked back down at the wreck. "Mr. Wolf...I'm sorry that I asked you to become involved. Now I'm asking you to stop. There may not be a conspiracy or some other guilty party but as you said, you have riled people up and who knows what's going through their minds or what they might do..."

"Like running me off the road," Wolf said, finishing her point. "You might be right..." Wolf stared at his smashed vehicle for a long moment. "Let get back to the car..."

The last meal with the Lewis family was breakfast the next morning. Wolf thanked them for their hospitality, assuring them he was sufficiently healed to return to Colorado Springs. Sarah drove him back to his hotel asking him one last time as he exited the car to stop his query about her and James, saying that she did not want any more harm to come to him.

"Please tell me you'll stop, Mr. Wolf. I know I'm not responsible for what happened to James, but I will feel responsible if anything happened to you."

"I will continue to keep my eye out for anything new and useful that might pop up about your case," Wolf said. "However, about harm coming to me, you must step back from feeling any responsibility if something happens for the simple reason that I have many, many enemies, some of whom would be delighted to bash my head in…or run me off the road. Promise me you will not feel guilty if something nasty happens to me…say it."

A reluctant smile grew on her lips. She gave a small shrug and nodded. Wolf leaned into the car and kissed her on the cheek.

"Thank your parents again for opening their home to me and take good care of yourself…and a safe ride back."

*   *   *   *

After a brief visit to his hotel room to change clothes and a quick bite of lunch in the hotel's restaurant, Wolf was back in a new rental car and on his way to Denver for a second visit to Colleen Silverstone. The ride up I-25 is a relatively placid one, no twists and turns through tight mountain passes skirting steep drop offs, but Wolf was not taking any chances, blocking stray thoughts and staying focused on his driving. The fact that he was moving faster than everyone else on the highway reduced the chance of anyone coming up from behind with the intent to run him off the road quite effectively, though it did significantly increase the possibility of being stopped for speeding.

To his amazement, he was allowed to pass through SSIS's security process without removing personal items, going through the X-ray scanner and sniffer or even surrendering his weapon. His next shock came when he was ushered directly to Colleen Silverstone's private suite, his escort retreating from the room and shutting the door leaving Wolf alone in the room.

He wandered to a wall of photos, drawn to those that included Silverstone. Closing in on the sole photo showing her in an evening gown, Wolf grinned at the thought that a casual observer might assume that she was some man's trophy wife, perhaps an actress, or to the baser minded, an elite escort to wealthy playboys.

She was attractive; dark, long wavy hair falling over bare shoulders, her skin glowing like bronze, enticing lips gracing a comely face. Looking more closely, our casual observer would spot well-toned arms and legs. As his gaze drifted to the sensual figure wrapped in her designer outfit, he'd spot the same firmness echoed by her torso and upon seeing her eyes glowing in that appealing face, would not fail to see they communicated an uncompromising toughness of mind.

It was easy for men, and certain women, to forget Colleen Silverstone's reputation when in her presence; finding themselves captivated by her looks, her charm and silky voice. Easy to forget that Silverstone was once a member of an elite military intelligence unit, that she single-handedly built a national security firm, that she could disable or kill a man with two fingers and shoot an assailant between the eyes at thirty yards.

Beauty, brains and brawn… what could be sexier than that?

"You keep staring at that photo I might think you have a thing for me."

Wolf froze. It was also easy to forget that Colleen Silverstone had the uncanny ability to appear and disappear without making a sound. He couldn't help but grin at the realization that he had been as distracted by her image as those captivated men he had been mocking in his thoughts. He turned casually around to face her.

"Thank you for seeing me."

She peered closely at him. "You've been in a fight?"

"Fight?" First rule of any discussion is discovering what the other knows and how she knows it.

A suggestion of a smile told him she knew that game as well as he. But she played along.

"Slight hitch in your stride," Colleen began, "favoring your right shoulder and the obvious bruise and scratches on your face."

"Car accident," Wolf said.

"But you don't think it was just an accident, which is why you're here." She gestured at a seating area near the windows and walked toward it. "What happened?"

Wolf took a seat opposite to her, lowering himself gently into it. His Ischium was mostly healed but sitting still resulted in mild protest from his nether region.

"I want to hire your firm to investigate a rape and a suicide." He was about to provide details when she spoke.

"Sarah Lewis and James Collins."

His eyebrows rose feigning surprise, delighted that his earlier visit did plant a seed in her mind after all. Of course, someone as thorough as Colleen Silverstone would wonder what he was up to showing up cold on her doorstep, so to speak.

"How did you know that?"

A smile formed on her lips. "Haven't you heard? I'm a crack investigator. And you being who you are, I could well imagine your visit as nothing more than one of your ruses to weasel your way into SSIS for a smear novel about security firms and the scheming woman who runs one."

Wolf leaned toward her. "Sorry to disappoint you, Ms. Silverstone, but you would in all likelihood never make an appearance in one of my smear novels."

"Because a gentleman doesn't smear a lady," she mocked, "or because you know I'd kick your ass?"

"Because you operate your business with honesty and integrity," Wolf replied. "I don't write fiction, Ms. Silverstone."

She stared hard at Wolf, he looking back at her relaxed and confident. She may feel animosity toward him over the way he portrayed her father in Screw You, Suckers! but he only depicted the lawyer exactly the way he acted in real life, nothing more, nothing less. And someone with the level of honesty, integrity and background like Colleen Silverstone would, however reluctantly if not publically—yet—admit that Wolf did not omit or distort facts inconvenient to his story, nor misrepresent the real people he wrote about in his fictional non-fiction exposes.

"Tell me about your accident," she said. "Begin by explaining why you were talking to Karla Grisham and staff at Overland."

"I was at a book signing in Colorado Springs last week when I was approached by Sarah Lewis who asked for my help."

Wolf told her the story as Colleen listened attentively. She took no notes but Wolf knew she was taking everything in, processing and weighing the information provided, considering possibilities, imagining scenarios. He was sure about what was going on in her brain because his mind worked in a similar fashion.

"And so now here I am asking for you to pick up where I left off," Wolf said finishing the account. "I promised Sarah I would continue to look into the matter and I do want to be able to give her a definitive answer about the rape and about James's suicide."

Colleen nodded. "What if the answer confirms the current facts of the case?"

"Closure is what Sarah needs, no matter which way things turn out," Wolf replied.

"You do know that in the majority of instances the facts are what was presented the first time around," she said, raising a hand when Wolf was about to reply, adding, "I won't pursue an investigation if we cannot find anything hinky in the file, uncover new information, discover a new witness or trip over a smoking gun within a reasonable time no matter how much money a client wants to throw at us to keep going."

"Then it's a good thing I don't throw money around," Wolf smiled. "You'll take my case then?"

"Yes."

"What happens if your people discover something that conflicts with one or more of your other clients?"

"We will bring that to your attention."

"Only my attention?"

"Yes, Mr. Wolf. Your case, your update—exclusively."

"But not the names and details of what your people have discovered."

"No, because we also protect their privacy, too," Colleen said. "If the information is criminal in nature then it will be turned over to the authorities. Every client, including you, sign an agreement to accept that as a condition for our service."

"Understood. Where do I sign?"

Colleen lifted an electronic pad from her desk; her finger scrolled across the screen then tapped it several times.

"The contract will be ready when you leave." She placed the device on the desk, came back and sat on the arm of the seat. "Thinking the accident is connected to your present query is a stretch considering that it's not the first time someone assaulted you with a motor vehicle Mr. Wolf."

"Just Wolf, please. May I call you Colleen?"

"No, Mr. Wolf."

"Ms. Silverstone," he stressed her name, "why did you admit me into your fortress without being subjected to a complete inspection of my body, my emissions and possessions?" When she didn't respond, he added, "I suspect you like to keep clients off balance; one of your Sun Tzu strategies no doubt. Or you're just messing with me in particular."

She gave him a droll look. "None of the above, Mr. Wolf. Your visit last week was your first and thus subjected to the full Monty. Subsequent checks are random; you could have easily gone through the process today, but you didn't. If my people discover evidence you're becoming hostile toward us in any way, admission would require full inspections from then on."

"Variation of trust but verify." Wolf nodded appreciatively. "I approve wholeheartedly."

"Considering your personal high profile and that of your organization," she said, "I'm surprised at the minimal level of security in your headquarters in Tyson's Corner."

"Minimal security?" Wolf scoffed. "The NRA's home office is just down the street."

Colleen ignored the goad. "Please leave a copy of your notes with the case worker before you leave. Unless you wish scheduled updates, we will only contact you if and when something arises— your choice." She stood up. "Now, unless there is anything else, I'll take you to Processing to get the ball rolling."

Wolf was sorely tempted to suggest a dinner engagement, but thought better of it. After all, the woman could kill him with her little pinky and he followed her obediently out of her office.

Chapter 5

Back to Business

Wolf's bags were packed and ready for his evening flight to Dulles. He stood in front of his hotel suite's picture window looking absentmindedly at Pike's Peak, thinking of the missed opportunities to hike along its trails and descending into Cripple Creek's earthen bowels exploring its gold mines. With his calendar rapidly filling with events, business meetings and affairs back home in Virginia, Wolf felt relieved to transfer the Lewis-Collins investigation to Colleen's firm thus keeping his promise to Sarah to keep an eye out for any new developments about her case. If there were any hidden evidence or witness to be uncovered, Colleen's crew would dig it up.

Wolf continued peering at the magnificent skyline filling the window feeling…. discouraged? Weary? Drained? Fifteen years immersing himself into human muck, raking, sifting, weighing its effluent had taken its toll. It wasn't all doom and gloom of course; he had uncovered any number of gems, people who chose not to imbibe the poison of compromise, settling for less as the only alternative presented by life, individuals like Sarah Lewis and her parents living honest lives, business entrepreneurs such as Colleen Silverstone who slogged through endless resistance to rise above the herd and on whom the stink of sludge never stuck.

Overwhelmed. *That* was the accurate description of the way he was feeling. Overwhelmed at the knowledge that the culture was drifting deeper into decay and decline with each passing year, that the opportunities for corruption in every field of human endeavor were expanding, that fewer and fewer individuals were inclined to stand against the rising tide of complicity, accommodation and justification for mooching, looting and every sort of white collar criminality.

He issued a snort at the thought that he was a modern Don Quixote titling at an endless array of windmills crowding in on him—

overwhelming him. Was it time to get off his steed, retire his lance and disappear from public life? Perhaps. Not today. But soon, perhaps?

His phone buzzed, the text message informing him the airport shuttle had arrived. He turned reluctantly away from the window, collected his things and made for the elevator.

The ride to the airport was uneventful; Wolf continuing to reflect upon his current state of affairs. He was approaching thirty-five, published author of fifteen books detailing the lives, actions, thoughts of CEOs, managers, lobbyists, lawyers, educators, politicians; insinuating himself into their businesses, organizations, firms and operations. Googling Grayson Wolf produced thousands of hits.

He had launched the Center for Individual Rights a decade ago to document assaults against individual rights as enumerated in the Constitution, fight to protect those rights and highlight those who failed to rise to the responsibility to defend these rights, whether their own or that of others. CIR's message was that freedom was not free and that it was everyone's responsibility to ensure the fundamental right to Life, Liberty and Property was defended now and forever.

Grayson Wolf had become far more successful that he had ever imagined back at twenty when he chose to abandon pursuing a career as a national-ranked tournament poker player and write about the consequences of choices made by the good, the bad and the really ugly. His work had brought him critical acclaim as well as deep animosity, millions of readers, media followers and also many tens of millions of dollars. His books covered issues and people so penetratingly that his novels were required reading in universities across the country including courses ranging from Economics and Education to Political Science and Psychology.

The shuttle arrived at the airport, dropping him in front of the entrance. Being a frequent flyer, Wolf secured a PreCheck pass years ago allowing him to pass through security without removing any article of clothing and sailing past all the electronic scanning devices. He also paid for premium boarding placing him at the head of the line, always choosing a seat in the front and on the aisle. Wolf could easily afford to charter jets but decided the money saved traveling on public carriers was better spent on salaries and bonuses for CIR employees.

He had surrendered his pistol and ammunition as required prior to proceeding to passenger security inspections and was breezing through the PreCheck when he spotted a pair of impediments in dark suits and polished Oxfords he guessed were planning to neutralize his speed and seating advantages. Lifting his attaché from the conveyer belt he made directly for the men in black, both holding up identification wallets with FBI boldly inscribed.

"Two federal bodyguards come to see me safely escorted to the gate," Wolf said, a big grin on his face. "I must be a really important VIP."

"Please follow us, Mr. Wolf," the one with slick dark hair said.

"No."

The agent blinked.

"We just need you to answer a few questions," he said.

"You first: Am I under arrest?"

"No sir. Just need to ask you a few questions."

Wolf was very curious what this was about, but right now he enjoyed playing hard to get. He peered at the agents.

"Gentlemen, I have a flight to catch…so I must decline your invitation for a chat."

"Mr. Wolf," the second agent said. His hair was curly—and receding rapidly. "We have been instructed to detain you if you fail to cooperate."

"Detain sounds a lot like arrested, Mr. FBI man," Wolf chided. "Knock yourselves out."

Sandwiched between the agents, he was escorted to a small conference room within the security center and took a seat opposite the agents. He produced his phone and laid it on the table in front of him, switching it to speaker.

"RJ, I've being invited to a gathering by two G-men at the airport and I need you to be my plus one at the party."

"10-4." Wolf heard the humor in RJ's voice. "Gotta warn you, though: I'm a terrible dancer."

"Beggars can't be choosy."

"10-4, Wolf. Love the one you're with."

Wolf looked at the agents. "Okay, gentlemen, let's dance."

The agents didn't look too pleased. Curly hair said, "Why did you visit Overland College?"

"If you're going to ask me questions you have the answers for then get to the point and state what you know," Wolf retorted. "I might or might not confirm it. Let's begin with, 'you visited Overland College'. My answer: I have visited Overland College."

"What was the reason you went to Overland?"

"Research."

"Why did you…" slick hair stopped, then continued, "You met with Karla Grisham. What was the purpose of your meeting?"

"Have you asked her that question?"

"Why are you stalking Ms. Grisham?" curly said.

"Far more importantly," Wolf replied, "why are two FBI agents at the beck and call of her father, Senator Grisham? Is he paying for this service or is the FBI, funded by public money, his personal go-to guys these days?"

The expression on the agents' faces shifted visibly; Wolf guessing their boss had failed to fully prepared them to deal with one of the most dangerous men in America—dangerous to those who cheat, lie, loot or misuse their public position to harass private citizens for personal gain or advantage.

"Considering how effectively your FBI head honcho has managed to shrink respect for, and confidence in, the agency over the last year," Wolf said, continuing to press his advantage, "it seems like you boys are up for sale to every two-bit hustling politician wanting a favor … looks like the FBI has handed me my next novel on a silver platter. Might title the book, G-Men for Sale or maybe, Federal Blunders Inc. how the FBI keeps tripping over their own incompetence."

The agents peered at him with stony expressions. When they didn't reply, Wolf continued his verbal aria.

"If you know anything about me—and you do—you know that I have a visceral reaction to the government messing and interfering with lives and businesses where they have no moral right, which unfortunately, is virtually everything and everyone these days. However, so I can fly home before the end of the week and you gents get to hassle some other innocent citizen, let's get your business completed: I was at the college to do research about the sexual habits of coeds. And I found a treasure trove in the form of Ms. Grisham.

I'd regale you with her come ons and promises of orgasmic nirvana, but you know all about the sexual mores of Karla Grisham. I think we're done here and now I'm going to make sure I board my flight this evening."

"I assume you recorded all that?" Wolf asked RJ, as he made for his Southwest gate.

"You bet your sweet bippie I did," the CIR media maven replied. "What the hell was that all about anyway? Are you working on a new novel?"

"No and no," Wolf replied. "I was just doing a favor for a friend, asking questions at Overland about an incident and Grisham's name came up in my inquiry. What the Feds were digging for I have no clue."

"Wolf, maybe this is the beginning of a harassment campaign." RJ sounded worried. "Two FBI agents intercept you at the airport because you happened to talk with Grisham's daughter? They've got nothing better to do these days?"

"Maybe," Wolf replied. "I'm thinking it's nothing more than what we've seen half dozen federal agencies doing over the last few years—abusing their position to meddle in the affairs of people they don't like."

"There's a name for that type of abuse: tyranny," RJ said. "Well I got news for them: I for one am sick of it and we need to have a meeting with the steering committee about what we're gonna do about it."

"In that case," Wolf replied, "I'll remind you that most likely everything we've said is, and will being monitored, by one or another surveillance agency—illegally by the way for the benefit of whomever is listening to this conversation at the moment. So, I'll say goodbye for now and talk with you tomorrow, Reg."

"10-4 boss man. Over and out."

*   *   *   *

By eleven, Wolf stepped into his penthouse on the tenth floor of the Patrick Henry Building five floors above the home offices of the Center for Individual Rights, making his trip to work one of the fastest commutes in Tyson. Built seven years earlier, Patrick Henry was located in a scenic area of Tyson, Virginia's western fringe. It housed sundry commercial offices in its first three floors, CIR on the fourth, five levels of condominiums capped by Wolf's lair, his rooftop garden and a two-seater helicopter resting on a pad near the far corner of the roof. Never know when one had to make a fast getaway.

Wolf checked his various communication devices for any new texts, emails, tweets, pokes, IMs or smoke signals then made for the shower. By twelve-thirty he fell into bed, thoughts about Sarah, Grisham, FBI and suicide keeping him awake well past two when he finally drifted off to sleep. His conscious mind freed from all rational constraint, his subconscious produced an avalanche of dreams, none following any particular rhyme or reason, many quite disturbing.

A passel of FBI agents was dragging him through the streets of Overland College, students screaming obscenities, a nude Karla Grisham walking alongside promising hot sex. An image of James Collins with a rope around his neck switched to Wolf standing on a chair in a radio studio with a rope around his neck, telling the interviewer about the advantages of suicide. Suddenly he was driving a bus followed by what appeared to be floats from the Macy's Thanksgiving Parade…transforming into a dark, hectic scene pursued by unknown assailants, running up a dark staircase, reaching the roof. Gripped by rising panic that "they" would soon be on the roof, he sprinted toward the far end of the roof in an effort to escape. Glancing over his shoulder he saw Colleen Silverstone, telling her to hurry. Looking ahead he ran off the roof, fell and hit the ground with a thud!

Wolf jerked upright in bed issuing a loud cry, his heart pumping, breath ragged.

"Holy shit!"

As his panic subsided, he checked the time—5:11 a.m.—and decided to get up, mostly because he normally rose at six but also to avoid another possible dream death. He had read somewhere that one would awake before being killed in a dream, but Wolf was dead certain that his dream-self was violently killed striking the ground. Musing further brought forth the idea that people who dream of being killed in some violent manner might actually die from a heart attack and cannot confirm or deny the dream-death claim. If there was such a thing as a dream-death survivor, Wolf might be among a tiny minority walking the earth after being killed in a dream.

Shave and a hot shower later, a refreshed Wolf chopped and sautéed half an onion, third of a green pepper, beat two eggs and cooked up an egg pie washed down with a hot cup of coffee. By seven thirty he walked down five stories to work, finding the doors to the Center for Individual Rights already unlocked. Scanning the area upon entry, he discovered the CFO's office door open.

"Good morning Annika," Wolf said, entering. "Got any extra bags of cash lying around from our fund-raising push?"

Annika von Hauzner peered at Wolf over raised eyebrows. "Ja, ja. Got a closet stuffed with money... I heard the FBI was hoping to lock you up in a dungeon far, far away."

"Many try, all fail."

"Good thing we've got bags of cash piled up here and there," she teased, though she wasn't smiling. As CIR's Chief Financial Officer, Annika would know better than anyone the cost incurred operating an institution that attracted condemnations, confrontations and lawsuits like moths to a very bright flame.

"You've done a wonderful job moving around those moneybags, keeping the operations fully funded," Wolf said. "Looks like we've already made our annual budget in the first quarter—a new record."

"Thanks Wolf," Annika replied, looking pleased. "We'll be able to fund several new initiatives the Steering Committee's been planning."

"Ah Ha! Another early morning meeting plotting against CIR's Executive Director, I see."

Wolf and Annika turned toward the voice standing at the doorway.

"We're doing our best to overthrow you, Diana but no luck," Wolf agreed. "How are you this fine conspiratorial Thursday morning?"

Diana Ruiz, CIR's shaker and mover, stepped across the threshold and joined them. "Wonderful feeling knowing that we've made our annual expenses in record time..."

Wolf shot her an ironic glance. "Because..."

"Because we can expand our college outreach programs, among other things," Diana said.

"Uh huh," Wolf said, peering at her. "And?"

"And because we can expect the cost of our legal defense and security to increase significantly this year," she replied, adding, "You personally and CIR generally being so popular with the Anarchists, Nihilists, social justice snowflakes and the growing herds of useful idiots brainwashed by our college Humanities departments."

Wolf shot her a humorous look. "You can always retire to the Bahamas and lounge around on the beach all day. You've raked in a tidy bundle over the past seven years."

Diana gave him one of her classic long-suffering expressions. "What did the FBI want from you at the airport? You didn't hang out with a local Militia again?"

"Still working on that story idea," Wolf said, sitting gently down on a chair, "but I'm about ten years too late; the subject has been worked to death. These days it's all about our neo-Brown Shirts and Red Guards being groomed in our universities."

"You okay?" Annika said, looking closely at Wolf.

Wolf nodded. "I'm fine...My ass is healing quite nicely."

Both women stared at him. "What?"

A contrite expression parried their surprise. He hadn't mentioned his close encounter with Mr. Grim on the highway to his associates because it would add to everyone's growing list of concern for his safety. It was also another reminder to think before speaking, especially in the company of friends where he tended to let his guard down.

"Where you attacked in Colorado?" Diana asked. She narrowed her eyes and added, "And don't give me some lame story about slipping and falling at the hotel pool or some BS like that."

"That's it." Wolf's expression brightened significantly. "I slipped getting out of the pool and busted my Ischium, that's the lower arches of the hip, the bones we sit on."

After a brief burst of sarcastic laughter, he told them about being run off the road, though neither woman believed that it was just a random accident, demanding he spill the whole story.

"I can't believe you hired Colleen Silverstone," Diana said, when Wolf finished his account of his Colorado investigation. "Her people dogged us hard for a year after Screw You came out. What were you thinking?"

Annika leaned toward him. "Having regrets about your portrayal of her father," a sly grin appeared, "or that she's one hot babe you couldn't resist getting a closer peek at?"

"Or just out poking the bear, maybe?" Diana added. "Maybe she's the one that ran you off the road—I'd run you off the road you portray my daddy as a looting, money-grubbing piece of shit."

"And you'd be justified because your father is as far from being a looting, money-grubbing piece of shit as they come," Wolf replied, grinning. "Larry Silverstone and Associates, however, is such a piece of shit."

"Did the police find out anything?" Annika asked.

"There was little traffic that morning and no witness of the incident has come forward," Wolf explained. "They've tested the black paint from the vehicle that struck me; apparently from a 2006 to 2010 Toyota Camry. Just about every fifth Coloradoan has a Toyota so not much help. The timing is suspicious considering I had been poking my nose in several hornet nests, but most likely it was just some drunk or distracted driver who decided that running was the better part of evasion from reality."

Diana made circular motions with her hands. "We're juggling over a dozen hornet nests already, so please leave the Overland hornets alone from now on."

"That's why I handed that nest to SSIS to poke and see what zooms at them from the hive," Wolf said. An impish grin appeared. "That, and the fact that Colleen Silverstone is one hot babe."

"Who will never, ever reach out and touch you in that special way you might be thinking of," Annika laughed.

"I can assure you, Annika," he replied, "I was far more concerned about her reaching out and beating me to a pulp... though I admit it would be hard to say no if she did reach out and touch me in the way you are suggesting."

"Hey!" Reginald Jano cried, entering the room. "You people ever going to stop jawing and get to work? We've got trouble brewing in one of the universities one county over."

"Tell me something I don't know," Wolf quipped. He got off the chair. "Which one is it now?"

RJ headed for the door. "VPC."

Diana followed Wolf to the exit. "Virginia Patriots College…what is it this time, RJ? Fainting spells over students viewing one of Wolfs' book covers?"

RJ stopped walking, pointed his phone at them and pressed play. A hectic scene appeared: groups of students screaming obscenities and epithets at a group standing behind a table displaying books and other materials. Hands grabbed books, hurling them about followed a few seconds later by the table toppling over and spilling everything toward the stalwart students who presumably had the audacity to display materials that others disapproved of.

RJ paused the video and waited expectantly.

Diana made a disgusted sound. "Nothing we haven't seen before."

"True," RJ agreed. "How about this…" He pressed play.

The mob surged toward the table's defenders pushing and shoving them when one of their victims struck back. A brawl ensued and with the assailant's quarry surrounded and outnumbered this battle was going to be bloody and in short duration.

RJ paused the video and waited expectantly once more.

"What?" Wolf cried. "Wolverine shows up to slice and dice?"

RJ grinned and continued the video.

The brawl continued for five seconds or so when the mob appeared to stop pressing forward, paused and fell back as several of their members were struck and went down opening a space around one of the defenders who was wreaking destruction upon the mob. It may not have been Wolverine, but whoever the young combatant was, he was clearly an experienced street fighter. He moved steadily forward, his fists laying low assailants with one or two strikes. Seconds later the mob dissipated, slinking back into the holes they crawled out of, leaving the fighter standing alone among half dozen bodies strewn at his feet.

"That was unexpected," Diana said, understating the surprising result. "This incident happened—"

"Twenty minutes ago." RJ interjected. "Eight thirty-seven, to be precise."

Wolf shot him a knowing glance. RJ was a huge Tintin fan and often made references to the characters' many adventures or quoted various characters from the books.

"Do we know anything more yet?" Wolf asked.

"Only that campus police showed up after the riot was over and that a bunch of people had been taken into custody," RJ explained. Seeing that Wolf was about to speak he added, "already taken care of. Notified Juan already. Whoever that punk punisher is, he will need legal representation for sure."

"Good work, RJ," Diana said. "In light of events and Wolfie here busting his ass getting run off the road in Colorado, I've texted the committee; we'll gather in the Executive Conference Room in ten."

RJ appeared mildly alarmed. "What's this about you getting run off the road?"

"Tell you later," Wolf replied. "Get that video to tech and get it out on the feeds and posted on Brown Shirt-Red Guard Alert now… everything but—"

"The punk punisher," RJ said, finishing the sentence. "Got it. See you in, um, six minutes and twenty-two seconds, to be precise."

"Thank you, Thompson and Thompson," Wolf replied, referencing the pair of comical police officers in Tintin, one of which always said, 'to be precise' if time or numbers were involved. He had seen the Tin-Tin movie years before and when he mentioned to RJ how much he enjoyed the show, he found a complete set of The Adventures of Tin-Tin on his desk the next day. He read them all in a week and became a fan, too.

Thinking it wise to secure a cup of coffee upon entering the conference room, Wolf made for the coffee machine choosing a Smooth & Silk coffee container which he inserted into the unit. Thirty seconds later—thirty-six seconds to be precise (he couldn't help but grin at how certain phrases stuck in one's brain,) he lifted the filled cup from the machine and made for an empty seat at the oblong table.

Half the Steering Committee was present and Wolf smiled and waved in greeting as he sat down. Juan Mendez, CIR Legal Counsel shot him one of his, it-never-ends expressions, then looked at a file in his hands. Brett Casings hand performed a random gesture, the computer software engineer's eyes glued on his computer screen. Hearing voices over his shoulder, Wolf saw Annika enter talking with Teena Sanoe, head of security, looking grimmer than usual. Not that he could blame her considering the multi-faceted threats she and her security team had to prepare for and defend against 24-7—CIR and Wolf being a popular target for the ideological wackos oozing out of the woodwork these days.

"Good morning everyone," Diana said, entering and taking a chair at the head of the table. "RJ will join us momentarily, but let's get started... I assume that everyone has seen the video from VPC ... right. Juan, if you would please..."

Juan looked up from his papers. "Already on it. Got a team leaving for the college as we speak. Latest is that about a dozen students have been detained by campus police. And we've identified the student who took on the mob—"

"Punk Punisher," RJ said loudly, entering the room. "Daredevil taken. Punk Punisher is the perfect name for him."

"His name is Lee Sterling," Juan continued, ignoring RJ. "He's a junior. We'll know more once my people get there and talk with him, assuming he accepts our assistance."

"His name doesn't sound familiar," Diana said, looking thoughtful. "I don't think he's a member of our VPC student group."

"Frankly," Teena said, "I'm surprised we haven't seen more physical confrontations involving campus thugs before today."

"Once these videos hit the Net in all its manifestations," Brett said, "we're going to see more students getting into these punks' faces."

"*Videos?*" Annika said.

Brett's fingers tapped his phone. He turned the screen at her.

"Videos," Brett repeated. "Several are already on the Net including this one which appears to have been taken in the center of the free-for-all." The images were jerky and abrupt showing little more than arms, heads and bodies being jostled hither and dither. Brett continued. "There's going to be plenty like this, a jumble of stuff. The video we've got is as good as it gets under the circumstances."

Diana smiled knowingly at the IT tech. "Tell us why, Brett,"

"Because, Diana," Brett grinned, showing a perfect set of teeth, "you and your radicals have done a fine job training CIR student groups, especially impressing upon them the importance of documenting altercations like the one in the video that was sent to us by the groups' media contact."

RJ pointed at the computer maven. "My team is working on the message which should be sent to your team shortly."

"And my people will get it on the Alert page and pushed out to all our members and followers five minutes after that and to all of you," Brett replied, "so be sure to push it out on all your social media immediately. This incident is going to be big."

"The blow seen around the world?" Wolf mused.

"What more appropriate place for the first shot of a new revolution against tyranny than in Virginia?" Teena quipped.

Annika looked troubled. "I really hate to see an escalation of violence in colleges."

"I certainly agree with you, Annika," RJ said. "But you can't expect people to be attacked and interfered with and just take it? That only encourages these thugs to become bolder and escalate their efforts."

"I understand that quite clearly," Annika replied. Her parents were children in Germany when the war broke out and survived the bombing raids, warfare and the difficult years afterward before her grandmother came to America in the late 1950's. Annika heard all the war stories and had no delusions about the outcome of violence. "What I hope for is that college administrations see this as a warning, because this the first shot in what could quickly turn into a war spreading across college campuses like wildfire."

"Chickens coming home to roost," Brett said, his tone icy. "I don't know what your college experiences were like, but I'm the youngest in this room and I can tell you that when I graduated three years ago I ran into these idiots all the time. They infiltrated virtually every campus group, hassling members, accusing students who didn't agree with them as being racists or sexists or some other crap, destroying the social cohesion of groups. I and just about everyone else dropped out of social groups and formed private ones. It was the only way to get away from these bastards. They're self-appointed Inquisitors, know-it-alls who spout their mumbo-jumbo as justification for burning us in their purifying flames... I'm with that Lee kid at VPC; my only regret about college is that I didn't kick their teeth in when I was still enrolled because these punks really deserve it!"

Everyone stared at Brett, the vehemence of his outburst silencing the group. The computer tech had a sharp wit and known to spice up his conversations, but this admission of raw emotion was new.

Teena broke the stillness that had descended on group. "Meet the new Puritans, just like the old Puritans. Infiltration is an accurate description and it's happening everywhere. Picked up a Cosmo magazine waiting at the doctor's office the other day. Did you know that men who enjoy giving women orgasms are selfish pricks because it builds up their ego and therefore diminishes women? Welcome to the neo-Puritan feminist scolds who hate men and hate fun while supporting by their deafening silence the herds of misogynic Muslim men who treat women as animals. Annika, this *is* a war and we better be prepared to stand and fight these new tyrants." She made a droll face adding, "Which is what we do here of course. Just feelin' Brett's energy..."

Brett grinned and held up a fist. "I hear you, sister!"

"Now that we've had our Kumbaya cleansing moment," Diana said sardonically, "Annika has some good news to share that will allow us to significantly build up our patriot armies."

Annika made her report about CIR's financial health and continued growth, the part about membership and support increasing by an impressive 20% the first quarter of the year being most encouraging. This was especially good news considering that her estimate for legal costs would most likely rise by 50% this year.

"Annika is right about the possibility of our legal costs jumping significantly this year, especially in light of this morning news out of VPC," Juan said. "I recommend that we immediately launch a strong fundraising campaign to build up our legal *and* legislative coffers because more litigation begets more legislation."

"I agree," Diana said. "And in light of this morning's events, we need to also double our efforts to build and support our campus groups. Litigation and legislation are often a visible symbol of the failure to win the intellectual battle where it must be fought: in the universities and in the media. All the lawyers in the world won't stop the Frankensteinian Leviathan assembled from evil ideological body parts over the past century from running over the nation. We must brainstorm ways to leverage our resources and take the fight directly to the colleges, to the media, to public schools, legislatures, and every organization working to undermine our liberty and rights." She paused and looked at each person around the table in turn. "A good place to begin is to organize a conference inviting every like-minded organization to send representatives to discuss a union of liberty-loving groups and organizations...our message is a simple one: united we stand, divided we fall. And you," she pointed at Wolf, "are goin to be the conference's Keynote Speaker."

Wolf gazed admiringly at CIR's Executive Director thinking that if most men had her philosophical understanding, intelligence, determination and balls, America would never have drifted into the collectivist quagmire it found itself stuck up to its neck in the first place.

Brett asked where this conference was going to be held.

"Philadelphia," Diana said, a wicked grin on her face.

Chapter 6

Round One

"Excuse me?"

Terrance Smith stared at the campus police captain wondering if had walked into some remote corner of Virginia where rights guaranteed by the US Constitution did not apply.

His associate stepped up. "Captain, you cannot prevent Lee Sterling from seeing legal counsel," she insisted. "Let us pass."

"Sorry, no go."

"Sir, you are breaking the law," Terrance insisted, raising his voice in frustration. "Mr. Sterling has a right to counsel and by preventing us from providing him with legal representation you are violating his Constitutional right to due process. I'd be happy to cite a host of Supreme Court rulings supporting a citizen's Constitutional rights for you, captain."

"I'm just follow orders," the captain replied, refusing to yield to the law of the land. "President Wilson says no one sees anyone. You want to see him, go talk with President Wilson. No one visits Sterling or any of the students we're holding out back without her permission. Sorry…"

Terrance turned to his associate. "Susan…"

Her phone was in her hand. "On it."

She tapped an icon and placed the phone to her ear.

"Are you serious Baker?" Juan said. "The campus police are refusing to allow you to see Sterling?"

"We've been arguing with the captain; he's deferring to the college president, claiming he's only following orders."

"The man is violating the law," Juan replied. "And if the president is ordering him to prevent Sterling from having access to legal counsel, so is he."

"She," Susan said. "The president is a woman: Dr. Wilson. And it's not just Sterling, it's all the detainees she's refusing anyone to visit."

"Go see her and read her the riot act."

"Happy to, Mr. Mendez. I'll keep you informed." Susan ended the call. In a low voice, she said to Terrance, "We're off to see the wicked witch of VPC."

The CIR legal team got as far as the outer office of the college president where they confronted a police obstacle in the form of two officers blocking the entrance. Susan made for the door managing to get her hand on the handle before being physically restrained, one officer escorting her several steps back.

"I insist on seeing President Wilson," she said, in her most authoritative tone. "We represent Lee Sterling and she is violating students' due process rights." Not exactly the whole truth, but close enough for the current situation.

The officer shook his head. "Sorry ma'am, but she is not seeing anyone at this time."

"Then allow me to enter to make an appointment with her assistant," Susan demanded.

The officer shook his head once more. "Dr. Wilson's secretary is busy attending to the president."

Terrance had enough of this obstructionism and decided to play his trump card. "Please tell President Wilson that Grayson Wolf will be stopping by in the very near future. Perhaps she'll be available then."

He stayed just long enough to see the officer's eyes grow larger. Very few people in the Washington DC metropolitan area weren't familiar with Wolf and invoking his name would garner immediate attention from everyone, even college presidents.

"Let's go," Terrance said, and the two lawyers retraced their steps back out of the administration building and to their car.

"Are you sure you ought to have dropped Mr. Wolf's name, Terrance?" Susan said. "Best to get permission from Mr. Mendez first."

"I'm more the, do it and ask for forgiveness later, kind of guy," Terrance said, shooting an evil look over his shoulder at the administration building. "Call Mendez and tell him we're going to a judge. This situation is totally illegal."

Susan looked pensive. "Maybe they're hiding something?"

"Well it's not their wanton disregard for the Constitution, that's for certain," Terrance quipped.

"Does Wilson think she's going to get away with this?" Susan mused. "I know the woman thinks she's the Il Duce of Virginia Patriots College, but locking away students and keeping them isolated from the outside is beyond the pale even for an old cow like her."

Terrance shot her a surprised look then flicked his eyes back on the road. Only takes a second or two of inattention to wind up in the ditch, or worse.

"You know Wilson, don't you?"

"My first two years were at VPC," Susan said. "Couldn't take her attitude and interference any longer and transferred to Georgetown."

"Oh." Terrance nodded and puckered his lips. He wanted to know more, but never liked to poke around in other people's lives—in the lives of colleagues that is. Clients and defendants was another matter entirely.

"Money," Susan continued, guessing what Terrance left unasked. "No way I could afford Georgetown so VPC it was. Later I applied and with a 4.0 GPA, excellent recommendations from professors and people at law firms I volunteered during high school and college, I was offered huge scholarship and here I am. You're Harvard Law, right?"

"Being a poor Black boy from the ghetto," Terrance replied, "they be fallin' all over theyslef to admit me and up their diversity cred, cause da brothers don't need no brains, just color and we gets da free ride anywhere's we's do go. Dat da reason we makeses so much progress."

Susan stared open-mouth at Terrance, who kept a straight face throughput his colorful account. He burst out laughing.

"That's why the Center hired you, you know," Susan replied matter-of-factly. "You Black, you in."

Terrance shot her a furious look. "That's bullshit..." He was about to wax on with indignation when he spotted her mischievous grin. "Girl, you don't know who you be messin' with!"

"Neither do you," Susan retorted, laughing. "What's good for the goose is delicious for the gander." Her phone jingled...

*   *   *   *

"It is unbelievable," Juan said, referring to comments about Dr. Wilson's stonewalling. "Baker was very clear about the campus police captain refusing to allow them to see Sterling, or any of the detained students, nor meet with Wilson. They weren't even allowed to enter her office."

"What's the plan?" Diana asked.

"Baker and Smith are seeing a judge within the hour," Juan replied. "We *shouldn't* have any trouble getting a court order to permit us access to the students…"

"But?"

Juan made a face. "But you do know how much those local yokel judges love us."

"Yes, I am; very aware," Diana said, looking disgusted. "We keep getting more politicized judges and the country will turn into a Banana Republic in no time. God, I want to bitch-slap them into the next county!"

"Diana." Juan paused and gave her knowing look. "Diana, you mentioned the other day about ratcheting up pressure on universities. What exactly do you have in mind?"

A suggestion of a smile touched her lips. "Best we discuss that at the committee in the near future."

"Best we discuss it real soon," Juan retorted, "because if my team doesn't get that court order we'll need a lot more than huffing and puffing to blow Wilson's door down."

Juan's prediction came true that same day when Susan informed him that the District Judge had declined to issue a court order allowing them to visit detained VPC students. He instructed Susan and Terrance to return to the college next morning and camp out at the campus police office and pressure every officer they encounter.

"I want you to demand access to the detainees, take officer names, inform each that they are violating due process of the detainees," he stated. "I want you to dog them; keep repeating your demands and remind them they're in violation of several laws. Maybe something will give."

Something did.

Shortly before noon the following day, after "dogging" campus officers as instructed, the captain ordered Susan and Terrance to leave the college grounds or face arrest for trespassing. Citing that Virginia Patriots College was a public institution, both lawyers refused to leave and were summarily detained.

"The captain backed off arresting us because if he didn't, Susan and I would be much wealthier in the future when we sue him and the school for false arrest," Terrance explained to Juan. "They're holding us for creating a public disturbance and interfering with the normal course of police business." He barked a laugh. "At least we got closer to the detained students; some are in the next room."

"They'll have to release you soon," Juan said. "When they do, take a seat in their lobby and wait. No hassling the cops. Keep an eye and ear out. I want Wilson to know that we're not going away."

Susan and Terrance were released shortly after talking with Juan, Terrance teasing the officer that he found it suspicious that they did so before lunch was to be served to the detainees. The officer ignored his protests and the lawyers had to secure their own lunch, though neither minded since the cost was a business expense billed to CIR and the food most certainly superior to what campus police would have provided.

They were sitting—according to Susan—in the best campus cafeteria sipping on the remainder of their drinks, when both received text alerts, followed by Terrance's phone ringing. He listened to the caller, confirmed the message and terminated the call.

"Lee Sterling has been expelled from VPC," he said. "Mendez wants us to pick him up at his dorm and bring him to Tyson." He checked his phone. "Okay, we've got the address. Let's go..."

The dorm was only minutes from the cafeteria but by the time they arrived several media vans were parked in front of the building, reporters and camera crew cluttering up the steps leading to the building's entrance. Terrance pulled his car behind the last van, parking along a red-painted curb signaling a fire lane. They got out and made for the stairs, weaving through the media crews, stopped at the entrance by several adults refusing entry to anyone. Terrance and Susan showed the dorm guardians their CIR identification informing them that they were Lee Sterling's lawyers and that he was expecting them. One of the women made a call, then permitted them to proceed to Sterling's room two flights up.

After packing an overnight bag, the lawyers hustled Sterling out a back door making their way gingerly around the building, across the front lawn and got him into their car without being spotted by the media mob. By three, the legal team safely delivered their charge to the secure offices of CIR in Tyson, depositing him in the Jefferson Conference Room.

Terrance shot Susan an occasional smirking glance at the fact that Sterling couldn't keep his eyes off her. She in turn rolled her eyes at Terrance who would wiggle his eyebrows in a highly suggestive manner. Their tit-for-tat ended when several CIR heavyweights entered the conference room.

"Thank you, Susan and Terrance," Diana said. "I'm sure you have lots of work waiting for you; we'll take it from here."

"Thank you for the ride, Ms. Baker," Sterling said, smiling brilliantly at her. "And, um, thank you, too Mr. Smith...hope to see you again sometime."

No one in the room had at any delusions which of the two young lawyers Sterling was hoping to see again sometime. Susan looked back, smiled warmly at him and exited the room.

Wolf and RJ came in and took a seat at the table. Diana introduced the men.

"*The* Grayson Wolf?" Lee asked, his eyes wide.

Wolf gave a brief nod confirming his identity. "Thank you for agreeing to come and talk to us about the incident on campus and the decision to expel you from VPC."

"That's totally bogus," Sterling shot back. "I get expelled and the bums get a slap on the wrist."

"Lee," Diana said, "tell us how you came to be involved in the fracas. Based on our records you're not a member of SIR—Students for Individual Rights—unless you joined very recently."

"No ma 'am I'm not," he confirmed. "I've been seriously thinking about joining, especially after what happened this morning... I was on my way to my nine 'o clock class when I see this knot of students crowding around a table displaying books and stuff. I could hear them shouting, cursing at the handful behind the table. They started knocking stuff off the table and others tossed books on the ground. At that point, I stopped and watched; others students stopped, too and a large crowd formed. Suddenly they pushed the table and it fell over and they rushed forward pushing and jerking around the ones behind the table; I decided that I'd had enough and went in swinging. Then the cops came and hauled us away."

"Where did you learn to fight like that, Lee?" RJ asked. "We have a video of you knocking 'em down like bowling pins."

"My dad, I guess," Sterling replied. "I work out, too."

"Is your father a boxer?" Diana asked.

"He's, um, a soldier. Special Forces. He's in Afghanistan, I think. They move him around without notice."

"Why did you get involved?" Wolf said. "You stepped right into a violent scene."

"When good men see evil being committed and do nothing, they are as guilty as the perpetrators," Sterling replied. "Heard my dad say that all my life. Those punks have no respect for other people's stuff and they attacked them. I hate bullies in all shapes and sizes."

"And you paid a price for standing up for what you thought was right," RJ said.

Sterling's expression darkened. "I'm not going quietly, sir and I hope the reason you' all asked me to come is that you're going to help me fight back."

"Mr. Sterling," Diana said, her tone measured, "we are going to do a lot more than help you. What happened to you, to our campus student group this morning, is happening in colleges all over the country, as I'm sure you are aware. You, however, are our immediate concern. Mr. Mendez will brief you about the options available for you to fight back. Later, if you are interested, we can have a conversation of how you can assist our efforts to protect the right of all students to hold views that may not be popular with others and to discuss and promote their views free from verbal and physical threats."

Wolf rose from his seat and smiled at Sterling. "What she said—in spades. Thanks again for agreeing to come, Lee. It's always a pleasure to meet someone possessing the moral compass to move him or her to defend one's principles..."

"Thank you, Mr. Wolf," Lee said, his expression communicating gratitude for being affirmed. "It means a lot to me that you think so."

"Once you and Mr. Mendez are done discussing legal options," Diana said, "our concierge service will take care of your overnight arrangements and bring you back here in the morning."

She asked Wolf to join her, tapping out a text on her phone as they walked over to her office. She made for a casual seating area adjacent to the windows.

"I've asked Annika to join us," she said, taking a seat. "The situation at Patriots has inspired me to speed up plans for a national convention." An aide stuck his head into the office looking expectantly at her. "What is it, Josh?"

The aide came over and handed Diana an iPad. "Thought you'd want to see this editorial by VPC's student newspaper right away..."

Ruiz's eyes flew across screen, her expression turning to one of revulsion. "What a bunch of sniveling hypocrites. Two weeks ago, they were trumpeting the justification of violence against people with whom they disagree as 'self-defense' now denouncing violence, whining about the poor students injured by Lee defending our group against violent assault by their friends. Where did these student propagandists passing for journalists come from, North Korea?"

"Just our homegrown garden variety commie-fascist," Josh said. "And they're growing like weeds."

Diana handed back the iPad. "Thanks Josh. Keep me informed of anything else oozing out of VPC—from any college about this incident."

"Yes ma'am."

Josh retreated from the office as Annika entered. "What's going on?"

"I think Diana is planning to go on the warpath," Wolf quipped.

"I am," she confirmed. "I asked you over to run financials past you."

Annika looked steadily at Diana. "I see. The short answer is fifteen million. That's how much we have in our war chest. What exactly do you have in mind, Diana—apart from our current efforts, that is?"

"I'm thinking I need at least one million, two tops," she replied. "RJ's been doing exploratory inquiry about conference space, room rentals, transportation, food and all the rest."

"Are you thinking about funding the entire conference?" Annika asked. If the CFO was alarmed, she didn't show it, not that she had a tendency toward becoming alarmed at multi-million dollar expenditures. Between the two women, Diana was the excitable one of the CIR outfit; Annika the cool, collected one, which upon reflection, was a good thing considering that the financial health of the organization rested in her hands.

"No," Diana replied. "The only risk I'm willing to take is the down payment required to reserve the conference center and a couple hundred rooms. I envision this gathering much like the first Continental Congress: liberty-loving groups sending a handful of representatives to whom we'll pitch the plan for a coordinated national effort to stop the creeping crud of totalitarianism propagated in our schools, universities, encouraged and supported by local and foreign corporate and financial interests."

"United we stand, divided we fall?" Wolf suggested.

"More like united we dramatically improve our ability to fight for our rights, divided we waste resources, time, money and continue to lose ground against the enemies of freedom."

"And you need up to two million for that plan?" Annika appeared skeptical. "Quarter of a million would cover the entire affair for two hundred people over a long weekend."

"A convention is only the beginning," Diana replied. "I'm planning a national campaign visiting cities, colleges. Couple dozen tour buses."

Annika held a hand above her head. "I think the nation has had it up to the proverbial here with demonstrations."

A wicked grin shone on Diana's face in response. "Not demonstrations, dear Annika; an invasion, a direct and prolonged assault on the enemies of freedom. Imagine a thousand supporters of the Constitution showing up on the first week at every Ivy League college as well as targeting colleges in every state housing the most virulent promoters of politically correctness. Imagine legions of supporters targeting administrators and professors poisoning the minds of students, challenging their premises, curricula and instruction. Showcasing the results of their propaganda along with their faces on every electronic medium across the globe. And I'm just getting started."

"You're going to ram their own words down their collective throats," Wolf said.

"Yes." Diana's eyes glowed with excitement. "We will expose their hypocrisy by inciting them to bitch and moan about us trying to curtail their 'academic freedom' then turn their teachings, premises and actions against them."

"Ivy League colleges are private entities as are many other colleges you will be targeting," Annika warned. "Invading their campuses would be trespassing, Diana. They'd have the invaders arrested."

Diana looked expectantly at Wolf who smiled like the proverbial Cheshire cat.

"Technically, Annika," he said, "there are only a handful of truly private colleges in the country. Hillsdale College is one of them. It's truly a private institution because unlike Harvard, Yale or VPC down the road, it does not accept one penny of government money in any form because to do so muddies the line between private and public making them subject to certain public demands such as the right of Diana's patriot army treading upon their hallowed lawns."

"According to Juan and his legal team, that's just one of any number legal options we can leverage to kick in their semi-private doors," Diana said. "For example, Tyson's Corner Center, along with every other mall or shopping center in the country, is privately owned. Yet, the Supreme Court ruled years ago shopping malls are today's parks and city squares and thus 'the home of free speech' and must allow access to anyone distributing leaflets on social issues."

"And," Wolf added, "it's only a legal baby step to argue that private colleges are free speech's ground zero that protesters must have access for distributing leaflets on social issues. Especially since private colleges such as Brown receive public funds in various ways including tax breaks, tuition, grants and so forth."

"The universities and their minions have worked diligently to break down the wall separating public and private in virtually every part of American life," Diana explained. She paused, as she often did to emphasize what would follow. "In their blind zeal to make private life and private property subject to public access or control, they have failed to see a fatal flaw in their crusade: that anyone can now use the public battering ram they have worked so diligently to build over the decades against them."

"Diana," Annika said, "aren't you failing to see the potential backlash that might arise to this plan invading college campuses? My kids are in college and they tell me that the majority just want to learn and get a degree. They roll their eyes at these nuts and think they're a joke. We wouldn't want to rile up that majority who might very well stand in solidarity with the nutters they know against the nutters they don't—not that you, we, are that, just that others might conclude we are."

"History weighs heavily against the view these true-believers are just a joke as your parents would confirm, Annika," Wolf said. "It's always a tiny minority—individuals even—that forge a path that soon an entire nation marches upon. Our organization is but one example of forging a new direction, a Constitutional back to the future, which an increasing number of people are choosing to walk upon."

"There is a reason the name Grayson Wolf is on the lips of millions of people, Annika," Diana said, "and it's not because he's some vacuous personality beloved by the paparazzi and the Twitterverse."

"What Diana is trying to say is that individuals can and do change the course of history for better or worse," Wolf said.

"Look Annika," Diana continued, "our plan is not about tilting at windmills. We are witnessing what its supporter and promoters believe is the triumph of political correctness in all its manifestations: social justice, systemic racism, identity politics, equality of outcome and all the rest of their collectivist nonsense. This is the perfect time to launch a counter attack for that reason alone...and the fact that I sense a fundamental shift happening, a growing sense of disgust and anger at what many are discovering is nothing but the old totalitarianism repackaged in shiny new wrapping spouting platitudes and intolerance and increasingly, violence against any opposition."

"Thus, your request for funds approaching two million," Annika said.

"I'm talking 1000 supporters on two dozen buses coming and going for a year," Diana explained. "With food, lodging and upkeep as needed."

It took Annika only a few seconds to calculate a rough estimate of the cost for this sustained assault on the institutions of higher learning. "That's easily closer to three million Diana," she said. "Most likely pushing four factoring in damage incurred to buses by thugs sabotaging the busses."

"I only need startup money; million tops," Diana retorted. "You know my iron rule: make every effort pay for itself."

A knowing smile formed on Annika's lips. "You're going to raise money for the campaign. Crowd funding, donation push, advertising and so forth."

"And a buy-in from all the organizations coming to our Liberty Convention," Diana said. "CIR will match their funds dollar for dollar. I think that might prime the pump sufficiently to get the money flowing. Even so, I expect to raise enough funds to not only pay for this venture, but to significantly fill our coffers."

"The last time anything of this magnitude was launched—"

"Was during the Civil Rights movement in the 50's and 60's," Wolf interjected, finishing Annika's sentence.

"Wait." Annika's eyes grew large. "Did you say you're planning this campaign to run for a *year?*"

Diana nodded and smiled in a very satisfactory manner. "That's correct. The plan is to hit targets at random times across the country. The colleges are just one target. We're going after the entire Unholy Progressive Complex, Annika. Draw international attention on businesses and their leadership who fund organizations that are anti-democratic. We'll go after institutions ranging from New York Wall Street financial firms, agricultural cooperatives headquarters in Podunk, Nebraska and colleges in every state. I see teach-ins, shaming, sticking microphones in their faces when they show up at work, leaking information about mistresses, tweets with photos of meetings with unsavory characters, tracking money supporting anti-democratic efforts, the lists go on and on. Once we begin, it'll capture the imagination of the country and this campaign will snowball with the speed of tweets until every one of these corporate hacks and college administrators are inundated with the consequences of their anti-American, anti-liberty ideologies and choices."

Annika's face turned a shade paler. "Ramming their words and actions down their collective throats. Jeezus, Diana, you'll start a war."

"No Annika," she replied, looking determined. "I'm going to raise an army large enough to effectively fight the war that these collectivists started."

"Then we had better be sure we fight to win it all, Diana," Annika replied, "because if we don't, the politicians and their cronies will undo every victory before the smoke of battle clears."

"Then perhaps what we need is a new political party," Diana shot back, "one that rejects cronyism, opposes special favors and restores our Constitutional Republic to some semblance of what the Founders envisioned. Perhaps *that* possibility will cause stools to sufficiently loosen to get the politicians in Washington to pay attention."

Annika seemed to become energized by the idea of a new political party. "People are increasingly fed up with being manipulated, divided, lied to 24-7; we see it everywhere," she said. "Perhaps the time is ripe for a new political party that represents Americans who want their government to function properly but also get out of their daily lives. I have serious doubts about the cost involved, however."

"I would think that a national convention calling for a new political party would draw financial support from sea to shining sea," Diana said. "Not from the big players benefitting from governmental favors and palm greasing, but certainly a sizable number of smaller firms who feel the brunt of regulations and tax policies and do not possess the political pull and influence big business enjoys with our moochers north of the Potomac River."

"Now all we need is a name for this new political party and someone with serious name recognition and the integrity required to become the presidential candidate of this new party." Annika looked pointedly at Wolf.

"Oh, yeah," Wolf scoffed, "just what I need; my mug dramatically featured on a hundred million TV, computer and phone screens so that I'd be instantly recognizable to every wacko and malcontent everywhere I go."

"But you are loved by millions, my dear Wolfie." Diana teased.

"And hated, despised, reviled, loathed and just plain disliked by millions more," Wolf quipped.

"Stop exaggerating," Annika said, a sly grin on her lips. "I'm certain the number is less than a million."

"One thing is for certain," Diana said, looking thoughtful, "we put your face on camera announcing a national convention to create a new political party we're going to have three hundred million mouths talking about it."

"The other certainty Diana," Wolf replied, "we will experience a dramatic uptick of hate mail and threats. I prefer to keep my face out of the public eye as much as possible."

"It's not like your photo isn't out there, Wolf," Diana said. "How could it not be? If someone was after you or any of us, they know where to find us."

"Fortunately," Wolf said, tamping down a feeling of agitation at the direction the conversation had taken, "all this bitching and moaning about CIR and me is just people blowing off steam 99.9% of the time…" He shook his head and sighed. "However, …"

"However, what?" Annika said, sensing a shift in Wolf's mood.

"We've been chipping away at the pile of collectivist dung collecting for the past century," Wolf shot back. "I wonder sometimes if the stress, the anxiety, the paranoia is worth it. Hell, we're packing heat in our own offices for God's sake."

"You've had a stressful week, Wolf," Diana said, trying to sound reassuring.

"Look, I get it," he replied. "If not us, who and all that. But sometimes I feel like I—all of us—are missing an important part of life, the part about just…*living*. Hiking up Pike's Peak, descending down a gold mine, driving leisurely through the countryside and *not* get run off the road. You know, stuff like that. At what point do we pause and actually enjoy the freedom we fight for 24-7? After we're dead?"

The silence that followed Wolf's uncharacteristic outburst continued for a long moment. They were not used to their leader uttering doubts and reservations and most certainly were digesting the import of his comment.

Wolf himself felt surprise at uttering such emotional-laden remarks and wondered where these feeling came from. Maybe he was getting tired feeling like he was immersed in an endless conflict that consumed most of his waking moments. Sure, he was successful; successful beyond anything he imagined fifteen years ago. He had few friends, but the ones he did have, Diana, Annika, RJ, Teena, Juan and a few others, his parents and siblings all were people of the highest caliber, individuals in whom he could—and did—trust with his life.

Wolf had found himself increasingly ambushed by thoughts of this nature for the past year or so, swatting them away like some bothersome mosquito buzzing in his ear. And like that pesky, annoying insect, kept coming back to annoy him at most inappropriate times.

Allowing these unwanted thoughts to continue buzzing in his mind, a strong sensation condensed from the emotions swirling in his head. He recognized the truth of the sensation immediately: he was lonely.

From the outset, keeping others at arm's length had become a requirement of his chosen profession. Firstly, when doing research for one of his books he had to operate underground for months at a time. More importantly was the fact that long-term entanglements with Grayson Wolf potentially placed one in harm's way, especially so were encounters with women. Love affairs were rare and brief and never with a woman who was one of his informants or connected with anyone or organization he was investigating. Years of experience dealing with the good, bad and ugly had taught him the length one's enemies would go to compromise reputations or worse, much worse. Diana's plan to possibly launch a new political party would cause his life and that of everyone at CIR to become more hectic and tense by a factor of ten, consuming whatever shred of personal time remained for everyone.

Coming out of his reverie he found the two women gazing intently at him. He smiled brilliantly.

"What?"

"That's what we want to know," Diana asked. "What were you thinking about; and don't say 'not much' because the look on your face screamed the opposite."

His smile faded, replaced by a look of resolve. "Shelf the political party, Diana: It's a dead end that will suck every bit of life out of you, all of us. And I'd advise we proceed very cautiously with organizing direct action on a national level, too. My books and the work we do here is having a positive impact across the nation; hitting the streets will only provide an excuse for the wackos to run amuck."

A confounded expression appeared on Diana's face. "I'm surprised, to say the least. I thought you were onboard with taking the next step in our fight for rights. What's going on? What changed your mind?"

Wolf looked thoughtful. "What's going on is that we're all vulnerable to being struck by flights of fancy but reason returns eventually. Think about it, Diana. You know that the large majority of voters are deeply invested in our contemporary sugar daddy policies and will not rally around the banner of liberty and individual rights. True, many give lip service to wanting a smaller government, cutting the national debt, draining the swamp and so forth, but don't dare touch one cent of their Social Security, ban lobbyists, eliminate ethanol, cut aid to schools or not fund NPR along with a thousand other goodies flowing from federal and state teats.

"Calling for a political party dedicated to restoring the original format of the Republic will distract every member of CIR, shifting our focus from defending and promoting individual rights to getting people elected who will be championing a political position totally out of step with the nation. It's not worth the time, effort and money we'll have to invest. Beyond the initial media brouhaha and a perhaps a spike in revenue, it's a lose-lose proposition long-term."

"I'm sorry, Diana, but upon reconsideration of the issue, I have to agree with Wolf," Annika said. "My objection is grounded along a parallel consideration. All of us at CIR are on over a dozen social media groups, many comprised of likeminded people who oppose the collectivist tide and speak or fight for freedom regularly. But look what happens when someone voices an opinion or makes a suggestion in these groups that others don't agree with or just don't like? They jump on some non-essential bit from one or hundred thoughtful posts and declare the writers to be either deluded or a malevolent troll and the infighting goes on unabated. It exhausting having to negotiate around these hacks twenty times or more daily; I can just imagine endless bickering about a thousand details as we move to launch a new political party. And that's just the people at the convention. Now try selling it to the entire country. Wolf's right on this one, Diana."

"And what about deep sea finishing rights, huh?" Wolf said.

Diana shot him a puzzled look. "What are you talking about?"

"Deep sea fishing rights," he repeated. "I want to make sure that my right to catch fish in the deep blue sea is not infringed upon. So, what's it gonna be? Yes or no?"

Both women must have thought he lost his marbles because they stared open-mouthed at him. He gave them a bright grin.

"Just illustrating Annika's point," he said, "and mine. The world of political activists is a witch's brew of every known idea, position and viewpoint to which a hefty pinch of irrationality is added keeping the cauldron bubbling and seething, thus my demand about deep sea fishing rights. That's a line from the musical 1776, by the way. On that note, I've made reservations to see Hamilton on Broadway this Saturday, so I'll be jetting to the Big Apple this afternoon. I'll be back Sunday evening. Questions?"

Wolf hadn't made any plans of that nature. It was a spontaneous remark that popped into his mind and escaping from his mouth before he realized what he'd said. But having uttered such plans he decided to act on the idea the moment he fled from the meeting.

After a brief flurry of questions including the one always asked of him when setting out on any form of entertainment, the one about bringing a date, he exacted a promise from Diana that she would not announce the formation of a political party nor launch a frontal assault on Virginia Patriots College while he was out of town.

Having parried all attempts to get him to confess to a tryst with an old flame or perhaps a fresh lover? he bade the ladies adieu, retreating into the stillness of his office. He managed to securing a flight, lodgings and reservations for Hamilton Saturday evening and do so without paying through the nose for the short notice.

Chapter 7

Unforeseen Encounters

Wolf's denials about the trip including rendezvous with women turned out to be glaringly wrong considering the inconvenient fact that he was lying next to one in—where was he? Then he remembered.

He hadn't been in his hotel room more than a few minutes last evening when his cell buzzed. Eyeing the screen, he recognized the name immediately and answered it. Though he was thinking of declining, but owing her a big favor, of course he'd like to join her for dinner and catch up on old times. After-dinner conversation turned into late-night dancing and drinks at a SoHo nightclub, the gentle swaying of bodies on the dance floor eliciting an invitation to come home with her.

Wolf reached over on the nightstand for his phone and watch, slipping the latter on his wrist and got up. Few people bothered wearing a wristwatch as the time is always displayed on everyone's digital displays, but he liked knowing that his timepiece was there providing backup during some unforeseen crash of the local communications network.

He looked down at the sleeping woman, a vague unease creeping into his mind. He hadn't planned meeting with anyone during his impromptu excursion, especially a woman and definitely not with any thought of sleeping with one. Yet here he was standing in a woman's bedroom feeling guilty, not about making love to her, but at his thoughtlessness for her safety. He should not have let his guard down, meeting her in such a public restaurant and worse, going partying with her in a Manhattan nightclub where they could be easily seen by unfriendly eyes.

It's been three years since Screw You, Suckers! was published, but Wolf knew there were no statutes of limitation for anyone leaking information and providing copies of documents to be safe from retribution by powerful individuals, such as the incensed treasurer for a green energy company who called Wolf a "fucking muckraking whore!" as federal authorities were taking him away. Miscreants like him would not easily forget or forgive anyone they knew to have shared even a most innocent encounter with the big, bad Wolf.

Any woman seen in his company for more than an occasional meeting was a potential target for revenge on Wolf and the Center for Individual Rights. Any woman or man connected in even the most remote way to one of Wolf's muckraking targets became suspect and might have his or her life turned upside-down by person or persons unknown. Payback for real or imagined offenses against an employer or organization might include exposure of previous arrest records or an extra-marital affair, identify theft racking up tens of thousands of dollar charges on credit cards, being fired (illegal) and blackballed from securing similar employment. To the best of his knowledge, none of Wolf's many informants and spies had been mysteriously killed, providing an important measure of psychological comfort and relief as he waded through the muck of the labyrinth of deceit, lies and malevolence which had produced a shelf full of fictional non-fiction exposes for going on two decades.

There was always fallout from his books, however: employees or contractor suspected of colluding with Wolf were demoted, placed on blacklists never to be promoted or summarily fired.

"Good morning," a mumbled voice said. "Not running away, are you?"

"Morning, Maddie." Wolf sat on the edge of the bed, leaned over and kissed her forehead. "Should I be?"

"What do you think?" she replied, a sly grin on her lips.

"I think I should get back into bed and have an intimate discussion about it."

A refreshing shower followed that satisfying intimate conversation with Wolf offering to make breakfast while Maddie got dressed. Wolf was an accomplished cook, whipping up tasty meals in short order. By the time Maddie came in the kitchen, a pair of Western Omelets with fried potatoes rescued from the fridge in the shape of crescent moons lined the rim of each plate. A mug of hot coffee stood at one o'clock position adjacent each plate of food.

"Wow," Maddie said, gazing at the table. "Grayson Wolf, chef extraordinaire. Who would have thought it?"

He shot her a look. "Lover extraordinaire also, perhaps?"

Maddie appeared to give his question serious consideration, then said, "Three stars…sorry but I always tell the truth. Most of the time."

"I'm not complaining," he replied, a smile lighting up his face, "considering my, ah, limited experience with intimate encounters."

Maddie shot him a shrewd look. "I have a difficult time trying to place limited experience and Grayson Wolf in the same sentence. You're rich, famous, ruggedly attractive, possessing a charming manner and disarming personality. You must have to ward off legions of women wishing to ravish you."

Wolf looked incredulous for a moment; then laughed. "Damn girl; you must be one hell of a lawyer because for a moment even I believed your description of me."

She gazed at him for a long moment, her expression inscrutable. "How do you see yourself?"

He shrugged. "Grayson Wolf: driving others to excessive drink, possessing a grating personality and charming manner of a rattlesnake who is delighted and honored to be in the company of the woman in this room." Maddie's composure changed as tears filled her eyes and rolled down her cheeks catching Wolf off guard. He placed his hand on hers. "Did I say something to upset you?"

She shook her head; a wan smile appeared soon thereafter. "Just your grating personality and charming manner of a rattlesnake…I wanted to sleep with you many times back then but I knew why it was unwise to get involved in that way. And the fact that you never gave any sign you wanted to, of course."

"If I didn't know any better, Maddie," Wolf replied, looking closely at her, "I'd say you regret doing so."

"Of course not," she hurriedly replied. "I'm surprised that's all."

"To be honest, I'm just as surprised as you are. What I do offers, um, limited opportunities to have a normal relationship with a woman due to the risk of their lives being disrupted."

Maddie looked askance at him. "So, am I a moment's weakness of your resolve or absolving a feeling of guilt?"

"I never act from a feeling of weakness and I always pay my debts," Wolf replied. "My resolve is sometimes subject to being overpowered, however."

"Like I said," she smiled warmly, "charming manner and disarming personality."

"Back at cha," Wolf said. He rose and cleared the dishes off the table.

Maddie eyes followed his swift and efficient movements. "Why do I get the feeling that our time together is coming to a close?"

"As much as I'd love to spend the entire weekend with you," Wolf replied, "further carousing is hard to keep secret. I won't risk exposing your connection to the infamous Grayson Wolf any further; I lug around plenty worry for the dozens of brave men and women who shared vital information about the scuzballs I write about without adding more."

He collected his things and made for the door. "Thank you, Maddie for being you: daring, resourceful and beautiful. Take care of yourself; I'm sure we'll see each other soon enough." He stepped into the corridor.

"Wolf." He turned to face her. "Five stars. Three for the whoopee a forth for your cooking and the fifth for being you. Remember that next time we see each other." She gazed at him for a long moment, her expression distant. She hugged and briefly kissed him, closing her door shortly after he started down the hall to the elevators.

The mild sensation of falling experienced as the elevator slid rapidly down the shaft, heightened Wolf's feelings of loss and deprivation as the elevator lowered him fourteen stories to the building's lobby. The doors opened...and closed. His finger jabbed angrily at the 14th floor button and the elevator lifted, stopping at its programmed designation moments later. The doors opened...and closed. His finger moved toward the 'open' button when the elevator began to descent, called by others some floors below. He took it as a sign that fate had decided for him and got out in the lobby with several others who had boarded the elevator at sundry stops on its trip down.

The morning reflected his mood quite perfectly: gray and dreary, a cold drizzle propelled by a blustery wind smacking his face and penetrating openings in his coat. By the time he managed to secure a cab, a thoroughly saturated and miserable Wolf entered his hotel room stripping off his wet clothing, tossing them in a pile at the foot of his bed. A call to the concierge brought a knock on his door five minutes later and an employee whisked away his bag filled with damp, rumpled clothing with a promise to return them cleaned and pressed no later than noon.

After a second shower that morning, Wolf was reviewing the collection of messages that had accumulated in his phone over the past twelve hours ignoring any that were not urgent, meaning life or death. Though he gave Maddie explicit directions not to text, tweet, poke or leave any message, he would have enjoyed seeing one from her nonetheless.

"Grayson Wolf: poor little rich kid," he said aloud, chiding himself for wallowing in self-pity. Not that he was wallowing, but these thoughts and feeling were starting to become an annoying intrusion in his life and he was getting angry about it. "It" being this upwell of mixed feelings composed of resentment, unhappiness and dissatisfaction with the direction his life was going—or gone?

Wolf concluded he had no regrets about what he had accomplished and the stunning level of success he attained. But after fifteen years of being on the road, burrowing into the background to avoid detection, deferring much of what makes life enjoyable—intimate and lasting relationships, love—Wolf had reached a psychological saturation point. He no longer was inspired as he had been for years, motivated by the purpose to ferret out and expose the hypocrisy, lies and malfeasance that propped up organizations and individuals claiming to do good works—saving the planet, promoting equality and a hundred other pretenses—when in fact their actions and objectives proved otherwise.

He saw what had been his mission slowly devolve into an expectation of continuation, an obligation, a duty—a sacrifice: the exchange of a higher value for a lower or non-value. He remembered vividly the aroma of Maddie's hair, the smooth silkiness of her skin, her warm embrace, the taste of her lips, the firmness of her breasts, the ecstasy of climax and he knew in order to have that life, a life of uncomplicated joy and happiness, he would need to stop.

The admission of what he would have considered impossible before filled him with a sense of indescribable joy, a sensation rarely felt since perhaps childhood. The realization that he needed to change and that he could choose to change any time he wished set him free that very moment.

Wolf jumped up from the bed, a bolt of electrical energy shooting through his body, making his fingers tingle and setting his mind on fire. He had no clue where he was going, but he was going somewhere new or different. A dozen possibilities popped into his mind, reasonable ideas such as picking up his quest to become a champion poker player or writing mysteries to nonsensical ones like becoming a decadent playboy jetting to and from exotic locations. Whatever it would be, Wolf felt confident the answer would present itself in the fullness of time. He knew he possessed the talent, motivation and diverse skills to tackle whatever was to come and looked forward to that moment of clarity whenever it struck.

The rain stopped, the day turned progressively brighter and he spent the afternoon playing tourist, beginning with a leisurely cruise circling Manhattan, followed by a visit to the National September 11 Memorial and Museum. Considering his state of mind, not exactly a prudent choice, though its somber atmosphere bristled with examples illustrating the triumph of the human spirit over what had been a challenging and dangerous time for New Yorkers and America. The ride up One World Trade Center and its magnificent Observatory did not fail to lift his spirits, as did the sudden appearance of brilliant sunshine when he approached the windows illuminating large swaths of the city laid out beneath his feet.

By the time Wolf got back to his hotel it was after six. He had to hurry if he was going to get himself ready for dinner and to the theater before the start of Hamilton at eight. It took him less than thirty minutes to shower, complete appropriate grooming and preening, the taxi delivering him at the entrance of the restaurant before seven—6:53 to be precise, as the Tin-Tin character Thompson would say.

Wolf declined his waiter's recommendations for wine and appetizers choosing a meal the attendant assured him would be ready within fifteen minutes. As promised, the meal appeared within the time allowed, handing his credit card to the waiter so as not to delay his departure for the theater.

Manhattan streets are crowded with vehicles every day, but especially busy Saturday evenings and today was no exception. After five minutes of waving and whistling at taxis that passed without stopping, Wolf took off by foot for the theater four streets west and seven north. Fortunately, most Manhattan blocks are relatively compact compared to other cities he had visited and he arrived at the theater with ten minutes to spare.

He had been lucky when he secured his ticket because the house was sold out except for several seats in the Lower Mezzanine freed moments before. It was a good seat, front row, though adjacent to the wall providing an oblique, but unobstructed view of the stage. The entire row was empty when he arrived and had just sat when a small party appeared and occupied seats in his row closest to the center. Wolf immediately recognized the elegant middle-aged man who sat in the middle of the group: Larry Silverstone of Silverstone & Associates law firm, Colleen Silverstone's father who was featured in Screw You, Suckers! in a most uncomplimentary manner.

Wolf bit his lip not to burst out laughing at the wild coincidence attending Hamilton on the same evening and sitting in the same row as Silverstone. Not only would such an outburst attract attention, God only knows what the man might do seeing his nemesis but a dozen seats away. He couldn't prevent the release of a low chortle, however, thinking about the chances of running into the man on this rare visit to the city. He would need to plan his moves carefully to avoid being seen during the intermission, or heaven forbid, wind up standing next to Silverstone at a urinal!

Wolf was thinking about how his evening was promising to be an especially interesting one when the improbable encounter transformed into the impossible encounter with the arrival of Justin Bellamy accompanied by a woman several decades younger. If there was such an entity as fate, Wolf mused, it had clearly orchestrated events as a cosmic joke.

Or… was he handed an exceptional opportunity on a silver platter?

The theater darkened, the overture played and the curtain rose. From the first lines and songs, Hamilton confirmed the adulations of the critics keeping Wolf's attention on the unfolding drama effectively parrying stray thoughts about the men sitting a dozen seats to his right. Aiding Wolf's enjoyment of the show was the need for no further contemplation about the men to his right, having conjured a plan within the minute the house lights went dark. He smiled, looking forward to intermission when *his* impromptu show would begin.

Ninety minutes later—it felt more like thirty—the lights came up signaling a fifteen-minute intermission. Wolf was careful to keep his face turned partially toward the wall pretending to read his program. When the row had emptied, he got up glancing surreptitiously at his departing target and proceeded to follow.

Staying in the midst of the shifting crowd, he kept an eye on Silverstone and Bellamy as they secured drinks from the concession stand and handed glasses to the women in their company. They retired to the rear of the lobby where they stood talking until their glasses were empty. Intermission would be drawing to close soon and as hoped, the men and women parted, each making for their respective restrooms.

Wolf waited outside the men's room, positioned away from the flow of traffic reducing the chance of Silverstone seeing him when the man exited the room. He was counting on the simple fact that, unlike little boys, Silverstone and Bellamy would not exit together and hoping that Bellamy would come out last. If not, he'd try to corral the man at the end of the show and do so without Silverstone being any the wiser.

There was the risk that Bellamy might recognize Wolf; he and Silverstone were partners in sleaze after all and the man's hedge fund was featured, albeit peripherally, in Screw You, Suckers! Unlike Silverstone, however, Wolf did not get up close and personal into the financier's life thus his hope that Bellamy would not recognize him. If he did, Wolf could imagine the man coming at him with both fists swinging.

Lady Luck was with Wolf, spotting Silverstone exiting the men's room first and proceed down the corridor. Wolf moved near the door waiting… several men came out then Bellamy. Wolf stepped forward and bumped into him.

"Oh, I'm terribly sorry sir," Wolf said, with a faint Western twang. He had years of practice switching to any number of accents and affectations. "Too busy thinking about things… an occupational hazard of my field I fear."

"Don't worry about it," Bellamy replied, brusquely.

"Excuse me," Wolf said walking alongside the man, "I'm sure we've met before..."

"I don't think so," he replied, and kept walking.

Wolf had to move quickly before Bellamy reached the lobby. "I remember now. You're Mr. Bellamy I believe. Your son Kerry is at Overland University."

Bellamy stopped and eyed Wolf. "You know my son?"

"My specialty is fiction and communication," Wolf replied, relieved to see Bellamy didn't recognize him—yet.

"You teach at the college."

Wolf smiled. "I suppose you heard about that unfortunate incident last December..."

Bellamy's face became very still.

"That poor girl, Sarah Lewis," Wolf continued, making a contrite face. "And recently ... you probably heard about the boy who went to jail for the crime committing suicide. Not the best of news for the college, I dare say."

Wolf had years of experience reading people's faces and though Bellamy appeared tense as he doled out his comments to amplify their impact, Sarah's name and the suicide remark didn't produce any reaction beyond general anxiety any father might feel toward a dissolute son like Kerry, the Overland bitch king.

Bellamy started to shift. "Nice meeting you, ah, I didn't catch your name, professor."

"Gray," Wolf said, mentally kicking himself for using part of his first name.

"Enjoy the rest of the show professor Gray," he said, and hurried away.

Flashing lights announced the end of intermission. Wolf waited until the theater lights went dark before entering the Mezzanine level, shooting quick glances at Silverstone and Bellamy as he made his way to his seat. The second act did not disappoint and Wolf was one of the last to leave the theater hooking a cab on the first try and back to his hotel without incident.

Resting on the bed with iPad in hand he entered the findings of his encounter with Bellamy, exploring different interpretations of his conclusions about the man's reaction, or lack thereof, for future reference; assuming that Colleen Silverstone found anything noteworthy in her investigation. He exchanged the iPad for a book about war and governing, read until two then went to bed.

*   *   *   *

Wolf stood at the window of his hotel room early Sunday morning gazing out over the expanse of Central Park thirty floors below marveling at the genius of its existence in the heart of Manhattan, totally encircled by a wall of stone, glass and steel. Unlike yesterday, it was bright and cheery; a perfect morning for a ramble through the park, its serenity providing ample opportunity to reflect upon the events of the past two days.

During breakfast, he imagined Maddie sitting across the table as she did yesterday morning, enjoying the simplicity of sharing a meal, having a normal conversation about nothing in particular, remembering her smile and every moment with her the night before. This time, however, his ruminations were not melancholy unlike those that had plagued him recently. Today was a new day, a day energized by the knowledge that he was open to new possibilities, free to actively seek other choices to explore.

Wolf was in no particular hurry as he walked along sundry paths through Central Park. He luxuriated in the knowledge that there was no agenda, no pressing engagement, no clandestine meeting, just a lovely stroll on a cool spring morning taking in the sights, sounds and aromas of the park.

His reverie was abruptly interrupted when he spotted Belvedere Castle as he skirted Turtle Pond. Looking up the slope to his left, hidden from sight, was the bench where he had met Maddie numerous times for the purpose of passing information, documents and rumors concerning Silverstone's law firm and Bellamy's hedge fund four years ago. He smiled at the coincidence, reflecting how so much in life seemed to pop back into one's awareness when least expected.

Wolf met no further coincidences the rest of his sojourn through the park that morning and by one was back negotiating across traffic and the press of humanity rushing—everyone hurries in Manhattan—to get to wherever they were going, which at this hour included a place to eat lunch.

Making his way south on Central Park West, Wolf crossed over Columbus Circle and aimed for Robert, a popular restaurant overlooking the circle with a nice view of the area and quality food. Though busy, he was quickly seated, ordered an eclectic assortment of dishes and a draft beer. He spent the time waiting for the food to arrive contemplating the degree of intimacy between couples at adjacent tables observing their body language, the distance between them and facial expressions. By the time lunch arrived, Wolf estimated that of the eight couples he had been studying, three were married, three were business associates and one was a new relationship. The eighth couple was most certainly a professional arrangement, Wolf guessing that the man was an escort, the woman paying for his company.

By half past two Wolf left the restaurant, took the elevator to the lobby, exited the building planning a leisurely stroll back to his hotel, when he was approached by two men he recognized immediately as federal agents. He slowed as they approached.

A mischievous glint appeared in Wolf's eyes. "I don't know why the agency insists you wear clothing that screams FBI. Why not just dress in uniforms and have it done with?"

The younger of the two spoke. "Please accompany us, Mr. Wolf."

Please go screw yourselves is what he wanted to say, "Thanks but I've already eaten lunch," is what came out of his mouth. Curious what this was about he pointed over at Columbus Circle. "Tell you what. I'll walk over and sit on one of the benches. Happy to talk with anyone that joins me."

He turned and crossed the street arriving at an unoccupied bench a few minutes later and took a seat. Within moments three agents approached, the two that had accosted him and a third, their boss no doubt. The third man sat down, the pair stood guard, their eyes darting back and forth over the ebb and flow of the crowd. Wolf rotated his body to better converse with the man.

"I'm all ears," he quipped, "but I do have a flight to catch in two hours."

"Why are you in New York, Mr. Wolf?"

This was becoming a tiresome déjà vu.

"You know my name," Wolf replied, "let's begin with you telling me yours and just so there's no confusion, please show me your ID."

"O'Brian." He produced a wallet and flashed his badge and identification.

"Well, special FBI agent O'Brian," Wolf said, eyeing the ID, "perhaps you can tell me why you and I are sitting on a bench in Columbus Circle wasting our precious time?"

"You had a conversation with Justin Bellamy," he said, ignoring Wolf's challenge. "What was the topic of your conversation?"

"The topic of my conversation with, ah, Bellman, was it?" O'Brian corrected him. "Right, Bellamy. Just happen to bump into him and apologized; he graciously accepted my apology, we exchanged a few niceties about the wonderful show and catchy music and parted ways once more."

"I know all about you, Mr. Wolf." O'Brian's tone was unmistakably hostile. "I know how you operate, skulking around the shadows and so on. You'll have to pardon me if I say that you're telling me a load of crap."

"Perhaps you haven't read the news over the past year, agent O'Brian," Wolf retorted. "Let me enlighten you: the FBI has been dishing out boatloads of crap about who did what and who did not and who did this, then did not and how evidence flutters from the sky one day only to magically disappear the next. Some might conclude that the FBI is one huge crap manufacturing machine."

Don't tread on Wolf, Mofo.

"I am warning you, Mr. Wolf," O'Brian shot back. "You are to stay far away from Bellamy or I will have you arrested for interfering with an ongoing investigation. Do you understand?"

Wolf's hardy laugh caught O'Brian off-guard. "Ongoing investigation? You mean the investigation regarding malfeasance, corruption, misuse of funds, money laundering and kicking helpless puppies to the curb that's been going on for six years? I recall writing *something* about it in one or two of my books a while back."

"I cannot speak to the substance or details of any ongoing investigation," O'Brian replied. "I am warning you to stay away from making any contact in any manner with Bellamy."

"I'm confused," Wolf said, his tone mocking. "I am not

allowed to have any contact with Bellamy, but scum ball Silverstone can do lap dances on him. Besides my esteemed self,
who else is banned from the honor of reaching out and touching Bellamy in whatever way they desire?"

"I cannot speak to the substance or details of any ongoing investigation," O'Brian repeated.

"Now who's dishing out a load of crap, agent O'Brian?"

O'Brian rose and shot Wolf a most malevolent look. "Last and final warning: stay away from Bellamy or I will have you arrested for interfering with an ongoing investigation." He spun around and marched away, the escort twins on his heels.

Wolf watched him go. This was a load of crap. The feds had been trying to take down Bellamy and his Hedge Fund for near a decade yet the man and his gang keep going full stop without an indictment on the horizon. All the while a hundred bankers and other Wall Street figures suffer arrest and drawn out legal battles only to discover that zealous US Attorneys or local District Attorneys looking to make a name for themselves have no real case and no sustentative evidence of any crime defendants were accused of committing.

And after a mere twelve hours after bumping into the man, Special Agent O'Brian appears warning Wolf off Bellamy.

Curiouser and curiouser.

Chapter 8

Round Two

Monday, Monday: A cry of distress heard from sea to shining sea as millions drag tired bodies out of bed after weekends that appears to blow past with the speed of a Chinook blast. Wolf didn't feel that way about Monday or any day because he never viewed work as drudgery although he had been struggling with doubts about his life as of late.

The events and subsequent reflections over the weekend had re-energized him, though not in the way that his friends and associates might understand or be inclined to readily accept. Wolf himself was unclear what the next phase of his life's journey would be and in the meantime, there was plenty of loose ends to tie up while waiting expectantly for a sign pointing toward a new direction.

By the time he arrived at the office, a mere five-floor commute below his residence, CIR's Steering Committee had already convened in the Jefferson Conference Room. He greeted everyone upon entering and headed for the refreshment counter figuring this was a four-cup coffee Monday.

Peering at the charts displayed on several TV screens and the packet of documents resting on the table by his seat, Diana Ruiz had been a very busy beaver over the weekend. But then he'd expect no less from an A-type personality and Diana was never one to disappoint. He was happy that the Center would be in her capable hands when the time came—if the time came.

Wolf became aware someone was speaking to him. "Excuse me?"

"How was your mini-vay?" Diana asked.

"Mini, but fun."

DJ shot Wolf a suggestive grin. "Fun, huh? Good Wolfie…"

Wolf rolled his eyes. "Thank you, Mr. one-track mind." He looked over at Diana. "We're gathered on a Monday morning so I assume there are new developments pursuant to Lee Sterling and VPC?"

Diana pressed her lips and made a satisfied expression. "You're on Brett; show us what you got."

Brett, CIR's computer maven, pressed a remote and all screens flashed to another scene, this one showing a section of CIR's website homepage. He scrolled slowly down the page.

"This will get everyone's attention," Wolf said. His eyes shot over at the head of security. "Might want to double up our muscle, Teena."

"Very funny, Wolf," Diana quipped. "This isn't any more inflammatory than other campaigns we've done...and before you ask: Juan?"

The counselor cleared his throat. "It's all legal. The photos were taken at various protests making them public. The names of the rioters were provided by other students; thus, obtained legally. Students have a First Amendment right to protest and we have a First Amendment right to publish their faces, actions and names. And if I may add my personal opinion, we should do this for every wanton demonstration at any college from now on. These punks have no respect for the rights of anyone and it's high time they were held accountable for their actions by *someone*."

"And that someone is us," Diana added. "Brett, continue please."

The tech's second broadside was fired at the VPC's faculty, showing each member's face and name under the headline, Furious at a President...Silent as The Grave and Meek as Lambs in The Face of Student Violence and Intimidation. His final volley was aimed at the administration under the headline, Enemy of Students for Individual Rights, Friend of Student Tyrants.

"Everyone okay with launching the broadsides?" Diana asked. There being no opposition she continued. "Brett, if you'll do the honors..."

"Roger that," Brett replied, and left the room.

"Where are we with Sterling?" Wolf said.

"We're going forward with a civil suit pursuant to several facets of Lee's Constitutional rights being denied by VPC," Juan explained. "We will simultaneously sue the school for damages; one hundred million and a jury trial."

"Hundred million." Wolf gazed expectantly at the attorney.

"There are five plaintiffs," Juan said, looking smug. "The four VPC students that were attacked; each sustaining physical and psychological trauma. We will show there has been a long pattern of failure by the administration to properly protect the student body from harassment, verbal abuse and increasingly, threats and acts of bodily harm." He paused, looked expectantly at the committee then continued. "For a while now I've been mulling a novel means of attack against complicit administrators; all that was needed was an appropriate event and the VPC incident and subsequent action by its president has handed us a huge, really huge, opportunity."

Juan stopped again, waiting.

"And here I thought Diana was the only drama queen on the staff," RJ said, resulting in an outburst of laugher around the table.

Diana shot RJ an, I-will-hurt-you look. "Please continue, Juan."

Juan smiled and held up a fistful of brochures. "According to virtually every one of their promotional literature and ads, college is far more than going to classes and getting a degree. They all promote the collegiate atmosphere, the social opportunities, the freedom to explore ideas and so forth. Not only their promotional material makes that promise..." He dropped the brochures on the table and picked up a larger booklet. "Upon enrollment, students receive the colleges' student handbook and campus guide that officially confirms what was cited in their promotional literature. In addition, the handbook articulates expectations, rules of behavior, consequences for breaking rules, and so forth ... the one I'm holding in my hand is the one given to Lee Sterling upon his enrollment. In addition to suing VPC on behalf of Lee pursuant to the school abrogating his Constitutional rights, we plan to press the claim on behalf of all five clients that their right to an *equal educational experience* as guaranteed by VPC's handbook, a de facto contract between the college and its students, has been denied." Juan took a breath and put the handbook back on the table and remained standing.

"That's not all, is it, Juan?" Annika said, a big grin on her face.

A very smug expression formed on the attorney's face. "Not by a long shot. We're planning to elevate the equal educational experience claim into class action status. What's been happening at

Virginia Patriots is echoed in colleges across the nation. Not only are administrators and faculty failing to take any punitive action against their campus thugs, many of them provide de facto cover and support by making excuses or lame comments about the right to express outrage to so called "hate speech," anything claimed as being racist, homophobic, sexist, etc., effectively silencing students holding differing opinions, ideas and viewpoints. It's intimidation; nothing more, nothing less."

RJ waved an open hand in the air. "Five VPC students does not a class-action suit make, I would think."

"It'll become many more, hundreds, maybe a couple thousand," Juan replied. "Damages will be sky high."

"Define sky high," Annika asked.

Juan looked thoughtful for a moment and smiled. "Maybe a billion."

Wolf barked a laugh. "Keep talking like that and I'll have to write a new not-so-fictional expose featuring you."

The smile vanished from Juan's face. "Oh, I'm just getting started."

Wolf knew exactly what the lawyer was thinking because he knew the ways of CIR. "We're goin to hire lawyers from every state of the union, aren't we?"

"What?" an alarmed CFO cried. "Why would we do that? What for?"

"We're going to need all those lawyers, Annika," Juan said, "because we will sue every college and university that's been violating the due process of their students and," he raised a finger, "allowing a thuggish minority to deprive other students of an equal opportunity to fully participate in what these colleges contractually offer every student—equally."

"It's going to take some time to assemble such a formidable legal army," Teena suggested. "And we'll also need to expand our security capability to offer protection to folks if and when they are threatened."

"Yes, it will," Diana said, a meaningful grin on her lips. "And VPC has presented itself as the test case for a legal frontal assault against universities on the proverbial silver platter."

"Like we don't have enough battles going on already." Annika laughed.

"I've been at this from the early days of CIR," Diana replied, her tone hard. "During that time, I've seen the transformation of colleges from centers of higher education where students learned the philosophical foundations of our nation become authoritarian hothouses producing mindless
puppets sucking their thumbs in designated safe spaces. And in the last five years we've got the neo Red Guards or Brown Shirts—take your pick—prowling our colleges terrorizing students and cowering the faculty. The time for talk and debate is not over, but the time for more than talk and debate is upon us whether we like it or not."

Wolf grinned and said, "What do you have in mind, Diana? Battering rams perhaps?"

"Something very much like that," she replied. "For years our goal has been to build opposition within the college walls by organizing and supporting student groups to educate, promote and defend individual rights. Important and critical, yes, but it takes a long time to change a culture. The time has come to ratchet up pressure on the institution itself and Virginia Patriots College is a good place to begin."

"What exactly do you have in mind, Diana?" Teena asked. As head of security, the woman was keenly aware of the geometric challenges pursuant to keeping people safe and sound. "A march onto campus? Rallies? Incursion via hot air balloons?"

"A mass demonstration lasting at least a week near the college for starters," she explained. "I'm talking one thousand; tents, latrines, meals, teach-ins and yes, marches and rallies. All of it broadcast live on every form of electronic communications known to man. Let's see what those mealy-mouthed, yellow-livered, spineless college administrators and faculty have to say and do about that."

"What about the kitchen sink?" Juan chuckled. "Going to throw that at them too, I hope?"

"Hell yes," Diana laughed. "I'm gonna bring a Mack truck full of them!"

"We're going to need tight security, Diana," Teena cautioned. "Some of those college Red Guards might get a bit frisky."

"I fully expect them to," Diana replied. "And we are going to be prepared to deal with them in some creative ways I've got in mind. We'll talk about that later."

"When are you thinking about launching this armada?" Annika said. "And how much money will you need?"

"Mid-April, before the end of the term while all the students are still in classes and before final exams," Diana replied. "Two weeks, from now. I'll sit down with you and we can go over numbers."

Diana adjourned the meeting. As everyone was leaving Wolf signaled RJ to wait up.

He grinned. "What's up good looking?"

"Hasn't anyone ever told you it's not wise to hit on your boss?" Wolf retorted.

RJ's lips twitched. "I think you might have mentioned it once or twice. But being a card-carrying member of our society's protected class, I can do what I damn well please, remember?"

"I think you did mention it once or twice," Wolf said. "Thanks for reminding me; don't want to run afoul of the PC block Nazi."

"So, what's the buzz?" RJ said. "No, wait, don't tell me. Using my special seventh sense only sexually oriented men like me possess, I'll summon the thoughts directly from your mind..."

His face went through a few contortions as he struggled to achieve this unique feat of mindreading. Wolf waited patiently for the media maven to do his thing.

"I've got it," he said, momentarily. "You're wondering how I knew you got lucky over the weekend."

Wolf gazed coolly at RJ, his bland expression revealing nothing. "Go on."

RJ cocked his head from one side to the other. "Blond, late thirties, slim but curvy...I'd guess Friday night." Looking smugger than usual, he added "and she called you."

This was way to accurate to be a guess. RJ either could read his mind or...

"You been stalking me, bro?" Wolf said, feigning anger.

"Don't need to do the deed," he replied, looking smug. "We have an extensive network of eyes and ears, you may recall."

"Which network are you referring to?" Wolf grinned. "The friends of liberty or the gay tribe?"

RJ puckered his lips and shrugged. "Whichever one is needed to get the job done."

"So why the surveillance?" Wolf said. "Some folks thinking I'm planning to run off with the treasury?"

"Some folks a little spooked about your sudden change of mood after you returned from Colorado, Wolf." RJ said.

Wolf made a droll face. "You worried about me, RJ? That's so sweet."

"I wasn't until I heard about Maddie," he replied. "Since when are you hooking up with informants? Thought that was a big no-no?"

"*Former* informant," Wolf retorted. RJ was about to object and he raised a hand. "Yeah, yeah, I know: no such thing as a former informant. Just a one-off, RJ; Maddie knows there's no repeats."

"We've been bosom buddies for twenty years, bro and I don't need my special seventh sense to know that something is stirring in that mind of yours," RJ said. "You're thirty-five and have arrived at the first of at least two life crises. You've done amazing things, Wolf: flying under the radar to investigate liars and thieves, write blockbuster books dramatizing the conflicts between the ugly and the beautiful, launch CIR to protect our rights. Then you wake up one morning and something has changed and you find yourself reflecting and evaluating everything you've been doing and discover that maybe you don't want to keep doing it. How am I doing, bro?"

Wolf nodded. "Batting a thousand."

A sweeping flourish of RJ's hand acknowledged Wolf's agreement with his assessment. "Maddie may be a no-no, but she's a good start to your new journey, wherever that may be. An intimate relationship—preferably a consistent one—is a crucial element of happiness and you, my good friend are years overdue."

"I have you, remember?" Wolf said, looking excessively appreciative.

"And I'd be delighted if that was the case," RJ replied, giving him the look. "But we both know that you are not of my tribe. What about that hot District Attorney in Colorado?"

Wolf made a sad face. "Married. But even if she were available, I sensed she was not exactly a fan of the Wolf."

"Colleen Silverstone?" RJ said, his infectious grin suggesting any number of intimate possibilities. "One hot looking mongrel."

Wolf shot him an alarmed look. "*Never* let Colleen hear you refer to her as a dog if you value your life, RJ."

"Oh, *Colleen* is it now?" RJ said, his eyebrows wiggling his approval. "For the record, I wasn't dissing her; quite the opposite. Mixed breeds often tend to be better looking and smarter to boot. Colleen Silverstone: Mother of Irish descent; Jamaican father— deceased; Jewish stepfather. And don't even pretend you didn't check her out when you visited her fortress—twice, I might add."

"Yes, I checked her out," Wolf admitted. "Impossible not to notice her." An image of a tall, impressive figure popped into his head possessing warm, radiant skin, a striking face with compelling amber colored eyes, golden-brown wavy hair, and a gorgeous smile. He heard RJ laughing from far away.

"You're thinking about her right now."

"Impossible not to notice her," Wolf replied, "and hard to forget her. But no use thinking about her because of that huge gap between us called Larry Silverstone."

"Flip side of hate is love, bro." RJ quipped. "You did visit her twice and walked away in one piece each time."

"Only because she was curious why I dared to enter her lair and the fact there were witnesses present," Wolf joked. "The only reason she accepted the contract to help me was because she felt sorry for me, having been busted up from the accident."

"Sure, the accident," RJ said sarcastically, drawing out the last word.

"Yes, accident," Wolf replied. "Until I find out any different."

"Opposites do attract and the more powerful the entities the greater the attraction," RJ said, returning to the previous topic. "Don't discount Silverstone; she'd be the perfect woman for you."

"Now you're a matchmaker?" Wolf said, in his best Yiddish accent.

"Think about it Wolf," he replied. "You have enemies galore; she's got a national security force at her beck and call not to mention she's a force to be reckoned with all by herself. Like I said, the perfect woman for Grayson Wolf."

"Well that settles it then!" Wolf cried enthusiastically. "I'll just catch the next plane, fly her to Las Vegas and get hitched. Wham, bam, thank you ma'am."

"Anyone ever tell you that you're one sarcastic bastard?" RJ retorted.

"Yes," Wolf said, giving him a sardonic look, "you do all the time."

"And it's a good thing you have me around to keep you in check and look out for you," he replied, "like marshaling muscle to prevent those shady characters you ran into at Columbus Circle from kidnapping you."

"They were FBI and I handled them quite well by my lone self, thank you."

"Like I said: shady characters." RJ insisted. "What is it with the feds hassling you since the Colorado Springs airport? You involved in some new venture you haven't mentioned beyond hitting on Karla Grisham, Senator Grisham's little darling?"

"At first, I thought it was about Karla," Wolf explained. "Maybe it made somebody nervous and sicced the feds on me. After the New York visit I'm thinking it's connected to Overland College somehow because the feds yesterday warned me to stay away from Bellamy. You know I was investigating a date rape and suicide and Bellamy's son may be involved; too many coincidences, RJ."

"Where did you run into Bellamy?" RJ asked. "Is that why you took off for New York, to see him?"

Wolf explained how he ran into both Bellamy and Silverstone at the theater and what occurred outside the men's room. RJ asked why the FBI demanded he stay away for Bellamy.

"They're investigating him," Wolf replied. "No specifics given, of course."

"That's a trainload full of enriched bullshit," RJ cried. "They've been *investigating* that SOB for, what, since he was born and yet he keeps walking free and clear? The feds are the ones needing investigation ... So, you think Bellamy's son is involved in a rape?"

"From what I was told, Kerry Bellamy is a piece of work," Wolf said, "but I have no leads or evidence that he was involved with the incident in question. And there's that little problem of the kid they arrested for the date rape admitting his guilt and committing suicide earlier this month."

RJ held Wolf's eyes for a long moment. "But you think there's something very stinky going on."

Wolf shrugged. "I did this on a lark, RJ. The victim approached me feeling quite distraught and I just stepped into it. Don't know what I was thinking."

His bosom buddy nodded sagely. "Yup, that's how these life changing events are, bro. You take an unexpected detour and one morning you wake up, look out the window and realize you're not in Kansas anymore. Doesn't have to be some traumatic event like surviving a plane crash. The transformation just sort-of sneaks up on you and find yourself walking that path every day."

"Your one insightful dude, RJ," Wolf said.

"It's my job to see behind the eight ball, look through a glass darkly and divine the real meaning what is conveyed between the lines and pauses," he replied. "I am the communications maven for the leading freedom fighting organization in the world, after all."

"And you also have that special seventh sense that only gays possess," Wolf quipped. "Don't forget that."

RJ shook his head and grinned. "You got that wrong, bro. Only one has that power and that is I."

Wolf held RJ by his shoulders. "I chose wisely twenty years ago."

"You mostly do, Wolfie bro."

*   *   *   *

Events moved at the speed of electrons over the week as plans for a demonstration were communicated to student and affiliate groups and interested individuals in the region. Others worked frantically organizing transportation, housing, care and feeding for a thousand protestors up to a week. CIR's legal team worked overtime pressing forward with plans to sue the college via a class action suit.

By the end of the week, Juan was ready with his presentation to the Steering Committee, explaining that the class action was a shot across the bow to complacent college administrations across the country, a warning that many more would follow. None of the legal precedents were novel, he explained, except that for the first time they would be applied to colleges and universities whose administrators typically operate under the—false—assumption that a university, being a non-for-profit organization, is immune from the rule of law and juris prudence routinely applied to for-profit corporations.

"Are college presidents really that dense or arrogant to believe they're exempt from having to comply with laws and regs that the rest of us are subject to?" Annika asked.

"Certainly not." Juan assured the group. "If anything, the colleges are the primary cheerleaders for regulating business back into the eighteenth century. And it's not that colleges are never sued because they deal with labor disputes, sex-based litigation and sundry unequal treatment cases. What's going to rattle them to their foundations is their darling business regulation chicken coming home to their roost. And it's the size of Godzilla times a hundred."

The counselor predicted his team would win a majority of cases with juries across the nation awarding billions in compensation for colleges violating the rights their students. Total settlements from hundreds of colleges across fifty states could approach half trillion dollars, conservatively. In response to the collective gasp that followed this announcement, Juan explained that judges could—and would—knock awards down by as much as ninety percent.

"However, that could still turn out to be fifty billion dollars or more," he explained. When no one said anything, he continued.

"We're talking about huge sums of money, true, but the most important bang for the buck, the real reason we are going forward with these lawsuits is, one," he held up a hand ticking off the reasons with his fingers, "a decisive victory for individual rights. Two, bringing the debate about the Constitution into every home in the nation and across the globe. Three, an assured process of review and replace of Constitutionally unsupported policies and practices. Four, a dramatic tightening of rules governing student protests with, hopefully, serious and immediate consequences for misbehavior. Five, a rebalancing of the humanities faculty infusing it with intellectual diversity. Six, the elimination of the re-education-camp style process promoting identify policies, embarrassing and targeting students because of their race or sexual orientation and another passel of un-American practices and policies promoted in colleges these days."

Juan took a deep breath and sat back in his chair.

The group silently digested this blockbuster report for a long moment. The Center for Individual Rights was a very successful organization generating an average fifty million annual income from various sources including speaking engagements, publications, advertising revenue from its website and donations from millions of its supporters. If even a tiny portion of the settlement money Juan predicted came to pass, billions would flow into the coffers of CIR.

Annika broke the silence. "What would we do with all that money? Billions?"

Brett slammed a hand on the table. "The first thing we'd do is organize one hell of a party! Then we'd upgrade our systems to NSA level because every hacker from around the globe will be working overtime trying to steal the money or F us up, because Juan is going to piss off every looter and moocher in the country."

"Piss them off? You mean more than they are already?" Teena quipped. "You ever hear of Grayson Wolf, Brett?"

"Thank you for reminding me how popular I am," Wolf said. "Juan, a question: why haven't bottom feeder law firms like Silverstone & Associates thought of suing the colleges? Considering they've been busy suing business for the crime of daring to exist, how'd they miss this super bonanza?"

"The college thug avant-garde is a relatively recent phenomenon," Juan explained. "It's been building for years, but has really become a disruptive force the last few years and becoming epidemic since the election. Our class-action suit pursuant to denial of an equal education as well as the failure of their contractual offer to provide an equal college experience itemized in student handbooks is novel. Lastly, I don't think it would ever occur to tort firms like Silverstone's of suing the higher education hand that feeds them; it would be like suing their mothers for nursing them."

"Makes sense," Wolf said. His lips twisted into a droll grin. "You 'all do know that this class-action suit will hit the country with the force of all my fifteen books combined, right? We'd better make an extraordinary effort to prepare the staff and families for the media cluster-fluck to come because we are going after their ideological reproductive organs."

"You have such a way with words," RJ laughed.

"Wolf is right," Juan said. "The subsequent storm will be like none we've had to endure before. But we've weathered dozens of them over the years and I'm certain we'll survive this one, too."

"Assuming the villagers don't burn down the place and string us up on the lampposts lining Leesburg Pike." Teena's comment caused a thoughtful silence to descend.

"Not counting our chickens before they hatch," Annika said, breaking the silence, "as a non-profit it's problematic to have huge sums rolling over from year to year. We'll need to plan for the possibility of billions flooding into our coffers and I'll explore options and vehicles to park the money. Best to be prepared so we don't get hit with huge tax payments and penalties."

"Still thinking about launching a new political party," Diana said, shooting a look at Wolf. "Especially in light of the cluster-fluck you've mentioned coming our way with the class-action suit."

To his surprise, Wolf found that he wasn't opposed to the idea as he had been before his weekend in New York. Things had definitely shifted and though he didn't have any idea where he was going, he was clear about the fact that he would not be a key figure in Diana's political plans.

"Then I suggest you put it on the Exec Team's agenda to discuss," he replied. "A billion dollars would definitely jump-start a new political party for sure."

It was Diana's turn to be surprised and her face showed it, though an expression of confusion was the more dominant feature. The others around the table were also surprised by Wolf's change of attitude, with the exception of DJ whose lips twitched a bit. He must have known what the others were thinking because he piped up.

"Wolf keeps flip-flopping like he's been doing lately, we'll have to call him Waffle instead of Wolf." He chortled at his own joke, adding, "And you 'all need to drop any idea of him running for president of the American Liberty Party because the last thing we need in DC is yet one more waffling President."

DJ burst out laughing as the members around the table shot him disapproving looks for uttering a disparaging comment about Wolf. He ignored their disapproval and looked pointedly at his life-long buddy.

Wolf gave him a droll glance. "RJ is correct; I have apparently entered a waffling stage of life. Furthermore, I have no desire to run for any public office, now or in the foreseeable future. Period."

This announcement resulted in a table full of shocked expressions, sans RJ, of course. Wolf sighed. Might as well get it over with.

"I've been at this longer and deeper than anyone and it's been an amazing journey…"

"Are you retiring?" Juan asked.

"Well, sort of. Maybe," Wolf replied.

"Waffle Man strikes again," RJ laughed.

Wolf shot him an evil glance. "What I'm trying to say is that I feel I've reached the end of that journey. Don't give me that look; you all have been running this show for years and doing one hell of a job. You do not need me and I'm not planning to disappear; I'm in this battle to preserve what remains of our Republic for life—I'm just not going to be leading the fight."

"What are you thinking about doing, Wolf?" Annika asked. "Traveling? Writing?"

"I really don't know yet, Annika," he replied. "Whatever it is, I'll figure it out sooner or later. Life is about the journey; we all know the destination, right?" Wolf smiled and looked warmly at each of the friends and colleagues in turn then added, "By the way, I like RJ's suggestion calling this new political party the American Liberty Party. My two cents for the idea."

The rest of the meeting that Friday afternoon involved updates from various department heads about progress made toward securing all the components needed for the Virginia Patriots College protest which now was barely a week away. The plan was coming together quite nicely. Transportation had secured twenty-four buses and created a schedule to pick up supporters across four states and deliver them to the rally site, a conference center barely a mile from the college's main gate. RJ and his team had completed the media campaign and Brett reported that everything was a go and waiting for the word to push it out into the electronic universe.

Logistics assured the committee that all the tents, latrines, field kitchens and first aid stations had been secured and ready for delivery twenty-four hours prior to the arrival of a thousand demonstrators. Power would be up on time and food would be prepared. Teena confirmed that sufficient security had been hired and would be under direct supervision of her people. Considering the short notice, everything was proceeding according to plan.

Jewel King, head of Scheduling & Reservations stood up. King was a vivacious young woman with a pleasing southern accent, glowing ebony skin and a warm smile. Wolf noticed she was not smiling as she prepared to make her report.

"I fear I have bad news about Philadelphia," she began. "I've been wrangling with the Convention Center all week, Diana. They do not want to book CIR and they've been evading the issue—and me—coming up with lame excuses why they won't accept our reservation."

"Perhaps it's time for me to get involved?" Juan said. "This is outright discrimination." He must have realized the contradiction he just uttered, adding quickly, "We can promote the right of a business to decline service to anyone for any reason *and* still have a conversation with them about the consequences of refusing to accept our business—though I'm loathe to do that."

"I've threatened legal action," Jewel replied, looking contrite. "I hope I didn't overstep my authority, but they really annoyed me, Juan."

"You have my permission to give 'em hell Jewel!" he laughed.

"What reasons did they give for putting you off?" Wolf asked, though he had a good idea what that might be having lots of experience skulking around Philly over the years. Very fertile ground, he had discovered, for gathering material about corruption, collusion and intimidation for several of his books.

"Oh, everything and nothing," Jewel replied. "'We're booked through next year,' for starters. I told them to check again because I was sure they got the year wrong being that he was referring to last year's booking. Next came nonsense about the number of hotel reservations, then confusion about the availability of large conference rooms. I allowed the manager to keep on like this for a while, each time countering his assertions or outright challenging his facts and figures."

"You're a very patient woman, Jewell," RJ said. "Did he ever admit to the real reason he doesn't want our esteemed presence?"

"Yes, he did, RJ," she confirmed. "Patience may be a virtue, but persistence pays off in the long run. When I pressed the manager he finally admitted that booking CIR was a high security risk due to the adverse attention we'd bring to the center." She rolled her eyes in a most skeptical manner. "This was cow poop because I've read the conference center's past schedules of events and they booked lots of controversial groups and I told him so. When I suggested that the real risk to the conference center and to him personally was the Philadelphia political machine he hung up."

Juan shook his head, making a disgusting expression. "I wonder if the manager realized the depth of irony by refusing America's foremost advocate for individual rights to hold a conference in Philadelphia, just blocks away from Independence Hall and the Liberty Bell."

"Thank you for doing your best, Jewel," Diana said. "Especially for cornering the spineless rat. Go ahead and look closer to home—Richmond, maybe."

A satisfied smile shone on Jewell's face. "Already done. I've booked the Richmond Conference Center for the third week in October. Deposit's already paid and the confirmation's in your phone. I'll get details out to the department heads so they can start planning."

"Excellent," Diana said, smiling happily. "A-plus on taking initiative and follow through. Thank you, Jewell ... It's Friday and we've had a busy day and busy week and next week will be a bear to be sure. I'm planning to go home early and I suggest everyone do the same." She stood up and looked over at her Executive Assistant Sheryl Baseman. "Sheryl, get a note out to the staff that they are welcome to leave by two. Thanks ... Wolf, a word, please."

Wolf gave Diana a thumbs-up and followed her to her office. He took a seat and waited expectantly, most likely for a pitch he continues his present capacity as CIR's chief bottle washer and most potent spokesman for freedom. Diana sat on the edge of her desk; he smiled placidly at up her.

"How involved do you see yourself as you begin this new stage of life?" She asked.

"I'm not sure because I don't really have any clarity about where I'm going or what I'll be doing, Diana," Wolf replied. "My commitment to the center, to you and to the cause of freedom will not change, that you can be certain of." He paused, then continued. "I'll always consider myself on call, so to speak. I'll come on a moment's notice and if not, I'll have a very good reason why or I'm dead."

Diana frowned. "That's not funny, Wolf. Just because you're stepping back from the front lines doesn't mean people will forget. You've had dozens of death threats; make sure that you keep a sharp eye out as you pursue new paths and experiences."

"Yes mommy," Wolf teased. "You're a good friend, Diana and I don't plan on disappearing, just exploring and see where it leads me. I have full confidence in your ability to lead CIR to bigger and better things and me stepping back clears up any confusion or doubt in the minds of anyone—in and out of CIR—who is in charge. I will formally resign as CEO and function as an advisor on the Board sharing my indispensable wisdom with one an all until all are sick of hearing it."

Diana looked at him, her expression clearly a mixture of sadness and reluctance. "I know you're not leaving, but I miss you already, Grayson."

"Oh oh," Wolf grinned. "My mom used to say my name just like that before she lowered the boom on my head."

"I'm not angry, just feeling your loss," she replied. "You've been my friend and mentor for ten years … I still remember the moment you approached me and asked me to be Executive Director and how scared I was and you told me that you had no doubt that I could do the job and do it better than anyone else you knew. Thank you for asking me; you had a lot more confidence in my ability than I had, that's for sure."

"I'm pretty good at reading people," Wolf said. "I knew you were going to lead CIR from the first day I met you. I knew you had the intelligence, integrity as well as fire and backbone; all an absolute requirement for heading CIR, and I was not wrong, was I? I'll help you in any way I can, you know that Diana. I'm not going anywhere, just taking a back seat."

"Thanks," she said. "I do need to hear that."

He rose from his seat and embraced her. "Works both ways, Diana. You've been there for me every step the last decade. Thank you."

His phone dinged and he stepped back, fishing the unit from his pocket. He peered at the text message for a long moment.

Diana shot him a quizzical glance. "What is it?"

Wolf looked up from the phone. "It's from Colleen Silverstone. I need to go back to Colorado."

Chapter 9

Stops & Starts

Wolf arrived at the front entrance of Silverstone Security & Investigative Services in Denver at high noon the next day. It was a Saturday, but SSIS never sleeps, a requirement for being in the security and snooping business since the nefarious minded didn't sleep either, the cat-and-mouse game continuing unabated. He identified himself at the entrance monitor, curious whether he'd get the full inspection treatment today or be allowed to saunter on through without the bother of X-ray or the sniff test. To his relief, the door slid open and he was waived through, following the guard to Silverstone's inner sanctum.

The company's owner and CEO looked up from behind her desk as Wolf stepped in her office. He smiled at her, more as a goad than a greeting; she ignored him.

"Please have a seat, Mr. Wolf."

He took a seat directly in front of the desk. "Good afternoon Ms. Silverstone."

He didn't bother to ask how she'd been since their meeting ten days ago nor compliment her outfit or comment on the shade of her lipstick. She had barely tolerated his presence last time and only agreed to investigate the Lewis-Collins case because he appealed to her sense of justice.

"I see you've recovered from the car accident," she said, peering steadily at him. "Last time you had difficulty sitting."

Touché; payback for his teasing grin upon entering her office. At least she was civil. Progress, he supposed.

"Thank you," Wolf replied, ignoring her dig. "Your text was disappointing, to say the least. Why have you decided to terminate the investigation?" He knew the answer, but wanted to gather every shred of information by engaging her in a conversation as long as possible.

"You may recall," Colleen began, "that I agreed to pursue the Lewis case as long as it did not conflict with any of our current clients or other ongoing investigations."

Wolf nodded. "Yes."

"This investigation has run into a conflict and as agreed, I am terminating it."

"May I ask who the Lewis case is in conflict with?"

"I'm sorry," she replied. "Client confidentiality."

Wolf gazed at her silently, nodding. "Don't you find it curious for the Lewis rape case and the suicide of James Collins to be even remotely connected any of your clients?" Colleen held his eyes and said nothing. "Take Senator Grisham for instance. He's one of your clients, yes?" She said nothing. "Now why would the good Senator invoke SSIS's conflict clause over something that most certainly doesn't concern him even remotely? His daughter Karla does attend Overland College." Wolf knew of Colleen's reputation as an impervious vault, her body language revealing not a shred of admission or denial, her expression blank. There was one more name to throw at her. "My guess is that the conflict has to do with Justin Bellamy." Not a twitch. "CEO of New World Hedge Fund and father of Kerry Bellamy, student extraordinaire, attending Overland."

Wolf had become a world-class reader of micro-expressions over the years as an underground expose writer rubbing shoulders with every personality type from saints to sinners but Colleen Silverstone was in a class all her own. The woman was a master of self-containment, leaking not a drop of reaction from even one tiny pore of her being.

Wolf suddenly became aware of some momentous shift. Colleen's lips twitched. Then a smile formed.

"What?"

Her smile grew revealing beautiful teeth. Teeth, Wolf mused, that had taken huge bites out of people's egos, reputations and bank accounts. No sane person messed with Colleen Silverstone and SSIS because the woman and her organization was bulletproof, not to mention ready and willing to fight back.

Her smile retreated. "It's entertaining to watch Grayson Wolf, the scourge of evil-doers everywhere, probing with his tiny instrument hoping to pry lose some tidbit of information."

"Tiny instrument?" He said this with as much allusion to certain male instruments as he dared, sitting within bitch-slapping distance of the woman. To his shock and disbelief, she actually laughed! Deciding to press his advantage, he added, "Fortunately I am not at all insecure about the size of my instrument and its ability to probe into the depths of the human condition."

What remained of her smile vanished. "Of that I am most certain."

She lifted a file from the desk and held it toward him. Wolf took it and sat back down.

"Interviews with prison officials; as far as we—as much we have."

Wolf glanced at the file noting its lightness. Not much indeed.

"Thank you," he said, simply.

There was no use pressing for more because she would never compromise a client's trust; one of the reasons he had approached her in the first place. That and the fact that her firm was one of the best in the country... and also that she intrigued him, Colleen Silverstone being the direct opposite of her father. Stepfather, he corrected himself.

"How much do I owe you?"

"No charge," she said, adding, "If we're not able to properly investigate the case because of an internal conflict we do not charge the client."

"Even if your people invested many hours into the case?" Wolf asked. "That's a lot of cash to leave on the table."

Colleen held his eyes. He was sure he could read her thoughts; to wit, Grayson Wolf was doing his thing, using his 'tiny instrument' to obliquely probe into her mind to extract whatever he might have loosened.

After a long moment, she said, "It's not the client's responsibility to ensure that his or her case is not in conflict with any of our other clients and they shouldn't have to pay if we discover later that it is."

Wolf found he was enjoying being in her company—she was rather civil this time compared to his previous visits—but there being nothing else to discuss he flashed her a warm smile and got up.

"Thank you again, Ms. Silverstone."

He gave a brief nod and made for the door, closing it quietly behind him. The guard in the waiting area rose out of his seat and proceeded to escort him to a nearby exit. Back in the car he studied the

file, the summary pages offering not much more information than he had managed to extract from the prison officials upon his visit two weeks back. But the file did contain much more. There were documents on every guard on duty in James Collin's section of the prison during the forty-eight-hour span of time around his suicide, the on-call doctor's report of Collins's injuries and a copy of a report describing several altercations between Collins and another prisoner during the last week of his life. It was far more information than Wolf had expected to receive.

"Thank you very much indeed," he said, to himself.

He gazed at Colleen's headquarters for a long moment imagining what the Center for Individual Rights could accomplish with Colleen Silverstone working alongside Diana Ruiz. The pair of women were driven to excel, valued integrity and honesty above all else and were utterly fearless in the face of adversity. Both also valued family and were loyal to their respective kin—to a point. SSIS's headquarters was, after all, in Denver and not in Manhattan where her father's firm was located. A distance of 1600 miles makes a statement...or maybe she just prefers mountains to skyscrapers.

Wolf made a low grunt and checked the time: a few minutes past one. From Colleen's text yesterday, he hadn't expected to get much information from the aborted investigation, but surprisingly the file contained plenty to chew on and explore in greater depth in the coming days. He took photos of every document with his phone, emailed them to DJ for safekeeping then transferred copies to his iPad containing all his case notes, photos and recordings pursuant to the Lewis-Collins case.

Reviewing his contact list, his gaze came to rest upon Richard & Carol Collins, James's parents, living in Ft. Morgan. Never one to waste a moment, he checked the route on his phone, noting that the town was eighty miles east on I-76—a good hour's drive.

Figuring one or both parents to be home on a weekend, he made the call and was rewarded when Ms. Collins answered the phone. Wolf identified himself as Mr. Gray, explained his reason for calling and was invited to come by anytime that afternoon. He started his car and made for a fast food joint back the way he had come, ate a quick bite then got on the road heading east to Ft. Morgan.

*   *   *   *

"Thank you for seeing me, Ms. Collins," Wolf said.

The woman peered closely at him and for a moment he wondered if she knew who he was. Considering that cameras were ubiquitous, Wolf had labored diligently to avoid getting his photo taken sans common disguises whenever he made any appearance anywhere, thus very few people could easily recognize one of American's most well-known personalities. Despite his best efforts, sundry photos displaying his face were out there, though most were dated and sporting one of his disguises. What surprised Wolf most, however, was not feeling relieved when the woman failed to recognize him.

Following Ms. Collins into the living room he came to the conclusion that perhaps unlike all his past investigations where anonymity was critical to his success, concealment of his identity in the presence of grieving parents was dishonest and disrespectful.

"Please have a seat, Mr. Gray. May I get you something to drink? Eat?"

Wolf sat down in a cushioned armchair opposite the sofa. "No, thank you, Ms. Collins. I'm fine."

At that moment, a man and a young woman entered the room. Wolf got up shaking hands with both.

"Carol tells me you want to talk about James," Mr. Collins said. "Did you know my son?"

Wolf shook his head. "No sir."

He wasn't sure what to say next, the second surprise in as many minutes. Hobnobbing with the high and mighty in the morning and sociopathic scumbags in the afternoon was second nature to Wolf. Inquiring about the suicide of a son while representing the woman he was accused of drugging and raping was an entirely different matter and clearly out of his comfort zone.

"Why are you here then?" The young woman introduced as James's sister asked. "Are you some kind of reporter looking for a story? If so, you need to get out!"

"Vicki," her mother said, in a disapproving tone, "please remember your manners."

The girl who wasn't more than sixteen or seventeen leaned back into her seat and glared silently at Wolf.

"Quite alright," Wolf replied, holding Vicki's eyes. "I'd feel exactly the way you do if my brother or sister, er, died."

"Murdered," she shot back. "James was murdered."

Wolf noticed that neither parent made any attempt to correct Vicki's assertion. He supposed that holding on to the idea of James being murdered was preferable to believing he'd committed suicide, such acts often dredging up any number of unpleasant associations by folks closest to the deceased.

"Why do you believe James was murdered?" Wolf asked.

"James would never hurt anyone," Vicki asserted. "He'd never even been in a fight...not since elementary school. He'd never drug and, and do something like that to any girl—ever."

Wolf weighed whether to mention a certain inconvenient confession when Mr. Collins spoke.

"Before we go any further Mr. Gray, would you mind telling us why you've come about James?"

"I was visiting Overland and was told about the incident that lead to the unfortunate death of your son," he replied. "I'm an investigator by profession and the case interested me so I decided to look more closely into the matter. I hope you won't object."

True lies yes, but often the best answer.

"Will you be writing about this for a newspaper or magazine?" the mother asked.

Wolf shook his head. "No ma'am. Happy to sign a statement to that fact if you'd like."

The family looked at each other for a brief moment then the father spoke. "Ask your questions."

Wolf learned about James's schooling, how well liked he was, how he never got into any trouble and received a scholarship to attend Overland and how successful he was academically at the college. Combined with what he'd discovered about James from his previous interviews, listening to his family talk about him, the more convinced Wolf became that James was innocent of the crime he confessed to.

"You can see why we can't believe James would do anything to hurt others, especially something this heinous." Ms. Collins said.

"He didn't, mom." Vicki insisted. "They made him confess to something he didn't do and then they killed him!"

"It's premature to say conclusively about what might or might not have happened," Wolf said, "but there's definitely something rotten going on. James's note to Sarah Lewis days before his death does
appear to suggest that he was beginning to have doubts about his involvement in the crime."

Seeing their surprised faces, Wolf realized the Collins's didn't know about the note. He gave a sanitized explanation how he came across that information, not wanting to possibly upset them further with the whole truth and nothing but the truth.

"See," Vicki cried, "that proves that James didn't kill himself; he was murdered."

"No honey," her father replied, taking her hand. "James is only claiming he has no memory of … of hurting that student."

"You think he killed himself?" Vicki said, incredulous.

"We only know what the medical report said and now with this note…" he hesitated. "James was very sensitive and sitting in jail made him depressed, Vicki. You saw that yourself when we visited him."

"Did he talk about what happened that night back in December?" Wolf asked.

"Not really," Mr. Collins said. "James is—was—a sensitive boy. I know he was embarrassed about the whole affair. He didn't want to talk about it, saying he much preferred to hear about us and life outside…"

"When was the last time you visited James?"

Collins scrunched up his face in thought. Ms. Collins responded first.

"The weekend before he died."

"How much later was it after your visit he died?" Wolf asked.

"Um… happened the following Thursday, so five days."

"Was James unusually depressed when you saw him the last time?"

Ms. Collins looked upward for a moment. "Didn't seem to be."

"Did he appear happier or more serene that visit than he usually did?" Wolf asked.

"Ah, I—oh." The woman's eyes grew larger. "I see what you're getting at. James was his typical self, just down about his situation."

"What does he mean, mom?" Vicki asked. "What are you saying?"

Wolf took the initiative and began to explain. "Often when someone begins to contemplate suicide they become increasingly depressed, irritable, angry and despondent. Once they arrive at the decision to proceed, their behavior can radically change during the days prior. They become calm, accepting, happy even. That James's behavior didn't change one way or the other tells us that he most likely was not thinking about committing suicide."

"Then he was murdered." Vicki replied.

Wolf held up a hand. "Let's just say that as the likelihood of James committing suicide drops, the possibility of having been murdered rises."

Vicki's expression hardened. "He didn't commit suicide."

"Mr. Gray," Ms. Collins said, "how long are you planning to keep investigating?"

"Until I find out what happened last December and the truth about James's death."

That announcement had them all peering at Wolf with skeptical expressions.

"I don't want to sound ungrateful, Mr. Gray," the father said, breaking the silence, "but that could take weeks and months. Are you telling us the truth about not working for one of those supermarket tabloids? I don't want to see photos of James or the rest of us looking back at me from a grocery magazine rack."

Wolf had to make a decision. It was rather a painless one.

"If I tell you something about myself, do I have everyone's promise that you will not tell anyone?" The parents nodded silently. "What about you, Vicki? Yes or no?"

"Fine, so long as you're not a crook or something."

Wolf grinned. Not a crook though many might claim that he was a thief, stealing their cover and exposing them to the naked light of day.

"My real name is Grayson Wolf." He paused giving them time to digest this bit of news, but also to prepare himself for any adverse reaction in case the family was related to someone who did not fare so well in one of his many books.

"Oh-my-God," Vicki exclaimed. "We're reading Lying & Cheating for Fun and Profit in Contemporary Studies."

"My first book," Wolf replied. "Hope it still stirs the passions."

"I'd say so," Vicki said, excitedly. "We have discussions about every page. I know some students who cheat like the devil and it's fun to see them squirm. Did you really write that while still in high school?"

Wolf nodded. "Senior year. I got tired of all the cheaters and liars and decided to do something about it."

"It's brilliant," she replied. "You show how cheaters and liars get away with it, making good grades and getting benefits they don't deserve and how school administrators turn a blind eye."

"I'm confused," Ms. Collins said, looking alarmed. "Is the book *encouraging* students to lie and cheat, because it sure sound like it from what you're saying, Vicki."

"At first it seems like Mr. Wolf is admiring the cheaters for their success, giving plenty of examples from a dozen schools, public and private," Vicki explained. "It's like he lures you in and then springs the trap! Mr. Wolf shows how lying and cheating undermines the integrity and even security of the liar because he's gotta keep lying to cover up lies and on and on making him afraid of being found out. Has many examples how lying and cheating can really mess up our future. He also shows how the schools are hurting themselves by ignoring the problem. It's pretty compelling, mom; makes us all think twice lying about anything."

"Are you writing a book about this, about prisons and colleges?" Mr. Collins asked.

"Been there, done that," he replied. "I found out about James and decided to look into it. The more I looked, the more questions came up. Like I said, I have the time and plan to find the truth. I can't promise you'll like what I discover, but I can promise you that I will discover the truth behind everything that happened to your son and hope to exonerate him from a crime I'm betting he didn't commit."

"Mr. Wolf." Vicki hesitated. "May I ask you for your autograph?"

"Tell you what." He leaned forward in his seat and smiled. "When I finish my investigation and James's reputation has been restored, we can talk about autographs and maybe something more interesting. Deal?"

"Will you keep us informed?" Mr. Collins said.

Wolf nodded. "Of course. I'll keep you apprised of my progress every so often. If I get a break in the case, you'll be the first to know. I may also need your assistance, too. I assume I can call you about that?"

"Anything you need, Mr. Wolf." The father confirmed.

"Thank you," Wolf said. "Please remember not to mention my name to anyone...I'm very sorry about your son."

$$*\qquad*\qquad*\qquad*$$

He got back to his hotel in Aurora shortly before five. Having checked out the excellent indoor pool and spa facilities earlier he decided on a workout in the gym followed by a thirty-minute swim. By the time he showered it was approaching seven and he ordered a meal to be delivered to his room.

The bedroom in his suite held two king beds and he used one to spread out the documents and photos from the file Colleen had provided. He was staring at the photos of James shortly after he was found when a sharp rap at the door sounded.

It would be his dinner, but Wolf learned ages ago not to blithely open doors. He removed the security doorstop and holding a pistol at his side, he stood with his back against the wall to the left of the door opening it with his left hand. Years ago, some incensed husband thinking that his wife—Wolf's informant—was having an affair forcefully shoved open the door knocking Wolf on his ass. Live and learn.

Wolf thanked the attendant handing her a generous tip, bolting the door after she left. He gazed at the door absentmindedly, pistol still in hand, wondering if this part of his life—endless vigilance—would ever change as he forged a new direction in his life. Paranoia was an old and reliable friend that had kept him reasonably safe from the inevitable fallout generated by his incendiary publications and CIR broadcasts to the world. He shrugged and replaced the security doorstop; there would always be someone holding a grudge no matter how many years passed and he was resigned to the reality of never living a normal life.

Nibbling aimlessly on a buttery roll, Wolf studied the prison doctor's report of James Collins's suicide gazing occasionally at the accompanying photos of Collins in the service closet where he allegedly hung himself. Peering at the close-ups, he noticed no post mortem bruises around or near Collins's neck indicating that he was strangled first then hung from the exposed pipes above his head. Close-up shots of his bare arms and hands did not show any signs of struggle, as most likely there would be if Collins was forced into the closet and hung.

The doctor's report confirmed what Wolf deduced from the photographs: James Collins entered the service closet with the intent to commit suicide, there being no evidence of foul play by parties known or unknown. Collins's death appeared to be an unassisted, singular affair.

Wolf read and re-read the report half dozen times, hoping to find something—a misprint, a suspicious omission—that he could use as a lever to force open a crack in the case, but the damn report refused to comply with his wishes. Not giving up, he employed the magnifying app on his phone to examine every millimeter of Collins's exposed skin on the photos in case his eyes missed a subtle bruise, a slight scratch.

Frustrated by his repeated failure, Wolf hurled the photos angrily across the room.

"Shit!"

He stormed out of the bedroom, his stomach tightening into a nasty knot from a feeling of rising powerless combined with a humbling sense of guilt at the possibility that he might fail. It wasn't failure per se that haunted Wolf; failure—repeated failure—was an integral part of the process mucking around to secure the information needed to fabricate the books that evolved from his efforts. Failure in this instance would be to James and Sarah's family and Wolf had never failed delivering upon a promise, pay a debt or honor a commitment, especially his commitment to securing justice, one of his highest values.

Perhaps James did drug and rape Sarah then kill himself in despair of what he'd done. Perhaps Wolf was too hasty—too cocky—making promises that upon reflection he should not have made. Emotions were never a means of cognition as he had often counseled others.

Wolf calmed his breathing, the slow, regulated breaths focusing his mind. Promises were made and promises would be kept. His highly tuned intuition told him that he was missing something important in James's prison file, something that were he a professional private investigator such as Colleen Silverstone he would most likely have spotted. He thought about hiring another firm or maybe a couple of them—he had the money—but without being properly vetted he might wind up with a huge mess on his hands. He thought about calling RJ and asking him to come to Colorado, but he was needed by Diana to bitch-slap Virginia Patriots College's administration.

He issued a snort. "Can't go back. Can't stay put. Won't quit. Forward it is."

Forward, for the rest of the evening, was watching re-runs of Rizzoli and Isles on cable. Sometime after one am, his eyes felt heavy and closed, drifting off to sleep listening to the murmur of dialogue from the TV.

Wolf woke with a start; the clock next to the TV glowed 3:33. He switched off the TV trying to remember what he just dreamt about. Images of hospital rooms, medical equipment and faces flashed thorough his mind. He closed his eyes and took long, slow breaths, falling asleep soon thereafter. At 5:42 he woke again; a dream remnant, image of bodies on steel tables in dimly lit rooms, fixed in his mind. A face appeared, one he recognized, having seen her just last night on TV: Maura Isles. Medical examiner. Performing—

"Autopsies!"

He slipped out of bed, turned on the light and made for the pile of documents strewn across the other bed. Wolf surveyed the mess of papers zeroing in on the one he was searching for in quick order. He lifted the doctor's report scanning rapidly across the pages finding what he was looking for, what was missing in the report: an autopsy.

Why was no autopsy performed? Wolf Googled Centennial State Prison searching for any mention of death protocol finding nothing definitive. He expanded his search to include all prisons discovering among other interesting facts that there are over 5400 federal, state and local prisons and jails in the United States. Then he found the answer to his question.

The standard protocol in the event of a prisoner's death while incarcerated regardless of cause included an administrative review, a clinical mortality review and a psychological autopsy in the case of suicide. Although the word autopsy was mentioned in the prison protocol, a comprehensive examination of the body to determine exact cause of death is not required and was not performed by the doctor on James's body. If James was murdered there was no way to determine how it was accomplished without performing a traditional autopsy thus allowing the culprit, or culprits, to get away with the deed.

Wolf was a highly successful investigator of civil misdeeds, ferreting information and data by immersing himself into whatever particular lake of business a company or organization swam in. Criminal detective work, as Wolf was discovering with every step he took, required a level of authority, experience and expertise he was lacking.

Not for the last time did he wish Colleen were helping him on this case, issuing a snort at his conceit she'd be *assisting* him. In reality Colleen would be leading and he'd be trotting along behind her, the thought immediately conjuring an image of seeing her shapely figure gliding ahead of him. He shrugged, accepting the fact that he appreciated the feminine form even if the woman in question gazed upon him with overt hostility.

Wolf stared at the name of the prison doctor in the medical report. He wished it were Monday so he could interview the doctor along with the guards on duty the day of Collins's death. This time Wolf was prepared to rain down righteous fire from the heavens if the warden refused to allow him to talk with personnel.

For a brief moment, he was tempted to Google the doctor, track down his address and visit him this morning, but thought better of it. Being served with a harassment complaint would impede his mission of getting justice for James Collins and for Sarah Lewis, too.

He resigned to spend the day swimming, working out in the gym, enjoying meals that took longer than two minutes to prepare and clicking around the Internet becoming more familiar with autopsies, prisons and particular individuals of interest as he waited for Monday morning to arrive.

Chapter 10

Conditioned Blindness

"My reason for visiting Centennial State Prison," Wolf replied to the guard at the prison's front gate at eight a.m. Monday morning, "is very important to warden Ragavitz's future."

When asked his name, Wolf chose to play his ace. "Grayson Wolf," adding in case the warden needed further incentive to open his door to him, "from the Center for Individual Rights."

It did the trick and the heavy gate slid open a few minutes later.

The sour expression on the warden's face warned Wolf this might become messy, but he hadn't successfully weaseled his way into the homes and lives of the people he was going to write about without learning finesse along the way.

"Thank you for seeing me again, Mr. Ragavitz." The man shot him a sarcastic look and Wolf continued. "Let me assure you I am not working on a novel about prisons nor am I here representing the Center for Individual Rights. I've been asked as a favor to a friend to look into the Lewis-Collins case and would like the opportunity to ask a few questions of the guards on duty when James Collins committed suicide and also of the doctor who examined the body. I'll only take up a few minutes of their time ... and as a thank you to your personnel for agreeing to talk with me I will write a generous donation to the prison's social fund."

"How generous?"

"Ten thousand dollars."

Ragavitz looked thoughtful for a moment then agreed, proving once again the adage that money talks, bullshit walks. He lifted the phone receiver from his desk and made the call.

"Follow me."

Accompanied by a guard, Ragavitz escorted Wolf to a small conference room. The warden took the seat at the head of the table,

Wolf choosing the seat directly opposite where any attempt by staff looking back toward their boss for visual cues permitting them to answer questions would be obvious. Wolf was determined to get every penny's worth of his donation to the prison social fund, Ragavitz's thin smile conveying the man's understanding of Wolf's seating choice.

Wolf placed his iPad on the table, but didn't bother to look at it for the first three guards he interviewed because none were included in the file Silverstone had provided. He asked each the same basic questions, were they on duty the morning of March 4th, when did their duty begin, what section each was assigned, did they deviate from their station at any time after the prisoners were allowed out of their cells and the body of James Collins was discovered. The guards answered all questions to Wolf's satisfaction and were soon on their way back to their stations.

The next guard was named Jesus Moreno, a name he recognized from Colleen's file.

"Mr. Moreno, thank you for speaking with me." Wolf peered purposely at his iPad for a long moment as if he was considering some important bit of information about the man. If doing so made the guard nervous, that would be helpful. Where there's smoke, there's a good chance of fire.

"You found James Collins in the closet on the morning of March 4th?"

"Yes sir, I did."

"What time did you discover the body?"

"Shortly after 9:30."

"Why were you in that corridor at that time?"

"It's part of my patrol route."

"Why did you open the service closet door?"

"Service closets and storage rooms are always locked," Moreno explained. "It's part of routine to check every door to make sure that they are locked. The nob turned; that meant it was not locked so I opened it to see what might be inside."

"Did you touch anything; Collins's body, for instance?"

Moreno shot him an absurd look. "That would be pretty stupid ... sir."

"How long have you worked at Centennial, Mr. Moreno?"

"Ten years, sir."

"Do you know why the door was unlocked?"

"No sir."

"Did you unlock that door?"

Moreno's face darkened. "Absolutely not. Guards don't have the keys."

"Based on your initial observation," Wolf continued, "did the lock mechanism appear to have been jimmied or forced?"

"I didn't look that closely," Moreno replied. "Didn't appear to be."

"What was the first thing you did after discovering Collins's body?"

"I called it in."

"How soon before others showed up at the scene?"

Moreno glanced toward the wall for a second. "Less than a minute."

"Did you remain at the scene or continue on your rounds?"

"I stayed until Doc Fallston showed up...five minutes at most."

The guard was relaxed and answered in a matter-of-fact tone. If he was involved in Collins's death, the man was a world-class actor.

Wolf smiled warmly at him. "That will be all, Mr. Moreno. Thank you."

Moreno rose from his seat and then hesitated. "Are you *the* Grayson Wolf... if you don't mind me asking."

"Yes."

Moreno nodded and smiled. "I've read your books."

"Critic or fan?" Wolf replied.

Moreno's lips twisted into a wide grin. "Critical fan."

"My favorite type," Wolf said. "Thank you."

After the guard left the room Ragavitz said, "It's sad and unfortunate, but James Collins hung himself, Mr. Wolf. Suicides kill more inmates than homicide, drug overdose, alcohol intoxication and accidents combined."

"How did he get inside a locked closet?" Wolf said.

"We have strict protocols for everything in this facility," the warden replied, "but occasionally someone slips up, something minor such as locking a closet. They become distracted by some commotion or a call and a door doesn't get locked. James might have been

134

looking for a convenient place and tried any number of doors finding one that was unlocked. Most likely if he didn't find that open closet it would have been his cell or a bathroom stall or some corner in the laundry room."

A pit formed in Wolf's stomach at the real possibility that once all the facts had been gathered, they may all point to the same conclusion: James Collins committed suicide. However, nothing is over and done until the fat lady sings and there were still several acts to come.

The next guard in Wolf's file entered the room.

"Mr. Ewing," Wolf said, after the warden introduced him, "you are the head officer in charge of the east wing surveillance room."

"Yes."

"You were on duty the morning of March 4th."

"Yes, I was."

"When did you begin your duty that morning?"

"Six a.m."

"How many monitors are there in the surveillance room?"

"A dozen."

"How many surveillance cameras feed those monitors?"

"Hmm..." Ewing hesitated for a moment. "About thirty-plus cameras. Most monitors are connected to two or more cameras."

"Two or more cameras," Wolf repeated.

"Cameras cycle every fifteen to twenty seconds," Ewing added.

"Something bad could happen in that twenty seconds until that same camera come back on screen."

Ewing gave him a stoic look. "Yes, it could, Mr. Wolf, but inmates often do bad things right in front of guards, too."

"I assume that images are recorded?"

"Yes."

"Is there a recording of Collins going to and entering the storage closet?"

"Yes."

That came as a rude shock to Wolf. A recording showing Collins walking to the closet and enter it; pretty definitive evidence for a ruling of suicide.

His mind blank. He said absentmindedly, "Alone?" When Ewing hesitated, Wolf added excitedly, "What are you not telling me?"

"Um, the camera is aimed toward the end of the hall cutting off a direct view of the closet door," he explained, "though it captures a slice of the door's top corner."

"Did the camera ever show the top corner of the door opening at any time after the prisoners were released to attend breakfast on the morning of March 4th?" Wolf asked.

"No."

"Could the door have been opened during the twenty seconds the hall camera was not sending a signal to your monitors?"

The guard blinked. "I suppose that's possible."

"If you can't see the door for twenty seconds at a time, how do we know Collins entered the closet alone? Maybe half dozen friends hustled him into that closet for a lynching party? Did any camera actually record him walking in the direction of that closet at all?"

The tech officer began to look uncomfortable. Wolf peered at him, waiting for an explanation.

"We have a recording of Collins, walking alone, making a turn into the corridor where the closet is located," Ewing said. "No recording shows him coming or going from that corridor after that. Collins must have entered the closet and hung himself..."

"When you said you have a recording of Collins entering the closet," Wolf said, "you naturally assumed he did since the recording shows him walking toward the hall where the closet is located."

"Um, yes," Moreno said, looking contrite.

Wolf's finger scrolled across his iPad. He enlarged the document he had selected and peered at it.

"Your surveillance system is a VizTec 2000," he said.

Ewing's eyes grew larger. "Ah, yeah. Why?"

"Do inmates assume the cameras monitor their activities continuously?" Wolf paused for dramatic effect. "Or are they aware that cameras only monitor them when the power light located on the front of the camera is glowing brightly and not when it dims?"

Deep silence descended upon the room. The look of surprise on both Ewing and the warden confirmed what Wolf had suspected: neither man—and by extension probably the rest of the staff—had any clue that some or all prisoners knew when a surveillance camera was down giving them a cool fifteen to twenty-second window of opportunity to conduct any number of illicit activity. Enough time to hustle James into a closest, after which there would be sufficient time to hang the poor boy, then when the timing was right, step back into the corridor and make an escape when the camera power light dimmed. The question forming in Wolf's mind was how many *staff* members knew about that glaring oversight of security.

Though both men looked at Wolf with alarmed astonishment at this blockbuster discovery, it had been Brett Casings, CIR's computer wizard extraordinaire, who tracked down Centennial prison's surveillance system, his review of the system's specifications revealing the power light quirk in VizTec 2000 cameras. In fairness to Wolf however, none of this would have come to light were it not for his habit of examining a problem from multiple angles and calling upon his people at CIR to do likewise.

"Did you know about this?" Ragavitz demanded.

"Hell no," a rattled Ewing cried. "But this is what we get for State policy awarding contracts to the lowest bidder, which, you might remember, I spoke against when we upgraded the system two years back."

"Jeezus." The warden shook his head. "When this gets out it's going to be a shit storm." He shot a worried glance at Wolf. "Excuse my language."

"Look," Wolf said, "I'm not interested in making your job any harder than it is. Knowing what I do, I'm pretty sure that every inmate in jail deserves to be there. No one will hear about this from me, but I would encourage you to upgrade the cameras as soon as possible. In the meantime, I'd consider killing the power light on every camera; at least then those who know about the quirk won't know when any particular camera is on or off the surveillance cycle."

A look of hope showed on the warden's face. "Is that something your men could do right away, Ewing?"

"I'll look into the second I leave here," the security officer replied. "I'm sure we'll come up with a fix before the end of today and get to work on it."

"During the night shift, Ewing," Ragavitz ordered. "The less eyes looking on, the fewer questions raised. Understood?"

"Yes sir…May I go and get started?"

The warden shot a glance at Wolf.

"Go. Thank you for your time, Mr. Ewing."

"How did you find out about the cameras, Mr. Wolf?" the warden asked after the guard left.

"I can smell compromise, collusion, duplicity and evasion from a mile away, warden." Wolf quipped. "Have twenty plus years studying it." When the man gazed at him with what appeared to be genuine respect he added, grinning, "And I have the best techies at my beck and call."

Ragavitz nodded. "Well I for one am most grateful for that … How could no one spot that flaw in the cameras?"

"It's called conditioned blindness," Wolf replied. "Our minds are tuned to notice the abnormal, not the normal. If these cameras buzzed and gyrated from day they came on line that becomes the baseline and we accept it as normal paying them no further attention after the novelty wears off. The power light dimming is far subtler and near impossible to spot unless it was your job to question everything you see and hear."

"Like your job, Mr. Wolf," Ragavitz said. "I've read a few of your books, too."

Wolf shrugged. "And why I'm here today."

The warden nodded. "Even if someone knew about the cameras, all the evidence still points to suicide."

"I'm not a conspiracist," Wolf replied. "I investigate, ask questions, follow leads and ask more questions. If all the evidence points to suicide, suicide it is."

There was a knock on the door. A man wearing a lab coat stuck his head in.

"You wanted to see me, Joseph?"

"Yes, thank you Jerome," the warden replied. He introduced Wolf. "Mr. Wolf has some questions for you about the Collins suicide."

The doctor's face became very still; pale even. It was a typical reaction by officials and professionals of every stripe when facing the man who had single-handedly exposed malfeasance, corruption, incompetence and collusion at the highest levels of business and government.

"Good morning Dr. Fallston," Wolf said. "Just to be clear, I'm not here to question your competence or findings." The man seemed to relax a bit. "I've read your report several times and studied the accompanying photos very closely and based on what I've seen, it does look like James Collins committed suicide."

When Wolf didn't continue, the doctor spoke into the expanding silence. "That was my finding, yes. There was no evidence on the body to contradict that conclusion. No contusions, no post-mortem marks that would indicate a struggle; nothing. Mr. Collins committed suicide."

"I understand the protocol in these cases does not include an autopsy." Wolf stated.

"That's correct." Fallston confirmed. "Unless there was some evidence contradicting the cause of death we do not perform routine autopsies on inmates who die."

"What about less invasive procedures such as routine blood and fluid tests?"

The doctor looked baffled. "No…considering all the evidence, what reason would there be to order blood and fluid tests?"

"To minimize the possibility of someone like me asking questions about a suicide?" Wolf replied. "From what I have learned about James Collins from my investigation, he didn't exhibit any of the typical signs displayed by those thinking about committing suicide prior to the act. His parents saw no such indicators—depression, despondency or serenity and acceptance—at their last visit with him five days before he died."

"Not all suicides exhibit typical symptoms beforehand," Fallston explained. "However, the subsequent psychological review of Mr. Collins did indicate he had become increasingly unhappy during the last two months of his life."

"That's consistent with the possibility that James had become increasingly convinced that he might be innocent of the crime he originally confessed to," Wolf said.

"Mr. Wolf," Fallston replied, looking knowingly at him, "you of all people must know that most incarcerated criminals claim to be innocent."

"Yet some are, Dr. Fallston." Wolf cleared his throat. "In James Collins's case I find it rather suspicious that he writes a note to his victim claiming he was innocent and commits suicide a few days later?"

It was a fishing expedition; never know what might be caught on the hook. Wolf didn't expect the doctor to know anything about this, the man's blank expression confirming his assumption.

"To quell any possibility of suspicion that a death is a sophisticated murder," Wolf continued, "perhaps it might be a good idea to add blood and fluid tests to the medical review protocol for suicides."

Fallston shot him a skeptical look. "That's quite a stretch, Mr. Wolf."

"One thing is for certain," Wolf replied, "without such tests we'll never know if a person committing suicide might have been drugged with psychological substances causing him to become so despondent that thoughts of suicide turn into actual suicide. There are hosts of chemicals that can work such evil, yes doctor?"

"Yes," Fallston agreed. "Where your theory hits the rocks is the part about 'sophisticated murder.' In all my years of working in the prisons, I cannot recall one example of a sophisticated murder. I can assure you, Mr. Wolf, that every murder I have attended to is quite common in every possible way: smashing a head with a tool, strangulation with a strip of cloth torn from a towel in the laundry, shanked with anything from a sharpened toothbrush to broken edge of a CD or forcefully drowned in a toilet. Sophistication does not enter the prison gates ... now if there's nothing further, I have a number of very common injuries inflicted by inmates upon each other to attend to." He got up and made for the door.

"Thank you, Dr. Fallston," Wolf called after the departing doctor. Turning back to the warden he said "One last staff member... Don Welling and I'll be gone."

Ragavitz waved a hand. "Unfortunately, officer Welling is on extended leave; won't return until end of next week."

"Any idea where he might be?" Wolf asked. "If he's in the area perhaps he might agree to see me?"

"Welling's a hunter; my guess he'll be out over the range shooting something or another," Ragavitz replied. "Give me a call end of next week and I'll arrange for a meeting." He got up. "I'll see you out."

"May I ask you for one favor?" Wolf said.

"Depends…"

"Would you show me where James Collins was found?"

The warden gave Wolf one of his long-suffering looks then jerked his head to follow him. Two burly guards escorted them through various hallways and rooms stopping by a door in a remote corridor some minutes later.

Looking up at the camera pointed over his head toward the doors at the far end of the hall, Wolf mused that one or more people could wait in the camera's blind spot, ambush James, drag him into the closet and string him up. He remembered the medical report showing no signs of struggle on Collins's body…he made a mental note to think about this quandary later.

Looking into the service closet, he noted papers supplies stacked on shelves covering the left wall, plastic storage cases to stand on and exposed pipes eight feet overhead where one could easily toss over a rope fashioned from strips of cloth or twine secured from the loading docks and hang themselves. Barring any definitive evidence to the contrary, the ruling of suicide stood firm.

Wolf followed the warden to the main gate. "A pleasure meeting you, Mr. Ragavitz; thank you for your cooperation… I'll call you next week for a meeting with officer Welling."

*   *   *   *

Sitting in the prison's parking lot, Wolf wrote a summary of the interviews and his impressions. The discovery about the prison cameras going dark every twenty seconds, the fact that there was no recording of James entering that closet alone or otherwise, did bolster expectations that a continued, diligent effort would in time uncover tangible evidence proving James's death was a murder. Persistence is ninety percent of success and Grayson Wolf was one persistent SOB.

Wolf debated his next move. He considered visiting the Collins's to inform them about his findings, but decided against it feeling that it would raise false hopes of vindication soon to follow. The death of a son and brother was too fresh, emotions too raw and the stakes of failure too high. Best to wait until he had hard, unassailable proof of foul play before presenting the family with what could simply be coincidental occurrences.

Wolf took a deep breath; too many lose ends. He still needed to press Kerry Bellamy and his infamous bitch boys along with Karla

Grisham and her bitch click at Overland College. Interview managers and employees at local college watering holes the night of Sarah Lewis's abduction who might have seen her or James Collins.

Last but not least, Don Welling, the guard whose profile Colleen had included in the file and who had conveniently taken leave after her visit to the prison last week. Gone hunting, the warden had suggested.

Hunting. Wolf had gone hunting a few times in his life, mostly as part of his ongoing incursion into one organization or another. He personally didn't care for the idea of killing an animal for sport seeing the hunter as having a huge advantage—tactical killing ability being just one—over the animal. He understood that hunters culled herds, preventing overpopulation and its consequences, starving animals and decimated corpses littering the countryside. Hunting game just wasn't his thing. Hunting human predators was quite another matter and Wolf was among the best at that task.

A question popped into his head and he reached for the phone. Googling hunting season in Colorado, he quickly discovered that the months of spring were not open for hunting any big game whatsoever.

"So, officer Welling," Wolf said, aloud. "Not gone hunting after all."

Applying simple mental triage, he counted the connections. One connection is chance: camera's that go dark for twenty seconds. Two connections a coincidence: camera pointed at the top of the closet door negating any chance to identify someone entering the closet. Three and more connections becomes an emerging pattern: James's suicide days after writing Sarah a note; Collins hanging himself in the one place where a killer could safely lie in wait and escape unnoticed; a guard in his file on leave after Colleen investigates.

Where there's a growing pattern, evidence is sure to be strewn along the way; Wolf just had to find it. He reached for his phone.

"Wazzzup boss man?" Brett's high-energy response blasted in his ear.

"Those files I sent you?" Wolf said. "Want you to track down one of the prison guards, Don Welling. Where he lives, where he hangs out, the women—or men—he plays with, where he goes to ground when he doesn't want to be found."

"Piece of cake, Wolfie," Brett laughed. "By the time my team is done with Welling he'll be standing buck naked on top of the Washington Monument at high noon for all to see his nasty bits."

"You do paint a quaint image, Brett," Wolf chuckled. "Remind me never to let you peek into me."

"Too late for that, my friend." His tone was somber. "How do you think I've managed to keep the creepy-crawlers at bay all these years? Having managed to cover your ass so effectively means having to first expose your ass. Sorry boss, but I know where all the bodies are buried and which side your junk hangs."

Wolf heard the man laughing haughtily. He wasn't worried, however, having never buried any bodies nor committed any egregious acts with his junk, though the thought has crossed his mind more frequently the last few months—not the part about burying bodies, of course.

"Okay then," Wolf said. "I guess I'll have to keep paying you my two bucks blackmail every month."

"You'd better," Brett retorted, "'cause I know some guys in Jersey—if you get my drift."

"Later…"

Wolf terminated the call. He fired up the car and got on the road heading back toward Denver. By the time he passed Limon twenty minutes later, he decided to call Sarah Lewis and see if there were any new developments on her end. He called out her name and the phone made the call.

"Hello Sarah… it's—"

"Oh! Hello Mr. Wolf," Sarah said, excitedly. "Have you discovered anything?"

"Bits and pieces," he replied. "Nothing definitive—yet. I'm working on it. Anything new on your end?"

"I'm afraid not," she said, sadly. "Have you discovered something that might point to James's innocence? Anything?"

"I've spoken with his family," Wolf replied. "They're convinced he didn't commit suicide—"

He wished he hadn't said that and stopped talking. The phone went silent for a long moment.

"If James didn't kill himself...then...then it's very likely that he didn't rape me; that he was drugged like me and it was all a set up."

She was quick. "A real possibility." A sickening thought struck him. "If he was—

Blasts filled the air as the driver side window exploded spraying the cabin with tiny cubes of glass. Wolf instinctively hit the brakes as another series of blasts created large holes in the windshield along with multiple radiating fractures obliterating his view.

Emergency maneuver training took over as Wolf calmly worked to keep the car on the road, while slowing as quickly as he dared. Once his speed was reduced, he pulled to the side of the road, slipped free of the safety belt and made for the passenger door while simultaneously slipping his pistol from his belt. Keeping his head down, he carefully peered around the hood spotting a truck stopped some thirty yards ahead.

A shot rang out, a bullet slammed into the car near his head. Wolf was about to return fire, when a series of shots came from behind him. Thinking he was trapped between two shooters, he was considering his options when a car rolled past, shots continuing from the moving vehicle. It was then Wolf realized that the person or persons in the car was shooting at the man or men in the truck!

"What the hell?"

Staying under cover, Wolf scooted back to the front and looked around the fender just in time to see a cloud of dust rising behind the truck as the driver hurried away. The driver of his rescue car performed a snappy turn, driving on the curb against the flow of traffic toward him.

Wolf rose carefully from behind his cover, pointing his pistol steadily at the approaching vehicle. He had no intension of being rescued from the frying pan only to be thrown into the fire.

The car stopped ten feet away. The driver's door opened.

Wolf lowered his pistol, staring at his rescuer who approached him purposefully.

"Best close your mouth, Mr. Grayson," Colleen Silverstone said, with amusement. "Got some nasty bugs flying around these parts."

"Where...?" he began.

"Later," she said, interrupting him. "I've already contacted the troopers; be here in ten." She glanced at his car. "Get your things; you can't drive this. We'll wait for the police in my car...you okay? Not hit?"

"I don't think so," he replied, doing a quick mental survey of his body. "Lucky he, or she, wasn't a crack shot."

"It was a he," Colleen confirmed. "One shooter. Even an expert would have some difficulty shooting a target with both in moving vehicles and do so from the driver's side through an open passenger window. So, yes, you are lucky, but it wasn't luck that maintained control of your car. You've had training."

Wolf slipped into the passenger side of her car. "A requirement of my, ah, profession. I'm a decent shot, too."

"I was a bit nervous when I saw you aim your piece at me," she said, restraining a smile, "considering our rocky relationship."

"I was sure I was trapped between two shooters when I heard shots coming from behind me," Wolf said, feeling relieved that was not the case. He turned in his seat facing her full on. "Would you care to explain why you happen to show up when you did?"

"After handing you the file Saturday," she began, "I became uncomfortable knowing you would most certainly follow up on the information in the file alone."

"So you decided to become my guardian angel." Wolf grinned. "Very sweet of you."

"Nothing of the sort," Colleen shot back. "The last thing I need on my conscience is you getting yourself killed over a file I handed you."

"Because *you* have a conscience." Wolf was immediately sorry for his offhanded reference to her father.

She held his gaze; there was no warmth in it. "Because you getting killed in connection to the name Silverstone would cause me no end of grief."

"I apologize," Wolf said, pausing to give the apology sufficient weight. "And thank you for coming to my rescue."

Her expression softened an increment. "You're welcome."

"Sarah..." Wolf reached for the phone and pressed redial. She answered on the first ring. "Sorry about that..." He gave her a sanitized description of the event, then: "Sarah...do your parents have guns in the house?" From the corner of his eye he saw Colleen glace sharply at him. "Good. Is your dad home right now? ... Oh, you are? Okay; strap it on and carry it with you at all times...your dad, too. Lock everything up and do not open the door for anyone...tell delivery men to leave packages on the porch...um, give me one second, Sarah—"

Wolf pressed mute and looked at Colleen. "I want her and family to have round-the-clock protection. Can I hire your company for that or will it be a conflict of interest?"

"I'll call it in now," she replied. "She's fifteen minutes west of Colorado Spring, right? I'll have security at her home in twenty."

"Thanks." He raised the phone to his ear. "Sarah, I've arranged for you and your family to have armed protection; someone will be there within half an hour...hold on, I'll let you speak directly to the head of the agency, she'll give you all the details."

Wolf handed the phone to Colleen who explained the protocol then gave the phone back to him. "You understand what to do...good, don't want you to shoot your bodyguard by accident...yes, call your parents right now..."

Five minutes after speaking with Sarah, the police arrived. Colleen Silverstone was well known to the troopers and after taking their statements and sending out a description of the shooter—white male, average build, about six feet—and his truck, they departed half hour later promising to inform Colleen of any developments.

"Must be nice to be appreciated," Wolf said, a teasing grin playing on his lips.

Colleen shot him a droll glance. "Comes from having a good reputation and not pissing people off."

"Thank you, thank you," he replied, in his best Elvis imitation.

She peered closely at him for a long moment. There was nothing in her look that suggested anything but professional curiosity, but Wolf felt his pulse quicken nonetheless. The woman had a magnetic presence; in the confines of a car her charisma filled the space challenging Wolf's concentration.

"I am impressed by how calm you were," she said. "You handled yourself very competently back there."

It took Wolf a second to realize she had just complemented him. He gathered his thoughts before replying; not wise to poke a bear twice within the space of forty-five minutes.

"Thank you. Comes from having to look over my shoulder for fifteen years." Never one to resist joking, he added, "You know, pissing people off as I'm wont to do." He swore he spotted a slight twitch of her lips, but supposed he was imagining things.

"What did you discover at the prison?" she asked.

Wolf almost blurted out a quip about foreplay, to wit, none, but bit off the words presenting Colleen a detailed account of the proceedings. She appeared impressed with his questioning of the guards and doctor, doubly so with the discovery about the cameras and hallway blind spots as Wolf explained the flaws and its consequences.

"What's our next move?"

"Excuse me?" Wolf said, genuine surprise on his face. "We? What happened to the conflict of interest having SSIS investigate this case?"

"My company is not investigating your case," she replied. "I am investigating your case on my own, thus none of my corporate clients have a conflict of interest with any other client."

Wolf shot her a suspicious glance. "Why are you so willing to help me all of a sudden?"

"What's the matter, Mr. Wolf—worried I'll kill you and bury your body in some remote mountain valley?"

He grinned. "Something like that."

"If I wanted you dead," Colleen leaned so close that Wolf involuntarily held his breath, "you'd be dead. Never see me coming."

Wolf gazed into those captivating eyes, his pulse ticking up a notch. "Thank you in advance for not taking me out and dumping my remains in a remote valley."

"You're welcome." She pulled the car on the road north to Denver, adding once she got up to speed, "Just don't push your luck; Larry Silverstone is still my father and you remain top of my shit list."

"You're not doing this because you find me irresistible?" Wolf retorted.

"Not even a Nano bit."

Her lips did appear to form what Wolf hoped was a semblance of a smile, which considering everything was a marked improvement in their relationship.

"Having had the opportunity to look into the case," she began, "I'm convinced there are too many hinky parts. I admit you're a top investigator, Mr. Wolf, but criminal genre is not your forte, though you're a quick study. Having provided you with specific information about potential suspects I've placed you in mortal risk. As I said, I don't want to be responsible for you coming to any harm, so here I am."

"Okay boss, what's out next step besides keeping a sharp eye out for another run at me?" Wolf asked.

"First stop is headquarters, Mr. Wolf," she replied.

"No," Wolf countered, "first stop is the Mr., Ms. thing, *Colleen*. And its Wolf, not Grayson or Gray."

"Wolf … predator extraordinaire," she mused. "Quite fitting."

"Wolf," he countered, "highly intelligent, fearless and tireless hunter, loyal, excellent parent … and mates for life."

"Wolf," Colleen repeated, mimicking his tone, "short life span."

"Comes with the territory," Wolf said, matter-of-factly.

She shot him a determined look. "Not if I can help it."

"I know you didn't recognize the shooter," Wolf said, "but might that have been Welling? He took leave last Friday so he's out and about."

"Unless the man lost a good forty pounds, no." She replied. "Welling's a solid 215 and tops out at six-five; big man. The shooter was thinner and maybe six."

"Great," Wolf said. "I was hoping it was Welling; I've got my people hunting him down so I can talk with him."

"Welling wasn't the shooter," Colleen replied, "but I don't think he's clean."

"How so?"

"Welling is one of the readers," she replied. "He's tasked to read all correspondence coming from and going to inmates."

Wolf's eyes got wide. "He would have read James's note to Sarah. He's probably James's killer—if I could find some damn proof—but there's not a mark on the poor boy's body to suggest foul play."

"Prison's don't perform autopsies."

Colleen's tone sounded a bit too innocent, but Wolf took the bait anyway. "Go on."

"If there is no physical evidence of James's being forced into the closet and killed," she said, "and your intuition screams he was murdered then...?"

"Then, what?"

"Then we need to perform an autopsy on the body to find evidence."

Wolf's forehead wrinkled in puzzlement. "But he's—oh! Exhume the body. Don't we need a court order?"

"You, me and every other citizen would need a court order," she quipped. "Next of kin, however need only file a request and pay for the service. I'll make arrangements for the autopsy and tests, but it's pretty straight forward if the parents agree to it."

"Oh, they will," Wolf said, emphatically. "They're certain James was murdered. I'll call them now if you think I should." Colleen shot him a surprised look and he added, "Wolves are pack animals. We recognize hierarchy and willingly follow a competent leader to successfully track and hunt down our prey."

Colleen turned her eyes back on the road ahead paying no further attention to her new, if problematic, partner. Wolf lowered the back of his seat, closed his eyes, allowing his slow, measured breathing to unwind the spike of physical and mental tension created by the attack an hour ago.

What surprised Wolf most as he closed his eyes was the surreal sensation of feeling unreservedly safe in Colleen capable hands, the daughter of a man he had (justly) eviscerated in his novel. Of his many experiences over the past fifteen turbulent years, this impression was perhaps unique ... conscious musings mixed with images blurred past and present as Wolf slipped into a state of welcomed sleep.

Chapter 11

Hunting Season

Wolf jerked awake, his gaze darting from scenes rushing past the window to the woman driving the car.

"Where are we?"

Colleen shot him a brief glance. "Fifteen minutes from headquarters."

He yawned. "How long have I been snoozing?"

"Half hour."

"Adrenaline burning off," he said. "You're a good driver; never felt even a jostle."

"You were out cold," she replied. "I could have driven like a drunken sailor and you wouldn't have noticed." Wolf yawned again and she added, "When did you get to bed last night?"

"One," he said. "But didn't sleep well, thinking about the prison interviews, imagining scenario possibilities. Kept waking up so I just got up."

"I would imagine you have many sleepless nights considering the business you're in…"

Wolf issued a low chuckle. She obviously couldn't stop herself from the opportunity to give him a jab, not that he could blame the woman. He'd probably feel the same if Colleen had skewered his dad's reputation for millions of readers across the globe to enjoy. Except Wolf's dad wouldn't wind up a central character in what New York Times reviewers routinely called his "muckraking drivel". Reviewers, Wolf reminded himself, who never produced one noteworthy literary work yet felt fully qualified to pass judgment on those who had.

"Experts at sex but missing the necessary tool," Wolf said, aloud to himself.

"Excuse me?"

"Just thinking out loud." Wolf said.

"Seven times a day."

She didn't continue and Wolf decided to bite. "What about seven times a day?"

"The number of times men think about sex," she said.

He caught a tinge of humor in her tone.

"You are misinformed, Ms. Silverstone," Wolf corrected. "Only common men think about sex seven times a day. Exceptional men act upon their desires daily."

A suggestion of a smile formed at the corners of her mouth; Wolf knew what was coming.

"Must be challenging not qualify for either category."

"Frankly my dear, I'm disappointed you'd swing at lobbed balls," he chided. "I would have thought someone of your caliber only went for a blazing pitch."

She shook her head as her mouth twisted into an authentic grin. "Well played."

"Never mess with a wordsmith proficient in crafting muckraking drivel," he replied.

She came to a halt at a red light and shot Wolf a droll look. "Impressive how well you know yourself."

He inclined his head. "Touché, madam. Touché."

After maneuvering several more streets, Colleen turned into the access road leading to SSIS headquarters passing the parking lot and coming to a halt at a heavily fortified gate. Lowering her window, she keyed in a code and waited. The accompanying screen came alive showing the hard face of one of SSIS's security officers.

"Identify your passenger please, Ms. Silverstone."

"Grayson Wolf."

"Thank you. Is there any other passenger in the car?"

"No."

"How much fuel in the tank?"

Colleen glanced at the dash. "Third of a tank."

"Please enter the access code."

She keyed in several numbers. The gate slid rapidly open and she drove through, the gate sliding shut the moment the rear bumper passed. A garage door twenty yard ahead barred her way. She stopped ten feet short and waited. Ten seconds later the door slid upwards and she drove into the building, the door closing behind her.

"What was that all about?" Wolf asked. "The waiting, I mean. I didn't see you do anything to open the door."

She looked over at him, hesitating. Wolf could tell she was considering telling him the secret behind the magic door.

"It's a scale," she said.

"In front of the door," Wolf said. "Weighs the vehicle and confirms whatever you told security at the front gate."

Colleen's eyebrows rose slightly. "Pretty good guess—unless you already knew." Wolf shook his head and she continued. "My car was weighed when I left this morning. Your name and vitals is in our system so adjusting to your weight, the computer expected the car to weigh X pounds more than when I left."

"Thus, the question about any other passengers and fuel level." Wolf nodded. "If the car's weight exceeded the expected heft the garage door would stay shut."

"Yes."

"I expect there's more to it," Wolf mused. "But you're not going to tell me and I don't want to know ... I will not discuss this with anyone—even my most trusted lovers, which are legion, by the way."

"Glad to hear it," she quipped. "Tiring to be around excessive testosterone day in and day out."

Wolf laughed at Colleen's swift retort, appreciating her dry sense of humor and also at the absurd idea of his legion of lovers, which upon reflection, he would find a most tiresome distraction. One steady lover would be nice, however.

"Why are you looking at me like that?" Colleen said, a suspicious expression on her face.

He felt the back of his neck burn. "Just thinking about my estrogen legion," he replied, hoping she didn't spot any awkwardness.

She opened her door. "Let's go."

"Your security protocol may be bordering on rabid paranoia," Wolf said, when Colleen faced yet another monitor scanning her face and keyed in another code to open the door leading out of the garage.

The door closed after them, followed by a very solid clunk confirming the door securely locked.

"Your business is about getting the information out there," Colleen explained as they strode along the corridor. "My business is keeping the information tightly locked in our vaults so that it never gets out."

"There is no secret and no defense," Wolf said.

Colleen shot him an amused glance. "Einstein; really?"

"Stuff always has a way of getting out," he replied. "Can't keep it safe anywhere for long. These days it has this nasty habit of walking out of the door electronically or in a tiny drive in a thief's stomach. There is no secret and there is no defense…the only option is staying ahead of the curve, or tsunami as the case may be."

"Our most secure data systems are air-gapped and drive snapped." She rejoined. "No data can be accessed by any means. Our critical systems are not online and cannot be accessed with any form of external drive. No way to send it and no receptacle to stick anything in."

"No sex, ever?"

He said it so innocently that she looked genuinely confused for a second—but only a second.

She burst out laughing, which caused Wolf to join her, the sound of their hilarity filling the hallway. Colleen was the first to regain control; turned and hurried toward the door at the far end Wolf trotting along behind her, chuckling.

Sweeping into her office, Wolf took the first seat across from her desk, Colleen slipping into her executive chair. He could see she was trying not to laugh.

"First order of business," she said, avoiding his eyes, "is for you to call James Collin's parents. I assume you have their number?"

The phone appearing in his hand answered her question. He pressed a number.

"Hello Mr. Collins, Grayson Wolf. I have a request and hope you and your wife will agree…"

He provided an update about his visit to the prison earlier that day leaving out the attempt on his life and explained about the importance of exhuming James's body. The father understood and promised to get back to him before the end of the day.

"Okay," Wolf said, terminating the call. "Made it to first base. What's on second?"

"What's on third." She replied.

"What's on third?"

"Yes." A smile appeared on her lips.

Wolf shot her an amused glance. "Who's on first?"

Colleen held up a hand, laughing. "A fan, I see."

"Every red-blooded American is a fan of that Abbott and Costello routine," Wolf replied. "Did you know the CIA uses Who's on First as a means to detect enemy spies?"

Colleen's smile lit up the room. "You pass the test." She appeared wistful for a second then added, "It feels good to laugh."

"It does." Wolf said. "Not enough of that happening these days."

Wolf felt blessed to have been born with a natural ability to view the world in a lighthearted way and he worked to cultivate his wit calling upon it during dark times, without which he'd never have lasted beyond the third or fourth book.

Colleen lifted the phone receiver and called one of her associates. A minute later the associate appeared at her door.

Colleen made a motion with her hand. "Come in Charlie…thank you for the file. Anything to add since yesterday?"

"No, Ms. Silverstone," the young woman said. "We'll keep searching."

The assistant retreated from the room as Colleen scanned the file, got up and walked over to Wolf, handing him the file.

"That's everything we got on Welling." She backed up and sat on the edge of her desk. "I've recruited one of my field agents to find him, but nothing yet; it's only been a couple days. Apparently, me poking around caused Welling to go to ground, assuming he's involved, of course. Might just as easily be standing in a stream enjoying couple weeks of solitude and good fishing as we speak."

Wolf examined the file in his hand and shook his head.

"Too much of a coincidence, Colleen. Prison cameras that signal when they are live; surveillance blind spots preventing security from seeing inmates sneaking through hallways and into closets; a key security guard takes off for a hasty vacation after you and I show up and I get shot at after visiting the prison; way too many coincidences to be just coincidences. This entire situation from beginning to end stinks to high heaven. Welling is involved and we are going to find him and if he gives me any attitude during questioning I swear I'll water board him."

Colleen peered at him for a long moment, perhaps wondering how dangerous he might become when riled up; or maybe just allowing him to blow off steam.

She tilted her head and said, "I am Wolf, hear me snarl."

He bared a canine tooth. "I bite, too."

"Have you ever had to shoot anyone?" she said. "In self-defense, I mean."

He shook his head. "No, though I've had to draw my pistol a dozen times. Mostly I'm showered with verbal abuse, pushing, shoving and the occasional physical assault. I sincerely hope never to shoot anyone...though I believe I'm capable push comes to shove." Seeing Colleen looking pensive he added, "What? Thinking I might faint at the sight of blood?"

She held his eyes; Wolf finding her scrutinizing gaze disconcerting to be sure. It wasn't just sex appeal, of which she had an abundance thereof, but something more potent and alluring to him: Colleen Silverstone exuded a degree of intelligence and competence becoming increasingly rare in contemporary culture. He realized she was smiling.

"What?"

"I was thinking I'm okay with schlepping you around tracking down Welling and unknown shooters," she replied. "Just don't fade out on me like that in tight situations."

"Fade out?"

"Your mind was somewhere else for a good five seconds a moment ago," she explained. "A ninety-year old suffering from severe arthritis in his hands could have shot you a dozen times in five seconds...So what were you thinking about?"

"That I'm lucky to have Annie Oakley as my partner," Wolf replied, grinning ear-to-ear. "What's our next move, partner?"

She checked the time. "I was thinking lunch."

Wolf was tempted to make some suggestive retort, but thought better of it. Like his own announcements, he sensed Colleen's statement were only the tip of the iceberg and he gazed expectantly at her.

"Have this favorite Mexican hole-in-the-wall a few miles south," she said. "Make some of the best Enchiladas north of the border."

"Few miles south…like near Castle Rock?" he replied.

"Yes, and you're buying." She slid off the edge of the desk. "Let's roll."

"Wait," Wolf said, remembering something. "I need to make a quick call to the rental agency about my car…"

"Don't bother," she said. "Already taken care of."

"Damn you're good."

A sly grin appeared on her lips as she walked toward the door. "You have no idea."

Wolf had to agree. He didn't have any idea.

There really was a tiny Mexican hole-in-the-wall restaurant at the outskirts of Castle Rock that did in fact serve some of the tastiest Mexican dishes Wolf had eaten in Colorado. He was just swallowing the rest of his beer when Colleen leaned toward him, smiling in an amusing way.

"Our first date."

Caught off guard, Wolf choked on a swallow of beer. Clearing his throat, he shot her a disapproving look, shaking his head for emphasis.

"You are an evil woman, Ms. Silverstone."

"You knew what I was when you asked me out to lunch," she grinned.

It took him a second to remember. "That was two weeks ago and I was teasing you."

"I take invitations seriously." She gazed at him so sweetly that his pulse really did skip a beat. "Careful what you ask of me in the future … you might get it."

Wolf thought it best to hold his tongue. Rising from his seat he held the chair for her and paid the bill—in cash; no credit or checks accepted.

Holding the door for her, he had no doubt that she could have any man she wanted, knowing with absolute certainty that *one man* would never be considered. You don't rip a woman's father to shreds and expect her to admire and love that man for doing so. Tolerate him, work on a case, sure. Become romantically involved? Sacrilege.

Wolf had no illusions about Colleen's reasons for helping him. Though she may smile and tease him, she was still Larry Silverstone's daughter who, he recalled, was proficient in various martial arts and reputed to be deadly with firearms and a blade. Vigilanti Semper.

"You keep staring at me with that severe look I might get the impression you don't like me," Colleen said, interrupting Wolf's reverie.

"Beauty, brains and danger. What's not to like?" he shot back without thinking. Her brilliant smile caused a burning sensation back of his neck. "I was referring to myself."

It was lame, but the best he could do finding himself in such close proximity with someone he would normally never be with considering the circumstances.

Colleen pulled the car on the road turning toward Overland fifteen minutes east. Approaching the college's sprawling complex with its ring roads and labyrinth of interconnected roads and alleys, Wolf was about to suggest a particular direction when she turned north into the Outer Ring and kept driving until reaching its apex, hung a right making for a spot somewhere near the college's center where she parked in a reserved spot.

"You do realize," Wolf cautioned, as she switched the engine off, "they will tow your car within half hour."

Colleen pointed at the glove compartment in front of Wolf instructing him to take out the bright red tag, which he did. She hung it around the back of the rearview mirror.

"VIP parking," she said. "Let's go."

"How did you manage that?" When she didn't answer, he added, "Overland is a client."

"Don't know why people keep saying you're terminally obtuse," she responded, though Wolf caught a tinge of respect in her tone.

"Isn't this a conflict of interest," he replied, "coming to grill Overland students and using your VIP pass to help you do it?"

"Let me worry about that," Colleen said.

"Just saying…"

She stepped in front of Wolf causing him to stop short. "Contrary to what you might think Mr. Wolf, not everyone puts the mighty dollar ahead of everything else."

Being with Colleen Silverstone might cause a rise in his pulse but Wolf was not easily intimidated or silenced.

"I am quite aware that you are not your father."

She became quite still; a look in her eyes suggesting the possibility of violence, while her calm demeanor clearly acknowledged the complement. Wolf almost smiled, restraining himself at the last moment knowing it would most likely be misinterpreted. She turned on her heels and continued down the walkway.

They walked through a wide, arched entrance into a beautifully appointed courtyard complete with gardens, exotic shrubbery and sections covered with colorful flowers one would expect to find at a luxury retreat. The grounds were enclosed on three sides by student residences, Colleen turning left and entering the building's lobby. Unlike the other dorms Wolf visited two weeks back, the security at this one reminded him of the airport with its metal detectors and baggage X-ray machine.

Passing through the first gauntlet they walked through a narrow path enclosed on both sides by chest-high Lucite walls to a reception counter staffed not by some common Resident Assistant but armed campus security.

"What kind of dorm is this?" Wolf said, approaching the counter.

"The VIP kind," Colleen replied. "Keeping children of the high and mighty safe from the Hoi Polloi."

"And what keeps the Hoi Polloi safe from them?" Wolf quipped.

"Colleen Silverstone," she said, presenting her identification to the officer behind the counter who looked at it, her eyes coming back to rest on Colleen's face.

The officer peered at Wolf who gave her his name, surprised to see no reaction. It wasn't vanity; it was a relief when anyone—especially someone in position of authority—didn't make any connection to his name since the alternative might often be a negative reaction.

When asked whom they were visiting, Colleen gave a name Wolf recognized. The officer nodded and handed both ID's to her.

"Thank you, officer," Colleen said, giving Wolf's ID to him. "Have a nice day."

"You too, Ms. Silverstone," the woman replied.

There was nothing special about the exchange; one hears such automatic greetings multiple times a day between individuals, except this one sounded a tad too casual to Wolf's ears having learned to spot all manner of sub textual references and nuances over the years. His suspicion was immediately confirmed when Colleen retrieved a small card from her ID wallet.

"Spies, Ms. Silverstone?" Wolf said, grinning.

Colleen ignored him and took the closest staircase to the second floor passing through a gauntlet of students loitering and chatting in the hall, lowering their voices and peering at the passing strangers with suspicion. They came to a halt in front of the last door along the corridor.

"Let me do the talking," Colleen said, rapping on the door.

To the untrained ear it sounded like a simple request. Wolf heard the order behind the tone.

It was a strange sensation—surreal in fact—for him to be ordered about as Grayson Wolf. Having spent years working undercover jobs ranging from lawn boy, cook and waiter to premier bartender and chauffeur to the stars, Wolf followed directives and orders with ease because he was playing a role researching the inner workings of individuals and organizations. Being ordered about by anyone as Grayson Wolf was another matter entirely and Wolf chafed at the idea.

The door opened revealing the surprised face of Karla Grisham looking back at them. She held the door saying nothing.

"May we come in, Karla?" Colleen said. A simply question, but one a rational listener would be wise to heed. The door swung open and they walked in.

Wolf's brief visual survey revealed this was no ordinary dorm room but a suite consistent with his initial impression of the dorm complex as a luxury resort. Karla's suite included a spacious reception area, a French door leading to the bedroom with an adjoining bathroom complete with a Jacuzzi no doubt. Tough to be a college student these days.

"Um," Karla said, eyeing Wolf with wariness, "why are you here, Ms. Silverstone? Has something happened? Am I in danger?"

Years of living and working in the company of men and women who saw themselves above the law and rules of civility, seeing others solely as a means to an end, suckers and cash cows ripe for milking to be discarded like trash, Wolf recognized the stench of moral decay instantly. He pressed his lips together to prevent a sneer of unqualified contempt from showing.

"Yes, and possibly," Colleen replied, taking a seat next to her. Karla's eyes grew larger in response to this alarming comment. "I believe you have met my associate, Mr. Gray some weeks back?"

Karla gazed over at Wolf, a knowing smile forming. "Freelance writer on the trail of hot college sex."

He saw Colleen shoot him a droll glance. "That's me, looking for love in all the wrong places."

"There are no wrong places for hot sex," Karla replied, looking smug.

"I'm glad you brought up sex," Colleen said. "That's why I came to see you, Karla. You remember that terrible incident back at the beginning of last December where an Overland coed was drugged and raped?"

Karla became suddenly very still. "What about it?"

No suggestive smile or cute expression this time.

"Did you hear about the suicide of James Collins back in March?" Colleen said. "He's the—"

"The one that raped Sarah Lewis," Karla interjected. "Yeah, everyone knows about that. What does it have to do with me?"

"Nothing, I'm sure," Colleen replied, sounding reassuring. "Apparently new information about that case has come to light and your name has come up..."

"What do you mean my name's come up?" Karla said. "How? I mean, why would it? I barely knew either one of them."

"I agree," Colleen said, keeping up the supportive routine. "It makes no sense why your name would be associated with something so horrendous. That's why I came here in person to tell you this; we don't want the press or Senator Grisham's political enemies to get wind of your name being anywhere near something so toxic as rape and suicide."

Karla's face was a shade or two paler than when she first opened the door. She glanced at Wolf and back again.

"What about him?" She shot a brief glance at Wolf. "He's a writer, right? Is he going to write about this, about me connected to Sarah or James? I'm not. Anyone says otherwise they're lying."

"You know my reputation, Karla," Colleen replied. "I assure you that Mr. Gray won't write one word about anything I do not want him to write about." She gave Wolf a threatening look for emphasis.

"She's the boss," Wolf said, doing his best to keep any hint of humor out of his tone. "No one crosses Ms. Silverstone and gets away with it."

"What should I do in the meantime?" Karla asked.

"First and foremost," Colleen replied, "tell no one. One Tweet is all it will take for this news to go viral and I don't have to tell you the political and personal ramifications of this to you and your family."

Karla gave Colleen a determined look. "No talking to anyone about this. Got it."

"We're going now," Colleen said. "Be sure to call me if you hear anything you think you I should know. Don't wait. Nothing is too insignificant or incidental. You understand, Karla?"

"Yes."

*   *   *   *

Neither spoke a word until they were back in the car.

"You were a well-behaved Wolf back there," Colleen teased, her smile lighting up the interior. "Almost house-broken even."

"Nice work," Wolf said, ignoring her taunt. "How fast do you think she's going to call her crew to tell them the news?"

"Sooner than later, for sure," she replied. "But I'll know in any case."

Wolf gave her a sharp look. "Oh? Certainly, nothing so pedestrian as having your agents dog her every move, so..."

She gazed silently at Wolf, waiting expectantly as he replayed the events of the meeting in his head beginning with Karla opening the door. As the movie in his mind sped forward he almost missed it because her action had been so very normal: Colleen had sat next to Karla. He saw the image clearly in his mind's eye.

"You cloned her phone laying on the table right at your elbow." Her silence confirmed his guess. "Where are going to next?"

"To the bitch boy cave to rattle more chains," she replied, exiting the campus and driving east on the main drag through Overland Downs, the name given to the amoeba-like growth of hotels, stores, coffee shops, restaurants, bars, tattoo parlors, apartments and sundry houses attached along the college's southern border.

Five minutes later she pulled into the circular driveway of an impressive looking two-story structure constructed from country stone and logs. A central pitched roof with large windows facing the driveway and a balcony wrapping its way around the building dominated the front.

Wolf craned his neck to look at the mixed roofline with its angles and pitches. "How humble of these boys to live in such a modest log cabin. Who would have thought it?"

Colleen pressed the doorbell, the door opening to reveal a pasty-faced pledge blinking at them. "We're here to see Kerry Bellamy."

The pledge made a face and shook his head. "He's not here."

Wolf saw Colleen slipping the boy a folded hundred-dollar bill. "I'm his very special friend."

"I'm not supposed to let anyone in." Colleen pressed a second C-note in his hand. He cleared his throat. "Room—"

"201. Left, top of the stairs; corner room," Colleen recited. "Special friend, remember?"

"I love it," Wolf said, scouting the interior with its Western motif, massive stone fireplace, a comfortable seating area facing it, wood paneled walls and spacious layout.

"You like this western ranch house look?" Colleen said, shooting him a sly look as they trod up the stairs. "I would think you'd lean toward the doomsday prepper style; you know: blast-proof underground lair hidden far from civilization where you can hide from all the people who are out to get you."

"Why would I need to hide?" Wolf retorted. "Polls routinely show that I'm universally loved and admired."

Colleen turned left on the landing and headed for the corner room. "A straw poll by its very nature is a small, informal opinion survey."

Wolf grinned knowingly at her, coming to halt in front of room 201. "Did you enjoy my interview on *Title Page Live* last month?"

She ignored him and knocked on the door. When no one answered after the second knock she tried the door handle, which opened. She stepped into the room.

"Ballsy," Wolf said, following her in.

Five boys were seated around a TV screen paying a videogame.

"Hey! Who are you?" a male student cried upon seeing two strangers entering the room. The group jumped up from their seats. "Get out! This is a private house and you're trespassing."

"Hello Kerry," Colleen said, ignoring his protestations.

"You can't just barge into my room, Colleen; leave or I'm calling the cops!" Kerry snarled.

"Yeah and maybe we'll play with you while we're waiting for the cops," one of the group threatened, leering at her.

Colleen stepped toward them so swiftly that several nearly fell as they stumbled backwards, surprised by her aggressive action.

"Sit down and shut your mouths."

Wolf heard the uncompromising threat in Colleen's tone. The boys blinked, their bravado retreating with them to their seats. No one spoke.

"You can't talk to us like that," a voice said.

Colleen casually retrieved her cell phone from her pocket. "Let's do call the cops and when they get here they'll arrest you for any number of violations beginning with the blow on the table and working their way up to conspiracy to cause psychological and bodily harm, drugging students without their knowledge, kidnapping, participating in rape and subsequent cover-up." She looked at Wolf. "Have I covered the charges sufficiently?"

"I'd add being sociopathic douchebags, though that's not a crime."

Wolf swore that he spotted Kerry Bellamy puffing up his chest as he walked up to Colleen. A sneer formed on his lips.

"Go ahead, call the cops," he said. "You've got nothing on us, cause if you did, the cops would be here with you. Besides, you work for my old man. So, what is this, a shakedown? Squeeze some extra cash from Bellamy junior?" His eyes groped Colleen's body. "Happy to hand over a fistful for some of what you got."

Colleen held Kerry's eyes. "Open your foul mouth again..." She waited for that to sink in, which it did quickly judging from Kerry's wide eyes and vanishing lurid grin. "What? Not so anxious for a fistful of what I've got?

"Who's he?" Kerry said, pointing at Wolf.

"My personal bodyguard," she deadpanned.

Kerry shot Wolf a quick glance, hoping Kerry and his cohorts were buying his steely, killer expression.

"Why have you come, Ms. Silverstone?" Kerry said, all polite now.

"To warn you and your friends," she replied. "With the unexpected suicide of James Collins, there is talk of reopening the Sarah Lewis rape case and certain names have been mentioned."

Wolf thought that Kerry's face appeared to pale a degree, though he'd expect a bigger reaction given the seriousness of the crimes committed. Either the boy had nothing to do with the rape, was a stone-cold sociopath or just a rich brat who had been allowed to get away with transgressions all his life.

Kerry's brow knitted. "Names? Like mine?"

"Yes, yours and others you hang with," Colleen replied, her glance sweeping the others in the room.

"Look," Kerry said, inclining his head for emphasis "I admit I mess around with people and have as much sex with as many girls I can get, but I have nothing to do with Sarah Lewis. Why would I bother? I'm Kerry Bellamy. The women folk line up outside my door every night."

"I'm sure the women folk get what they deserve," Colleen replied. Seeing Kerry's quizzical look, she added, "I mean, you are, after all, Kerry Bellamy. What girl wouldn't want to get a piece of that, right?"

"Very funny Ms. Silverstone." He replied. His face brightened. "Though I have to agree with you. The girls get what they deserve from me which they not soon forget."

"Your extra-curricular activities aside," Collen said "Your father is a client and I felt it my responsibility to inform you of the fact that new questions about the Lewis-Collins case are being raised. Having so informed you, I bid you all a good day."

Wolf shot everyone a threatening glare and hurried after her. She trotted down the stairs and out of the building without saying a word. Once in the car, however…

"I feel in dire need of a shower."

Wolf didn't have to guess her reason. "My place is closer than yours."

Colleen shot him a droll look. "Nice try...but no. Make that never."

"Never, Ms. Silverstone," Wolf began, "say never."

"Not ever in a million years, then" she retorted. "I have to say that you were surprisingly convincing as a bodyguard."

"I can handle myself," he replied.

A skeptical expression formed on her face. "Really?"

He held her eyes. "Want to try me sometime?"

She stared at him long enough for him to feel his temperature rising, close proximity to the woman having that effect, but his expression remained inscrutable.

"Perhaps once our temporary partnership is over," she replied. "It's not good for business for me to be pummeling a client into submission."

"You and what army?" Wolf wondered why the hell he uttered such juvenile remarks.

Colleen rolled her eyes and issued a brief snort as she pulled the car on the road. They hadn't gone far when they spotted a young man standing at the side of the road ahead waiving at them. She pulled the car to the shoulder and stopped; the student—Wolf recognized the boy as one of the residents of back at the house—came up along the passenger side as Wolf lowered the widow.

"What's going on?" Wolf said.

"Can I get in?" he replied. "I want to talk."

Wolf jerked his head toward the rear and he got in. "What's your name?"

"No names," he replied. "I room at the Lodge, the house you just came from and get enough crap from some of the residents. So, no name. Please drive; don't want anyone to spot us."

Colleen pulled the car back on the road and drove out of the housing area toward the main boulevard. "What do you want to talk about?"

"The bitch boys," he replied immediately.

"Not a badge of honor, I take it." Wolf quipped.

"Oh, they think so," he replied. "They're proud of the moniker. But the rest of us feel that Bellamy and his crew and Karla's bitch click represent everything that is wrong at Overland: drugs, drinking, fucking; I say fucking because that's what they do. Not sex, not love or enjoyment, just fucking. Each other and the stupid boys and girls who feel honored to be invited to their fucking parties."

"Sounds like you might be a bit envious?" Wolf ventured, trying to prod something lose.

"I have a girlfriend; she's great and we make love," he replied. "Often. I wouldn't want to be part of their snake pit. And it's much more than just that. It's the endless haranguing of anyone who don't act like trash, who want to do something with their lives. People like James Collins and Sarah Lewis. Not everyone at Overland is some billionaire's kid. Many of us just get by. When I first came here last year I was like, really stoked about the college and living in this fantastic house. Now I want to get the hell out as fast as I can. The college is turning in to a cesspit filled with more and more Bellamys and Grishams, which is a shame because I have fantastic professors and I'm in an exciting entrepreneurial program."

"Thank you for sharing your view about your experience at Overland," Colleen said, "but I think you wanted to tell us something more about the goings on at the Lodge."

"Yeah," he said. "I've got the name of the drug dealer that provides all kind of shit to students. The campus cops know him but no one does anything about him and his crew. Little Richie needs to have his goodies and we don't want to upset the money train rolling into the college now, do we?"

"What's his name and where can we find him?" Wolf asked.

"Here," the boy said, handing him a slip of paper. "Everything you need including a description of the guy. I don't know what kind of cops you are, but I hope you can get something on Kerry or Karla and their flunkies...Ah, you can drop me off right here; thanks."

He got out and made his way toward a nearby open-air mall. Wolf watched him walk away thinking that Overland would be the fantastic college it once was if the large majority of its student body was composed of student like him, Sarah Lewis, James Collins and Jennifer Park.

Colleen pulled back onto the road. "What's the address of our dealer?"

They arrived at the address given by their unnamed malcontent twenty some minutes later only to find half dozen state trooper vehicles cluttering up the street, light flashing. Pulling over, they got out and made their way toward the scene where they were stopped by a trooper from proceeding toward the house in question.

Colleen smiled at the officer, producing her identification. "I'd be ever so grateful if you'd give a holler on your radio to Captain Jeffrey's over yonder. I'm sure he'd want to see us."

The officer did and moments later Wolf was introduced to Colorado State Trooper Captain Jeffrey. They men shook hands, Wolf making sure he applied sufficient pressure to assure the officer that he was a solid, upstanding citizen. Wolf had learned many things over the years including the fact that a handshake could very well be the difference between effusive acceptance as a fellow traveler or rejection as though one was harboring a social disease.

"What's going on, Ken?" Colleen asked.

Jeffrey gave her a probing look. "And what bring the amazing Colleen Silverstone to a drug infested dump like this?"

"Looking for the source of the infestation," she replied.

A smile creased Jeffrey face. "A disagreement of terminal proportions. Three dead, two more wounded. The wages of criminal sinning."

"One of them," she looked at the slip of paper, "named Paul? Black stingy hair, pasty face, tattoos around his neck?"

"Grazed," Jeffery replied. "Medics patching him up now."

"May I...?"

"I'd never say no to a lady who askes so nicely and one who ..." Jeffrey grinned and gave her a suggestive wink "has the level of access to the Governor that she has."

Colleen rewarded the Captain with one of her brilliant smiles. "I owe you one, Ken."

"And I'm gonna collect them all one of these days," giving her a look that made her laugh.

"You know where to find me."

"Yes, I do, missy. Yes, I do."

When they arrived at the ambulance, the EMT had just finished patching up the injured drug dealer. Two troopers stood nearby their captive to ensure he remained there. Colleen told them the Captain had cleared her and her sidekick to speak to the prisoner.

"Sidekick?" Wolf said. "I prefer bodyguard, please."

Colleen continued what Wolf assumed was her policy of ignoring him and approached the prisoner.

"I'd like to ask you some questions, Paul."

"Got nothin' to say, cop."

"I'm not the police," Colleen replied. "Nothing you say to me will constitute you losing any Miranda rights."

"Lawyer."

"Some questions, first."

Paul looked confused. "What?"

"You answer my questions, I will get you a real lawyer," she replied. "Not some public defender flunky."

Paul looked at her with suspicion. "How I know you not some undercover bitch?"

"Because I'm a private investigator bitch," she replied, producing her ID. "I'm not interested in what went down here today or what shit you've been playing with. I have a couple questions about some college kids buying stuff from you. Give me clean answers, I promise I will call a lawyer right here and now. Well?"

"Wadda wanna know?"

"You know Kerry Bellamy?"

"Maybe?"

"Not the way to get that good lawyer."

"Yeah, I know the punk."

Colleen shot Wolf a look that conveyed that Paul gave a very "clean" response. "You ever sell him any Rofis? Rohypnol? Ketamine?"

Paul scrunched up his face. "Nah, just the usual. Blow mostly. Lots of weed."

"Think, Paul. Are you certain you never sold any Rofis to Bellamy—or to his crew?"

"Nope."

"What about to some of the coeds? Karla Grisham or her crew?"

"What da hell they want with Rofis?" Paul snorted. "Dudes screw any of 'em anytime they whistle for da dogs."

"So, no Rofis to any of these students." Colleen stated. "Any to adults? Teachers?"

"Look," Paul said, becoming annoyed, "Shit like that is, like, special order. I deal in main product: coke, smack, weed, uppers 'n downers. No demand for Rofis. You want that you gotta put in a special order and it take some days to get it. I'm not the only dealer 'round, though."

"Thank you." Colleen pressed a key on her phone, explained her request to the person on the other end then handed the unit to Paul. "As promised, a real lawyer."

Five minutes later they were back in the car. Colleen's hand rested on the wheel, pondering the situation.

"Another dead end."

"I suppose it was too much to hope that we'd nail the bitch crew this afternoon," Wolf replied. "But the elimination of one trail reduces the number of trails to pursue. We know in all likelihood the date-rape drug came from elsewhere. A small step, better than no step."

Colleen nodded, pressed a button on the steering wheel then called out a name. Wolf heard the phone ringing filling the cabin from ten speakers encircling the interior.

"Colleen," a deep voice said.

"Hi Cooper. Any news on Welling?"

"In fact, yes," he replied. "Came in just a minute ago. Was just about to call you."

"What's the scoop?"

"We think Welling's hiding out in a hunting cabin, ten miles northwest of Creede...about two hundred fifty miles southwest."

"Good work, Cooper," Colleen said. "How did you discover that?"

"Digging for prizes," he quipped. "Welling has a childhood friend who owns the cabin. He's gotta be there."

Colleen looked at the dashboard clock. "We'll load for bear and run at him in the morning."

She gunned the engine and headed for home.

Chapter 12

Wolf v. Bear

Wolf awoke to the sound of his phone buzzing. Instantly awake, he snatched it off the bed stand.

"Good morning, Colleen. What's the buzz?"

"Something important has come up and we'll need to delay our run at Wellington."

"Anything I should be aware of?"

"Nothing that concerns you or our mission," Colleen replied. "I do have other clients besides Grayson Wolf."

Wolf grinned. "And I believed you only thought about me."

"Why Mr. Wolf," she said, matter-of-factly, "I never think about you at all."

"Upon reflection, Ms. Silverstone," he retorted, "that might be very comforting."

That remark elicited a low chuckle. "You have no idea … Most likely we won't get going until afternoon sometime; I'll give you a heads-up as soon as I know."

"I understand," Wolf said. "Colleen, would it be okay for me to come by your office later this morning and look at what your people have on Welling's friend and location?"

"Of course; I'll let Connor know," she replied. "Feel free to wait at the center and have lunch…we have gourmet chefs."

"I knew if I waited long enough you'd invite me to lunch eventually," Wolf teased. "Thanks. Hope to see you before sunset."

"Thanks for the warning," she retorted and terminated the call.

"Funny woman," Wolf said, to no one in particular. He pressed a number and moments later the recipient answered.

"Good morning partner," Diana said. "Making any progress in your extracurricular investigation?"

"Been tough row to hoe, but we've caught a break," Wolf replied. "Key suspect, a guard, went on an extended 'vacation' and disappeared. We think we've found where he's hiding."

"Tell me you're not going alone, Wolf," Diana said. "Going after killers is not like hunting down typical sociopaths."

"I'm bringing serious backup," he replied.

There was a pause, filled with a faint buzzing. "Serious as in Colleen Silverstone."

"The one and only."

"Wolf ... be careful."

"Don't worry, we will be."

"I'm not talking about the man you're going after."

"Colleen is not enamored with me, sure," he replied, "but she's not going to hurt me."

"You know exactly what I mean," Diana said.

"That I have a weakness for women?" Wolf grinned.

"That she's exactly the *type* of woman you have a weakness for," she replied, "and who has the, ah, wherewithal to manipulate men for her own ends."

"Not to worry," he said. "Yes, she's hot in so many ways that appeal to me, much like you, by the way—except you ran off and got married—but our relationship is strictly professional."

"Until it isn't."

"If it ever comes to that," Wolf replied, "it won't be because of her Jedi mind tricks. Besides, I'm pretty good at manipulating men and women for my own ends, too ... enough about me; how's the siege shaping up?"

"Ahead of schedule actually," Diana said. "Tent, kitchens and restrooms expected to arrive Tuesday and the avant-garde arriving in busses Thursday."

"Any problems?"

"Curious people looking on at the site as we prepare, but no trouble—yet," Diana explained. "Considering that Virginia Patriots College is a national leader when it comes to Progressive activism, I'm sure things will get interesting sooner than later. Hope you get this guy and wrap up this case; I'd feel a lot better with you at my side."

"I'm working on it," Wolf replied. "The body of the student who committed suicide in prison will be exhumed tomorrow or the day after, then a battery of tests run and if we get Welling today maybe we'll get some answers about what the hell is going on. Keep me informed of progress and I'll let you know immediately if we break this case open."

Wolf terminated the call. Diana's plan was a bold one, brilliant really, but he had a bad feeling about how the student crazies and their professional protesters backed by money from financiers such as Soros, the man's history illustrating his willingness to support and profit from dictatorial regimes and seeking to undermine America at every possibility. But a decisive stand against the disease of political correctness and appeasement had to be taken and to do so in Virginia, the cradle of American independence, was most appropriate.

*   *   *   *

It was past twelve when Wolf rolled into the parking lot of SSIS and admitted with minimal hassle. Inquiring about Cooper's location, he was informed the Head of Search and Recovery had just gone to lunch, and having not eaten since seven, headed for the main cafeteria.

Colleen had not been exaggerating about gourmet chefs preparing meals, even the selections at the buffet wing for employees desiring a faster meal, looked and smelled delicious. Not being in a hurry, Wolf opted for the main dining room where waiters served employees sitting at linen-covered tables adorned with fresh cut flowers and glowing orbs of light. An attendant escorted him to a table for two, an array of which lined the outside wall. Thick windows rested on high sills, clearing the heads of seated guests, protecting them from flying shards of glass in the event of an attack from the outside—assuming the windows even shattered. SSIS was a fortress in many more ways than obvious to its visitors.

He finished his excellent meal and asked for the bill when the waitress informed him there was no charge. Reaching into his wallet he drew out a large denomination note and handed it to the server who smiled and declined.

"I apologize for the insult," Wolf said, pulling out a second note and pressing both into her hand. He held her eyes, then said, a sly grin on his lips, "I can keep doing this all day."

The waitress made a sheepish face and thanked him, adding as she removed some dishes from the table with a big smile, "Next time I'll take you up on that threat."

Wolf returned her smile. "I wouldn't expect any less."

Exiting the cafeteria, he was making for the reception desk to inquire where Cooper's office was when the man himself intercepted him.

"Mr. Wolf, I'm Cooper Adkins. Call me Cooper, please."

"Cooper...great. Just going to look for your office," Wolf replied shaking his hand. "Just Wolf is what everyone calls me."

Cooper was a burly looking man with a wicked grin. "Not according to Colleen."

Wolf issued a snort. "The price of fame, I fear."

"Please follow me," Cooper said, turning left into a vestibule with a door at the far end. "You want to study the maps where the cabin Welling is probably hiding out is located. Got satellite images, too."

He approached the door, faced a monitor and keyed in a number. The heavy door slid open revealing a staircase.

"I think you folks have more security than the NSA or the Pentagon," Wolf said, as they descended the stairs.

"We do," Cooper confirmed. "The brain of the complex is underground, safe from everything but a guided 500-pound bomb dropped from high up."

The entered a circular shaped space with four doors leading to rooms. There were no windows. Cooper made for the door on the right and keyed in a code opening the door. Large monitors hung on the walls, computers filled the center of the space with sundry equipment clustered in several alcoves. Half dozen techs were busy working.

"Here you are, Wolf," Cooper said, stopping in front of a large wall screen showing a top-down view of a rugged landscape. He handed him a controller. "Just like any TV control...arrows, etc. Press Zoom and you'll get close enough to the cabin to see the raindrops on the roof."

Wolf zoomed in, rapidly narrowing the field until the roof of a small house appeared. "This is not Google Earth."

"That is live satellite feed," Cooper said.

Wolf peered at the man with incredulity. "You have your own satellites?"

"We have contract for blocks of satellite time," Cooper replied. "Gives real-time surveillance capability and helps pay the bills of private companies putting them up there."

If Wolf had questions about Silverstone Security and Investigative Services from his first foray through the firm's extensive security protocol weeks back, it was becoming clear that SSIS was far and beyond any security or investigative firm he had ever encountered.

"This is very impressive," Wolf said, reflecting on his conclusion. A stray thought about global cybercrime popped into his head. "What about cyber security? It's clear that barring a massive military-type assault on this place no one is getting in, but the growing threat these days is cyber-attack." His hand swept across the room. "This is all online and therefore vulnerable to being breeched."

A faint smile touched Cooper's lips. "Colleen said you'd ask questions about everything and anything you see, hear or touch. Said it's in your DNA ... and that I was allowed to answer—prudently. Yes, some are online. And vulnerable to hackers. Let me ask you a question: how does disease spread through population?"

"Some form of direct or indirect contact," Wolf said.

"And in the world of electronic technology?" Cooper replied.

Wolf smiled. "Some form of direct or indirect contact such as hard lines or Wi-Fi. Colleen said something about cyber security here." His eyes swept the room. "Some are connected, you said. But ... not necessarily connected with each other."

"Ever." Cooper added for emphasis. "Our business is security, Wolf. We've seen cyber vulnerability coming way back and are prepared for it. How prepared are your people in Virginia? I'd bet if I call across the hall to Cyber Unit to find out, they'd hack into the Center for Individual Rights' system in two minutes."

Wolf stared at the man. He knew that CIR had good cyber techs who had successfully foiled previous attempts to mess with the centers computers, but there's always someone better or more determined. He thought about the demonstration Diana was organizing at VPC and the backlash it would provoke which would most certainly include a highly organized and well-funded assault on the center's computer systems.

Wolf nodded. "You're right, Cooper. What's the most immediate action we need to take to diminish the damage a concentrated attack would incur?"

"Disconnect any vital computers from the network." He replied. "Crack the server and the body is wide open to infection. Do that now. It's a pain, but better than the alternative."

"I'll let my people know today," Wolf replied. "And I want to hire your cyber team to upgrade our system."

"You'll need to speak with client services," Cooper said. "I'm sure they'll be happy to discuss services and fees."

Wolf thanked the man and turned his attention to satellite images and maps of Creede. Perhaps the discussion with Cooper about the vulnerability of computer systems increased his sense of paranoia and he carefully studied the cabin's position, terrain in the area, nearby landmarks and fixing their position in memory. Wolf had absolute confidence in Colleen's skill and experience pursuing her quarry whether it be dark alleys in the inner city or box canyons in badlands, but shit happens. There were too many what-ifs once in the mountains miles from rescue and Wolf would rather be modestly prepared than not when Murphy strikes at he does, usually at the most inconvenient time.

Colleen got back by two-thirty and off to Creede by three, the Toyota 4-Runner loaded for bear. The bulk of the 250 miles to Creede was smooth open road and after some negotiation through tight mountain passes into the old mining town they stopped at the first gas station, Wolf pumping fuel while Colleen spoke with Cooper for the latest update about Welling.

"Okay," Colleen said, terminating the call, "no sign at moment at the Cabin all afternoon. Welling is either hunkered down inside furiously whittling wooden sculptures of Western villains or he's out and about hunting or fishing."

Wolf made a shocked face. "Did you just make a joke?"

"Must be oxygen deprivation," she retorted. "Probably from being cooped up with you breathing the same air for hours."

She pulled the car out of the station and headed northwest on 504 out of town. The road came to a fork a mile or so, Colleen abandon 504 taking the left fork. Five miles later the road came to a dead end.

"Must have missed the trail." She turned around and drove slowly back. "Ah ... no wonder I missed it."

"It's a glorified Elk trail," Wolf said, looking at the narrow dirt road.

She took a breath. "And we're going to bounce along that trail for about four miles."

Wolf peered skeptically at the road. "You sure this car's up to the task? Looks like a rough track."

"Wanna walk instead?"

"You're really enjoying poking the greenhorn, aren't you?"

She smiled. "Not every day I get to be entertained by Grayson Wolf. Tighten your loins because here we go."

The first mile was up a twisting incline, Colleen weaving past large stones and larger potholes. The next couple miles were mostly downhill, the trail punishing car and passengers every foot of the way.

Holding on to the handgrip to prevent head and shoulders from striking the door, Wolf said, his speech broken with the jerking of the car "This ... gives a ... whole new meaning to the phrase... rock 'n roll. How ... much further?"

"Half mile, or so ... fifteen minutes."

Wolf checked the time. "6:15. At this rate it'll be dark by the time we reach the cabin."

"Stop your bellyaching, greenhorn," Colleen said, stopping the car. She checked the satellite photo on her phone. "Okay, I think we need to turn into that elk trail hundred feet ahead. The cabin should be fifty feet or so in."

The road to the cabin went over a low rise, Colleen halting the vehicle the moment she spotted the cabin thirty feet ahead. "Okay, we need to proceed very carefully."

They exited the vehicle, quietly shutting the doors. Colleen swung open the rear door, reached for a pair of armored vests and utility belts holding pistols, folding knives and extra magazines of ammo. Vests and belts on, Colleen did a pistol check.

"Chamber a round ... fine, we're hot. The only safety on these pieces is your trigger finger. Got that?"

"Yes, captain my captain," Wolf intoned. "Wolf knows how to handle a peashooter."

"We'll see about that. Take the right."

Colleen raised her pistol and started to walk carefully toward the cabin, Wolf doing likewise on the other side of the driveway.

They had gone only a few yards when gunshots rang out from the direction of the cabin.

Colleen hit the ground, Wolf bounding off the road taking cover behind nearby trees. Peering around a trunk, he spotted a figure hustling away from the cabin and took advantage of the break to rush toward the cabin firing several shots as he ran down the driveway.

Colleen got back on her feet and hustled after him. Wolf fired several more time reaching the cabin where he waited for Colleen to catch up.

"What the hell were you thinking!" A very annoyed Colleen cried.

Wolf pointed west. "He went into the woods that way. Let get him!"

"One second..." Colleen edged to the door and swung it wide, peeked carefully inside and stepped in. She was back out a moment later. "Empty... Don't want to be shot in the back ... okay, there's a deer trail. I lead you follow. No more cowboying, got it?"

"Yes ma'am."

Two miles back the trees and undergrowth was sparser, but this area sat in a valley and they had to content with denser vegetation providing a measure of cover for the shooter to make his escape—or to ambush them along the trail.

Colleen's left hand made a fist and dropped on her knees. Wolf did likewise having seen enough special ops shows to know the meaning of hand signals. Unlike Wolf, who saw nothing but trees and greenery as he peered through the undergrowth, Colleen's military training would allow her to see far more than he, confirmed seconds later when she shot off several rounds. After a moment of silence her volley was answered from some distance away, the bullets ripping through vegetation ahead of Wolf's position, some thudding into tree trunks behind him.

"He's got to be over thirty yards ahead and widening his lead," Colleen said. "He's going to get away."

"We could make a run at him," Wolf suggested. "Very hard to hit a moving target."

"All he needs is a lucky shot and one of us will be carrying the other couple hundred yards back to the car," she replied.

"You suggesting I can't carry you over my shoulder?"

"No … I'm saying I'm not looking forward to hauling your ass back to the car," she retorted. "Might be tempted to leave you for the coyotes—or wolves."

"We've got to at least pursue him a little while longer," Wolf said, ignoring her. "Maybe he'll trip over a root and hit his head."

"Fine. A little longer. Stay behind me."

The trail weaved in and out between clumps of bushes and tightly packed trees following a path of least vegetative resistance. However quickly Colleen dared to followed, their assailant would be escaping twice as fast. After a while Colleen called a halt.

"We're wasting our time." She looked toward the west. "And the sun is setting. It's going to be dark within the hour and we do not want to be wandering around the woods. We're going back." She stepped around Wolf and headed back down the trail.

They had gone about fifty yards when Wolf thought he spotted a shadow off the trail on the right. He called Colleen to halt with a loud whisper. Raising his pistol, he moved toward the shadow.

"Wolf, freeze!"

"What?"

His question was answered by a rumbling grunt followed by the shadow rising to its hind legs fifteen feet ahead of him. Black bears are notorious for being peeved when surprised and far more likely than Grizzlies to attack humans. Wolf froze and pointed his pistol at the growling animal, knowing that his nine millimeter bullets would do little to stop the bear and most likely infuriating the animal further.

"Back up slowly and get ready to follow me at full sprint," Colleen said.

Wolf retreated carefully, keeping his eyes glued on the bear. He made it to the trail when the bear uttered a piercing roar and came after him. He started to run down the path, turning west at the last second following Colleen cutting through the forest, zig-zagging her way through denser vegetation in hopes of slowing down the bear by forcing the much larger animal to circumvent stands of trees too tight to barrel through.

Nonetheless, the bear was gaining on them, Wolf hearing the beast crashing through the forest close behind him. Very soon, Colleen and he would be forced to turn and empty their pistols into the animal and hope that several strike a vital area.

Wolf was so focused on the doom rushing in from behind he almost ran into Colleen who had skidded to an abrupt halt in front of him. He didn't need to ask why. He was standing on a precipice overlooking a rapidly moving stream, fifteen feet below his feet.

Colleen leaped.

The bear was upon Wolf. He jumped.

He struck the water, hitting the streambed seconds later. Fortunately, the depth of the water was sufficient to break his fall and he quickly pushed his head above the surface in time to see the huge hulk of the bear crash into the river some feet behind him. Panic set in and he struggled to get distance between him and the ravening animal that would most certainly pursue him downstream.

But the bear did not move, his bulk a heap of black fur resting in a few feet of water, the stream flowing unperturbed around the sudden obstacle nature had placed in its path. It took Wolf a moment to realize that a fifteen-foot drop, even into deeper water than the few feet the bears' momentum plunged him into, would most likely kill an animal of his size. As the current carried Wolf away from the scene he hoped the bear was dead, a quick death being far more preferable than the alternative of broken bones and a slow, painful demise.

He was having difficulty staying afloat and looking ahead saw Colleen tossing her vest, Wolf doing likewise. A bulletproof vest may keep one from being killed when shot, but they do not substitute as a floatation device, the seven-pound vest working to drag Wolf under the surface.

Some moments later he saw Colleen making for the bank, waving wildly for him to do likewise. By the time he managed to drag himself out of the stream the current had deposited him ten yards further downstream and he walked back to join her.

Colleen pointed downstream. "Hear that?"

There was a faint whooshing sound. "Rapids?"

"Yes, and some very energetic ones by the sound of them," Colleen said. She gazed at Wolf, a grin forming on her lips. "You look like a drowned rat."

"I've been called much worse," he quipped. "You on the other hand..."

"I what?"

Even the thickest of men wouldn't miss the warning look her eye.

"You look great wet or dry," he replied, matter-of-factly as possible.

Colleen looked up the bank. "We floated a good quarter mile from where we jumped putting us about a mile south of the cabin's location. It'll be faster to walk back upstream along the bank, at least until we get to the turn in the stream where we'll have to hike up into the woods and find the trail leading us back to the cabin." She looked hard at Wolf. "Do try not to rile up anymore wildlife." Before Wolf could reply, she pulled out her cell and shook her head. "Crap. Works fine if it gets doused or rained upon, but not after an extended swim. Let's get going or we will be spending the night in the woods yet."

Wolf noted the sun was beyond the mountains setting the western sky on fire, the encompassing trees casting long, dark shadows over the stream. The thought of spending the night hugging a tree for comfort did not appeal to Wolf one bit, much preferring the relative comfort of even the dumpiest motel barring any other option.

"Hold on." He tried his cellphone. "Mine works ... unfortunately no reception."

Colleen started upstream. "I've got a satellite phone in the car."

She set a fast pace, making good time. It didn't take them long to reach the point where the river made a sharp bend, the centrifugal force pressing the water around the outside of the turn cutting a steep bank over time into the hill that stood in its way. Looking up at the edge of the drop where he and Colleen had jumped, Wolf realized that had they come charging out of the woods sixty feet either direction the story of the rampaging black bear would most certainly have turned into a tragedy. Not only was that location one of the few high spots along the stream's banks, but the force of the water rushing through the turn cut a deeper channel just below the cliff, creating sufficient depth to break their fall and prevent serious injury. He glanced at Colleen just as she looked at him and he knew she was thinking the same thing.

They scrambled up the slope and into the woods, finding their surrounding considerably darker than walking under the open sky along the stream.

"Stay close," Colleen warned. "Daylight vanishes rapidly after sunset in the mountains … no, no. Holster your weapon. Hopefully your fuzzy friend was the only one in the area and besides, we need larger caliber guns to stop one. Let's move."

Wolf's eyes adjusted to the dim light soon enough and thankful when Colleen found the deer trail they unceremoniously abandoned fleeing the bear earlier. By the time they made it back to the cabin the light was rapidly failing and Wolf was genuinely relieved to see it's darker silhouette, knowing that the car with dry change of clothing lay ten yards away.

Colleen stopped next to the cabin. "We need to search it before we leave; we might find evidence Welling left behind or clues to where he's gone."

"He couldn't have gotten that far on foot," Wolf said. "He's in the woods somewhere."

"The shooter was not Welling," Colleen said. "Thinner by forty pounds and shorter by half a foot; sound familiar?"

"The bum who ambushed me leaving the prison," Wolf concluded. "He couldn't have known we were coming and been waiting here to ambush us."

"He's here to clean up," Colleen said. "Only had a quick look in the cabin and it's a mess from him looking to destroy any evidence no doubt. The only question remaining is, where's Welling?"

"Could we go to the car?" Wolf said. "Wet and cold is not my favorite condition."

The first thing they spotted approaching the car was the smashed driver's side window. Next came a groan from Colleen as she walked to the front.

"Oh, oh."

The hood was unlatched and she raised it. Even in the darkness she must have seen they weren't going anywhere.

"Bastard ripped off the ignition cables." She slammed the hood shut. "Grab our gear; I've got flashlights and high energy lanterns stowed away; the phone, too. Looks like we're staying over at the villa."

Wolf opened the cabin door waiting for Colleen to come up, which she did a minute later sliding apart the TekLite lantern in her hand. It emitted a bright, white light illuminating everything within ten-yard radius and entered the cabin, Wolf following and closing the door.

"Don't get too comfortable," she said, facing him. "There's only one room…you need to go back outside while I change."

"Oh, come on," he protested. "We're partners."

"Nice try, greenhorn. Now get out."

Some minutes later the door opened and a dry attired Colleen appeared, phone in hand. "Your turn. There's a towel hanging on a chair."

Wolf walked in and shut the door. He gladly stripped off the heavy, damp outfit, dried himself with the towel and got dressed, feeling immediately warmer.

"Much better," he said, to himself, calling out in a louder voice, "I'm decent; safe to come in."

"I've spoken with my people," Colleen said, walking through the entrance. "They'll have a team here by eight tomorrow morning."

After a quick decluttering of the mess that the shooter assumingly created, it became clear whatever evidence there might have been was no longer in the room. Dinner came next, consisting of a selection of protein bars with bags of chips for dessert, washed down with containers filled with water or sundry flavored liquids containing electrolytes to replenish cellular loss during extended exertion.

There was only one bed, Wolf volunteering to sleep in the car, which Colleen nixed. "The night temps in the mountains goes into the thirties this time of the year. I'm not waking up to find you suffering from hypothermia. We stay in the cabin. Get a fire going in the stove, I'll handle the bedding."

Wolf pulled two seats near the stove inviting Colleen to join him. "I admit It's far more pleasant sitting here than huddling under a blanket in the car."

"Who says A-type personalities can't work together?" Colleen replied.

"Many psychologists, apparently."

"Many psychologists have children with multiple psychological issues," Colleen rejoined, "so I don't take much stock in psychologists' pronouncements about, well, pretty much anything."

"Daddy sent you to therapy as a child, did he?" Wolf quipped.

She leaned provocatively close. "Let me review my iron-clad rule of our *temporary* partnership: no references about my father to pass your lips." Her eyes narrowed slightly and she added, "Especially when cooped up in close quarters … if you get my drift."

"You'll pummel me into mush?"

"Nothing so pedestrian." Her smile was devoid of warmth. "I'll break one of your fingers for each reference you make."

"It's a good thing that rule isn't retroactive," Wolf grinned, "because I'd need to purchase dozens of extra fingers for you to snap."

Colleen ignored his comment, something he noticed she was very good at doing, providing him an update by Cooper from her phone conversation earlier. Satellite images had caught the shooter approaching her car, reach into the vehicle, raise the hood for a brief moment, lower it then run down the lane and get into a vehicle parked behind thick clumps of bushes and drive away.

Colleen sighed. "We missed him by no more than five minutes."

"Obviously he and the bear were in league," Wolf joked. His smile faded. "That was pretty intense. Thanks for your quick thinking … I always thought black bears were the good bears."

"It depends," Colleen said. "The rule when walking through backwoods is to be loud, talk, hum, sing. Unless the animal is wounded or rabid, bears hear you coming and ignore your presence or move further away. Surprise a brown bear, he's defending himself. Rear up on hind legs, roar at you, but not necessarily attack you. Best response with brown bears is to stand your ground and not back off. Black bears, on the other hand, become predatory and attack, thus my call for you to run."

"Didn't the bear hear the gunshots?" Wolf asked. "Why didn't he go and hide deeper in the forest?"

"He was hidden if you recall," Colleen replied, "until a certain Wolf headed off the trail and surprised him. It's spring; bears are hungry and the two of us would have made a tasty snack. Well, I'd be tasty…"

Wolf shook his head and held his tongue. "Did Cooper manage to track the shooter after he drove off?"

"On the way to Creede we assume," she replied. "We didn't track him after because it would require re-ordering the satellite camera coordinates. Besides, the tourist season is upon us—this area has lots of natural and historical attractions—he'd most likely vanish in the crowd."

"Did the satellite ever spot Welling today at all?" Wolf asked. "Cooper told me earlier this afternoon when I saw the satellite images that there was no movement around the cabin that day."

"That's not fully accurate," Colleen replied. "It's a hefty fee to keep a satellite camera focused on a target for hours on end. We do that occasionally when we are tracking a high valued target, but mostly it's intermittent bursts of live imaging then the satellite switches to tasks paid for by other clients of the company. In this case, the camera was on the cabin for five minutes on a twenty-minute imaging schedule. Catching the guy messing with my car was lucky timing."

"Welling might have been here all along and escaped when he spotted our shooter."

"Yes," Colleen agreed, "or he didn't escape and the shooter killed him in the woods somewhere. I want to spend some time in the morning searching the area before our rescuers come." Her gaze softened and she added, "You need to get some sleep."

He felt exhausted. Wolf considered himself to be in good shape; he swam, lifted weights and did various cardio routines. But there is a world of difference between being in good shape and being tough, a condition that comes from consistent physical training and engaging in diverse types of rugged activities. Compared to Colleen, he was soft. And tired. Wolf glanced at the bed then at Colleen, his expression forming a question.

Her lips twisted into a grin. "That's right; we're sleeping together. Might as well get something out of you for my trouble."

"Sorry to disappoint you," Wolf said getting up, "but I'm impotent."

He made for the bed, edged as close to the far side of the narrow mattress as possible and fell promptly into a deep sleep.

The image of a giant bear's snarling and drooling image that appeared in front of his face out of nowhere caused Wolf to jerk upright in the bed, his heart pounding, breath ragged. For a moment, he had no clue where he was. He was alone in a dark room, dim light seeping through the shutters on the windows and edge of the door. Then he remembered.

Where was Colleen?

He got off the bed and opened the shutters to one of the windows, pale light flooding into the small room providing enough illumination to see adequately. He found his phone: 5:09.

He was about to call Colleen but bit the name off at the last second. What if the shooter had returned and she was in trouble? Glancing at the table he noticed her utility belt gone, at least she was armed. Putting his belt on, he checked the pistol—one round in the chamber—and stepped toward the door, the pistol lowered at his side. He was within arm's reach of the door when it swung open, his gun hand moving instinctively pointing the pistol at Colleen's surprised face.

"Jeezus!" Wolf cried, stepping back and lowering the weapon. "Why would you open the door like that and not say something! I almost shot you, God damn it!"

"Sorry," she replied, seeing genuine horror on Wolf's face. "I thought you were asleep."

Wolf retreated to a chair, placing the pistol on the adjacent table. He placed his hands on his knees and lowered his head; his breathing was labored. He felt sick and on the verge of vomiting. Taking deep, measured breaths he fought back the rising nausea and started to feel better.

Colleen placed a hand lightly on his shoulder and gave him a bottle of water. "Take a few sips."

The water helped and he sat back in the chair thinking that of all his frightening experiences over the years—being attacked, getting beaten, shot at, run off the road and yesterday's bear attack—this incident at the door was his most terrifying moment ever.

His extended silence must have begun to worry Colleen, asking if he was okay.

"Not really," he replied, shaking his head slowly. He reached for the pistol on the table, popped out the magazine, ejected the round in the chamber then replaced the magazine. "I never want to be in that position again. I'll take my chances taking the extra second to chamber a round."

Colleen pulled a chair up and sat facing him. "You didn't shoot me," she said tenderly, "and I'm not angry with you. You did exactly what I would have done given the circumstances."

He held her eyes and sighed loudly. "I'm prepared to defend myself and shoot someone if I have no other choice. As a rule, I don't hunt down killers and kidnappers. You're a highly trained professional, Colleen; this," he swept a hand across the room, "is what you do for a living. But I'm certain you'd not shoot me because I jerked open a door and surprised you ... my finger pressed the trigger, Colleen. The *trigger*. No round in the chamber unless we get shot at or you tell me to pull my gun."

"I really am sorry that happened." She stood up. "It's plenty light outside; if you feel up to it, let's search the area."

He got up and holstered his weapon. A sly smile creased her lips.

"About you thinking I'd not have shot you opening the door...I may not have been able to restrain myself, so be sure to wear a bell or call out before entering any room I'm in."

"You're part Irish, I understand," Wolf replied, in his most understated tone. Colleen ignored him and walked out of the cabin.

It was cold. He very much appreciated her insistence he stay in the cabin instead of sleeping in the car, though had he done so would have avoided the sickening jolt of almost shooting her.

His almost victim stood in the clearing surveying the area, apparently lost in thought. Wolf walked up and stood silently next to her, waiting.

"Welling's dead," she said.

"How can you be sure?" Wolf replied. "I didn't see a car anywhere when we drove up, so maybe he was gone when our shooter arrived; stocking up on supplies in Creede, or maybe he got antsy and took off to points unknown."

"You forgot that Cooper did spot movement here two days ago—" She abruptly stopped speaking and lifted the satellite phone from its holster on her utility belt and pressed a key. "Good morning...all good...Cooper, did you see a car parked at the cabin when you first got the satellite feed couple days back?" There was a pause… "I see, but you did see movement after that … you sure with acute angles from that height? Okay, thanks." She terminated the call and slid the phone back in its holster.

Wolf gave her an expectant look. "What's the verdict?"

"There was a car parked by the cabin three days ago and images of Welling out of the cabin," she explained. "Late yesterday afternoon, 5:15 when the satellite image went live, that's an hour or so before we got here, the car was gone."

"That means Welling is gone and we've got nothing," Wolf said, frustrated.

"Not so hasty," Colleen warned. "Cooper just checked a larger area and spotted a car with a similar shape as the one that was parked next to the cabin in the woods at the end of the road hundred feet up where we turned around when we first got here. And," she held up a hand to stop Wolf interrupting, "checking the 5:15 satellite recording caught a man walking up to the cabin and entering it. Cooper assumed it was Welling when he confirmed shortly before we approached the cabin yesterday that there had been movement around the cabin."

"Okay," Wolf said, puzzled. "So where in the world is Don Welling?"

"Pretty sure he isn't walking around on the world," she replied. "Cooper said the BSCRP—Body Shape Composite Recognition Program—produced a 98% certainty that the figure walking to the cabin during the 5:15 time frame and the figure leaving after incapacitating my car is the same person. So, let's see if we can find where in the woods our shooter dumped Welling's body."

Colleen's eyes scanned the area, a slight crinkle at the outer edge of her eyes revealing the weighing of possibilities in her mind. She was looking in the direction they had chased the shooter when Wolf broke her reverie.

"Not that way," he said. "One, it goes uphill. Human tendency is to follow the path of least effort. Two, the shooter would want to draw us away from the body dump, not toward it and three—"

"Downhill," Colleen interjected, walking north into the woods.

It didn't take long before they intersected a dry gulch paralleling the trail where they discovered a body slumped across boulders in the streambed twenty yards further along the trail. Making their way carefully down the steep embankment, they came upon the body, Colleen agreeing with Wolf that the corpse was Welling.

"Head shot," she said. "Okay. We have a mystery shooter hired by person or persons' unknown over what we assume has something to do with Sarah Lewis and James Collins."

Colleen slipped on a pair of latex gloves and proceed to check Welling's pockets, coming up empty handed.

"Nothing, not even spare change," she said. "I guess the shooter didn't want to chance anything showing up such as a fingerprint on a dime that wasn't Welling's."

"Now what?" Wolf said.

"Now we go back to the cabin and wait to be rescued."

Chapter 13

Breakthrough

An hour before the rescue team arrived at the cabin, Colleen and Wolf were being interviewed by the local Sheriff whom they notified about Welling's murder. The lawman listened politely to their story, though like any good police officer, with a skeptical ear. He inspected their pistols confirming that both had been fired then sat in his vehicle corroborating their identifications on his on-board computer.

"You both check out," he said, handing back their IDs and pistols, gazing at Wolf with undisguised awe and smiling warmly at Colleen. His reaction to her had been one she no doubt was very familiar with; one which Wolf knew she'd not fail to take advantage of to move a case toward a successful outcome.

"Thank you, Sheriff," she said. "I would appreciate it ever so much if you'd keep me informed of anything you discover during your investigation," she handed him her card, "and I will, of course, do likewise."

Wolf heard the silk in her tone, his lips twitching knowingly as he watched the officer walk back to his vehicle. There were many reason for Colleen's success, not the least of which being her physical appearance and seductive voice.

Colleen must have spotted his grin. "What?"

Wolf jerked his head toward the departing Sheriff.

"Nothing wrong with being nice to the man," she said, adding as she walked back to the cabin, "Besides, he's a real hunk."

"Fortunately for him he's got a gun," Wolf teased.

"Most men I know carry one," Colleen replied.

Wolf issued a low chuckle. "Like I said, fortunate for them."

She reacted in her usual manner—ignoring him—and made for the cabin. They stood in the room for a moment, Colleen's eyes scanning the space. Stepping toward the small dresser she pushed it away from the wall.

"Let's do one more search. I don't expect we'll find anything; Welling's killer did a good job tearing the place up, but one never knows."

Wolf tackled the walls, sliding his hands along the wooden planks, his fingers probing, pressing and pulling on any crack or space that might act as a hiding place or cover one up. He had completed his inspection of the wall adjacent the bed when Colleen uttered a profanity.

"Should have asked you to check the stove before starting a fire," she said, holding up a scrap of paper. "The shooter burned papers; might have been some unburned bits inside."

Wolf came over and peered at the scrap of paper in her hand—a remnant of a photograph—only a smudge of a man's partial forehead and a lock of hair remaining.

"Maybe the shooter?"

"Perhaps." Colleen looked closely at the scrap. "Definitely not Welling." She placed it on the table, wiped it clean, took photographs with her phone then uploaded the images to SSIS. "I'll have my people do a search of our database and see if we can ID this guy. For what it's worth, our shooter is a white male with dark hair like the man in our partial photo. Maybe we'll get lucky."

By the time Colleen and Wolf finished searching the cabin, their rescue team arrived bringing with them new ignition cables for the Toyota allowing Colleen and Wolf to drive themselves back home rolling up to SSIS's gate by noon. Checking in with Cooper, the S&R tech had nothing new to add since his talk with Colleen hours before.

"I aimed the satellite's cameras toward Creede hoping I could spot the shooter's vehicle, but no luck," he said. "My guess is he hightailed it out of the area. I can keep the sky eye on Creede the rest of the day if you want, Colleen; maybe he's got his car under cover and we might spot him if he leaves."

Colleen shook her head. "Not worth the cost, Cooper. Ten to one he's long gone. Maybe the imaging team has something...thanks. Anything pops up, call me immediately."

"Sure thing, boss."

Wolf followed Colleen out of one room filled with electronic equipment into a similar one across the way. Three technicians were busy working on various projects, all of which involved images of one sort or another. She headed for an adjacent door, knocking as she opened it. A sweet face looked up from her computer and smiled.

"Hi Colleen," she said. "Nothing so far, I'm sorry to report."

"No surprise there, Kat," Colleen replied. She looked at Wolf. "Kat, this is Grayson Wolf; Mr. Wolf, Katherine Simmons, head of Imaging."

The technician's eyes flicked to Wolf and back to Colleen, Wolf spotting the subtle stillness of her expression and compression of her lips in the glance. Reaction to his presence had become as natural as breathing to Wolf, the years refining his skill ascertaining nuances of a person's reaction. His immediate impression was that Simmons's reaction wasn't about animosity toward him, rather loyalty to Colleen. Admirable and understandable considering Wolf's literary assault against her employer's father.

"You're a very talented artist, Ms. Simmons," Wolf said, looking at the unique paintings on the walls he assumed were created by her.

"Thank you," she replied, her tone cool.

"It's fine, Katherine," Colleen said, looking amused. "Mr. Wolf is behaving himself—if he knows what's good for him—and he promised to autograph copies of his books that I know are hidden from sight in your bedroom."

Katherine's eyes got very large. "How did you know about, um—"

"Crack investigator, am I," Colleen intoned in a very respectable Yoda impression. "Relax. I own all of Mr. Wolf's books; I so much enjoy using them to refine my sharpshooting skills."

"Better my books than me," Wolf retorted, more from surprise that she had all his books than banter. He pointed at the art on the wall. "May I?"

Katherine grinned and nodded. "Sure."

Wolf was impressed by the quality and diversity of Katherine's art, most impressed with her oil paintings of living subjects and less enamored with her impressionistic pieces, though some where striking. Then he spotted the distinctive signature looking closely at one of the paintings, the mark always reminding him of a Japanese logographic.

"You're Kat." Wolf said, his tone conveying surprise and genuine respect. "I own several of your pieces…"

She smiled and said, "Let me guess: Wolf Call and Wolf Hunt?"

"Talented artist, Head of SSIS Imaging and clairvoyant, too." Wolf presented her with his brilliant smile. "But you missed one."

Katherine's brow wrinkled as she considered the matter. She looked up at him with expectation. "Wolf Pups."

"My favorite, though I cherish all three," Wolf replied.

"They're a family, you know," she said, her tone surprisingly flat. "Center piece in my study."

Wolf's face brightened with excitement. "I'd love to see it sometime."

She hesitated, shooting a glance at Colleen. "I'll think about it."

Colleen's phone dinged. She lifted it from its holster and read the text.

"James Collins's body is being exhumed," she said, looking at Wolf. "Sooner than I thought."

"His family is anxious to find the truth about his death," Wolf stated. "How soon—"

"Tomorrow morning," Colleen interjected, answering his unfinished question. "The casket will be on its way to the Centennial Forensic Lab in Denver within the hour. I've scheduled a rush job on the examination; we should hear something definitive before the end of tomorrow."

"What do we do in the meantime?" Wolf asked.

"Wait. Katherine's team will keep expanding the search looking for a facial match to our forehead snippet. Meanwhile, I expect Welling's killer will be busy fixating on being discovered or upon the possibility he'll be next to be 'cleaned' by our mystery conspirator. The autopsy results will come in tomorrow and then the hunt begins anew."

Wolf reached over to shake Katherine's hand, thanking her for her wonderful contribution to art and followed Colleen out of the room. Going up the staircase he asked about Katherine, saying he sensed a sadness in her expression when she mentioned the painting of the wolf family.

She remained silent until they reached the main floor above and the bolt securing the door sounded.

"My office."

Wolf shut the door behind him. Colleen made for the bar and poured herself a glass of wine, a wave of her hand indicating he help himself. Selecting a Belgian pilsner from the cooler, he joined her at the seating area, took a long draught and waited.

"Three years ago, Katherine's husband, young son and daughter were killed by a truck driver who fell asleep at the wheel," she said. "Killed instantly."

"A blessing, I suppose." Wolf replied.

"She hasn't painted since," Colleen said.

"Two kids..." Wolf mused aloud. "Two pups...the wolf family painting."

Colleen nodded. "Yes."

"The truck driver walked away without a scratch, I assume?"

"Yes..."

Wolf heard the missing rest-of-the-story in her pause. "Yes, but he what? Got run over as he stepped out of his vehicle at the scene?"

"Was arrested, got out on bail, went home and shot himself." Colleen took several swallows of wine. "The driver was working overtime trying to provide for his family. It's a Greek tragedy: everyone loses."

"You have two sisters." Wolf didn't know why he said that.

Colleen gave him a sharp look. "Yes. Why?"

"I have two younger siblings," he said. "Sister and brother."

"Stop right there," Colleen snapped. "I'm not interested in bonding with you. Our arrangement is temporary. *Very* temporary." She stood up. "There's nothing for us to do but wait for the autopsy results to come back tomorrow and in the meantime, I've got other business demanding my attention."

Wolf nodded and got up from the chair. "Of course." He walked over to the bar, drank the remains of his beer and tossed the bottle in the trash. "Thank you for the drink and saving my life— twice." A tight grin appeared and he added. "I hope you won't regret that too much."

Colleen shot him an icy look. "You may leave."

There was a twinkly in his eye as Wolf inclined his head and swept out of her office. More like hurried, but swept sounded more dramatic and drama was most certainly the keynote to his temporary, his *very* temporary, arrangement with Colleen Silverstone.

Googling something on his phone, Wolf made a satisfied grunt, slipped it back in his pocket and retraced his steps to the door leading down into SSIS's secure electronic center only to realize as he stood in front of the shut door that it would not open for him. Walking to the lobby, he asked the attendant for Katherine Simmons's telephone number, informed she was not authorized to provide any information about staff.

The attendant smiled and said, "I am authorized to call her and tell her you wish to speak with her if you'd like."

Wolf did like and Katherine did accept his call.

"How may I help you, Mr. Wolf," she asked.

"Did you know there is a fantastic exhibition of Dutch Masters at the Denver Museum of Art?" he said. "According to my source, the Dutch plan to pack up and leave for El Paso at the end of the week, so it's now or never. I'd love to take you to dinner followed by a tour of the Masters."

An extended silence followed. "Your source named, Google?"

Wolf heard the humor in her voice. "As I said earlier: clairvoyant…I would love to hear your perspective and I promise not to embarrass you by wolfing down my food or make a mess on the floor."

She laughed. "May I think about it and let you know before the end of the day?"

"Of course," Wolf replied. "I'm not going anywhere— literally. I don't have a car."

"Oh, I see," she said, her tone lively. "What you're really asking for is a ride."

Wolf laughed. "Just can't manage to pull the wool over your eyes, can I?"

He gave Katherine his cell number, encouraged her to consider his offer and terminated the call. The attendant smiled at him, wished him good luck and directed him to a quiet sitting room where he could relax, work or just take a snooze if he wished.

Checking the time, he had over three hours wait until Katherine was off work, hopefully accept his offer for dinner and Dutch Masters or call for a ride to take him to his hotel.

Wolf could lounge around with the best, but this was no time for "relaxing." Retrieving his iPad from the attaché he reviewed case notes, adding new questions and musings to a growing list of maybes, what-ifs and perhaps'. Satisfied that no new insights were to be gained by going over details yet one more time, he closed the file and checked email, answering a few, ignoring most. Next, he perused several online national newspapers, his attention captured by a headline about student mobs at Virginia Patriots College.

Worried at first that Diana's plans for a massive, week-long free-speech event was already under attack, he was relieved to find the story was about an Engineering professor who dared to publically challenge the conspiracy of silence rampant among the faculty and found his classes interrupted by mobs of students shouting obscenities, calling him racist and demanding his resignation.

Wolf grabbed his phone and sent a text to Diana asking her about the issue. He didn't have long to wait for her reply.

"Perf timing. Prof a fighter & pissd. Camp up Wed. LOD!"

"Liberty, yes," he texted back, grinning, "no death, please."

"Come soon?"

"Soon," he texted. "Maybe."

"Waffle-man!" Diana texted back.

"Mean B!" Wolf retorted.

"BOTC"

It took Wolf a second to decode Diana's text. "Bitch Of The Century," he said, aloud. He chuckled and texted, "100% XO." He waited for a return text, but none forthcoming he slipped the phone back in its holster. He enjoyed his texting repartee with Diana and others at CIR but worried about the upcoming battle at VPC because Diana took Patrick Henry's clarion cry for liberty of death as a personal challenge.

The CIR Executive Director had never backed down from a fight yet, but the situation at these colleges and universities was becoming increasingly volatile since the national election. Wolf was justifiably concerned about what might happen once the student thugs at VPC realized the true purpose of the demonstrators massing a mile from the college's main gate.

He pushed such thoughts out of his mind and went back to perusing his online papers and newsletters, eventually reading through CIR's Twitter and Facebook pages and groups, pleased to see a huge uptick of comments critical of the students harassing the engineering professor at Virginia Patriots College. Wolf was so engrossed wading through the various social media sites he didn't notice a woman walk up and stand next to him for some moments.

"Are you coming or not?"

Looking up from his iPad, he saw Katherine smiling sweetly down at him. He shut the unit off, placed it in his attaché and stood up.

Wolf inclined his head and swept an arm toward the exit. "Lead on, me lady."

Exiting SSIS required passage through a security screening, the process for employees being as extensive as it had been for Wolf the first time he entered Colleen's fortress. He watched Katherine remove all items from pockets and place them in a tray along with her handbag and shoes, next was the X-ray body scan then passage through a Sniffer. When Wolf commented on the tight security after leaving the compound, Katherine informed him that if the security process suggested even a hint of irregularity, personnel were subject to a complete physical examination.

"That must be quite arousing," he quipped.

"Cheap thrills, I assure you," she joked.

Katherine lived ten miles southeast of SSIS, away from Aurora, so she drove Wolf to his hotel first, promising to return before seven. Driving up to the main entrance, Wolf asked her if she had a favorite restaurant. From the faraway look in her eyes he knew she was thinking of a special place, a restaurant whose threshold she'd most likely never cross again.

"Surprise me," she replied, adding, "In Denver only."

"Thank you for the ride," Wolf said, stepping out of her car. "I'm looking forward to our evening together."

"Me, too."

When the minute hand on Wolf's wristwatch edged past ten minutes after seven, he wondered if his date got cold feet.

"7-11." He said to no one in particular. "Always been lucky for me."

He watched the second-hand sweep inexorably across the dial rushing to put another minute behind it. Nine seconds remained of that lucky number when the phone dinged. He picked it up and read the text.

"In the lobby-K."

The second hand passed 12. 7-11 continued its lucky streak for Grayson Wolf who understood luck was a matter of fortunate coincidence and who rarely left anything to chance. He glanced at the mirror, his eyes peering at the left cuff of his pant leg satisfied that all appeared normal, opened the hotel door and stepped carefully into the corridor. He walked past the elevator to the stairs at the other end of the hallway and made his way down to the lobby. Wolf learned long ago that routines could get one pummeled, doused with paint or even killed. It had become a habit to *routinely* make arbitrary changes in schedules, direction and routes thus not taking the staircase adjacent to his hotel room. Paranoia was an old and trusted friend.

"You look lovely," he said, surprising Katherine by coming from behind. His gaze took in all of her.

"Thank you." She looked uncomfortable.

"I'll be happy to drive if you'd like me to," Wolf said, "or I can upload the location into your GPS."

"I'd rather drive, Mr. Wolf," Katherine replied.

He shot her an amused look. "*Mr.* Wolf? Are we going on a date or to a business meeting?"

"I confess to being rusty at this," she replied, looking embarrassed.

"That makes two of us," he said. "Please call me Wolf." He took her by the arm and escorted Katherine out of the hotel.

Wolf uploaded the address of the restaurant into her car's GPS and buckled up. She started the vehicle and placed her hands on the wheel.

"I'm not sure I'm ready for this."

"Eating at a restaurant can be a tricky affair in Nepal or Viet Nam," Wolf joked, "but I can assure you it's relatively painless in downtown Denver." He spotted her lips twitch and added, "There's nothing to worry about, Katherine. It's just dinner, a walk through a museum and my good company. My name may be Wolf, but I'm not a wolf."

Katherine looked over at him and smiled. "I know you're not."

"Excuse me?" Wolf said, an exaggerated expression on his face. "You do know who I am, right? Women swoon at my feet when I walk by."

"And you do know I work in the heart of SSIS's intelligence center," she replied. "I know pretty much everything about you."

"Therefore, you would know that you are perfectly safe going to dinner with me," he retorted, adding, "and I want you to tell me all about myself over dinner, so put it in drive and let's roll."

By 7:47 they were seated in the Mercantile's attractive main dining room, Katherine doing her best to restrain her laughter listening to Wolf reading the entre selection in a most affected tone.

"...next we have pan roasted Arctic Char, avocado sorrel purée, fresh chickpea & sheep's milk whey dressing, topped with a dusting of shaved fennel 28." He made a jaded face and continued. "For the more discerning palate, I recommend pan roasted broccoli, fruition farms sheepskyr, chickpea panisse..."

"Please stop," Katherine pleaded, issuing low snorts. "I'm going to make a spectacle of myself if you continue."

"As you wish, madam," Wolf said, inclining his head.

The waiter arrived and took their order, Wolf going with the Boulder natural chicken, Katherine choosing the pan roasted broccoli.

His droll routine having succeeded in making Katherine feel at ease, he returned to her earlier comment about knowing all about him.

"So, tell me, head of SSIS Imaging service in the heart of its intelligence brain, what you know about my dating habits, having declared knowledge of all things Grayson Wolf."

Her face became still. "I should not have said that; I apologize."

"Not to worry," he grinned. "I'm certain your boss has spent significant company resources delving into my life since Screw You was published three years ago."

"Why me?" Katherine asked, holding his gaze.

Wolf leaned toward her, a warm smile forming on his lips. "I'm drawn to beautiful, intelligent and accomplished women ... But you know that already, yes?" He caught the slight blush on her cheeks. "And I have three of your magnificent paintings, which makes me even more interested in enjoying your company for an evening and I'm especially interested in how you came to work for Colleen of all people."

"Painting only pays some of the bills," Katherine said. "I'm also well versed in computer imaging, graphic design and programming. I have a good eye for detail and working for Colleen does pay all my bills. And it's interesting, rewarding work."

Wolf listened attentively and nodded. "Do you miss it—painting, I mean?"

Her expression became guarded. "What makes you think—"

"I'm a fan, remember?" he interjected. "I'd guess you haven't touched an easel for three years and the world is poorer for it."

Katherine shrugged. "Perhaps I'm not inspired."

"Perhaps you're hiding," Wolf replied.

"Perhaps you should mind your own business," she retorted.

"What I'm best at," he quipped, "minding other peoples' business. But you know that, too." He took her hand and studied it. "You spend many hours at your piano—playing solos. But not because you're planning a new career."

Katherine's expression hardened. "Change the subject or I will leave."

She tried to withdraw her hand from his grasp but he held it tighter, his brilliant smile illuminating the cubby they were seated in.

"You and I have a lot in common beginning with the fact that both of us are rusty at this dating thing."

Katherine's eyebrows rose alarmingly. "Since when are you given to exaggeration, Wolf? You went on a date in New York less than two weeks ago … it's been…a little longer for—." She must have realized what she had just revealed and stopped talking.

"I like you, Katherine," Wolf said, squeezing her hand, and I think you're enjoying yourself, too."

She looked away, a restrained smile forming at the corners of her mouth. Dinner was served, Wolf spending the time between bites of food being careful to avoid saying anything to wind Katherine up. He had tested her resolve and patience concluding that, though she was still suffering the loss of her family three years ago, she had plenty of life—and fire—remaining, a positive sign for a happier future.

Declining dessert, they walked back to the parking garage across the street and drove to the art museum. The exhibition of the Dutch Masters was better than promised, Wolf commenting on the stunning quality and skill of the various artists, Katherine talking animatedly about style, lighting and brush strokes.

"Your paintings should be displayed right along with these," Wolf said at one point. "You are as talented as any of them." Gazing at her upturned face he said aloud what he was thinking, "And as beautiful."

Katherine's looked at him funny and laughed.

"What? What did I say that's so funny?" he said. "You are beautiful."

She pointed to the image of one of the famous Dutch Masters adjacent to his painting. "As talented and as beautiful, am I?"

"Oh," Wolf grinned. "I meant as beautiful as their works of art."

She smiled warmly at him. "Thank you..."

It was ten thirty by the time they got back to the car. "I had a really good time," she said, looking over at Wolf. "Thank you."

"The evening is not over yet," he replied. "You drive, I'll direct you. Begin by turning left at the street..."

For the young and restless of any age, Denver offers its share of exciting night life—jazz clubs and sizzling dance spots for those seeking to let loose and get down. For couples seeking a more intimate and sophisticated experience, After Hours was their destination. The nightclub was an oasis in a sea of pounding music, crush of sweaty bodies and inebriated couples looking to "hook up" for another weekend evening of meaningless sex in their personal Groundhog Day existence.

"How do you know about After Hours and more importantly, manage to get us in on such short notice?" Katherine asked. "I've heard one needs to make reservations far in advance."

Wolf shot her a look of mock surprise. "I guess you don't know everything about me after all."

An attendant led them to one of the many cozy alcoves that honeycombed the establishment, a waitress appearing shortly thereafter, halting at a discrete distance until called upon. Wolf ordered a dessert platter and coffee.

"Would you care for something else?" Wolf asked. "Less sweet, perhaps?"

"Dessert is fine," Katherine replied. "I would like to know how you could have gotten a reservation so quickly."

"I'm a large investor," he replied. "Got in when the owners were looking for private capital to expand the concept to other cities. Besides this one, there are four more After Hours in major cities, some connected with hotels for a more seamless romantic experience."

"Seamless romantic experience" she said, mimicking his tone.

"What wrong with that?"

"Nothing at all." She smiled. "Just having difficulty connecting 'romantic' with Grayson Wolf—um what I mean, it's just that, um…"

"The first step when finding oneself in a hole," Wolf quipped, "is to stop digging."

"I plead terminal rustiness," Katherine said, looking contrite. "I am sitting in the most romantic nightclub in Denver…" She sighed.

Wolf took her hand and led her to the dance floor.

"You're a good dancer, which is a good thing since I'm not," she said, after the second dance.

Wolf grinned. "You didn't know that about me either?"

"No, I didn't." She smiled, adding, "Colleen's interest in you was more about—" She stopped dancing, her expression turning hard. "That's what this evening is all about, isn't it? Doing what Grayson Wolf does best: using people to gather information by any means necessary."

Wolf escorted her back to the table where she reached for her purse.

"Please sit," Wolf said.

Katherine heard the steel underneath his request and hesitated. "I think we're done here."

"Not by a long shot," he said. "I may be many things, but I do not use people for any purpose whatsoever and if you think so, then it's abundantly clear you know far less about me than you think." Katherine sat down and Wolf continued. "Let's get one thing straight: I asked you out on a date, not a fishing expedition. If Colleen wants to waste valuable resources hoping to ferret dirt on me and mine, I say, good luck because you will not find much—as I'm certain you know or you would never have agreed to come on this date ... I like you, Katherine. You're smart, attractive and yes, rusty at this dating thing," he lifted the plate and leaned toward her holding her gaze, "so stop using me to beat yourself up for enjoying yourself ... Dessert?"

"You're a real hard ass, aren't you?" Katherine said, a smile creeping across her lips. She selected a tart and took a bite, followed by a swallow of coffee. Her eyes shifted from peering at her cup to Wolf's face. "You're the first man I've gone out with..."

"Colleen provided a thumbnail sketch of what happened," Wolf said, treading very carefully into this emotional minefield. "Some never get over it."

She shook her head slowly. "I'm not sure I can."

"Au contraire," Wolf replied. "You can if you choose to do so. The fact you're here with me, one of America's most dashing characters is a good first step, don't you agree? Not many women would be brave enough to risk being seen with me...or dare to dance with me...shall we?"

It was well past midnight when Katherine insisted it was time to go, Wolf reluctantly agreeing. Since his tryst with Mattie earlier in New York, he reveled in his new-found freedom to take a woman on a date, enjoy her company, engaging in intimate and interesting conversation, holding her close during dance interludes, luxuriating in the aroma of her hair and skin.

Being in the company of two women in the span of two weeks was a record, his past rendezvous being necessarily rare and brief. Asking a woman for a date required ensuring there was no possibility of her being connected to any person or organization past or present that had been included in Wolf's novels, and absolutely never an informant. He simply could not take the risk of putting a target on any woman seen regularly with him. For years, random liaisons met his most basic emotional and sexual needs but rarely left him emotionally or psychologically fulfilled.

Coming out of his reverie, Wolf sensed they had been driving much longer than it took to come to Denver at the start of the evening. He noticed an expanding darkness beyond the windows where a better lit urban landscape ought to be.

"Katherine, where are we? I think you missed the exit to my hotel."

"We're going to my house," she said. "I want to show you something."

"Show me what?"

"You'll see," she replied.

Were Katherine not employed by SSIS and that he asked her out on a whim, Wolf's inner guardian would have him reaching for the pistol in his ankle holster. He put his suspicion on hold, focusing instead on the type of surprise waiting for him at Katherine's place, imagining any number of pleasant possibilities.

"I hope you don't feel I brought you here under false pretenses," Katherine said, standing in her den ten minutes later.

"On the contrary," Wolf said, admiring the stunning painting hanging on the wall. "This is a most wonderful surprise; thank you. What did you title it, Wolf Family?"

"Just, Family," she replied.

"Of course." Wolf studied the various subjects, the playful energy of the pups romping between their parents; the alert face of the male, his gaze looking beyond the frame for possible danger; the female peering affectionately over at her brood.

"It's a masterpiece, Katherine, worthy to hang alongside any Dutch Master," Wolf said. "You've captured your subject perfectly; the tenderness and affection, the inner strength of the adults, the glow of their faces evoking joy at being alive ... if you ever decide to sell it, please think of me first."

Her expression was resolute. "I'll never give it up."

Wolf shot her a humorous look. "I guess the only way I'll ever own that painting is by marrying you."

"That's not going to happen, either," she grinned.

"It's late; tomorrow is a work day," Wolf said. "I'll call an Uber to drive me to my hotel."

"You are welcome to sleep over if you wish," she said, adding quickly "in my guest room."

Wolf gazed at her. "You sure?"

Katherine nodded. "Yes. Follow me..."

Upon rising the next morning, Katherine texted SSIS informing Personnel she'd be two hours late. Wolf made breakfast, surprising his host who silently held his eyes for a long moment.

"It looks and smells great," she said. "It's been many years since someone made me breakfast."

"Sit." Wolf filled a plate and cup with coffee, placing them in front of her. "It nice to have someone to serve breakfast to." Seeing her incredulous expression, he continued. "I've known many women in my life; never would have written fifteen exposes without them. Doesn't mean I made breakfast for them. That number I can count on one hand."

"You are a very, um, attractive, intelligent man," she said. "I would think many of those women would want to, er, eat breakfast with you."

"Some wanted to, but I wasn't playing secret agent man," Wolf explained getting a plate of food and sitting across the table from her. "I didn't need to seduce women to get what I needed. I insinuated myself into people's lives, listened to their conversations, made connections, asked questions and found informants more than willing to talk about their bosses and ex-lovers."

Katherine looked skeptical. "You never slept with any of them? Ever?"

He leaned forward, holding her gaze. "You do know who I am, yes? A critical part of that is my iron-clad rule: never sleep with, date or spend more time than required with any woman—or man. Keeping them safe from retribution for accidentally or purposefully giving me information that later exposed bosses, friends and lovers was my number one priority."

She appeared to consider some idea that had occurred to her. "I understand now why…"

"Why what?" Wolf said, suddenly alert. "What do you understand?"

Katherine sipped some of her coffee and smiled. "Why Colleen is helping you with this case."

"That's because," Wolf began, "she's a person of integrity with a strong passion for justice that transcends personal and familial loyalties."

Katherine's smile widened. "Yes, she is and why people were surprised and concerned when the word spread that Grayson Wolf had come to see Colleen Silverstone. After everything you wrote about her father and his firm, you were not exactly the most popular person around SSIS, you know."

"I saw that in your face when we first met in your office," Wolf replied. "People who live and act upon principles like Colleen are in the minority and the people who work for or with them tend to be very protective and loyal."

Katherine looked at Wolf for long moment. "I had a great time, and," she made an amusing expression, "I can tell everyone that I slept with Grayson Wolf."

"And I," Wolf retorted, "can tell everyone that Katherine Sessions, one of America's most talented artist, is painting my portrait to memorialize her most intimate encounter the past three years."

"That's both accurate and generous," she replied, "except for the *most* intimate part. *Only* intimate encounter. Thank you for asking me out."

Wolf raised his cup. "Here's to the beginning of many more intimate encounters to follow for America's premier artist and Imaging technologist who deserves to be happy."

"Thank you." Katherine gazed at Wolf, adding, "You're surprisingly sweet and thoughtful considering you're America's most notorious novelist."

"Ah, thank you?"

"Your welcome," she replied. "But if I don't get going I know of a boss who will be even less happy than she probably is already."

Katherine declined to explain her comment, Wolf discovering soon enough what she meant when they entered SSIS and the receptionist informed him that Ms. Silverstone had requested to see him immediately.

Katherine shot him a droll smile. "Good luck, Mr. Wolf."

He winked at her and made for Colleen's inner sanctum. Seeing her expression as he entered her office sobered him up fast.

"Just what do you think you are doing sleeping with Katherine? She demanded.

"Define sleeping."

She got up, walked aggressively toward him and stopped within striking distance of him. "This is a joke to you?"

Wolf stood his ground. "I was delighted to discover one of my favorite artists residing in the bowels of your fortress and asked her out to dinner."

"Dinner?" she scoffed. "I see it more like, having nothing better to do you saw a vulnerable, grieving woman to take advantage of."

Wolf had learned ages ago to parry attempts to push his buttons, but Colleen's accusation that he acted dishonorably felt like a slap in the face. She must have seen the anger flare up in his eyes because her expression softened somewhat.

"I've been accused of many things over the years, Ms. Silverstone," he said, keeping his voice even. "Lying, cheating, bribing, assault, corruption, seduction, even attempted kidnapping. Comes with the territory. But what you are accusing me of is a new low and frankly, disappointing." His reproach having caught Colleen off guard, he continued. "Katherine is an attractive woman who has lost much three years ago. *Three,* years ago. Cooped up in your basement impervious to penetration by anything less than a 500-pound bomb, apparently, I asked, she accepted and we had dinner, went dancing and she drove me to her home allowing me to see Family, the painting of the wolf pack that I so much admire. And yes, I slept over. Emphasis on sleeping, as in resting comfortably in her guest bedroom. Would you care for further details? About breakfast perhaps, or how expertly I led her around the dancefloor or a thrilling blow-by-blow account of dinner?" He noticed Colleen looking at him with increasing suspicion. "What?"

"You only sleep with women that have absolutely no connection to anything related to one of your investigations."

"Yes, among other things."

"And you didn't sleep with Kat."

"Correct," Wolf confirmed. His eyes widened. "Not even remotely."

Her eyes narrowed. "Really? Invite woman from target organization to dinner. Wine, interesting conversation, dancing cheek to cheek, get invited to sleep over, decline because a gentleman does not take advantage of a tipsy lady. Makes her breakfast accompanied by conversation with the charmed and disarmed lady from the target organization who soon tells all kinds of stories she has no business divulging. Does that sound like anyone you know, Mr. Grayson Wolf, expose novelist extraordinaire?"

"So, you do think I'm an extraordinary novelist." Wolf teased.

She took a step closer. "I think you had better tell me the truth because I am this close to hurting you."

"I'm not secretly investigating you or SSIS," he replied. "In fact, I'm done with that part of my life." Colleen expression became very still. "As for Katherine, I didn't sleep with her, nor suggest, nor signal such desire because I'm not a dog, Ms. Silverstone. I am, however, happy she decided to go out with me because we both had fun and got to know each other better... Full disclosure: I did find out something very important about Katherine pursuant to my prodigious efforts to charm and disarm the lady..."

"Oh? And what was that?"

"I'll have to marry her if I want to own Family because she will never sell that painting for any price."

She made a knowing look. "Do I have your word that you are not working on some novel about me or my company?"

"Yes," Wolf said. "I'm done with all that."

"Care to explain that?" she asked. "Are you seriously saying no more exposes, no more novels?"

"Correct."

Colleen studies his face. "I assume you'll be more involved with CIR?"

"No," he replied. "Resigned from administrative duties, but will remain on the Board of Directors."

"You've just cleared your work calendar for the year," she said, genuinely amazed. "Not my business, but why are you doing this?"

"I know your peeps have been digging into my life for a while now," he held up a hand to stop Colleen from interrupting, "and it's okay, I understand; I've had my peeps go through your life, too. The point is, you know more about me than just about anyone, so let me ask you: am I married? Have a family? No? Engaged perhaps or steady girlfriend? No? Perhaps I like to play the field, hit on all the hot women as I fly to and from all the swanky exclusive sites across the globe? Again, no?"

Colleen continued to gaze silently at him. Wolf knew he was opening himself up his fiercest adversary, a woman who might take everything he was revealing and use it to get even for what he had done to her father. It was a risk, sure, but what better way to break the tie to his old life than by burning the bridge that connected him to that life?

"I'm good at what I do and have no regrets, but it's time to move on."

Colleen shot him a questioning look. "Do you think you can?"

"I already have," he replied. "In the last two weeks, I've dated two women, a record and since I'm on a roll, I'm compelled to ask you out for date, too, but only because I feel bad about nearly shooting you the other morning."

"That's true, you do owe me," she grinned. "But I'll pass. I prefer my men emotionally stable when using utensils in restaurants and twirling me around on a dance floor."

"I suppose even Colleen Silverstone likes to play it safe once in a while," he replied, nodding sagely.

"I play it safe every day or I would not be standing here talking," she retorted. "There is another reason why I asked you to see you the moment you set foot in the lobby. The results from the Collins autopsy and lab tests will be available after lunch. I've scheduled a videoconference with the director of Centennial Forensic Lab at 1:30."

"That's great." Wolf said, excitedly. "Anything else?"

"Yes," she replied, a sly grin playing on her lips. "You're taking me to lunch…imagine that, Wolf taking out two hot women back to back. A personal best, I'm sure."

Wolf shot her a conflicted look. "You're hot?"

If looks could kill he'd be a dead man and Wolf wisely retreated from Colleen's office.

Chapter 14

Revelations & Suspicions

Lunch was a reasonably successful (and safe) affair considering Wolf's jest about Colleen's hotness, or lack thereof. Lunch was in SSIS's restaurant at no cost to him, though Wolf did hand the waiter a sizable tip. Colleen confessed she enjoyed tormenting her luncheon date, having him worry about possible retribution she might bring down upon his head. Expectations of hearing some positive news from the forensic lab about James Collins's lab tests following the meal buoyed Wolf's spirits.

"What?" Colleen said, when Wolf gazed silently at her for the third time within five minutes. "First you dare question my decisive hotness and now you can't take your eyes off me."

Wolf laughed. "Just thinking about the lab report. I really hope they found something definitive about James's death. I would really hate to tell his family that it was suicide after all."

"Centennial Forensics is one of the top labs in the country," Colleen assured him. "If there is anything on, in, or hovering around James's corpse, they will find it." Seeing Wolf's sudden frown, she added, "Don't worry, they'll find something, I'm sure."

He held her gaze and slowly shook his head. "Looking at you, suddenly I'm back in the cabin seeing your face in the doorway and, um..."

"It's normal," she said. "It'll take some time; it will fade eventually but never be forgotten. It's not a bad thing so long as it makes you more careful."

"Or so cautious that I'll hesitate next time it's the killer stepping through a door."

"Or that," Colleen agreed.

"Thank you for that; a real confidence booster," Wolf quipped.

"Would you prefer I pat you on the head instead?" she retorted. "The truth is even highly trained soldiers have choked when the shooting started and some got killed because they did."

"Did you?"

"Once, early on." She admitted. "Life and death situations are not like a video game or an action flick. Real people are really trying to kill you." She stopped, her expression suggesting she was weighing what to say next. "You acted and reacted competently under fire and duress for a civilian, Wolf. I'd have no problem with you having my back anytime."

"Does that mean you'd consider hiring me to work for you if I decided to apply?" Wolf grinned.

Colleen's face brightened. "We do need a new janitor."

"Been there, done that," Wolf replied. "I've had it with taking out the institutional garbage."

She held his gaze, then got up. "Time for the show to begin."

*   *   *   *

"The link is hot, Colleen," Katherine said, as they entered the Imaging Department. She shot Wolf a welcoming expression.

"Thank you, Kat."

Katherine led Colleen and Wolf into a private room. "The Director is standing by." She left the room, shutting the door behind her.

The image on the large monitor showed a portion of a laboratory behind a man's face dominating the screen. He smiled, presumably upon seeing Colleen's face on his monitor.

"Hello Ms. Silverstone," he said.

"Dr. Yi, nice to see you," Colleen replied. "Thank you for the quick turnaround of our request. We hope your people have found something definitive?"

Yi didn't immediately respond, staring instead at his screen. He looked stunned.

"Excuse me," he said, "but the man with you is a dead ringer for Grayson Wolf!"

"It is Mr. Wolf," she replied. "I apologize for not introducing him."

Yi appeared to be struck dumb. He blinked several times.

"I see…" he finally managed to say.

Wolf understood the man's reaction. He imagined every single person in Colleen's circle of friends, acquaintances and professionals knew about Wolf's book excoriating her father.

"Perhaps we can proceed with the report?" Colleen said.

"Ah, of course," he replied, his eyes flicking to and fro the section of his monitor where Wolf's image would be. "We started by examining tissue for the full range of Rofis—Rophenol, ketamine, gamma-hydroxybutyrate—but he was clean. Based on the prison doctor's report, Mr. Collins didn't show any post-mortem bruising suggesting he was forced into the closet and murdered. We also ran tox-screens for a category of drugs that in low dosages can incapacitate a person's mobility, which could permit a second person to hustle them into the closest and hang them. Nothing. Then we aimed at some of the more exotic toxins—tetrodotoxin from pufferfish for instance—in hopes of finding some trace of anything. All negative."

"So, we have nothing," Wolf said, discouraged.

"We have no evidence of toxins or typical drugs," Yi confirmed. "But we did find something that is quite common in virtually every person having access to city water: Chloroform."

"Chloroform?" Wolf said.

"Comes from the chlorination process," Colleen said. "Drinking tap water, baths and showers exposes us to chloroform by inhaling mist and through skin contact."

"Very good, Ms. Silverstone," Yi said, looking pleased. "We all get a tiny dose, but the body eliminates it rapidly. In larger doses the chemical affects the central nervous system, liver, and kidneys which we discovered after years of using chloroform as an anesthetic."

Wolf always appreciated learning something new, but he was anxious for the doctor to get to the point.

"Since we all have some of the chemical in us, what's it got to do with James Collins's death?"

"You see, Mr. Wolf," Yi replied, "test showed Mr. Collins had higher levels of chloroform in his oral and nasal tissue than he would receive through normal contact with water. Had Mr. Collins been alive for several hours after being exposed to a higher dose of chloroform his body would have eliminated it through normal functions such as respiration. Because we found a much higher level of the chemical in his oral and nasal tissue tells us firstly, that he died shortly after being exposed and secondly, the substance was delivered by placing a cloth across his mouth and nose. Therefore, it is my professional opinion that James Collins was dosed with chloroform to incapacitate him so that others could stage a suicide."

"That's great," Wolf said, excitedly.

"There is one little problem," Colleen said. "If the killers used chloroform to knock Collins out, then they'd have to manhandle him: carry him into the closet, prop him up, and jerk down to break his neck."

"Damn," Wolf said. "There are no post-mortem bruises on his body and manhandling him like Colleen suggests would have left lots of evidence."

"Excuse me," Yi said. "Why do you believe Mr. Collins was manhandled?"

"He'd be unconscious," Wolf replied. "How else could they drag his body around and stage a suicide? Use levitation?"

"Levioso!" Yi laughed, making a flourish with his hand. "Harry Potter fan anyone?" He must have caught the frustration on Wolf's face because he continued. "Levitation spells aside, using chloroform is not necessarily *dose and drop* like in movies. Brief exposure can disorient sufficiently to allow someone to steer the victim much like if he were drunk. One or two people could have guided Collins into the closet, got him up on something, placed a rope around his neck and gently pushed him off. No post-mortem bruising, thus no suspicious death."

Wolf stared at the screen. "You said brief exposure. Wouldn't someone need sufficient medical knowledge to understand how much chloroform to use and for how long?"

"The only thing the perpetrator needed to know is how to Google chloroform and do a little reading," Yi explained.

Wolf and Colleen looked at each other; both were smiling.

"Dr. Yi, you are the best," Colleen said. "Thank you very much. Please convey my gratitude to your team and tell them their contribution will bring justice to the victim and ease the minds of his family."

Yi's face crinkled in appreciation. "My pleasure, I assure you, Ms. Silverstone. I will email the full report to you immediately."

"The invoice for your service, too," Colleen replied. "Funds will be transferred within three days."

"Always a pleasure doing business with you, Ms. Silverstone," Yi said, nodding. "Have a terrific week and good luck finding the culprits responsible for this young man's death."

"You can be certain of that, doctor," Wolf said. "A pleasure to meet you and thank you again."

Wolf saw the man's eyes shift from him to Colleen on his screen. A thin smile formed on his lips.

"They say politics makes for strange bedfellows. I suppose so does hunting down criminals to bring them to justice."

Colleen lifted both hands making a helpless gesture and grinned. "I suppose it does. Good afternoon." She pressed a remote, terminating the connection.

"What's our next move?" Wolf asked, following Colleen out of the room. "Visit the prison? Get the DA to re-open the case?"

"All of the above," she replied. Her eyes flicked over to a monitor against the wall showing the time. "We need the forensics' report first; can't to rush this. I'll have my assistant make arrangements to visit the prison and an appointment with the DA in Castle Rock for tomorrow. Right now, there are other pressing matters I must attend to."

They were on their way out of the Imaging Center when Katherine intercepted them at the exit. "Is there anything else you need from me today, besides continuing to search facial images looking for the killer?"

"No, thank you Kat. Proceed with your other tasks," Colleen replied. "Do let me know the moment you get a hit."

"Of course," she said. "May I have a word with Mr. Wolf please? I'll send him right up."

"He's all yours," Colleen said. "No rush, our business is finished for today."

"Hi." Wolf smiled as Colleen left the center. "Everything okay?"

Katherine nodded. "Yes. If you're not otherwise engaged this evening, I was wondering if you'd like to come over for dinner?"

"Absolutely," Wolf replied. "I do need a change of clothes so I've ordered a car. Text me your address and I'll be at your house at the appointed time."

"If I may ask, did the lab discover any new evidence about James Collins's suicide?

"Yes, they did," Wolf said, happily. "Looks like he was murdered. Tomorrow Colleen and I will be making the rounds to the prison and the DA, so I'm afraid it can't be dancing until the wee hours of the morning."

Katherine held his eyes. "You could bring a change of clothing."

Wolf was very tempted to "bring a change of clothing" but remembered that this woman had lost her entire family in a tragic accident. Were his situation different, were his name not Grayson Wolf, he would very much enjoy an intimate evening with Katherine.

"A simple yes or no would suffice," Katherine said.

"Not that simple," he replied. "Couple weeks back I was run off the road and almost killed. Last week I was shot at leaving the prison, shot at again in the backwoods in southern Colorado and nearly killed by a bear. Tomorrow Colleen and I will get the Collins case re-opened, visit the prison again and actively pursue James's killer and most likely the person who actually raped Sarah Lewis."

The reality of what Wolf was saying must have hit home because her expression turned thoughtful. After a brief moment, she smiled and said, "Your name might be Wolf, but you're not a wolf … Please do come for dinner and you're welcome to bring a change of clothing if you change your mind."

Wolf inclined his head. "Done and done."

*   *   *   *

Colleen stood in her office deciding whether to make the call pursuant to that other pressing matter she told Wolf and Katherine she needed to attend to. A matter that had been pressing on her since last week and getting heavier with each passing day.

Sitting behind her desk would provide psychological support by reminding her she was the founder and CEO of the nation's leading security and investigation firm. On the other hand, making the call from the informal sitting area near the windows was a more appropriate setting for the personal nature of the matter.

Personal, yes. But also, pressing. Very pressing, in fact. Desk it is.

Lifting her cell, she pressed a name.

"Hi Dad."

"Well it's about time," Larry Silverstone said. "I've left you a dozen messages since last week."

"I've been rather busy." It was a lame excuse but far better than what she might have said.

"I bet you have," Silverstone retorted, "busy hob-knobbing with the person who single-handedly destroyed my marriage to your mother and almost my business. What the hell are you doing, for God's sake!

"I'm doing my job: investigating a rape and a murder," she replied. "Mr. Wolf is a client; no more, no less."

"Client my ass!" He shot back. "That weasel is working on another smear piece, Colleen! Why would you ever invite that snake into your house? Are you insane?"

"He's not working on a novel or any hit piece," she replied.

"Oh yeah? Then what was he doing in New York ten days ago spying on me and Justin while we were watching a Broadway show?" Silverstone said.

A knot formed in Colleen's stomach. She knew how far Wolf had gone to investigate people and organizations in the past. It wasn't hard to imagine him seizing upon the Lewis-Collins case as subterfuge for insinuating himself into SSIS for the purpose of ripping her apart for her three-year campaign to discredit Wolf and failing to do so, harassing him at every turn.

"And that's not all," her father said. "He approached Justin coming out of the men's room pretending to be a professor from Overland College asking him questions."

"What kind of questions?"

"What difference does that make?" he cried. "The point is the bastard is stalking us and he's in your house! You know how good he his, Colleen. People talk, he asks a couple innocent questions next thing you know one of your people is in his pocket and you are royally screwed a year from now when his hit piece on the corrupt Colleen Silverstone and her evil security firm hits number one on the best seller lists."

An image of a woman's face popped into her mind. "Jeezus."

"What? You think of something?"

"He went on a date with the head of my Imaging department," she replied, her tone flat.

"Honey," he continued, "if she's sleeping with that dog she's compromised for sure. You had better get your people all over him and her the second we hang up. I really do not want to see you featured in his next novel."

Neither did Colleen. "Dad, I gotta go; talk with you later…"

She placed the phone on the desk, thinking long and hard about her unexpected partnership with Wolf. If his goal was writing a novel about private security firms using the Lewis-Collins case as a pretext to get inside her headquarters, it was classic Grayson Wolf modus operandi. Recalling the attack on him after leaving the prison and the near-death experiences in Creede, she found it hard to imagine that even he would go to such lengths to gain her confidence; that his claim of seeking justice for James Collins and Sarah Lewis was all a pretense.

If it was all a ruse, then she had willingly compromised a critical part of her security protocol, revealing basic security procedures such as weighing her vehicle before allowing her access into the garage. But far worse than that breech was permitting Wolf access to SSIS's most secure intelligence facility where he was free to talk with Cooper about God knows what. And last night he stayed over at Kat's house. Katherine, the head of her Imaging section also located downstairs in the SSIS's highly sensitive intelligence complex. Katherine, whom Wolf denied sleeping with.

Then she remembered: Wolf never sleeps with his informants!

"Son of a Bitch!"

Colleen sprang out of her chair, snatched the secured transceiver from its cradle and pressed a button. She instructing the person on the other end to find Grayson Wolf and escort him to Interrogation Room #2 immediately.

"Call me when it's done." Then she remembered she allowed him to retain his pistol. "Ask him to turn over his weapon first; be prepared just in case."

Within four minutes the call came and she made for the interrogation room. Wolf shot her a very convincing quizzical look when she entered.

"What's going on, Colleen? Is this about Katherine?"

She sat down on the opposite side of the table facing him. "Did you sleep with her?"

"You know the answer to that," he replied.

"Tell me again."

"I did not have sex with that woman."

"Kat is attractive, intelligent and talented," Colleen said, ignoring the Clinton reference. "Your ideal type of woman."

"Yes. And…?"

"And you chose not to sleep with her."

She said it so matter-of-factly that Wolf's paranoia alarm blared in his head. He leaned across the table.

"I—am—not—writing—a—book. Period." He leaned back into his chair.

"Did you attend a Broadway show in New York the weekend before last?" Colleen asked.

Wolf decided to go on the offensive. He stood up.

"I'm leaving."

"Sit down," Colleen ordered.

"No," Wolf snarled, and turned toward the door. "If you or your goons try to stop me you will be holding me against my will and *that* is a criminal offense."

Colleen held his stare. "Feel free to walk out of that door. But if you do, we are done … Sit down—please."

Wolf's smile lit up the room. "See, that wasn't so hard." He sat on the corner of the table. "Yes, I was in New York. Yes, I was seeing a show, Hamilton to be precise. Yes, I saw your father and Bellamy and yes, I accosted Bellamy outside the men's room. You know, Justin Bellamy, father of Kerry Bellamy, one of our prime suspect bitch boys?"

"Go on." Colleen said, after Wolf paused for a long moment.

"No, I was not stalking them," he continued. "I just happened to be there when they showed up. I enjoyed the show and took advantage of the situation by engaging Bellamy in a brief exchange, my goal being to see his reaction when I mentioned Sarah Lewis and James Collins."

"What did you learn?"

"That he looked uncomfortable when I mentioned the names of our victims, a reaction I interpreted as a father who is knowledgeable of his son's transgressions."

Wolf slid the legal pad from underneath Colleen's palm with one hand and her pen with the other. He began writing, reading aloud as he composed the note.

From: Grayson Wolf, author extraordinaire
To: Colleen Silverstone, hot investigator extraordinaire
Subject: Declaration of Intent. No date of expiration.
Date: April 13

This is to certify that I, Grayson Wolf, author extraordinaire, being in sound mind and exceptional physical fitness hereby declare that I, nor any of my usual suspects and associates are currently engaged in writing any expose, hit piece, novel, essay, paragraph, or sentence pursuant to anything or anyone part, parcel, family member or employee of, or associated with, any business, client or plans, innocent or nefarious, of Colleen Silverstone, hot investigator extraordinaire, currently or in the future.

Further, if I, Grayson Wolf, author extraordinaire, fail to honor the article of declaration above, I give Colleen Silverstone, hot investigator extraordinaire, authority to seize all profits made pursuant to this breach of contract and give her full authority to dispense any and all products published relating to her specifically or SSIS in any manner she so wishes plus pay a penalty of $1,000,000.

I make this declaration free from inducements or coercion of any type by her or anyone else."

Wolf signed the document and pushed the legal pad back across the table.

"Sign it, call in some of your goons to witness it, then let's get back to the business at hand and track down these scumbags."

Colleen tore the page off the pad, crumbled it up and tossed at his head.

"That's not necessary."

"The hell it isn't," Wolf retorted, smoothing the paper on the tabletop. "Whatever this was about, it's just the beginning and I'm not interested in being interrogated by you every few days. Take the document, sign it, have it witnessed and put it in your safe or stuff it under your mattress. Do it or I'm done ... Oh, full disclosure:

Katherine invited me to dinner this evening. And just so you know, if she invites me into her bed, I might just say, yes. May I leave now?"

*   *   *   *

"Are you okay?" Katherine said, studying Wolf's face over the dinner table. "You did like the meal, I hope?"

"Absolutely," Wolf asserted. "Sorry about my mind wandering off; lots of moving pieces happening right now. Dinner was scrumptious and dessert delicious."

Katherine took the dishes, Wolf clearing the table then following her to the kitchen. He started to place silverware into the dishwasher when she stopped him.

"No, no. Leave it," she said. "I'm not wasting one second of my dinner date with Grayson Wolf having him clean my kitchen. Come outside; it's a pleasant evening." She reached in the fridge, took out two beers, handed him one and led him to the veranda.

"You have a nice spread here," he said, looking at the spacious back yard. "Very private, quiet and serene. I bet you spend a lot of time out here."

Katherine looked wistfully toward the line of trees demarcating the property line a good hundred yards away. "Yes … quiet and serene."

They spent the next hour chatting about their childhoods, school experiences and college. Katherine told Wolf of her passion for painting and graphic art beginning from her earliest memories wearing out boxes of crayons scribbling colorful pictures, her mother referring to her as "my mini-me Pollok." Wolf confessed he hated writing essays in English, avoiding writing anything until his rising disgust with cheaters drove him to put fingers on keyboard and write Lying & Cheating for Fun and Profit.

When Katherine mentioned she rode dressage during high school, Wolf's eyes went to the barn in the meadow some distance to his left.

"Do you still keep horses?"

"No more," she replied. "We had six beautiful steeds; I sold them soon after the accident."

"When's the last time you went on vacation?" He didn't know why he asked that; perhaps because it had been some time since he'd gone on a real holiday himself.

"August, 2013," she said. "Spent the entire month at the beach in New Jersey. We all loved it. Four months later…no more family vacations."

"Virginia Beach is quite lovely, too," he replied, surprising himself. "I've seen you in your party dress; I bet you look fantastic in a bathing suit."

Katherine held his gaze. Her expression darkened.

"I'm not any man's reclamation project," she said, coldly.

"No, you're not," Wolf replied. "You're an attractive, talented and accomplished woman with whom any man would want to spend time with. It's been years since I've had beach sand between my toes and surf in my face and I'm planning to do more of that kind thing in the future."

Katherine held his gaze and nodded slowly. "I think I'm ready for more, too. I'm glad you asked me out and glad that I didn't allow myself to slink back into my cozy and lonely cocoon. You're the first man I've cooked for in a long time."

"We are more alike than you think, Katherine," Wolf said. "Because of my work, I have had to put a lot of my life on hold, retreating into my own little cocoon, as it were. Like you said, it's lonely in there."

Wolf had little choice but to place a tight leash upon his desires because a failure to do so placed others at unnecessary risk. Even now he felt a tinge of guilt being here with Katherine for a second time, considering such an act as sheer recklessness as recently as a month ago. But he was tired of denying himself once again the simple pleasure of being with a woman for fear of remote harm coming to her. Gazing at Katherine, he imagined he'd be happy spending a month with such an interesting woman in a summer adventure—no stings, no deceptions, no secrets. Just fun.

He leaned over in his chair, his face close to hers. Her face became very still, her eyes large. She leaned forward, her lips meeting his and a tender kiss was exchanged. Then another. Wolf was more than ready but proceeded gingerly, restraining his hand to gentle stroking of her shoulder and arm, not sure how Katherine might react to exploratory forays into areas of a more erotic nature.

Concerns about her response to his amorous act became moot when her lips pressed harder and she removed his hand from her shoulder placing it on her breast. Wolf got up from his chair, lifting Katherine from hers, embracing her fully, his lips working their way from her mouth along her neck, one hand drifting down her back pressing her against his firm desire.

"Inside," she breathed, leading him to the bedroom.

Wolf took his time, lips working their magic on her mouth, skimming tenderly across them then pressing harder, making their way along her neck, teeth gently nibbling here and there, taking his time to savor the moment.

He made his way along her smooth abdomen, enjoying every inch of his journey, his mouth finally coming to rest on its objective, tongue probing and penetrating until her breathing became ragged and irregular. In one swift movement, he raised himself above her and slipped inside, Katherine's gasp announcing the union.

She raised her hips to allow him deep entry, the intensity of their passionate dance rising and falling until Wolf felt himself getting dangerously close to the edge of losing control. Just then Katherine's movements slowed then stopped, her body tense and rigid followed by swift, hard pushes, Wolf matching her rhythm until gasps filled the room, movements slowing as bodies came to an exhausted and most satisfying rest.

"That was wonderful," Katherine said, Wolf spooning her and nibbling on her ear. "Don't you wish now you'd brought a change of clothing after all? I do…"

"I did," he replied, feeling very relaxed.

"Boy scout?" she teased. "Be prepared?"

"Being Grayson Wolf," he replied, "means always being prepared if he knows what's good for him."

"Sounds stressful to be Grayson Wolf."

"In so many ways," he replied.

"One of those ways Colleen calling you to her office this morning?" She made a dismissive wave. "Sorry, that's none of my business. Occupational hazard working in intelligence."

Wolf rolled Katherine on her back. He stroked her hair and cheek, his fingers caressing her lips, which he kissed subsequently.

"You're beautiful; a living work of art," he said. "A living work of art that needs to stop hiding in Colleen's dungeon and get out into the world and—" An idea struck him and he sat up. "Katherine, would you be willing to paint my portrait? And others at CIR, too; for a commission, of course."

"You're joking?" she said, looking at him with a mixture of surprise and incredulity. "I haven't touched a paintbrush in over three years."

"It pains me to see enormous talent like yours languishing in limbo instead of expressed and celebrated," he insisted. "Katherine, do you not see the cultural decay spreading like a toxic fog throughout the nation? It permeates our homes through all the malevolence-soaked entertainment glowing on TV screens and infects our institutions turning them into amplifiers of lies and dispensers of dung. In a hundred insidious ways, it seeps into our very souls, a corrosive acid dissolving, layer by layer, our values, beliefs and freedoms, all working to destroying our future and happiness."

Katherine stared at Wolf who had gotten out of bed standing naked in front of her, his impressive six-foot two-inch, muscular frame commanding her attention. If she had wondered before this evening what an intimate relationship with Grayson Wolf was like, she was getting quite an ear and eyeful.

"I know you're in pain," he continued, "that circumstances have knocked the wind out of you and you might feel I'm asking too much of you too soon. I can tell you this: I've put much of my personal life on hold for too long ... life is time punctuated, there are no guarantees and I'm not going to defer my pursuit of happiness for one second longer." He pointed his finger dramatically at her, intoning, "Katherine Simmons, pick up that paintbrush and paint my portrait!"

She peered at him with large eyes, made a sputtering sound then laughed merrily. "You're absolutely crazy, do you know that?"

He hopped back on the bed. "Promise me—promise yourself—you'll start to paint again." He took her hand pulling her toward the edge. "In fact, let's begin right now. Show me your studio. Come on..."

"Fine, but we need to do something first," she replied, grinning knowingly.

She took his hand and led Wolf to the bath where they enjoyed a hot shower, hands washing each other, gently caressing sensitive areas, enjoying the experience of wet skin on skin contact. Katherine switched on the unit's waterfall option disgorging a wall of water cascading over them, both struggling not to drown as they embraced and kissed standing under the torrent from above.

"That was the most challenging shower ever," Wolf said, collecting his clothes. "You should consider installing an alarm that sounds for at least three seconds prior to being deluged and possibly drowned."

"It does come in handy for self-defense," Katherine said, smiling happily watching him get dressed.

"Oh?" Wolf said, shooting her a suspicious look. "And just how many men *have* you attempted to drown?"

"Just you." She smiled, though he detected a hint of sadness in her eyes.

He was dressing when she saw the pistol on the night table. "I guess that's a part of your life, too."

Wolf gazed at the gun. "I'm afraid so. At least for the foreseeable future. You okay with that?"

She reached behind the headboard and produced a small caliber handgun. "I work in Colleen's dungeon, remember? Never had to use it, but being a member of SSIS's highly sensitive intelligence team, potential danger comes with the territory."

"Comrades in arms and in the sack," Wolf quipped. "What more could any red-blooded man ask for?"

Chapter 15

Hunt Begins Anew

"Good morning Wolf," Colleen said, meeting him in SSIS's lobby. Peering closely at him, she smiled and added, "Successful date I see."

"I'm successful at all my endeavors," he retorted. "How about I drive this time."

She puckered her lips. "Is your rental bullet-proof? No? My car it is. We've got a ten o'clock appointment with Castle Rock's DA. Let's roll."

They drove in silence until Colleen merged on I-25 South when she mentioned Katherine's name, Wolf saying a gentleman doesn't kiss and tell.

"I'm not interested in hearing about your undercover exploits," she replied. "I've been gently prodding Kat to get out of the house for a while now without much luck. I was surprised when I found out she was going on a date with you and shocked about her going dancing. And if your expression earlier suggests what I think it does, then I'm very delighted. It's tough to rebound from a life-changing tragedy like the one Kat experienced; that you managed to do what you did in two dates places you in the miracle worker category in my book."

"Katherine is fun to be with," Wolf said, "and I've engaged her to paint my portrait."

Colleen's head jerked toward him. "You're kidding."

"Engaged is a rather strong assertion," he admitted. "Strongly encouraged is more accurate. She did show me her studio and we talked art, so I'm hoping she'll get back to painting. I'll keep after her every so often."

"I'm glad; Kat deserves to be happy..." she paused, adding, "About grilling you yesterday—"

"Forget it," Wolf said. "If you came to CIR working with me on a case and started dating one of my key people I'd be all over you, too."

Castle Rock is barely a twenty-minute drive from Aurora and Colleen pulled up to the Municipal Center with fifteen-minutes to spare. Entering the DA's outer office, Wolf once again faced the severe expression of the middle-aged keeper of the keys who he still suspected of keeping a sawed-off shotgun concealed in easy reach under her desk.

"Good morning, Ms. Silverstone…Mr. Wolf." The receptionist's tone plunged when she spoke his name. "Ms. Catelli is expecting you. First door to your left."

"What did you do to that poor woman?" Colleen said, under her breath as they approached the door. "She has it on for you; I can sympathize."

"Suspected serial killer, that one," he said.

She gave him a look and knocked on the door. "I'd steer clear of her I was you."

A voice from within called for them to enter. Wolf opened the door and followed Colleen into the room.

"Nice to see you again Colleen," District Attorney Catelli said, coming up to her and giving her a hug.

"It's been too long, Sylvia," Colleen said.

Wolf held out his arms and grinned.

"Good morning, Mr. Wolf." Catelli stuck a hand out, Wolf settling for a handshake. She pointed at a small table near the window. "Less formal; please have a seat."

Colleen drew a file from her attaché and slid it toward Catelli. "The lab report from Centennial Forensics I told you about, Sylvia. Findings are solid: James Collins was murdered and his suicide staged. The more we look into his case the more we are convinced he was not guilty of drugging and raping Sarah Lewis but is himself a victim of that crime."

Catelli read through the report and sighed. She didn't look happy.

Seeing her expression Wolf wondered if the DA was being pressured to keep a lid on the case. "You need to reopen the Lewis case, Ms. Catelli. James was murdered and the guilty party or parties are at large thinking they've gotten away with rape and possibly murder, too." He glanced at Colleen who gave him an annoyed look.

"I know my job, Mr. Wolf," Catelli replied, her gaze frosty. "What you need to understand is that our police department has two full-time detectives for the entire district, each with a stack of open cases weighing down their desks. I'll do my best to nudge the captain, but cold cases wind up on the bottom of the pile. It'll be lucky if they get to it before fall…sorry, but that's the best I can do."

Silence filled the office. Catelli must have seen what appeared to her as an aggressive expression on Wolf's face because she said, "Please don't do anything rash, Mr. Wolf, it will only complicate matters further."

"Do something rash?" Wolf shot her a sly look. "Never. How quickly can you re-open the Lewis case?"

"By the time you exit the building. Why?"

"The department's detectives are swamped," he said, repeating Catelli. "Perhaps you can encourage the police captain to free a uniformed officer to work on the case."

"What you really mean," Catelli said, looking at Wolf knowingly, "is ask the captain to give you one of his officers to act as your point man allowing you and Colleen to use the officer's uniform as a means to apply pressure on whomever you plan to question. Am I warm?"

"Quite hot, in fact."

Wolf's infectious smile ensured the DA didn't miss the double entendre and she couldn't help but smile in acknowledgement of his compliment. Wolf's notoriety wasn't just based upon his "ruthless" pursuit of his prey, his boyish charm and wit just as effective at disarming friends and opponents alike.

Gazing over at Colleen she conveyed a you-are-unbelievable look over her eyebrows. "I think what Wolf has in mind is working collaboratively with an assigned officer with that officer clearly in charge."

"And I'll be happy to make a generous donation to any police fund the captain designates." Wolf added.

"Careful about that," Catelli replied. "Could sound like a bribe."

"It is a bribe," Wolf quipped. "For a good and just cause."

"I'll pretend I didn't hear that," the DA replied. She stood up. "I'll call the captain and tell him you're coming down to discuss a mutually beneficial arrangement ... nice seeing you again Colleen."

"Ditto, Sylvia."

Catelli was making the call before they exited her office and whatever she said to the captain, the officer's assistant whisked Colleen and Wolf into his office shortly after introducing themselves.

"So, you're the infamous Grayson Wolf." The captain looked and talked like a lawman of the old west: rugged face, rough hands, iron grip and steely gaze. Wolf knew he had better be totally straight from the get-go cause this man would detect the faintest whiff of bullshit from miles away. He liked him immediately.

"Yes sir," Wolf replied. Normally he'd continue with some light banter but sensed that less was much more.

The captain eyed Colleen. "Always a pleasure to see you, Ms. Silverstone."

Wolf heard the absolute sincerity in his tone, not that he could blame the man. It was a pleasure to be working so close with Colleen, though he was certain the pleasure of her company was a one-way affair only. Even if she hated his guts (a strong possibility) she was still delicious eye-candy.

"Pleasure seeing you, too, chief Holcomb," Colleen said.

Holcomb's eyes went to Wolf and back to her. A wry grin spread across mouth.

"You must hear this quite often, but what the hell are you doing with Grayson Wolf?"

"We're engaged." Wolf heard himself say before he realized it.

The poor man almost choked. "What?" he croaked.

"Pay no attention to him, chief," Colleen calmly said. "Mr. Wolf has developed a tendency to spout babble while in my company."

"A condition many men are struck with while in your company," he snorted. "So, what is going on and more importantly, what kind of bribe are you gonna offer me, Mr. Wolf?"

"Depend upon the quid pro quo, captain" Wolf said boldly.

"What do you want and what are ya offering?" Holcomb said, grinning humorously.

"District Attorney Catelli has re-opened the Sarah Lewis rape case," he replied. "She told us your detectives are buried under live cases and have no time to pursue a cold case." Holcomb didn't dispute the statement. "I want Sargent Hernandez to lead the Lewis investigation in collaboration with Colleen and myself. In exchange, I will make a sizable contribution to any police fund you designate."

Holcomb scrunched up his face in thought. "Why Hernandez?"

"He's quick, got a good sense of humor, knows all the dirty little things going on at Overland and I like the man."

"How long and how sizable a donation?" Holcomb said.

"Maybe a week or two," Wolf replied. "Three on the outside."

"Then thousand per week or any part of a week," Holcomb said. "And you feed and drive Hernandez."

"What do I write the check to?" Wolf said, shaking the man's hand.

"I was thinking Mitchell Holcomb, but the Review Board might be a bit peeved," he laughed. "The police social fund could use an infusion of cash. Use the money for families who need some well-deserved R and R. When will you be needing my good sergeant?"

Wolf looked at Colleen who answered. "Depends on our schedules. This afternoon we'll be over at Centennial Prison … tomorrow's Friday, that's a busy time for me and my weekend is slammed. I've got a couple days open next week … Wolf?"

"I'd really like to get started with our Overland suspects, but rather we do it together, Colleen," he explained. He remembered the action at Virginia Patriots College was now underway and he was on stand-by. "As much as I hate to say it, I guess we'll wait until next week."

"Next week it is," Colleen said. "Is a twenty-four-hour notice sufficient and will you inform sergeant Hernandez about his new role, chief?"

"A day's notice is good," Holcomb confirmed. "I'll cue Hernandez in today. I like doing business with you two." They said good bye and were on their way out the door when Holcomb's face lit up. "You two do make a striking couple 'case you ever thinkin' about getting hitched."

Wolf issued a low snort while Colleen strode silently into the hall and toward the exit. By the time he caught up to her she was at the car.

"It's perhaps the oldest cliché in history," she began, pulling the car out of the space, "but not if you were the last man on earth."

"Commitment issues, huh?" Wolf quipped.

Colleen shook her head. "Do you ever not have a retort?"

"The answer to that is, no."

"You must really be enjoying this."

"This, being…?"

"Messing with the daughter of…"

"Let me stop you right there." His tone was so firm she actually turned her head to glance at him. "I am not messing with you, Colleen. Teasing you, yes, but most of all I'm thankful for your willingness to put aside you're, ah, distaste for me personally to help me get justice for two young people who have been cruelly wronged. I consider it an honor to work with you; for that and a dozen more reasons I could list."

"Thank you."

"You are more than welcome," Wolf replied. "Also, even though you wouldn't if I were the last man on earth, I would and you wouldn't even need to be the last woman on earth."

She laughed at that and after driving silently for a while, said, "Not feeling guilty one nano-bit."

"Good. Neither am I."

Wolf felt the temperature drop in the car but Colleen didn't issue a rejoinder to his comment alluding to her father, his firm and associates. But it was true: he didn't feel guilty exposing their shady deals, their grossly insensitive attitudes toward their victims and callous disregard for the welfare of the community at large they resided in. Even if every woman in the world felt like Colleen did and shun him till the end of his days, Wolf did not regret one word of what he had written in his fifteen non-fictional-fictional exposés.

Shortly after one, Colleen parked the car in the visitor's lot of Centennial State Prison. First order of business was meeting with the warden and presenting him with a copy of Collins's forensic lab report.

"Has my county prosecutor seen this report yet?" Ragavitz asked.

"No," Colleen said. "I coming to you first as a professional courtesy to launch an internal investigation. No one wants a rat in their house and Mr. Wolf and I are here to help."

The warden looked at Colleen and nodded slowly. "Thank you, Ms. Silverstone, Mr. Wolf. Your right about that. I'll open an investigation and if any of my people are involved I will personally make sure they wind up behind bars. This is a tough job and I'm sorry to hear about Welling, but nothing worse than a dirty officer; can't have that. Now, how can I help you?"

"I need a list of any employee or contractor who was off or did not show up to work on Saturday, March 25 or left early that day and three days prior," Colleen replied. "Whoever tried to kill Mr. Wolf after leaving the prison that Saturday afternoon is most likely the same man who killed officer Welling the next day."

"Hmm..." Ragavitz looked thoughtful. "We've got near 800 employees and contractors at Centennial. That list you're asking for might be a hundred or more people ... you looking for a man?"

"Yes," Wolf said. "White, about six feet; maybe one eighty?"

"Okay," Ragavitz replied. "Take out the women and non-white males you're looking at maybe less than fifty. I'll have my data people get that list before you leave. What else?"

"We'd like to take a close look at the service closet where Collins was killed," Colleen said.

"Not sure what you'd find that would help, but no problem." The warden raised the phone receiver from his desk and made a call. "Two guards will be here in five to escort you ... Mr. Wolf, I want to thank you again for spotting that security glitch in the cameras; that's been fixed. Still gives me nightmares to think who knew about this and what they got away with doing."

"My pleasure, I assure you."

Just then there was a loud knock at the door, opening seconds later. Ragavitz instructed the guards where to take the guests and to bring them back to his office afterward. The trip was a short one and within minutes Colleen and Wolf were standing in the service closet.

Wolf peering at a wall of shelves holding paper goods and sundry cleaning supplies. Below the last shelf on the bottom rested a collection of sturdy storage bins each about twenty inches in height. He dragged one to the middle of the floor and stepped on top.

"OK," he said, "this is what James supposedly used to hang himself. Except in his drugged condition James would never have managed to get up on this. The killers would have struggled to lift him up, and—"

"And that would most likely have left post mortem bruising," Colleen said.

"See anything in here that could be used for steps?" Wolf asked.

Colleen shook her head. "No."

He walked slowly along the closet's perimeter looking for anything that could be used to enable the killer or killers to get James up on that storage bin.

"What about one of the shelves?" Colleen suggested.

Wolf studied the shelves holding the paper goods. "Too long and too thin; they'd break the second James's full weight was brought to bear and he'd crash onto the floor causing serious post mortem bruising."

"Hey," Colleen called. She was looking at something near the edge of the cabinet along the wall. "Look at this." She pointed to an inch-thick strip of wood between the top and side of the cabinet used to close the space between the unit and the wall. "See the scuff marks along the wall? This spacer had been pulled out and replaced."

"Give me your key," Wolf said.

Using the car key, he easily wedged the horizontal spacer upwards. Inserting his finger, he pulled on the vertical one which slid easily outward producing a ten-inch wide, thirty-two-inch-high board an inch thick. He brought it over to the storage bin and laid one end on its top forming a ramp.

"Well, lookie here," he quipped. "We've got ourselves a makeshift ramp wide enough, long enough and strong enough to guide a moving James on top of the bin." She shot him a questioning look. "What?"

"Next time don't manhandle possible evidence: fingerprints." Seeing his flustered expression, she added, "I think you're off the hook this time, Sherlock. Considering how much handwork was involved—plastic bin, moving boards, handling James, touching the pipes above and ten more items I'm pretty sure they wore gloves."

"Sorry about that."

Wolf started up the makeshift ramp when the bin tilted and the board crashed on the floor. He was about to say something when he noticed Colleen looking toward the ceiling and saw what she was looking at: the exposed pipes from which James was hung. Pipes that ran parallel to the edge of the wall. He slid the bin against the wall, angled the board on it and successfully walked up the ramp.

"Colleen..."

"Yes...?"

"I want you to give me a try."

"Excuse me?"

"See if you can hustle woozy me up the ramp and keep me steady on top of the bin."

Colleen guided a swaying Wolf into the closet, holding him with just enough pressure to keep him from falling—and bruising him. Using his forward momentum, it took several runs at the ramp get Wolf stumbling up the ramp. Once up she had to press her wobbling victim against the wall to prevent him toppling over with one hand while trying to place an imaginary rope over his head with the other was challenging and time consuming.

The conclusion of the experiment was that James's murder required at least two perpetrators. Like Colleen, one killer would have faced too many challenges to accomplish his task quickly and silently.

Colleen took numerous photos with her phone of the space between the cabinet and wall from where the ramp was secured. She asked Wolf to replace the ramp board and top spacer closing off the space then take it all apart once more while she took photos of each stage. She took shots of him placing the makeshift ramp on the storage bin, standing on the ramp and on top of the bin.

"Okay, that should do it," she said. "Let's put it all back again and we're done here for today."

When they got back to the warden's office the man had the list of absentees Colleen had asked for.

"Fifty-seven white males not working on Saturday, March 25 and the three days prior as requested," Ragavitz said, handing her the printout.

They thanked the warden and headed back to the parking lot and got in the car. Colleen fired up the engine and heading out of the lot when Wolf mentioned he had called James's father earlier, saying that they would come by this afternoon to give them an update about the investigation.

Colleen pulled the car off the driveway and stopped. She turned to face him and peered silently at him.

"What?" Wolf said, looking at her hard expression. "I promised the family I would keep them informed of any new developments. It's only about ten miles out of our way back to your office and I thought it would be convenient for us to stop by and let them know what we've found." Colleen continued to stare silently at him and he added, "Have I done something wrong? I rather tell them the news in person than over the phone."

"Look, I understand that in your business doing your lone Wolf thing is critical for your success," she began, "but in my business, we often operate in pairs and when we do, partners do not act first and tell second. That creates doubt and doubt leads to second-guessing which leads to someone getting killed. I'm not averse to stopping by the Collins's; *I am* averse to my partner having conversations and making plans without first checking in with me. Don't do it again."

"I won't. Sorry."

It was rare for Wolf, as Wolf, to be chastised, but he understood and appreciated Colleen's point. This operation was not a lone Wolf affair where it was only he who made his way stealthily through social and organizational terrain but a joint effort requiring open and timely communication to keep both partners safe.

He caught a bare hint of amusement in her face as she turned back to the business of driving. Was she just pulling his chain?

"What's so funny?" he said. "I saw that little grin just now. Was this little lecture another one of your digs?"

She shot him a brief glance, pulled the car on the road and accelerated. "You're amazingly observant," she said, passing a slower vehicle. "I was not kidding about what I said; just surprised how well you took it."

"I see," he said. "I admit to having a red in tooth and claw rep—with my adversaries. You're right about me operating like a lone Wolf; it's what makes me successful. As for this partner thing— at least the part about working in the field—is new to me, but I'm a quick study so no more lone acts without informing you first ... You may be mistaken, however, about me being obstinate and uncooperative. Wolves do hunt in packs very effectively, you know."

Colleen came to a halt adjacent to the Collins's garage just as Mr. Collins pulled in his driveway after them. Wolf introduced Colleen and the group walked into the house, where he introduced Colleen once again to Carol, Richard's wife and her daughter, Vicki.

"I've Googled you, Ms. Silverstone," Vicki said, looking impressed. "You're quite famous, you know, though," she glanced at Wolf and grinned "not nearly as famous as Mr. Wolf."

"You mean not as *infamous* as Mr. Wolf," Colleen said, her smile lighting up the room.

"Not as famous," Vickie corrected her. "But thank you so much for helping Mr. Wolf."

Colleen shot a look at Wolf who sat there looking smug.

When her mom asked her to elaborate, Vicki provided a brief overview of Silverstone Security and Investigation Services, its stellar reputation and Colleen's role in creating the firm and turning it into one of the most successful security firms in the country.

Her parents gazed at Colleen with genuine respect and appreciation, both thanking her, too.

Wolf provided a sanitized version of events the past week, omitting the attack on the highway leaving the prison and the high drama in Creede, providing just the bare facts about Welling and his death.

"I'm going to let Ms. Silverstone tell you what we discovered pursuant to James's exhumation and lab tests," Wolf said, "and also correct Vickie's perception about Ms. Silverstone's help, to wit: if it not for her, I would have very little new information to report." He gazed over at Colleen, she holding his eyes for an extended moment.

"Thank you, Mr. Wolf…"

Colleen told the family about the lab results, the confirmation that James was murdered, their discovery of how the perpetrators managed to kill James in the prison without leaving any post mortem bruising and what was next in the hunt for the murderers.

"I knew James didn't kill himself," Vicki cried, "and I know he didn't hurt that woman, either!"

"Tough I'm inclined to agree with you, Vickie," Wolf said, "we don't know that for sure, but I'm hoping once we solve this case he will be vindicated for that crime, too."

"He will." Vicki insisted.

Carol insisted they stay for some light refreshment and thirty minutes later were back on the road heading west to Denver. Wolf remembered he had not informed Sarah Lewis of everything that had transpired within the last week and slipped the phone from its holster.

"Partner," he said, holding up the phone, "do I have your blessing to call Sarah Lewis and give her an update? She and her parents have no clue about anything new since my off-road event."

"Knock yourself out, partner," she said, grinning.

Sarah was surprised, delighted and thankful upon hearing the news, Wolf thanking her for her courage to approach him back in March and share her story.

"None of this would have happened were it not for you, Sarah. Thank you."

"Just be careful, Mr. Wolf," she said, just before terminating the call.

"What did she say at the end?" Colleen asked.

"For us to be careful," he answered.

"That's an understatement," she said. "I noticed you didn't mention your near misses since the road incident."

"Don't like worrying people unnecessarily," he replied. "I do plenty for all concerned."

Colleen appeared to digest that remark and kept hauling silently west on I-76. Wolf made another call.

"Hi Kat, how are you; any hit on our elusive killer?"

"Would you mind putting the call on speaker?" Colleen said.

"Kat, I'm with Colleen; we're on the way home. I'm putting you on speaker..."

"Hello Wolf and Colleen," she said. "No hits yet. We've got the top imaging software of anyone south of the NSA, but the scrap we're working with may just be too little and the image too poor. We'll keep trying, of course."

When Colleen didn't say anything, Wolf continued. "Are you busy this weekend?"

"You're funny." They heard the humor in her tone.

"Not at all; considering you're going to paint my portrait, I naturally assumed you'd be busy mixing paints and working on your brush strokes during your free time."

"I should feel insulted by that remark," she replied, "except I do need to seriously bone up on my skills."

"So, you will be busy all weekend after all."

"I am allowed to take long breaks between brush strokes. What do you have in mind?"

"Dinner tomorrow evening," Wolf began, "lunch at Cripple Creek on Saturday, dinner and dancing in Denver."

"If I do all that you'll have to wait an extra year for your portrait."

"A man's gotta do what a man's gotta do," he intoned, "and this man needs wild dancing. Pick you up at your house at seven good for you?"

"I'll be ready ... gotta get back to work before the boss finds out and docks my pay. Bye!"

Wolf put the phone back in its belt holster. "You still okay with me dating a key employee?"

"Absolutely," Colleen confirmed. "I haven't heard her sound this happy for years..."

"I sense a but coming." Wolf quipped.

"No but," she said, "just tread carefully into Kat's emotional minefield, Wolf."

"It's not serious, just fun for both of us." She nodded and said nothing. "Feel free to tell me anything, Colleen. You know Kat far better than I do and I trust your judgement implicitly."

She made a conflicted face. "Please don't say things like that."

It sounded almost like a plea. Wolf heard it and understood it's import.

"I do trust you implicitly," he said. "I'd never have approached you otherwise. I know how you feel about me personally and you have my permission to hate my guts; I'll not hold it against you. So, tell me what you need to tell me about Kat and me."

"Kat lost her entire family in one fell swoop," she said. "Within three weeks you have nearly been killed by being run off the road, a drive by shooting, taken fire in Creede and nearly eaten by a bear. I'd go very gently into that relationship and frankly have an exit plan for sooner than later."

"I like Kat and I do hear you," he said. "I've had to tiptoe around intimate relationships most of my adult life Colleen, and it really sucks. I'm not complaining, it's just the logical consequences of the reality I've created for myself. You're right about Kat. I'll begin the disengagement process this weekend before either one of us invests more emotional commitment into the relationship." Wolf shook his head. This definitely sucked. "You're loving this, aren't you?"

"Just a little bit," she replied. "I might hate your guts, but you're also an honorable man who deserves to be happy, too. You told me you're done with your old career; things will cool down; people will forget and move on and eventfully you'll find the right woman who can take the residual heat that comes with hanging out with Grayson Wolf."

Wolf punched her gently on the shoulder. "For a major badass, Colleen Silverstone is pretty cool." A compelling thought struck him. "You know, whether you or I like it or not, we are bound tightly together. You came to help me because you felt responsible for my safety after handing me that file not wanting the name Silverstone connected to my possible demise because of it. Just imagine had I shot you at the cabin: Grayson Wolf, not satisfied with destroying Larry Silverstone in print decides to kill his daughter in reality. Face it partner: for the foreseeable future, our destinies are wrapped up in a pretty black bow. You watch my back, I watch yours—or else."

Colleen's frustrated expression confirmed his formulation.

His phone rang. "What's up RJ? ... Shit ... Understood. First flight I can get ... Right. Call you the moment I've got arrival time. Later, dude."

"What's happened?" Colleen said.

"I'm needed back at the ranch," he replied. "Remember me telling you about the free speech event CIR has organized at the gates of Virginia Patriots College? Some people don't like the idea of free speech when it's speech they don't like and the situation is rapidly deteriorating."

"I see..." She held his gaze. "I think you need to call Kat now before you leave and kick your disengagement plan in high gear."

Colleen was right. He slipped his phone from its holster once again and pressed Katherine's number.

Sometimes life does suck.

Chapter 16

Siege

Wolf spent the late-night flight to Reagan National Airport thinking about the potential for real violence as he viewed video on CIR's website of confrontations at Diana's self-proclaimed, Camp Liberty, a mile north of Virginia Patriots College's main entrance. The event had been operational for a mere three days and facing rising overt hostility from the outset, the irony of opponents exercising their right to speak and protest in order to shut down a free speech rally obviously lost on what Diana referred to as, "Lenin's contemporary useful idiots". Whatever the outcome of this confrontation between the forces of freedom and politically correct bullying, Wolf knew his plan to retreat into the background of social awareness would most likely be placed on the back burner, or more likely, shot to hell.

Breakfast Friday morning was a large mug of coffee which accompanied Wolf's five-floor commute down to Center for Individual Rights' headquarters. His first surprise came in the form of armed guards at the Center's main entrance, Wolf spotting further armed backup at the far end of the lobby. He was certain armed personnel were stationed outside the building's entrance and within its lobby, too. Fortunately, the Patrick Henry Building attracted commercial clients and condominium owners very much aligned with the Center's mission protecting individual rights including most notably, the Second Amendment. The majority of owners and occupants carried concealed weapons or supported that right and few, if any, would feel uneasy at the sight of heavily armed security stationed around the building.

He identified himself and after a visual scan was permitted to enter. It was very early and the place was already abuzz with purposeful, but undeniably nervous energy. CIR's associates were accustomed to working under pressure in the equivalent of a public fishbowl, but Diana's free speech camp had clearly ratcheted up the heat substantially.

His cell dinged. RJ's text read: "in the war room". Wolf headed to the Bret Casings' IT lair finding the place humming with activity.

"Over here, boss!" RJ cried.

"Good morning everyone," Wolf said, joining a small group assembled in front of a computer looking at videos and data on its multi-screen monitor. "What's this?"

"Hi Wolf," Brett said, looking up. "Just preparing the morning's blasts to the teeming masses. Tweets, clips, policy statements and so forth. How was Colorado?"

"Making progress," he replied. "Things heating up at VPC, I see."

"You could say that," RJ answered. "The whackadoos been trying to disrupt the rally, but Diana and Teena are several steps ahead of their nonsense … if you're ready I'll drive you over to Camp Liberty."

The college was an hour's drive west, fortunately against the morning rush which typically could add another thirty minutes to the trip. After updating RJ about developments in the Lewis-Collins case, RJ told Wolf about the free speech rally at Virginia Patriots College on Tuesday morning sponsored by that school's Students for Individual Rights and its aftermath.

"Camp Liberty, at Lawson's Conference Center, was ready for participants this past Sunday and people started arriving that afternoon," RJ began. "By next evening there were about five hundred people at the Center. Diana and a few dozen supporters went to the college, the rally held on Patriot's Green where SIR had set up tables and a sound system. The event attracted hundreds of students, Diana along with selected students and several college professors spoke, answered questions and distributed lots of literature."

"And everything went peacefully?" Wolf asked.

"It went as expected," RJ replied. "Of course, there were hecklers, spouting typical PC crap, name calling; the usual mindless, intolerance of the right of others to voice their opinion and views. A thug contingent rushed the display tables and tried to do their vandal thing, but Teena and her team interfered with their plans. When a couple tried to shove their way past them, they found themselves face-down in the dirt."

"Did Teena hurt them?"

"Sore wrists and grass between their teeth," RJ said. "Just defending our property from the riff-raff."

From the top of a ridge over a mile away, Wolf spotted the tight cluster of structures comprising Diana's free speech colony. Most puzzling was what appeared to be a multi-hued wall enclosing the settlement within.

"What is all that around the camp?" Wolf asked.

"The palisade," RJ replied. "After the rally on campus, Diana and her group retreated back to the camp. Later that afternoon and early evening, groups of students kept raiding the camp screaming obscenities, throwing bottles and breaking stuff. It was clear the punks had no respect for private property, pushing their way into the compound, so Diana told Teena to launch the palisade. By Wednesday morning the shipping containers rolled in and the wall was operational by noon. Yesterday evening a bunch tried to breech the barrier and ran into Teena's rubber hose brigade. Ever get hit by a rubber hose? Stings like hell."

"Where were the cops?" Wolf asked.

"Oh, they're there, keeping peace and order—at the campus gates," RJ said, disgusted. "Why I called you back; thought you better be here and see this shit up close and personal."

Wolf looked at RJ, not sure if his friend was teasing him, a reasonable assumption given his joker reputation.

"Teena actually clipped them with rubber hoses?"

He nodded vigorously. "Hell yeah; warned them she would if they tried to scale the wall."

This was worse than he thought. Wolf had expected trouble: screaming, throwing objects, blocking streets and the like. That the police stood aside allowing rioters to trample across private property, harass people and destroy property was unacceptable.

Approaching the conference center, they were met by a group of people effectively blocking the access road to the center's entrance a hundred yards away. RJ rolled up to the human barrier stopping a few feet short of them. A representative of the group sauntered up to RJ's window her face—Wolf assumed it was a female—sporting an expression of bored distain, her black makeup, piercings and slovenly appearance destroying any hint of a comely face she may have possessed once upon a time.

A grin spread across RJ's face as he lowered his window.

"The road is closed."

RJ's grin grew larger.

"You can't enter."

RJ's grin grew to maniacal proportions. "Five seconds."

"What about five seconds?"

"Four seconds."

"What the fuck is wrong with you?" she sneered.

"Now it's two seconds."

RJ rolled up his window and pressed a button. A high-pitched piercing scream exploded outside the car, it's volume so loud Wolf clamped hands on his ears. The crowd blocking the access road fell back, scurrying away from the car as fast as they could, hands pressing on ears in a futile attempt to block the nauseating, earsplitting screeching. RJ drove the car down the now cleared road, terminating his primal scream machine and rolled up to the wall, one of the shipping containers sliding open sufficiently to allow the car to pass through, sliding shut behind it.

"Welcome to Valley Forge," RJ shouted, a requirement considering their own hearing was compromised by the intense sound. He parked the vehicle next to others in an open area.

"Jeezus RJ," Wolf said, rubbing his ears, the ringing retreating to a loud buzz. "That was loud enough to burst eardrums!"

"They're trespassing on private property, preventing access to those who have a legitimate right to come and go," RJ replied. "It's either the Primal Scream or run over their collective asses."

RJ was quite capable of doing what he threatened, Wolf silently agreeing that the scream was preferable to tire tracks over prone bodies. They got out of the car, RJ escorting him to a large, single storied structure at the far end of the parking area. A picket line of American and Gadsden flags lining the walkway fluttered in the breeze.

"Welcome to Camp Liberty," RJ cried, entering the building. "The place used to be a farm, the Lawson family transforming it into a conference center and nature retreat back in 2002." He led Wolf through a corridor entering a large room. "Our fearless alpha wolf has arrived!"

Diana and Annika came forward, happy to see Wolf, each giving him a tight hug. Teena, standing with a group of security personnel in the far corner, raised a hand in greeting.

"Glad you could get back so soon," Diana said. "I'm sure RJ has briefed you about the challenges we're facing, not that I didn't expect trouble, just surprised it started so quickly."

"What's up with the local police tucking their tail and hiding behind college walls?" Wolf asked. "Call the governor and have him get on their ass before conditions deteriorate further."

Diana made a resolute face. "Not doing that. I'm not going to let the County Executive and his police captain off the hook for whatever mayhem these Bolshevik wannabees commit."

Wolf looked worried. "You do know there will be violence."

Diana shot a glance over at Teena. "And we're prepared. They've invaded our private space on day one causing destruction and threatening people so we erected the wall complete with no trespassing signs plastered everywhere. Being the law-abiding citizens they are, yesterday they stormed the barricades, throwing rocks over them. When some managed to scramble on top, they got a nasty surprise as our security force wacked them with rubber hoses, the barbarians beating a hasty retreat. Getting hit with a three-foot hose stings. We've got lots more surprises in store for these brats if they fail to conform to our laws."

"They'll retaliate by becoming even more violent." Wolf warned.

Diana held his eyes. "Yes, they will. And we will defend ourselves. When it becomes hot and heavy and the shit hits the fan, questions will be asked why the local police failed to act, sitting on their hands allowing these punks to riot without responding."

Wolf glanced at Annika. "You need to get out of here now. We can't have our CFO get hurt, or worse." Seeing Annika's expression harden, he added, "Today, Annika. We need you be back at the Center ... and that's an order. RJ?"

"Annika will go out the way she came in," he said, sounding mysterious and grinning. "Helicopter."

"Even better," Wolf replied, feeling relieved. "Get it done."

"Righto, boss."

Wolf turned his attention back to Diana. "I thought you were expecting at least a thousand people? What happened?"

"And I thought you resigned as CEO, shouting orders nilly-willy," she said, grinning happily. "We had a thousand; after groups of punks invaded the camp that first day and the failure of local police not to uphold the law, we knew the insurgents saw that as a green light to run amok at will. Many of our people were families with kids and older folks, so we discussed the issue and the risks associated with staying. I added a push, saying that anyone not prepared to stand and fight should leave. About six hundred did, mostly older folks and those with families. Currently we have about 350 remaining." When he didn't say anything, Diana added, with a glint in her eye, "You want to join Annika in the copter?"

Wolf gave her a most sarcastic expression. "Say that again and I'll kick your ass."

She laughed. "Now that you brought it up, how's Colleen Silverstone's ass?"

"Magnificent, if you must know," he retorted. "It appears she and I have been handcuffed together by converging interests of critical importance as we work together solving a crime of rape and murder."

Wolf explained how each had to make sure the other wasn't killed because both had much to lose in terms of reputation, negative media attention and possibly even criminal proceedings against the survivor of the pair.

A humorous expression appeared on Diana's face. "You should marry the girl; she'd provide serious protection, that's for sure. Add a prenup cutting off the survivor from inheriting a dime from the dearly departed and you've eliminated a key motive for doing in a spouse when the cops suspect the survivor."

"I think you have a vivid imagination," he replied. "Perhaps you should become a writer of fiction."

"Stranger matches have occurred," Diana rejoined. She looked at him knowingly. "Opposites do attract and complementary opposites form the strongest bonds."

Wolf gave her one of his long-suffering expressions. "Now you're a matchmaker? Just because you found *your* perfect complementary opposite doesn't mean most people ever do. How about we put a pin in the Colleen-Wolf nuptials and talk about the barbarians at our gates instead?"

"Not just at our gates, Wolf. In the college, too. Yesterday, we got news that a student mob rushed into Professor Alexander's engineering class, shouting invectives and refusing to leave."

"He sponsors the colleges' Students for Individual Rights group," RJ said.

"Yes," Diana replied. "No coincidence there. They wanted to interrupt his teaching, but the man used the digital overhead to write comments and instructions for completing lessons."

"Very resourceful of the good professor." Wolf agreed.

"Until they smashed the unit," Diana said, looking pointedly at him.

A sarcastic grin slid across Wolf's mouth. "Anything and everything is acceptable when one is a member of the Nazional Widerstand fighting for the right to maintain terminal stupidity."

Diana's expression became resolute. "When I launched this project, I knew we'd face blowback. How could we not? President Wilson and her useful idiots have turned Virginia Patriots College into a center for Progressive foment. What a joke; there's absolutely nothing progressive about them and their Marxist-Leninist ideology. The irony of a college founded in honor of American patriots who fought and died for liberty being turned into a national cheerleader for totalitarian ideals is totally lost on Wilson and her ilk."

"You're too generous, Diana," Wolf said. "It's not irony; it's intention. Wilson and her goons want to smash any association with the word patriot much like ISIS smashes historical sites, churches, mosques and cultural antiquities. They're all nothing more than cultural and ideological barbarians."

"And I'm sick to death of the whole lot," she retorted. "Wilson allows her student thugs to scour the campus intimidating peers and the few professors like Nicholas Alexander who refuse to be silenced."

Wolf was about to ask about Lee Sterling when RJ called her name from across the room.

"Time for your broadcast," he said, walking toward them.

"Gotta go and rile up the Ethernet," she said. "RJ, you and Teena take Wolf on a tour of the battlements—whoops, I mean camp." She grinned mischievously and made for the far exit.

RJ corralled Teena and the tour of camp liberty got underway, Wolf following them to the roof of the building providing an unobstructed view of the makeshift settlement. Looking east, behind the building, he saw clustered tightly together five concentric arcs of tents facing two large tents that stood close to the building. A distance beyond the last row of tents were a bank of portable toilets beyond which stood the shipping container ramparts, enclosing the entire camp in the shape of a huge square.

"There's got to be a hundred shipping containers," Wolf said, genuinely awed by the scene. "Where'd they come from and tell me why this display of defense is not way over the top?"

"One hundred twenty containers make up the wall," Teena answered. "Thirty for each side. The extra ones you see to your left contain food and medical supplies and other materials needed to survive in this island for weeks. As for the wall, it's not over the top any more than police or soldiers wearing armored vests is over the top. Keeps us much safer than without it and it's my job to keep us safe."

"As for where," RJ said, "twelve miles west is a huge transport facility storing over two thousand used containers. Being former military, Teena knows how to plan for a mission, reserving two hundred containers weeks back and paying a generous fee for expedited delivery when called. Check this…"

He produced his phone and touched the photo icon and handed the unit to Wolf who scrolled through the array.

"This must have been an awesome sight," he said. "These pics reminds me of the Red Ball Express during World War Two with hundreds of trucks rolling through France bringing supplies and ammo to the Front."

"And just as fast," Teena said. "Took a morning to haul 'em in and set 'em up. Each unit is forty feet long, nine feet high and unmovable, short of using a Mack truck."

"What's under the tarps on the flatbeds near the parking lot?" Wolf asked.

"Just one more surprise for our North Korean friends on campus," Teena grinned.

"What kind of surprise?" Wolf said, hoping it wasn't a battery of rocket launchers she'd found at an Army surplus store. Not that such an item would be sold by any, but Teena was a most resourceful individual with numerous contacts in the military and private security and push comes to shove, she'd secure rocket launchers and rockets.

Teena handed him a pair of binoculars. "Take a look toward the college, west of the main entrance."

Wolf lifted the field glasses, adjusting the focus ring to his eyesight. Though a mile distant, the powerful military-grade glasses allowed him to see people and detail as though they were standing across a room. Scanning right, he saw what he supposed Teena wanted him to see: a long line of media vans and trucks sporting satellite dishes and long antennas that under the compressed image, made the row of vehicles looks like a horned caterpillar.

He scanned back along the road leading to the college until he passed the access road to the camp and a length further north. A wry smile appeared on his face and he lowered the glasses.

"Cops and media everywhere, but not one in sight of our gate." He handed the glasses back to Teena. "We've got the local constabulary hugging the college perimeter and their media pals standing at the ready with bated breath to report every sneeze, cough and bathroom break."

"That's pretty harsh, boss," RJ said, displaying a toothy grin. "Them being grossly underpaid public servants and all."

"I assume we're documenting all this, RJ?" Wolf asked.

"Absolutely," he replied. "In living technicolor. That County Executive is handing us his head on a plate, because when shit happens—as it already has—and the country discovers he ordered the police to stand down and let things take their course—he's up a very shitty creek without a paddle."

"I guess it's true what Forrest Gump said." Teena interjected. "Stupid is as stupid does."

"I just don't understand what he hopes to gain by letting punks run amok in his district?" RJ said, shaking his head. "Maybe he thinks no one cares what happens out in the sticks?"

"Or maybe he's banging the college president." Teena said.

Wolf and RJ peered at her. Wolf spoke first.

"Is this true?"

A tight smile played on her lips. "Something about politics and strange bedfellows."

"Truth or fiction?" Wolf demanded.

"Truth … fiction … truth … fiction…" Teena chanted, moving her hands up and down like scales in time to the words. Seeing Wolf's impatient stare, she added, "Rumors, rumors, but where there's smoke, most likely some hot 'n heavy fire happening. I've got my peeps on it."

"That would make one hell of a story in your next novel," RJ said, giving Wolf the eye.

"It'll make one hell of a story when our legal team comes down upon the Executive and Wilson with flaming sword in hand," Wolf replied. He sighed. "Let's hope any future disturbances are limited to gnashing of teeth and stamping of feet."

"I'm good with that," Teena said. "But if they come at us violently, they'll be sorry."

RJ must have gotten a call because he fished the phone from his pocket. He looked at the screen for a moment.

"Text from Diana; she done with the morning report. Let's go down."

RJ delivered Wolf to a small room that had been turned into Diana's field office. She pointed to a pair of comfortable seats near the window.

Once seated, Diana said, "What do you think of fortress liberty?"

"Impressive," Wolf replied. "How was your daily report?"

"Also, impressive," Diana replied, a satisfied expression on her face.

Changing the subject, Wolf asked about the latest developments regarding Lee Sterling and wondering if he was at the camp.

"No," she replied, firmly. "We're keeping him far away; do not want him involved, period … Juan's team has assembled a law suit against the college, waiting for the most auspicious moment to file it. Once things get hot and heavy we'll use the lawsuit to add pressure on Wilson."

"And the class action? How's that going?"

"Being assembled piece by piece," she said. "One clarification about my student comment earlier: it's not just students; it's a passel of outsiders—*paid* protestors."

"Paid," Wolf said. "By whom and how much?"

"Donations to ultra-liberal websites for starters," Diana replied, "and millions from sources such as Soros, though he denies it."

"Much like he denies working with the Nazis in Hungary then with the Communists after they took over." Wolf scoffed. "Will the class action include financial sources as part of the suit?"

"It would dilute the effort; that might come at a later time, however," Diana replied. "A keystone of the suit against VPC is the fact that Wilson has not only done nothing about outsiders on campus, she has actively invited non-students to participate in campus activities and events. We'll be going after her lock, stock and stinking barrel."

"And the other colleges?" Wolf asked.

"Juan is forging the largest class action wrecking ball ever," she said, her eyes glowing with excitement. "It'll make the cigarette and asbestos class actions look like peanuts in comparison. Juan and his team are working twenty-four seven every day to get ready for a broadside at the colleges and universities leading the PC-Progressive bullshit first, then work our way down the list. It will have the impact of a thousand legal neutron bombs."

Wolf had been so preoccupied with his personal quest for justice back in Colorado, he had failed to grasp the full import of what Diana and his Center for Individual Rights were in the process of implementing. Studying her face, he saw the determination expressed in the set of her jaw, the resolve in her eyes and the warrior-like stillness and posture. He recalled RJ's quip about the camp—Valley Forge—and saw in Diana sitting across from him that first and greatest American general, his back to the wall, facing overwhelming odds, overcoming every adversity to triumph in the end. He smiled approvingly at the thought that nearly 250 years later a woman by the name of Ruiz would be leading the next American revolution for individual rights.

"What are you smiling at?" Diana said, looking at Wolf suspiciously.

"You're an amazing woman and a true Virginia patriot," he replied. "I know you're disappointed in me ending my career as an expose novelist, but I want you to know I will always stand shoulder to shoulder with you in our fight for liberty."

Her expression softened. "Wolf, I've never been disappointed in you. I get it about rooting around in cultural cesspools; one can only stand so much exposure to human sludge. You've done much to expose the intellectual scum seeping into our culture for decades and made it possible for us, here, today, to shine the disinfectant light of day upon their vile, rotten ideas and we're going to keep doing it until they slink back into the sewers from whence they spawned."

Wolf nodded slowly, thinking about the consequences of these vile, rotten ideas over the last century, rising like ideological zombies, time and time again spreading decay and death with every touch. Several hundred million innocent souls murdered by knife, gun and starvation by mass murderers proclaiming a worker's paradise or a Europe cleansed of Der Untermensch. The rot created by Collectivism under any name kills and stinks the same.

He saw Diana looking at him with that knowing smile, having gotten used to Wolf's mental pauses over the years.

"Sorry, just thinking about what you said. It's Liberty or Death. It always comes down to Liberty or Death, Diana. Look were a century of compromise has gotten America: approaching two hundred trillion unfunded debt, Presidents bowing and scraping before dictators and misogynists, our universities gleefully transforming our children into enemies of Western culture while the media panders to tribalism, the lowest form of racism."

"It's disgusting to see so much of the media pushing division instead of unity," she replied. "And even though a majority of the country recognize the media lies, distorts information and produces fake news, I see too many people being complacent, sitting on the sidelines, watching as their culture passes away in front of their eyes and do nothing. We can't let it go, Wolf. We *won't* let it go."

There was a loud rap on the door, opening a second later. Teena took a step into the office.

"Just got news from our people on campus," she said, her tone crisp. "A mob stormed into Professor Alexander's office, attacked the man and ransacked the place. I've got footage of the mayhem from inside and out. They were tossing books and papers out of the professor's windows."

"And no one did anything to stop them?" Diana said, disgusted. "How badly was the professor hurt?"

"According to our people, it was all over in a couple minutes," Teena replied. "Alexander was roughed up, pushed into a corner and the office trashed. He'll be okay, I think."

"Has Wilson made her, children behave, announcement yet?" Diana scoffed. "Followed, of course, by blathering on about respecting each other and running to one's coziest safe space comforted by hugging a favorite stuffed animal?"

"Mean, unfeeling woman," Wolf chided, shooting her a look of mock disapproval.

"That's not all," Teena said, redirecting their attention. "The word is that a contingent of the Red Fascists—"

"Red Fascists?" Wolf interjected. "Blended accuracy. I like it."

"What these punks are," Teena agreed. "Don't want to be accused of discrimination, so Red Fascists fits the bill. Anyway, I've alerted my minute men and women to man the barricades because Lenin's useful idiots are marching our way."

Chapter 17

Stand Your Ground

Wolf required no military-grade field glasses to spot the horde snaking its way north, blocking both lanes of the highway forcing drivers onto the shoulder where they crept slowly along to their destinations. Being experienced with mobs, he guesstimated its size at several hundred. He also needed no binoculars to tell him there wasn't a police officer or cruiser in sight.

"Why do I feel like I'm living in Jamestown colony all of a sudden?" Wolf said, peering over the shipping container palisade from the roof of the conference center.

"And like that Jamestown colony," Teena said, "our little colony requires a wall to keep the Vandals out." She shot Wolf a droll look. "Feeling better about my makeshift bulwark, are we?"

"Why is it heads of security all seems to sport a smart mouth?" Wolf retorted.

A bright smile lit up her face. "Getting to know Colleen Silverstone better, are we?"

Wolf shot her a knowing look. "Like I said, smart mouth."

Teena raised her field glass. "Oh, oh. Looks like the restless natives are bringing gifts."

Wolf squinted to get a clearer view of the marching horde. "What are you talking about?"

She ignored him, tapping her finger on a small unit in her ear. "Attention everyone: our uninvited guests are carrying assault paraphernalia. Fire crew on standby; repulse crew to your posts."

"Did you say they're armed with assault weapons?" Wolf said.

Teena shook her head. "Not guns—yet. Bows, sling shots, ball launchers: dog owners use them to fling balls downrange, except it's not balls they're going to launch over the wall; rocks, most likely, though *great flaming balls of fire* is a possibility."

"Thus, the fire brigade on standby," Wolf said.

"There is nothing we are not prepared for, Wolf." She gave him a sober glance. "Nothing."

The adage, out of the frying pan into the fire, popped into his mind having been shot at several times recently. "I sincerely hope it doesn't ever come to that."

"Copy that," Teena replied. "I do want to remind you the local police are busy tickling their personal organs a mile south. That's a green light for the riffraff to express their views in a more explosive manner."

"The wall is a large perimeter to cover, Teena," Wolf said. "If my crew were planning to employ deadly violence, I'd have them scale the wall at numerous points."

"And if you and your crew climbed on top of the wall and began shooting," Teena said, her tone icy, "the snipers I've position on this roof will end you and your armed assault in short order."

Wolf stared at Teena. She didn't smile and she didn't blink; her glistening ebony face calm and serene. A different face popped into his mind, her skin color two shades lighter than Teena's but that same steely look in her eye warning the stupid or foolish to stand down, or else.

Teena must have been thinking that Wolf's silence suggested he didn't really believe her about the use of deadly force, adding, "In the words of Capt. John Parker at Lexington, April 19th, 1775, 'Stand your ground. Do not fire unless fired upon. But if they mean to have a war, let it begin here'. If they fire upon us, Wolf, my people will return fire. If you don't agree, you need to tell Diana right now."

Wolf held the warrior's eyes and nodded slowly. "Just make sure your shooters do not fire indiscriminately."

"Not to worry," she replied, her smile lighting up her face. "My shooters are among the most discriminating marksmen and women found anywhere."

Teena excused herself, Wolf remaining on the roof observing the crowd swell as it came to a halt near the access road to the camp, their chants filling the air as hundreds of voices joined the verbal barrage. Wolf couldn't make out much in the rumble of noise emanating from the highway, but he did catch the shout-out about hate speech, that free pass permitting one to righteously and justifiably exercise their own hate by violently striking out at person or persons deemed guilty of hate speech. All in the name of protecting freedom of speech, of course.

The crowd shouted, gnashed its teeth and stomped the ground for some time, when Wolf spotted a large contingent was making its way up the access road, treading on private property, waiving arms and shouting for the others to follow. More and more did, and the group split into two columns, working their way around the perimeter much like a swarm of ants encircling a lump of ice-cream that had fallen from a child's cone.

"Excuse me, sir," a male voice said.

Wolf turned to see a squad of heavily armed security agents joining him on the roof. The one who had spoken to him came up while the others took positions at corners.

"I'm going to have to ask you to clear the roof," he said. "You're totally exposed up here and make an easy target. Thank you for your cooperation."

Having been a target of vitriol in the form of "hate speech," flying objects and a few common assaults most of his adult life, Wolf readily agreed he didn't want to be an easy target for someone to take a shot at.

"Of course. Please stay safe...and thank *you*."

Looking for Diana upon returning to the main floor, he was directed to the largest of the big tents out back, nicknamed Big Top as a joke in consideration for the circus-like events surrounding—literally at this point—CIR's free speech rally. Approaching Big Top's main entrance, he heard Diana's voice talking to the supporters inside, taking a position at the rear. She was standing on a stage, cameras pointed in her direction, hand movements underscoring her comments.

"...long past the point where college administrators can claim their polices are designed to keep all students safe. Administrators like Dr. Wilson of VPC promotes required 'sensitivity' training and supports student protestors who want to punish students and faculty for so-called 'offensive speech' because it may be a threat to student safety. Yet President Wilson doesn't exhibit much concern for behavior and actions representing a *genuine* threat to student safety. This is especially true when the threat of harm is directed at students or faculty who don't toe President Wilson's party line."

A murmur of agreement filled the Big Top. Diana took a drink from a bottle of water, put it back on a nearby table and continued.

"Three weeks ago, members of Students for Individual Rights, a registered campus organization, were attacked by other VPC students for the political crime of displaying materials expressing ideas contrary to the thugs who attacked them."

Diana told how the few students defended themselves against physical attack and the injustice of SIR students receiving far harsher treatment and subsequent punishment than the any member of the assailants that initiated the violence. She explained that disruptions of SIR activities, events and disruptions of invited speakers holding contrary views to the politically correct monopoly of VPC, had been going on for years becoming especially prominent since the last presidential election.

"What we are witnessing in the media, social networks and on many college campuses," Diana said, "is the triumph of emotion over reason. Unlike a few years ago, today colleges actively promote the idea that if you *feel* threatened by ideas you don't like, then you're justified—*righteously justified*—in taking action against those who hold or speak these ideas." She paused, and peered into the cameras pointed at her.

"College administrators like Dr. Wilson of Virginia Patriot's College actively pandering to emotional excess, 'safe spaces' being a perfect example, contribute to infantilizing young adults under their charge. Ayn Rand, better than anyone, understood the difference between reason and emotion: 'When men abandon reason,' Rand said, 'they open the door to physical force as the only alternative and the inevitable consequence.' Dr. Wilson supports emotion over reason and the outcome, as Rand predicted, is physical force and violence..."

As Diana continued, talking about the attacks on Professor Alexander and on the camp, Wolf became aware of a metallic rumbling sound that rose in volume, becoming loud enough to interfere with the meeting in the tent. Having grown up around a deaf aunt, he had become sensitive to sounds and knew immediately what was happening.

"The barbarians are emoting on the wall," he said, to one of the security guards near him. "Using hard objects, mostly stones I imagine."

The center of the camp was a hundred yards from the nearest wall, but several hundred trespassers banging stones on hollow shipping containers raised a racket loud enough to be annoying, to be sure. Diana included this latest violation in her presentation, pointing out that these people had no respect for private property and no regard for anyone's right to peacefully assemble and exercise their right to discuss ideas and issues.

The meeting broke up ten minutes later, Wolf following Diana back to her office inside the conference center. The building's brick walls and double-paned windows muffling the rumbling sounds substantially.

"They're going to keep this up for hours," Wolf said.

"And we're going to ignore them for hours," Diana retorted. "Eventually their arms will give out."

"What's next on the agenda?" Wolf asked.

"A march to the college for a free-speech rally tomorrow morning on Patriot's Green, VPC's main plaza," she replied. "Right in front of the media. Of course, we'll have our own media there to report on them."

"Report on the media?"

"Yup," Diana confirmed. "We're going to give them a taste of their own medicine. Stick mics right in their colluding faces."

"You're going to march a couple hundred people a mile through a gauntlet of unbalanced Red Fascists?" Wolf said, looking alarmed. "You're asking for trouble."

"No, I'm not," she replied. "What we're doing, Wolf, is exercising our damned right to peacefully march to the college, rally and protest Wilson's policies."

"A mile-long trek with no police protection," he protested.

"That's right, Wolf," Diana replied, her tone underscoring her words. "Exercising our rights while the police sit on their asses at the college gates instead of doing their job to ensure a peaceful march and rally."

"Quite a risk to make a point," Wolf said.

"And livestreamed every step of the way," she said, a wicket grin on her face. "We'll have camera crews stationed all over the place documenting this entire fiasco and when we're done, we'll sue the County Executive and his lover back to the Stone Age!"

"What if you or others get hurt, or killed?" Wolf said.

Diana held his eyes. "We're not the only ones that bleed, Wolf. They become violent and attack us, they're gonna be sorry."

Wolf was about to reply when several shots rang out.

"What the hell?" Diana said, face whirling toward the window.

"Shotgun fire," Wolf said. "Came from the area of the northern and eastern walls."

They hurried to the door and making their way across the main room when Teena intercepted them coming from the stairway leading to the roof.

She made a dismissive gesture. "Took out several drones crossing the walls. Probably just trying to take photos, but we're not taking any chances because drones have been used by the Red Fascists in Berkeley and elsewhere to drop Molotov cocktails. Far easier than shooting clay pigeons, for sure."

"Hopefully the media team captured the drones?" Diana asked.

"Yes, they most surely did," Teena replied. "Got eyes and ears everywhere—we'll capture every indiscretion."

"Every indiscretion?" Wolf said, sounding dubious.

Teena shot him shrewd stare. "They piss on the wall, we'll record it. Floozy gives a blowjob in the bushes, we'll capture his and her close-up. The Lemmings saddle up and swarm, we'll get the footage and it's all going to be broadcast worldwide to mega-million electronic teats. No one is going to get away with anything, anywhere, anymore."

Wolf started to laugh. "After this reality show you've got going comes to an end, I'm moving to a remote cabin in the far reaches of Alaska where no electronic unit is seen or heard and the skies are devoid of drones all day."

"You can run," Teena said, a bright smile on her face, "but you can't hide from the electronic beast ravening to suck out every last remnant of your private life for public consumption."

"I think I'd rather face the Zombie apocalypse than your swarm of electronic terminators, Teena," Wolf said, grinning. "At least the Zombies just want to eat my brain, not get inside it turning me into some mindless robot twitching to every electric stimulus."

"So says the man who has wormed his way into the very private affairs of man and the edifices he's erected, exposing the whole lot for public consumption." Diana reminded him with a glint in her eye.

"Keep poking the Wolf, Diana and you may become the feature attraction in one of my novel yet," he teased.

"You're done with that, remember?"

"Keep poking me and the Wolf might just bite that finger off," he replied. "Figuratively speaking, of course."

"And my electronic eyes and ears will be recording that event for posterity," Teena promised.

Wolf peered at the security chief thinking about another head of security. "Remind me never to introduce you to Colleen Silverstone, because the woman would snap you up in a heartbeat." Spotting a subtle change in Teena's expression, he said, "What don't I know?"

Her face lit up; the subtle expression blossoming into full drollness.

"Been there, met that, rejected offer," Teena chanted. "Trice."

"What?" Diana said, clearly surprised by this alarming news. "Silverstone's been trying to poach you?"

"Not poach; recruit." Teena replied. "After my term of enlistment was over. That woman has her tentacles imbedded in every branch of the Service; that's how she snaps up the best of the best making her company the leading security firm in the country—in the world, probably."

"The leading security firm in the world. Imagine that." Diana shot Wolf a droll look. "And its owner takes time off running her billion-dollar business to go slumming with little insignificant Wolfie."

"Little and insignificant?" Wolf said. "I will remember this indignity."

Several shotgun booms brought everyone's focus back to the business at hand.

"More drones, I suspect." Teena taped a finger on her earpiece and listened for a few moments. "Not cameras; incendiary:

gasoline. The good news is that it takes a more powerful, therefore more expensive, unit to lift a bottle full of liquid plus detonator. Blasting three of them out of the air sets the owners back at least $600 to $1000."

"Your shooters see them in the daylight. What about nighttime?" Wolf asked.

"My shooters see them long before they get near the wall," she replied. "We've got camera arrays hooked to AI programs that spot movement, identify it and project a path within a mille-second, so we know it's coming and from what direction. At night, their heat signature lights the little buggers up quite nicely and our shooters see them and take them out. I've got other ways up my sleeve, but best policy is need to know and what you don't know won't come to bite you in the ass later."

"Are we going to let them drum on the wall all night?" Wolf asked.

Teena shot a look over at Diana who answered.

"Yes, we are. It's annoying, but not enough to interfere with us sleeping," she said. "Might even act as white noise helping everyone to drop off to a restful sleep. We'll have lots of tired punks in the morning as we march to the college gates, though I suspect they'll get tired by nightfall and give it up."

*　　*　　*　　*

Diana's prediction the rabble at the wall would eventually tire of hammering on the metal palisade came to pass shortly before midnight when the last of the metallic rumbling ended. Wolf spent a restful night sleeping on a cot tucked into a corner of a small room along with eight other CIR personnel.

By the time he made an appearance in Big Top, the lines for breakfast had receded substantially, securing a tasty-looking plate filled with eggs, bacon and hash brown potatoes. He filled a large insulated cup with hot coffee adding a shot of Half & Half and made for the reserved tables standing near an adjacent edge of the tent.

"Good morning everyone," Wolf said, taking a seat next to RJ. "Looks like Diana was right about it being a quiet night. No drone invaders either, I take it, since no gunshots were heard."

"You'd be wrong about the drones."

Wolf looked at the woman dressed in a uniform sitting diagonally across the table. He'd seen her around the office back in Tyson's Corner, but didn't recall her name.

She smiled and said, "Naomi Brown, sir. We took down five drones: three before two a.m., two more before sunrise."

"Naomi," Wolf said, deliberately repeating her name, peering at her for some handle to help him connect the name with the face for the future. "Five drones. How come I didn't hear any gunshots? I'm a light sleeper."

"Didn't use firearms because we don't want to startle people sleeping," she replied. "Used multiple-shot HCAG on the buggers. Smashed them to bits." Seeing Wolf and some others around the table looking confused, she explained. "HCAG: High Compression Air Guns. Looks a lot like a M32 grenade launcher, five cartridges filled with various sized pellets, air compressor powered. Effective range of fifty yards. It's pop and drop."

"Why not use them during the day, too?" Wolf asked. "Why use shotguns?"

"Deterrent, Mr. Wolf," Naomi replied. "Air guns are considerably quieter than firearms. The sound of shotguns is unmistakable and heard well beyond the barrier." A cute smile appeared. "Besides, the drones provide target practice for the shooters."

Wolf held her gaze. "Shooters, like yourself, I assume."

"Took out two yesterday," she replied.

Wolf gave her a thumb's up. "Thank you—and congratulations."

"They put 'em up, I'll shoot 'em down," she quipped.

RJ leaned closer to Wolf. "I'm nervous about the march today. There are serious wackos out there and I can see people getting hurt. We've got our own security tagging along, but they're not the police."

Wolf knew RJ was right. People were going to get hurt. He also knew Diana would make sure the entire world would be watching. He made a snorting sound thinking about something.

"What?" RJ said, probably thinking Wolf's noise dismissed his concerns.

"Oak trees," Wolf replied, enigmatically.

"Oak trees," RJ repeated, looking confused. "I appreciate their shade and fall colors as much as the next man, but what's that got to do with the march?"

"The nation's Founders planted a healthy seedling, feeding it the most nourishing and powerful ideological fertilizer formulated in the history of mankind," Wolf said. "The oak grew tall and strong, but many—Franklin being one—were skeptical about the Republic lasting longer than a few generations, humans being fallible and all."

"Go on," RJ said. "Please."

"The thing about oak trees, RJ," Wolf said, smiling knowingly at the meaning of RJ's 'please', "they take many decades to grow to maturity, last for centuries and look as healthy at 250 as they did at twenty-five. Then without warning, during a passing storm, the mighty oak splits and crashes to the ground. That's when all can see and understand why that healthy, vital oak appeared to die so suddenly."

RJ grinned, shooting him a long-suffering look. He was very familiar with how Wolf loved drawing out a story, feeding the listener more and more information, building up to a climax.

Wolf got the hint and continued. "Standing next to the corpse, the people discover that the mighty oak's heart had been rotting away for decades, weakening the structure, until the shell shattered under a stiff breeze. Over time, the oak's remains decompose becoming undifferentiated matter, absorbed and digested by weeds and other vegetation, while any of its acorns that dare to germinate, shrivel and perish in toxic soil never to rise again. Nature and toxic ideologies both being a harsh and unforgiving mistress."

"Damn, man," RJ cried, "I feel *so* much better now. I can't tell you how much I'm looking forward to traipsing through the gauntlet of toxicity on the way to the VPC this morning!"

Wolf barked a laugh. "Anyone ever tell you that you're one sarcastic bastard?"

"Mr. Wolf," Naomi said, "by toxic ideologies; you're talking about fascism and communism?"

"I'm referring to the premise all collectivist ideas and schemes are based upon," he replied. "Altruism, the belief that individuals are sacrificial animals, a cog in the social fabric to be used and dispensed of as seen fit by the great and all powerful Collective."

Naomi peered at Wolf, her expression strongly suggesting she believed he was pulling her leg. He smiled and continued.

"I see you're skeptical about the great and powerful Collective," he teased. "Think, Borg. One big, collective brain. Individuals need not apply."

"That's nonsense," she retorted. "I don't work for some great Collective; I work for CIR, hired by my boss, who was hired by her boss who in turn was hired by you. Individuals all. Collectives need not apply."

"What's more moral: selflessly jumping into a river to save a stranger or selfishly keeping your feet firmly planted on terra firma?" Wolf challenged. Seeing Naomi hesitate, he pressed harder. "Come on! He's drowning. So what if you're a poor swimmer? Jump in!" As she considered her answer, he said, "Too late, he's gone. What a kind of selfish, unfeeling, bad, immoral, evil person are you anyway! It's your duty to risk life and limb for others and instead you did nothing but stand there watching as that poor person drowned!"

Wolf and RJ both gave Naomi the most uncompromising, judgmental glare they could muster. Wolf noticed her eyes were looking at someone behind him.

"Leave the poor woman alone, you two troublemakers," Diana said. "Allow me to give you the thumbnail version to Wolf's epic rendition, Naomi: no one has a moral claim to your life and you have no moral claim to the lives of others. Period. Now, if you are done with breakfast, the event Steering Committee is meeting in the main conference room in five."

"Copy that," Wolf said, shooting a humorous look at Naomi, "my great and all powerful Collective."

The meeting lasted an hour, various heads of committees making their respective reports about expectations, readiness, and security during the march, at the rally and the march back. Because of the volatile nature of their opponents and being high profile personalities, Teena insisted Diana and Wolf wear armored vests in addition to the padded jackets and helmets that every marcher would have on. The objective was to achieve a successful demonstration, not be walking ducks exposed to Red Fascists hurling objects causing serious injury.

Wolf marveled at how Teena marshalled two hundred marchers into two tight columns of a hundred people each. She barked orders, reviewed march protocols in clear, crisp language, finishing up by walking around each column ensuring that everything was ready and everyone knew their role.

At precisely ten 'o clock, the shipping container gate slid open and the lead vehicle slowly rolled down the access road, the mass of bodies marching behind it. Diana was at the head of the first column, Wolf at the head of the second. By the time his column cleared the gate, followed by several trucks protecting their rear, the first group had reached the highway, smartly executing a left turn. Looking at the disciplined marchers ahead and around him, Wolf saw the fruition of Teena's tireless efforts and thoughtful planning: she had transformed two hundred civilian protesters into a tightly knit army marching toward their objective.

The Red Fascists wasted no time, harassing the marchers from the moment they exited the gate, hurling invectives, obscenities and the occasional handful of rocks, which, thanks to Teena's foresight, struck heads and shoulders with little effect. RJ's vision of marching through a mile-long gauntlet proved accurate, each tenth of a mile bringing increasing resistance and assault from hundreds of students joined by a flotsam and jetsam of locals along with what Diana dubbed, professional protesters that routinely appear at confrontations from sea to shining sea.

Half way to the college, conditions began to turn increasingly ugly as the mob realized the free-speech marchers were unfazed and pressing forward, a hundred Gadsden and US flags in their midst fluttering above the fray. Large groups rushed the marchers' flanks trying to disrupt the flow, only to be rebuffed by marchers closing ranks and pushing their way down the highway.

At least a dozen times, masked thugs attacked the marchers swinging clubs and batons, meeting stiff resistance from Teena's disciplined army defending themselves with rubber hoses, beating the assailants back under a flurry of painful strikes. The barrage of stones ebbed and flowed as the columns wound their way toward the college, the helmets worn by marchers fortunately preventing most head injuries. Wolf was struck several times by flying stones, his head and body gear absorbing the brunt of the impact. During a particular intense bombardment, a stone clipped his cheek, causing blood to flow freely down his chin, which he stemmed by pressing a cloth on the wound. Looking at the marchers around him, it was clear from the way some were limping, holding or massaging limbs and attending to cuts and bruises, many had sustained injuries. Catching sight of Teena in the column ahead, he wondered why she had not turned loose her dogs of war on these Sonsobitches long ago.

Within sight of the college, a mob flooded onto the highway blocking further progress. The lead vehicle continued to crawl toward the human barricade, everyone wondering if the driver would roll over anyone not getting out of the way. Suddenly there arose the intense, primal scream blaring from the vehicle's sound projector causing the human barricade to dissolve into a panicked retreat, people tripping and falling over their comrades in an effort to escape the piecing screech assaulting their ears.

Once within range of the local police huddling against the exterior parameter of the college and within sight of the unenthusiastic national media convoy strung along the college walls, the captain of the constabulary must have realized that failure of his peacekeepers to shield the incoming marchers from further assault would not be in his best interest and a contingent of officers fanned around the marchers. Wolf knew the feeble efforts by the police was too little and way too late, certain that the police captain and county administration would soon be facing a backlash not experienced in this part of Virginia since the Civil War.

Entering the campus grounds on their way to Patriot's Green, the protesters initially encountered stiff opposition by large groups of students and what Wolf assumed were members of the faculty performing their usual three act plays: shouting invectives, shaking signs sporting contradictory and/or vulgar messages and physical assault. After being pelted with stones and struck with clubs during his mile-long march from Camp Liberty, Wolf had reached the end of his patience, his hand tightening around the rubber hose at his belt, ready and willing to pummel the next punk getting into his face when a loud roar erupted and the scene turned into an all-out riot.

Thinking the marchers were being attacked, he prepared to enter the fray when he heard the columns' security commanders order everyone to stand down and keep moving forward. At first incredulous at being told to stay calm and carry on, so to speak, it soon became clear to Wolf that something else, something quite unexpected and extraordinary, was happening around the marchers: the hunters had become the hunted. A large wave of students coming from the direction of Patriot's Green surged past the columns of marchers attacking the Red Fascists, the clash escalating into a major free-for-all with combatants employing fists, feet and teeth as they swept through the surprised goons smashing and ripping signs, trampling through and over the doomed thugs with the speed and fury of a hurricane. Looking back, Wolf saw dozens of police hurry onto the campus, but the march defenders melted away in short order leaving the police with the task of cleaning up the dozens injured in the surprise assault.

By the time Wolf's column entered Patriot's Green he was struck by the eerie silence of the multi thousand-strong audience crowding the open space. Approaching the soundstage, Wolf made for the stairs as the rest of the marchers continued to encircle the stage, creating a protective phalanx for the protest's organizers and guest speakers as planned. Wondering what caused this sudden change of temperament as he peered across the throng, the answer became self-evident seeing a cellphone in virtually every hand.

CIR's media team had been livestreaming the mile-long march giving viewers a close-up view of the violence perpetrated upon the marchers for daring to exercise their right to peacefully assemble and protest. Must have been a sobering sight to witness protesters marching for freedom to be beaten and bloodied by unruly mobs of anarchists, nihilists—Teena's Red Fascists—and the criminal elements that cling to them like shit on the sole of one's shoe. The counterattack upon entering the college was an unexpected surprise—shock, really—Wolf wondering what else Diana and Teena had up their sleeves yet to be revealed.

A young man stepped up to the microphone.

"Good morning. I'm Casey Voss, head of Students for Individual Rights; welcome to the first of what I hope will be many more rallies for individual rights." He paused and gazed across the audience. "I want to thank you for having the courage to show up today. I say courage, because if you've been watching the marchers traverse that dangerous mile from their camp to this college, you should have no doubt that these enemies of freedom, these thugs, would not hesitate to bash in your skull for daring to hold views contrary to whatever they want you to spout.

"Thank you for choosing to listen with an active mind to the speakers this morning. I say, active mind, not open mind. An active mind strives to identify the validity of ideas, judges their value and ponders the consequences of ideas. An open mind, on the other hand, is like an open sewer, allowing all kinds of garbage to flow into to it unprocessed and undigested. The consequences of accepting the premise of keeping an open mind are writ large on every college campus, on social media, national politics and on full display on our phones this morning and over the past four days as a disruptive minority decide they are the final arbiters of what ideas and opinions are acceptable and act to suppress contrary views by force.... At this time, I'm honored to introduce Diana Ruiz, Executive Director of the Center for Individual Rights, America's unwavering defender of the smallest minority in the world—the individual...Ms. Ruiz..."

Diana gave Casey a brief hug and approached the microphone.

"Thank you, Casey, for choosing to approach life with an active mind and for having the courage to stand shoulder to shoulder in solidarity with the individual—the forgotten man and woman doomed to irrelevance by the mindless Leviathan named collectivism." She paused, then continued. "Students, faculty and guests, we are at war. For the past week, our group has been harassed, verbally accosted and physically assaulted by hordes of thugs representing an ideology inimical to a free, civil and prosperous culture. An ideology that has brought nothing but misery, poverty and death everywhere it has been tried. It has many faces: Nazism, Fascism, Maoism, Communism, Socialism; the list goes on, but in the end, it's all collectivism, the ideology that only the group matters; the individual—you and me—is nothing more than a cipher to be sacrificed for any or no reason at all. Everyone, that is, except for the few who control the levers of power. The pigs who are more equal than the collective of pigs from which they suck the lifeblood drop by drop ... there is no safe space, no golden mean, no compromise, no middle ground between liberty and slavery, between life and death. Sooner or later each of you will have to choose. But the time is growing short. Wait much longer and you will discover that there is no choice to be had as you trudge along to the collective Gulag we have allowed to be assembled year after year, idea by idea, vote by vote..."

She paused to allow the crowd to digest her words. After a long moment, she introduced the next speaker, Marcus Jefferson.

He thanked Diana for her welcoming remarks. "It's been 52 years since I marched with Martin Luther King from Selma to Montgomery, Alabama on that fateful March day in 1965. Fifty-two years ago, and I still bear the physical and mental scars from the beating I got that day from the police and their attack dogs. They beat on young men, on men older than I am today; women, White, Black, anyone who dared to march for the right of all Americans to live, work and interact wherever and with whom they wished. This morning, like I did at Selma, I carried my nation's flag during that mile-long journey to this stage. Like at Selma, I was assaulted by rabid dogs— the two-legged kind—who pelted me with stones, struck me with clubs, pushed and shoved, knocking me to the ground several times ... Unlike Selma, it wasn't the police knocking heads, but it was the police nonetheless. It was the police failing to their job protecting my right to peacefully march, to make it to this stage, to exercise my right to tell you my views. Fifty-two years and I—all of us today—are back at Selma 1965 where some people are allowed to use physical violence to prevent others from exercising their right to their own views and share them with others freely and peacefully. Shame on the county executive! Shame on the police! Shame on the college president! Shame on the hoodlums! Well, I've got news for them all: my legs might not make it from Selma to Montgomery anymore, but they damn well still carry me a mile or more. I'll be walking back to the camp today and back to this college tomorrow and every day after that for as long as it takes the police to rein in these rabid dogs. Freedom isn't free. Never has been, never will be. Like Ms. Ruiz said, there's no compromise, no middle ground, between freedom and slavery ... choose wisely ... your children will inherit the consequences."

Mr. Jefferson retreated back to his seat accompanied by tremendous applause. Casey Voss introduced the next speaker, Susan Baker, CIR lawyer and former VPC student who addressed specific legal issues, followed by three more speakers. The last scheduled speaker was Engineering Professor Nicholas Alexander who began by giving the audience an account of the deteriorating freedom and personal safety on campus, laying the blame squarely on the college's faculty, Board of Directors and President Wilson herself.

"To paraphrase Martin Niemöller, the Protestant pastor who spoke out against Hitler," Alexander began, "when the cultural war began many years ago, first they attacked ideas, ideas such as freedom of speech and we smiled, dismissing the assailants as ignorant children. Then they attacked organizations and business for providing the values and products they and us—literally—depend up for our comfort and survival and we shook our heads and went on with the business of teaching. Then they verbally attacked people, shaming them with their own values, with their professions and most of all, their personal success. And still we sat silently doing nothing, confident that the totalitarian tide would falter and recede as it has done so often time and time before. And now, we have arrived at the final solution that every totalitarian turns to when meeting even the suggestion of noncompliance: the use of brute force to implement their will upon any who dare to object to their brave new world overrun by ignorant, irrational, whim-driven, power-lusting sewer rats..."

Professor Alexander detailed quite graphically what his listeners can expect living in this brave new world. He called on every American patriot to stand and speak out in the classroom, on social media, in dorms, with friends and family, ending with promising to fight, "Today, tomorrow, for as long as it takes to drive this ideology of death back into the gutter from where it spawned!"

Alexander was the final speaker of the rally and Diana was approaching the podium when Wolf cut her off.

"What are you doing?"

"Looks like you have one more speaker," Wolf replied, taking the podium. Skipping welcoming comments, he dived right in. "My name if Grayson Wolf..." The name electrified the crowd, sounds of astonishment washing over the square followed by countless hands rising above heads holding phones, taking photos of this rare occurrence. "You know who I am and what I do. I've spent fifteen years exposing the bad, the really bad and the absolute dregs of society. Take my word for it: there is no person, no company, no organization in our country as toxic, as evil, as the collectivist ideologies Diana Ruiz mentioned earlier: Nazism, Marxism, Communism, Fascism and all its bastard offspring. It is the ideology of envy, of theft, of extortion, of violence and mass murder. You would not willingly take a drink you know to be poison, yet so many gleefully swallow this intellectually corrosive poison by the case full ... Friends, it's freedom or something far less palatable. It's freedom or the block Nazi. It's freedom or the house Commissar. It's freedom or a version of Iran, Venezuela, North Korea, Russia or China ... Patrick Henry said it best for all time: it's liberty or death. Yes, it's that serious. Liberty or death. It always comes down to liberty or death sooner or later...."

Wolf looked at the crowd for a moment, then started back to his seat as the chant, liberty or death arose, growing louder with each repetition until reverberating from every building on campus.

The rally continued for several more hours, students crowded around display tables, taking pamphlets and sundry event tokens, many dozens signing up to join the campus's Students for Individual Rights and downing gallons of liquid and handfuls of solid refreshment. By three 'o clock, the marchers got ready to return to Camp Liberty, forming a pair of tight columns in preparation of walking the mile-long gauntlet once more.

Everyone, that is, except Wolf who was approached by a pair of officers near the soundstage. He interrupted the officer speaking to him, watching as Diana took her position at the head of the first column and the group snaking their way out of the college, accompanied by a large contingent of students.

"Looks like my freedom marchers picked up a thousand fellow travelers escorting them north to Camp Liberty," Wolf said, though the police didn't seem to care. "Okay, so what is this all about, officers?"

"We have a warrant for your arrest," the one holding a folded sheet of paper said, handing it to him

"Arrest?" Wolf said, looking droll. "For what? Unscheduled speaking?"

The officer did not smile.

"Sexual Assault."

Chapter 18

New York Hustle

Wolf couldn't resist grinning at the thought that within the span of a mere four hours his fortunes changed from revolutionary hero to common felon in handcuffs sitting between two lawmen on a plane bound for New York City. He found nothing amusing about being arrested for sexual assault, but being arrested and extradited to New York, now that was a most interesting development. It was also ironic, considering the number of Wolf's romantic liaisons the past decade did not exceed the digits on one hand.

By the time Wolf's police escort delivered him to a Manhattan police station it was pushing nine in the evening. His situation became even more curious when the precinct captain placed him directly into an interrogation room instead of lockup until morning. He supposed their plan was to interview him now, in the late evening, hoping Wolf's lawyer would assume the interrogation would begin with the morning shift next day.

He was handcuffed to a chain bolted to the floor under his feet, issuing a snort at the thought of being considered sufficiently dangerous to warrant such restraint. He could imagine next day's news headlines: Rabid Wolf in Police Custody. He sighed, hoping the charade would begin sooner than later when the door opened and two detectives entered, taking a seat across the table.

"Good evening Mr. Wolf. I'm Detective Clark," the one on the left side of the table said. "This is Detective Vanderhelm."

Wolf smiled placidly at the two detectives and said nothing.

"Mr. Wolf," Vanderhelm said, "You have been charged with Sexual Assault upon Madeline Talbot on the evening of March 31, a felony. In New York, that will get you between ten to twenty years of jail time."

Wolf held the detective's gaze and said nothing.

"I know what you're thinking, Mr. Wolf," Clark said. "You think your money and fame will get you off. And, I'm sad to admit, I've seen too many rich men walk away without any time or maybe a slap on the wrist." He paused a long moment, then continued, leaning toward Wolf with a satisfied grin on his lips. "Unless we have them dead to rights."

Vanderhelm spoke into the silence that followed. "By dead to rights, my partner isn't talking about a, he said, she said case, Mr. Wolf. He means we've got solid evidence. So solid, Mr. Wolf, that your future for the next ten to twenty years is going to consist of a small, bare room without a view."

Wolf listened and said nothing. He was certain that neither detective was bluffing. Whatever evidence they had, it was probably as solid as it gets in this business.

"You talk with us now," Clark said, "you write us a confession, the DA offers six years maximum with probation after three."

"One time offer only," Vanderhelm said. "Expires the moment we walk out of here. Best deal you're ever going to get, Mr. Wolf. Beats the hell out of pushing twenty years ... Wadda ya say, Mr. Wolf? Now or never..."

Wolf shrugged. "I've got to pee."

*   *   *   *

By two the next day Wolf was standing in front of a judge listening to his lawyer argue with a New York Assistant District Attorney over his release on bail and the exchange was becoming quite heated.

"Seriously?" The ADA cried, glaring at the woman representing Wolf, "release your client on his own recognizance? Your Honor, Mr. Wolf is charged with forcing himself on a hapless woman, with *raping* the woman. Your Honor, considering the severity of Mr. Wolf's crime, the District Attorney of the State of New York strongly urges you to deny bail to Mr. Wolf."

The judge turned his gaze on Wolf's attorney. "Ms. Wallace?"

"Your Honor," she began, shooting the ADA an incredulous look, "ADA Korbin must have my client confused with a serial child molester considering his draconian demand for denying Mr. Wolf bail—oh, wait, didn't Mr. Korbin agree to bail for a serial child molester a scant three months ago? Perhaps the ADA considers my client to be far more dangerous than a serial child molester and if so, I'm most interested in hearing his reasons.

"Your Honor," Korbin said, ignoring Wallace's sarcastic comments and shooting Wolf an icy look, "Mr. Wolf has the means and the international connections to vanish much like terrorists can and do."

"Your Honor," Wallace retorted, "please instruct Mr. Korbin to refrain using the term, 'terrorist', in connection to Mr. Wolf."

The judge gazed at Korbin who made an acquiescent expression.

"Your Honor," Wallace continued, "we submit that Mr. Wolf has no prior convictions, is an outstanding and valued member of not only his local community, but our national community. He is not a flight risk and is more than anxious to appear in court to protect his stellar reputation and clear his good name."

The judge peered at Korbin.

"Your Honor," the ADA said, "the State does in fact consider Mr. Wolf a flight risk and recommends that bail be set at a minimum five million dollars and restrict him to travel in the continental US only to ensure that Mr. Wolf does not decide to take a permanent vacation in a nation without an extradition treaty with the United States."

"That's totally absurd and unfounded," Wallace rejoined. "There is nothing in Mr. Wolf's history to suggest he'd run away from anything; quite the opposite in fact. I can personally assure the court that Mr. Wolf will appear in court at the appointed day and time to fight this specious and unfounded accusation of sexual assault."

The ADA was about to speak when the judge cut him off. "I've heard enough. Bail is set at one million and the defendant is restricted to movement within the continental United States." The crack of his gavel loudly concluded the bail hearing.

Wolf accompanied Wallace to post bail. She had giving him a blank certified cashier's check and a release form. He completed the pertinent sections, filled out the check for one million dollars and handed both to the bail clerk. Ten minutes later the clerk handed Wolf a receipt, clearance papers and a pre-trial date.

"We're good to go," Wallace said. Peering at the trial document, she added, "Curiouser and curiouser. They've scheduled your pre-trial hearing three days from now."

"That's good, yes?" Wolf said. "Better sooner than weeks from now. Get this over with."

"No, it's not," Wallace replied. "The New York Prosecutor's Office has a sizable backlog of court cases, yet they are pushing your case to the top of the pile, Mr. Wolf. That being the case, you can expect them to push for a jury trial before the end of next week. This is not good for many reasons.... Let's get to my office and discuss your case; I've got a car waiting in the underground garage with midnight tinted windows to foil the press and paparazzi swarming a block deep."

"Maddie, Madeline Talbot, is a successful lawyer representing various clients including New World Hedge Fund headed by Justin Bellamy," Wolf explained, sitting in Wallace's swanky law office thirty floors above the Manhattan streets. "She was a key informant about Bellamy's company and his connection to Larry Silverstone's operation during my investigation for the book, Screw You, Suckers!"

"Where you intimately involved with Ms. Talbot during that investigation?" Wallace asked.

"Absolutely not." Seeing her skeptical expression at his adamant reply, he explained. "I have a cardinal rule never to become involved with any informant or any woman even remotely connected to one of my investigations. It might place them in harm's way; my expose subjects looking for payback."

"I understand," Wallace said. "Yet you did sleep with Ms. Talbot four weeks ago."

Wolf smiled at his attorney's inquisitive tone. Getting him ready for the trial, he supposed.

"I didn't plan to," Wolf said. "It just happened ... Maddie isn't an informant anymore and it's been three years since the book came out. She just caught me during a vulnerable moment..."

"What do you mean by 'vulnerable moment'?"

"I've been re-evaluating my life, thinking about terminating my expose novel writing career," Wolf explained. "Decided to go to New York on the spur of the moment and Maddie called me out of the blue shortly after arriving at my hotel in the city."

"Excuse me," Wallace said, her eyebrows rising. "Did you say Ms. Talbot called *you?*"

Wolf nodded. "Called and asked how I've been and suggested dinner. Owing Maddie many favors, I agreed and one thing led to another and I wound up making breakfast for her. I've always like Maddie and almost went back, but my old habit of protecting informants and contacts kicked in and I didn't go back."

"Was sex consensual?" Wallace asked. "Did Ms. Talbot ask you to stop at any time?"

"Yes, consensual. Maddie invited me to her condo and invited me to her bed," Wolf said. "The word 'stop' did come up, prefaced each time with 'don't', as in 'don't stop, don't stop'."

Wallace shot him a droll look. "Is there any reason you can think of why Ms. Talbot would claim you sexually assaulted her?"

Wolf thought back at all his interactions with Maddie during the year she was his informant and anything he did or might have done to make her angry enough to punish him in this vile manner. He came up blank. It was Maddie who had made the decision to help him back then. It was Maddie who called to invite him to dinner and suggested he stay over. He liked her and she liked him. Therefore...

"It's got to be the evil twins," Wolf quipped. "Silverstone and Bellamy. The only way this makes any sense is that they've got something on Maddie. But I'm the prize ... Do they really think this charge is going to stick? If she got a rape test done that day, it's not going to show anything beyond intercourse: no bruising due to being forced, no restraint marks on her wrist or body and so forth. DNA, sure, but it's going to come down to her word versus mine and that's not going to be enough to convict."

"They put her on the stand and she gives an emotional, tear-stained description of what you did to her," Wallace said, "a sympathetic jury has been known to convict."

Wolf's face darkened. "Of what I did to her? You suggesting I forced Maddie to have sex? That I raped her?"

"Not at all," Wallace said, looking pleased. "Happy that you're paying close attention to what is being said. Many of the people you have skewered in your books live in New York, as I'm sure you know. This sexual assault charge is tailor made for payback and the speed the DA is pushing this case to trial is testimony to that. There is a good possibility I will have to put you on the stand and you will need to listen carefully to the questions and comments made by the DA and his witnesses to spot the innuendo inserted and spouted, because there will be plenty. But be assured, any you miss, I won't and will knock them down as fast as they pop up."

Wolf issued a snort. "I've had to look over my shoulder most of my life, Ms. Wallace. I'm used to being verbally and physically assaulted, but this attack I never saw coming." He shrugged, adding, "Made my bed. Should have slept alone in it."

"I've made arrangements for you to stay in Manhattan," Wallace said, getting out of her chair. "We have several suites reserved for company clients and guests. Give them this card. They will not ask for your name nor check your ID. Anything you need—meals, transportation—is a call to the concierge desk. Unless you have any questions, a taxi is waiting for you outside the lobby to take you to your temporary residence. We'll meet again tomorrow afternoon, Mr. Wolf." A droll smile lit up her face. "Be sure to sleep alone."

"A lawyer and a comic," Wolf retorted. "Can't wait to see your stage performance during the trial." They shook hands and Wolf made for the elevators.

Thinking about the situation on the way down, he was sure Maddie would never voluntarily set him up, that she was coerced into doing so. He was also quite certain the culprits behind this had to be Bellamy and Silverstone. But why, and more importantly, why now? Why not closer to the release date of Screw You, Suckers: two years ago? A year ago? months ago?

A far more disturbing thought struck him: is Colleen Silverstone involved? If so, why bother to save his life, accompany him into the forest, get shot at and nearly eaten by a bear just to, what? Set him up and watch him squirm? Enjoy the thought of him rotting a decade in jail for a crime he did not commit? Colleen is tough and unforgiving, but far from a sociopath—unlike her father and his vile pal, both men easily capable of orchestrating this farce. They have the connections, money and most certainly the motive to engineer a way to harm Wolf in a manner most rewarding and enjoyable to that pair of human degenerates.

Wolf exited the lobby and reached the taxi waiting at the curb without attracting the attention of any reporters or paparazzi hiding in the crowd hoping to pounce on him. The first thing Wolf did entering his hotel room was to empty everything from his pockets, strip off his clothes, call down for the concierge to take them to be cleaned and took a much-needed shower. Being one of Manhattan's premier hotels, Wolf slipped into one of the comfortable bathrobes hanging in the adjacent closet and headed for the seating area, phone in hand.

"Since you're using your cell to call, I assume you made bail," RJ said. "How's Mia Wallace? Hear she's the crème de la crème defense attorney."

"Well, she's funny; that much I know for sure," Wolf replied.

"She can be whatever she wants to be, bro, because she agreed to take you on."

"I feel so special."

"Special enough," RJ said, "because Mia's very, very picky."

"Picky, huh? Maybe she's fond of wolves."

"Picky in that she never represents dirt bags unless she's convinced they are innocent," RJ replied.

"I'm an innocent dirt bag?" Wolf retorted.

RJ issued a humorous snort. "Dirt bag is in the eye of the beholder and to the darlings you've skewered in your novels, you are a dirt bag extraordinaire ... like I said, in the eye of the beholder. So, sexual assault, is it? Like you'd ever even kiss a girl without written permission from her father."

"My first inclination was to assume payback," Wolf replied. "One of the reasons my nasty bits rarely come out to play. But the timing of this event reeks of Colorado. Someone has tried to violently stop my investigation of Sarah Lewis's rape and James Collins's murder at least twice, three times if I count the bear attack, though I suspect the bear's an equal opportunity mauler. Colorado must be the real reason why they've pressured Maddie to accuse me of rape; hoping they can generate enough heat to put me behind bars."

"What could they have on Maddie to pressure her?" RJ asked. "She's squeaky clean based on my peeps."

"No clue, RJ," Wolf replied. "But it's got to be something substantial for her to do this."

"Pressure or no pressure," RJ retorted, "what she's doing to you is unforgivable, Wolf."

A sad smile formed on Wolf's lips. "Maybe. We'll see. She's going to have to take the stand."

"I sincerely hope Mia Wallace fries her lying ass," RJ cried.

"Not going to let her do that, RJ. Maddie's a victim, too."

"Oh-my-God!" RJ cried. "The woman kicks you in the nuts and you still have feelings for her? Maddie should have contacted you right off the bat, bro, and you know it."

"If she were not connected to one of my books, I'd agree," Wolf explained, "but I allowed Maddie to be my informant...and..."

"And?" RJ said, his tone rising with suspicion.

Wolf sighed. "Maddie was clearly taken with me from the start and I liked her, too. And no, I didn't break my rule about sleeping with informants, but I was attracted to her and allowed my feelings to leak during our meetings. I'm going to give Maddie some slack and trust that whatever's grabbing her by the throat will be exposed sooner than later."

"Jeezus, Wolf," RJ replied. "Here's my take on that: sooner than later you're going to have to bare your fangs and rip her to shreds or be sitting in some New York jail where one or more of your skewered friends are going to have you killed before your first week in. That's the risk you are taking giving Maddie some slack and hopin' the truth shall set you free."

*   *   *   *

RJ's words came back to Wolf loud and clear during the pre-trial hearing Thursday morning when the prosecutor presented a flash drive containing images purportedly showing "the defendant using his superior strength to force his victim to engage in sexual intercourse." When challenged by Mia Wallace, the prosecutor claimed that his office received the images on a flash drive two days after the news account of Wolf's arrest, source unknown.

"Your Honor," Wallace continued, "since these images were sent by an anonymous source, the court can conclude they were taken in Ms. Talbot's residence without her knowledge, a serious invasion of her privacy and that of any of her guests and therefore cannot be used as evidence."

"Cannot be used as evidence against the *owner or renter* whose privacy was violated," the prosecutor said. "In Delaware v. Smith the

Fourth Circuit Court ruled the admissibility of visual evidence within a private residence by a third-party committing a crime. In that case, local police had set up court-authorized surveillance inside a suspected drug dealer's home which was subsequently burglarized by a man unaware his crime was being caught on camera. Mr. Wolf's assault of Ms. Talbot in her home was captured by cameras, that, though illegally installed in Ms. Talbot's home, is not a violation of Mr. Wolf's privacy and therefore admissible in court."

"You Honor," Wallace objected, "a flash drive allegedly showing images of my client forcing himself on Ms. Talbot appears on Mr. Korbin's desk shortly after Mr. Wolf's arrest from an anonymous source with no explanation. I need not elucidate to the court the ease digital experts can manipulate images and videos that originally showed innocent activities, transforming them to display malevolent acts."

"Your Honor," Korbin interjected, "our technicians have validated the accuracy and integrity of the images and the State is confident that Ms. Wallace's visual experts will corroborate its authenticity."

"If it pleases the court," Wallace continued, ignoring the prosecutor. "In light of the anonymity of the person or persons behind the video, its appearance coming so conveniently immediately after my client's arrest and the ease of digital manipulation of electronic images and videos, I ask the court to exclude this highly suspect video *in limine* to ensure my client receives a fair trial. I ask the court not to risk a jury being exposed to what most certainly is tainted evidence and most likely found inadmissible later on. Visual images are among the most powerful influencers of human decision making and once seen, even the most sedate visuals proven to be false have been shown to influence members of a jury."

The judge ruled in favor of the prosecutor and the pre-trial hearing finished soon thereafter, the video and upcoming personal testimony of the victim being the key components of the prosecutor's case. The jury trial was scheduled for May 8, two weeks hence.

Their first act at returning to Wallace's law firm was viewing the visual evidence that had magically appeared on the prosecutor's desk earlier that week. There were a dozen photos organized into a timeline beginning with one showing Wolf appearing to yank a surprised Maddie toward him inside the entrance of her condo, the next one appearing to drag Maddie through the living room toward a hallway. The remaining images where in the bedroom starting with appearing to shove Maddie on the bed, Wolf's teeth bared and looking quite ferocious, the rest showing acts of intercourse, two close-ups of Maddie's face, her expression registering distress.

"If I wasn't there," Wolf said, "I'd might believe that I did assault Maddie."

"Used to be," Wallace began, "a picture was worth a thousand words. These days a picture tells a thousand lies. Ever watched porn, Mr. Wolf?"

"If I say no, then you'll say I'm a prude," Wolf replied, smiling. "If I say yes, then you'll call me depraved."

Wallace issued a sniff. "Have you observed the faces of the women actors as they pretend to achieve orgasm? Of the dozens I've observed, none look like this—" she pointed to Maddie's face on the monitor.

Wolf looked at the photo then over at Wallace. "You mean, none have the genuine expression of a woman in the throes of climax."

"Correct," she said. "Pornography, especially high-quality porn, is tightly directed and choreographed, just like any decent movie shown at the local theater. If producers of porn were to accurately portray how bodies engaged in sexual intercourse *naturally* moved and gyrated followed by accurate facial expressions approaching and during orgasm, they'd be required by law to provide a viewer warning to have barf bags handy."

Wolf made a comical expression and burst out laughing. "Remind me never to invite you to watch any porn with me."

"Admitting to depravity, then," she said, shooting Wolf a 'gotcha' look.

He smiled and made a helpless shrug. "Caught red handed and bare assed, apparently ... not looking so good for me, is it?"

"Can't promise you a walk in the park, Mr. Wolf," Wallace said, "but we only need to show reasonable doubt. The prosecution must prove their case beyond reasonable doubt to twelve people on the jury. As far as these images go, by the time I'm done with them, no one will take them for anything but what they are: fiction."

Wolf looked thoughtful. "And Maddie? I'm sure she's not a willing party to this; she's being pressured somehow."

"I will proceed as gently and carefully as I can," she replied. "But my job is to represent you, not Ms. Talbot."

Of course," Wolf said. "Unless you need me to stay in New York to plan for the trial, I believe the conditions of my bail allows me to travel domestically, yes?"

"Correct," Wallace said. "But please be sure to get back at least three days before May 8."

Wolf promised to return no later than May fourth, thanked the lawyer for her service, returned to his hotel to pack his meager belonging and catch a flight back to Virginia. Reservations made, bag packed, he reached for the small crystal decorative bowl where he tossed items such as change, keys and whatever he fished out of pockets. He retrieved his keys and sunglasses when he stopped, remembering his last visit to New York, seeing a different bowl where he'd stored his small personal items and how happy he felt that morning after. Shrugging, he issued a nondescript noise, emptied the bowl and dropped the items into his pants pocket.

The TV was still on and Wolf reached for the remote to turn it off when a news alert flashed on the screen, followed by a reporter informing her viewers about a shooting at a northern Virginia college. Wolf didn't need to hear more, switched off the TV and grabbed his phone.

"I'll be there in a couple hours."

Chapter 19

Fog of War

Wolf stood in Diana's office shortly after arriving home from his flight to Reagan National Airport.

"What exactly happened at the camp?"

"We're still not sure," she replied, looking vexed. "Over half dozen Red Fascists were shot outside the camp's walls this morning; fortunately, no fatalities—at least not yet. Teena is adamant that none of our security personnel, nor any of our supporters, shot anyone. Campers are not permitted on top of the palisade; our armed security does patrol on top of the wall and the punks are claiming they're the shooters."

"What about all the surveillance cameras all over the place; were they not working?" Wolf asked.

"The cameras are mostly aimed at the rabble trespassing on private property beyond the wall," Diana explained. "They do sweep across chucks of the wall occasionally, but there was plenty of opportunity for a shooter or shooters from our side to fire and not seen by surveillance."

"I assume the police did a GSR test of our security personnel?" Wolf asked.

"According to Teena, police detected no gunpowder residue on our people," she replied. "A significant number of participants have their own weapons, but Teena convinced the police that none of our people are allowed near the wall and never on top. We have strict rules that must be followed; any attempting to climb on top would be taken into custody, questioned and asked to leave immediately. No exceptions."

"Glad to hear that," Wolf said. "What's your next move?"

"The camp is on temporary lockdown as police investigate the matter," she replied. "We've got nearly three hundred people and if the police decide to question each one, it'll take days. Everything is on hold for now pending the investigation. But we're not going away, that I can promise you … Your turn: what the hell is going on, Wolf? Sexual assault? This is payback for all your good deeds, hands down. How could Madeline accuse you of something so heinous anyway? This is ridiculous—no way would you ever do anything even remotely like this."

A droll grin slid across his face. "I'm relieved to know you don't think I'm a rapist."

"Don't be stupid," she retorted. "What do they have and any idea who's behind this?"

"Photos good enough to sell the tale and testimony from my victim," he replied. "Mia Wallace, my lawyer, promised to reduce the photos to ashes and light up Maddie, though I told her to take it easy because I'm certain that Maddie is being blackmailed or threatened in some way."

"You're such a romantic," Diana chided. "What if she's part of the conspiracy to take the great and powerful Grayson Wolf down?"

"Why now?" he countered. "Why not set me up when I was investigating Silverstone and Bellamy or soon thereafter? Three years later? Nope. This is about my investigation in Colorado and they've found a way to get to her."

"Considering how that tryst turned out," she quipped, "you might want to avoid inviting old contacts to dinner, dancing and bedding in the future."

"I didn't invite Maddie, she—"

"What? What is it?" Diana asked, seeing Wolf's alarmed expression.

Events had moved so fast he hadn't had the opportunity to think beyond his arrest and subsequent proceedings. Now, standing in Diana's office in the Center for Individual Rights it became crystal clear.

His gaze flew toward the office door to ensure it was shut. "How did Maddie know I was coming to New York? It's not like it was planned in advance; it was an impulsive decision made hours before leaving. How could she—anyone in New York—know I was coming to visit?"

Diana's eyes widened significantly. "Shit."

"We have a mole," Wolf growled. "Everyone in that meeting was on the Executive Board. This is not good, Diana … Call them in now."

An hour's-interrogation of the seven-member Executive Board revealed exactly what Wolf had expected: nothing. Short of Waterboarding the lot, all of them were genuinely shocked to hear about a possible mole at CIR, all vehemently denied contacting anyone about Wolf's trip to New York back in March, all were certain they did not discuss Wolf later that evening with friends or family and none could think of anyone they suspected of being a mole.

The interrogation over, the Board wanted to hear about Wolf's arrest, the particulars about his defense, followed by a discussion of possible futures for CIR pursuant to a guilty verdict. Considering Wolf's arrest and the shooting at Lawson Conference Center, the general mood was gloomy.

"You know," RJ said, biting his inner lip, "if we have a mole, why haven't critical plans leaked regularly? I'm thinking it might a recent hire."

"Nope," Paul Onaka, head of Human Resources, said. "We haven't hired anyone for eight months. We have engaged the services of several new contractors since January, though none would be roaming around the Center or be interfacing with this Board, especially during our conferences."

"There's another possibility," Juan Mendez said. "Perhaps the mole's job was to report only on Wolf's comings and goings for an opportunity to spring this trap. That might explain why we've had no critical leaks. It also means it could be anyone that's worked here for a long while."

"I wish Teena was here," Diana said. "She's super at finding needles in haystacks."

"Come on," Juan said, "we can do this. The meeting that Friday afternoon was almost over when Wolf dropped the bomb about no more novels. There was a brief conversation about how he felt it was time to go in another direction, ending with him announcing he was going to see a show in New York that same evening. Think, everyone. See the meeting in your mind. Try to remember any non-committee member in the room or anyone entering the room shortly before Wolf mentioned New York. Go through it image by image and see if you can spot anything different, or something very normal that's easy to overlook..."

There followed a long pause as the assembled thought about that March Friday meeting. One by one, the faces of the Board members registered a blank, including Wolf who could not recall anyone entering the room to deliver a message or pick something up. Nothing.

"Sheryl." Brett Casings said.

"What about Sheryl," Diana challenged. "She's my assistant. She's often at meetings."

Brett made a determined face. "Juan said to think of something different or the same. Besides the Board members, Sheryl is the only non-executive that's the same ... and she was in the room during Wolf's lament." Wolf shot the computer maven a mock hurt look, Brett giving him an ironic expression in return. "Come on; I know you appreciate alliteration."

"I'll talk with her," Diana said.

"Let me do it," Juan said. "Me asking to speak to her might be enough to get her to talk. If she did inform on Wolf, his lawyer will have a witness to bolster any case she might make that you were set up."

Diana agreed and Sheryl was summoned to Juan's office. Observing her face as she entered the room and sat down in front of his desk, Juan concluded that the woman was either clueless why she'd be asked to come to the legal center or a hardened operative. Having known Diana's executive assistant for nearly three years, Juan leaned toward the former appraisal.

She peered expectantly at the head of CIR's legal department. Juan cleared his throat, suddenly feeling very self-conscious, as though he were doing something unsavory. But what if Sheryl Baseman was not the wide-eyed innocent she appeared to be as she sat calmly facing him?

"Um, thank you for coming so quickly," Juan said. "I assume you know about Mr. Wolf's arrest in New York?"

"Yes; it's absolutely ridiculous," Sheryl replied, indignant. "Mr. Wolf would never do something like that. It's either a sick joke or someone trying to get back at him for writing about them."

"That's what we're trying to find out, Sheryl," he replied. "We'll be talking with everyone over the next couple of days asking them about anything they might know or heard."

"I see," she said, nodding. "I'm not sure I have anything to tell you, Mr. Mendez. No one's approached me asking about Mr. Wolf or about the Center, either, though if they did, I wouldn't tell them anything, of course. And besides, if I thought it was suspicious or worrisome, I'd let Teena know right away."

"Glad to hear it." Juan wasn't sure what to say next, then a thought struck him. "I hear you have a boyfriend; been with him for a while now, right?"

A warm smile appeared on Sheryl's face. "Yes, Charles. We've been seeing each other since New Year's."

"Things getting serious between the two?"

Her smile grew wider. "It is, I'm happy to report. I'm inclined to think he might be the one. I know he's crazy about me."

"I hope he is," Juan replied, smiling cordially as he steered the conversation. "I remember when I first saw Ashley; I knew I had to marry her—and I did! Fortunately, she's happy where I work, you know, Grayson Wolf and all the brouhaha that comes with him and the Center."

"Charles thinks what I do—what we do—is real cool," Sheryl said. "He's a real fan, read all of Mr. Wolf's books."

"What kind of work does he do?" Juan asked. "My wife's a paralegal, though these days her main job is taking care of our two children. But she loves it—we homeschool them, you know. That's a full-time job, for sure."

"I bet it is," Sheryl said, looking impressed. "Not sure I could teach my own children."

"Doesn't have to be you," Juan said. "More and more fathers are staying home educating their children than ever before."

"That probably wouldn't work for Charles," she replied. "He's in advertising and travels regularly to New York where his firm is located."

Juan felt his pulse quicken. "Advertising can be a tough business, that's for sure. What company does he work for?"

"Simon-Stellar. Been working for them for a couple years," Sheryl said, proudly. "Apparently Charles is a star; he does really well."

"I've heard of Simon-Stellar." He lied. "What's Charles's last name? Might want to talk to him about our advertising needs."

"Mandeville. Charles Mandeville."

"Great," Juan said, standing up. "Thanks for your help, Sheryl. Wish you all the best with Charles … make it a great day."

The moment Sheryl closed the door to his office, Juan lifted his cell and called Diana to tell her the news. He opposed her request to meet immediately, insisting that doing so would very likely make Sheryl suspicious meeting immediately after talking with her, suggesting they eat lunch in her office and invite Wolf and RJ.

By the time all four principals were free to meet, lunch was had in Diana's office short of two o' clock. Juan's report of his meeting with Sheryl took all of a minute, Diana being the first to comment.

"Sheryl is the best assistant I've ever worked with," she said, clearly not happy about what Juan had found out. "I know it looks suspicious, Juan, but it might just as easily be a coincidence. I've known ad people who work for New York and Chicago firms but live in the DC area. I don't want to lose Sheryl—she's fantastic."

"Juan, you said Mandeville works for Simon-Stellar advertising firm, right?" Wolf said. Juan nodded affirmatively and Wolf continued. "What law firm represents Simon-Stellar?"

Juan typed into his phone, swiped the screen a couple times and said, "Simon-Stellar is represented by Cookson & Hudson."

"I'll have my peeps do some very quiet sniffing and see if there's any stink on Mr. Mandeville and the ad firm," RJ said. "He'll never know and neither will Sheryl."

"Don't bother." Wolf interjected. "He's the one."

A crooked smile formed on RJ's lips. "I know wolves have a superior sense smell, but no way can you pick up the man's stink all the way from New York."

"I most certainly can pick up on New York stink when it's connected to Silverstone and Associates law firm," Wolf retorted.

"What are you talking about?" Diana asked. "Juan said Cookson & Hudson represented Mandeville's ad firm."

"Cookson & Hudson does represent Simon-Stellar," Wolf said, looking quite smug as he took a drink. "Cookson & Hudson is an affiliate, a front, if you will, of Silverstone and Associates. Our friend Larry has several more laws firms doing his bidding. Enough stink for you 'all? It's Charles Mandeville."

"I can talk with Ms. Wallace and give her all the particular to have her subpoena him for the trial," Juan said.

"Thanks," Wolf said. "Ask her hold that subpoena until the last possible moment. Most likely Charles is just a Gofer making a few extra bucks for passing on information. Don't say anything to Sheryl right now, don't want Chucky boy to know we know."

"Okay, but as soon as the trial is over, I've got to speak with her about her Charles," Diana said. She did not look happy. "I hate this. I've got a super assistant that I've got to keep sensitive information from. Her boyfriend will have to go or she will..."

Changing the subject, Wolf asked if there was any news about the shooting at Camp Liberty.

"I spoke with Teena just before we met," Diana said. "The police were planning to run ballistics tests on our security personnel's weapons, but shelved that, deciding to do a visual check of their weapons instead—no clue why. The good news is that the shooting has finally brought police to the camp to provide protection and clearing the bums off the property, most of which seemed to have oozed back to the college according to Casey Voss of SIR."

"Seven people were shot," Wolf said, though it sounded more like a question.

"Yes; fortunately, no fatalities," Diana said. "According to what the cops told Teena, none of the wounds are serious; mostly legs, couple in the lower torso."

"That's strange, don't you think?" RJ said. "All shot in the legs or lower part of the body. It's almost like the shooters were purposefully trying not to kill anyone."

"That's what Teena thought, too," Diana said. "The police are considering several scenarios but we won't know anything definitive until the police investigation gets done and that will take a few days or longer."

"None of this makes much sense," Wolf said. "When I first heard about the shooting this morning, I supposed it was our people that were the targets. Frankly, I'm puzzled by it."

"In the meantime, our free speech campus rally will continue as planned," Diana promised. "I'm leaving for the camp early tomorrow and the moment the police give us the green light, plan to march to the college for another rally where we plan to spout all manner of 'hate speech'."

"Meanwhile back at the home front," Juan said, "CIR will sue the County Executive and the Police Chief for putting our people at risk during the march last Sunday and the rolling riots at the camp prior to the shooting this morning after failing to respond to numerous request for police protection."

"And you," Diana pointed at Wolf, "are to remain here and stay out of trouble. We do not need you to become embroiled in some incident at the camp or at VPC. Consider this a good time to catch up on your reading, contemplating your future and keeping up with developments of your court case."

"Yes, mommy," Wolf said. "I'll strive to be a perfectly domesticated Wolfie."

The lunch meeting adjured, Diana waving her visitors out of the office. RJ suggested they visit Brett and see what's new in the organization's intelligence center. Wolf was especially interested in hearing what, if anything, Brett's people had discovered digging around Larry Silverstone and Justin Bellamy's electronic accounts, a favor he had asked of Brett the evening of his arraignment in New York.

"Bupkis," Brett said, disgusted. "We've got bupkis. I had my best hacker, um, I mean, *algorithm program adjuster*, go back a year. Assuming Silverstone and Bellamy are behind this frame-up, they've made sure to keep their actions old school: no electronic communication of any type."

Wolf nodded knowingly. "The reason your *adjuster* hasn't found anything incriminating is that the evil duo is a client of Colleen's security firm. Colleen's people are security paranoid and savvy like no one I've ever seen."

"Just how friendly were you and Colleen out there in the wilds of Colorado?" RJ said, his eyebrows raised in a suggestive manner.

"She tolerates me," Wolf said. "And I'd never ask her under any circumstances."

RJ made a face and shrugged. "Just a suggestion, bro."

"Sorry Wolf," Bret said, looking sympathetic. "It's pretty bad, isn't it?"

"My lawyer feels confident she'll destroy the legitimacy of the photos," Wolf said. "There's still Maddie's testimony and the thought of having Wallace going after her with both guns blazing makes me feel sick to my stomach. I'm sure she's being blackmailed or threatened somehow."

"All the more reason for your lawyer to hit her hard and long," RJ said. "Let me ask you a question: do you think Maddie would have called you on her own volition to hook up?"

"I think so. There's always been a spark between us."

"If you really believe that, bro, then you've got to let loose the dogs of war upon her when she's on the stand." RJ held up a hand to cut off Wolf's objection. "Don't you get it? If Maddie's being blackmailed, the *only* way she can help you—and herself—is by appearing to falter and crack under an intense barrage of questioning and cross-examination." RJ placed both hands on Wolf's shoulder and got into his face. "Bro: let her help you help yourself. Tell Wallace to go at her with both barrels blazing."

*　　*　　*　　*

Wolf spent the next few days doing what Diana suggested, relaxing around his roof-top condo, catching up on his reading and contemplating his future. By Sunday he had become rather antsy and fired up his two-seater copter for a flight along the Potomac River, hovering above Great Falls admiring the massive flow of water cascading over the rocky barrier caused by excessive spring rains. Refueling at a small local airport, he decided to head southwest and fly over Virginia Patriots College and as a lark, buzz over Diana's Camp Liberty several times. His exploit garnered a stern rebuke from his Executive Director informing him that if he did that again she'd give Teena a green light to shoot him down!

"I said stay away and I mean it, Wolf!" she warned. "Things are relatively calm at the moment and the last thing I need is for Grayson Wolf to rile up the natives complaining of an aerial assault upon their precious safe spaces. Stay home and write something, anything."

A chastised, though not penitent, Wolf took Diana's off-handed quip seriously and wrote something that very afternoon. It all started when perusing his home library and Wolf came across The Communist Manifesto. The slim volume had gathered a fine film of dust over a decade resting on the shelf and revisiting the document inspired him to write a manifesto of his own reflecting the struggle of the 400 people at Camp Liberty and the efforts of CIR. He titled it, *Stand and Fight: An Individualist Manifesto* modifying Marx's opening lines of The Communist Manifesto:

> A specter is haunting America — the specter of collectivism. All the powers of the West have entered into an unholy alliance to bring this specter to fruition: Pope and Presidents, Prime Ministers and Legislators, Media and Cronies, Professors and Administrators, bureaucrats high and low.
>
> Collectivism by any name—Communism, Nazism, Socialism, Fascism—enslaves and kills the same.
>
> Where is the party in opposition? Red, White or Blue, which has not colluded with this vile and evil specter, offering the enslavement of entitlements in exchange for freedom? Trading promises of safety for shackles? Where is the opposition that has stood against this abhorrent specter—killer of hundreds of millions—hurling its toxic waste back upon the dung pile of history where it belongs?
>
> Will Liberty be doomed to drift into that long goodnight, extinguished not with a bang, but a whimper? Or…will we, one by one by one, stand and fight for our life, liberty, property and pursuit of happiness?

By the time he finished, it was two in the morning and Wolf had written a fifty-page manifesto divided into three parts, the first identifying and defining key terms and ideas of the battle for the minds of the populace and their outcome in the real world. Part two identified key figures ranging from captains of industry to obscure professors guiding the transformation of America into a collectivist hellhole. The final section of the manifesto, titled *Stand and Fight*, was a call to action by freedom-loving individuals, itemizing a list of actions one could take to resist the "creeping sludge of totalitarianism" and reverse the Red Fascist toxin backwashing from sewers across America.

With minimal changes by RJ, *Stand and Fight: An Individualist Manifesto* was published and distributed to millions of CIR supporters worldwide that Thursday with general distribution to the public at large planned for a week later.

"Absolutely brilliant ramming Marx's words down that misanthropes' lousy throat," Brett gushed, during lunch after the first release of the manifesto that morning. "I've read Grundrisse and others books by that killer of the human spirit and place it just below Joyce's Ulysses for its endless gobbledygook and sheer nonsense."

"I'll have to disagree, Bret," Annika said, taking a long swallow of sparkling water. "Marx's gobbledygook tops the pile by a wide margin. James Joyce's Ulysses was a malevolent literary travesty; Marx's tomes resulted in far worse than killing the human spirit...and the slaughter continues unabated in half the world's nations today. Joyce, you can safely ignore; take your eye off Marx and his Hydra-headed offspring at your own peril."

Of the assembled around the lunch table, Annika von Hauzner and Diana Ruiz were most familiar with the death and destruction associated with the wages of collectivism. Annika's grandparents lived through the Nazi era in Germany, her grandfather perishing shortly before the end, her grandmother escaping death several times. Her mother married a German engineer, the couple emigrating to America in the early 1960's. Diana's parents came from Venezuela eighteen years ago and she has relatives living, if that's what it could be called, in that prison run by looters propped up by the Cuba's military to maintain the cocaine pipeline that Raoul Castro and his thugs profit from.

Wolf felt good about composing the manifesto, but sitting in front of his computer that evening peering aimlessly at nearly twenty folders, each containing notes, drafts and completed document for every one of his novels and other literary works, he felt at a loss what to do next, assuming he'd be set free at the trial to have any next at all.

He got up, apprehensively pacing around the room. Wolf had been living on the edge for fifteen years, constantly on the move, always having to look over his shoulder, running from one project to another and another. He was a man of action and this level of enforced inactivity, of waiting, was wearing on his nerves. For the first time since his announcement retiring from being the nation's muckraker, Wolf felt the full weight of the uncertainty looming in his future bearing down on him.

Reflecting on his published works—fifteen expose novels and dozens of essays written for CIR—Wolf accepted the fact that writing would continue to be his future. His expose novel career was definitely over and what remained was to figure out what type of creative writing inspired and excited him sufficiently to devote weeks and months to the task. The possibilities were extensive: Mysteries, movie scripts, historical, even biographical might be an option.

Mulling the choices, the words of his writing professor popped into his mind after handing Wolf back the first chapter of a fictional work with a grade of C-, a shock to Wolf who had rarely garnered less than excellent grades: *write about what you know*. A happy grin lit up his face because Wolf knew exactly what he could write about.

Rushing over to his computer, Wolf opened a blank Word document and began to outline ideas for a series of fictional stories about a brainy female insurance claims investigator named Tara Mason. Her job is supposed to be routine examination claims ranging from fire damage to ordinary row houses to theft of million-dollar private jets. Yet the quiet, unassuming five-foot-two heroine never failed to get herself embroiled in conspiracies, controversies and, more often than not, physical danger.

Having flushed out the plot, characters, setting, point-of-view and theme he keyed in the title, *Underwater,* and wrote the opening sentence:

> Barely awake and groggy, Tara Mason wondered why she felt cold and wet, realizing to her horror she was alone in a flooding basement, hands bound to a heavy table and water creeping up her chest.

Lines of prose flowed like the water threatening to drown our heroine, completing 19,000 words by midnight. Up by five the next morning, he wrote throughout the day stopping only for a bite of food, the occasional bathroom break and for brief stretches pacing rapidly back and forth on his roof garden to quicken his pulse, oxygenating his brain to help solve conundrums or entertaining valuable tangents. Not brooking any interruption of his creative endeavor, he had shut off his phone, switched all electronic devices to unavailable and wrote straight through the next three days. By

Sunday evening Wolf had completed a 369-page draft of *Underwater*, ready for the proofreaders to sink their teeth into.

He had just sat down to eat a late meal when he heard someone pounding on his door. He turned on the TV selecting the security mode to see who was interrupting his dinner, seeing a well-known figure huffing and puffing on the mat.

"Jeezus Wolf," RJ cried. "Been trying to call, tweet, poke, email and send smoke signals all day! Thought for sure you cracked you head open in the shower or fell off the damn roof. What's with the dead silence all of a sudden?"

"Can't a man have some private time to himself?" Wolf said, grinning at RJ's constipated expression. "So, what's the buzz? Is the building on fire?"

"Not our building," RJ replied, his tone ominous. "But a bunch of building at VPC are."

"What? You mean actually on fire?"

"Yes, like flames pouring out of windows and billows of smoke rising to the sky," RJ said, excitedly. "Started couple hours ago when a bunch of thugs ransacked the office of our student group on campus and set their library on fire. Word of the attack spread like wildfire—no pun intended—and hundreds of students supporting SIR—who knew—marched from one safe space to another making them far less safe by setting them on fire. I'm not making excuses, but these Red Fascists have pushed students over the edge with their endless haranguing, bullying and increasingly attacking anyone daring to disagree with their totalitarian views."

"What's happening at the camp?" Wolf said, worried about Diana and the others.

"All quiet on the western front, bro," RJ quipped. "After the shooting earlier in the week, the cops are there in force. I bet they were surprised when the riots started at the college since the bulk of their officers are milling around Camp Liberty." His phone jingled. He listened to the caller briefly then terminated the call. "That was Diana. The Governor has ordered the State Police to help restore order on campus. You can bet he'll call for an investigation and the second he does, Juan is going to file Lee Sterling's law suit against the college, Wilson and the county police and executive."

"Diana wanted to *ignite* national attention on our Red Fascist menace," Wolf said, a droll expression on his face, "and it looks like she's succeeding spectacularly. Any news about the shooting?"

"That's old news, which you would know about if you'd not shut yourself up in your wolf den up here," RJ replied. "Forensics showed there were at least two shooters both using twenty-two's, not nine calibers like our people carry. But here's the real poop: the shooters were standing on the ground with their backs to the palisade making it look like the shots came from our people."

"From the look on your face," Wolf said, "you think the Reds shot their people to incite outrage hoping for a general uprising to occur."

"Standard modus operandi when reality refuses to comply with the wackos," RJ replied. "Ever since the rally the day you were arrested when to everyone's surprise hundreds of VPC students massed in support of the freedom marchers, the Red Fascists have become more and more desperate and desperate people think and act irrationally and do stupid things like shooting their own supporters in hopes of garnering sympathy for their plight."

"You are assuming it wasn't any of our supporter from the camp or from the college," Wolf said. "Look what happened today: mobs of students attacking Red Fascist safe spaces. The shooters could just as easily be some of the same pissed-off students setting fires this morning."

"Maybe," RJ replied. "But if I'm angry enough to start fires on campus, I wouldn't use .22 shorts and shoot at people's legs."

"Good point," Wolf agreed. "We'll just have to wait until the police arrest the shooters to know the truth."

"Right," RJ said. "Meanwhile back to incommunicado Wolf: inquiring minds want to know what you've been doing the last three days holed up in your lair."

"I'll show you."

Wolf led him to his den and opened the draft to *Underwater*, letting RJ read the first chapter.

"You wrote an entire novel within three days?" RJ said, astonished. "It's great! Love the character. How did you come up with, ah, everything?"

"You know I've been frustrated about what comes after quitting writing exposes," Wolf said. "Banished to my room by

Diana, it became clear writing was what I do best. The words of my writing professor telling me to write about what I know came to me and I know an awful lot about how the world operates. So, no more exposes, but I've got dozens of adventures I can write mining my fifteen years muckraking. Tara Mason is just the beginning ... and the good news is I can easily write my books sitting in a prison cell; nothing much to do there anyway."

"If anyone can get you off, Wallace is the woman to do it," RJ said, looking worried. "By the way, Diana's been making occasional comments about you being worried and depressed when Sheryl is present. Assuming she shares that with Mandeville, it'll give Bellamy or whoever is behind this a sense of false hope that you believe you'll be found guilty. It's not much but every bit of misinformation can be helpful."

The trial was now only eight days away and in three days he'd be flying back to New York to prepare for his defense. Unlike his friend, Wolf was far from certain that his lawyer would be able to overcome the visual evidence and the prosecution's star witness. Though he did not relish the idea of being sent to prison, he'd have many books to write and that required little more than a cell and a computer.

Assuming, of course, he wasn't killed first.

Chapter 20

New York v. Grayson Wolf

Wolf checked into the designed hotel Mia Wallace assigned him to and settled in for the battle to come. He very much appreciated her picking a suite overlooking Central Park, finding an expanse of greenery less distracting and more effective for contemplation than peering at glass and concrete towers. To keep his mind off the upcoming trial, he had brought along the second installment of his Tara Mason series, this one titled, *Bulldozed*, a tale of demolition gone terribly wrong and he wasted no time picking up where he left off back in Tysons Corner.

Thursday and Friday was spent discussing strategy and being prepped for taking the stand. When he encouraged Wallace to hit Maddie hard and the reason why, she agreed, saying that it was the best chance for Ms. Talbot to help him, if in fact she was being blackmailed.

"However, Mr. Wolf," Wallace said, her tone sober, "if Ms. Talbot is involved in setting you up, pressing a rape victim on the stand will make the jury even more sympathetic to her and potentially increase bias against you."

Wolf said he understood the risk and gave her a green light to come out swinging at Maddie. Saturday was a day of rest, Wallace giving him strict instruction not to go roaming the streets, exploring the park or sneaking off to a Broadway show. Sunday morning, he was back in the law office reviewing strategy, discussing options and getting everything ready for Monday morning, May 8.

Wolf was up by six, shaved, showered and dressed by six thirty and working on *Bulldozed* until eight when he closed his laptop and made for the lobby where he met his escort who'd accompany him to the courthouse. Wolf had successfully avoided the media, paparazzi and the general public as he came and went pursuant to his arrest and pre-trial. Escaping detection this morning would be far more challenging with crowds mobbing the courthouse steps, entrance and adjacent sidewalk; but Wolf had a plan.

Two blocks from the courthouse, his vehicle pulled into a parking garage. Two men got out. One was dressed in plain clothing the other in dark overalls, dark cap and carrying a tray filled with tall containers of cappuccino that he held chest high, the cups obscuring the lower part of his face.

"Even without the limo distraction," Wolf's bodyguard said, "no one's going to bother looking at a deliveryman while expecting Grayson Wolf to step out of a car any moment. But I'll be right on your heels just in case things get dicey."

"Thanks Jerry," Wolf said.

The escort checked his phone. "She's five minutes out. Let's roll…"

Manhattan blocks are short and within minutes they approached the courthouse, their first challenge struggling through a large crowd as they made their way to the right side of the steps butting up against the building. Wolf the coffee deliveryman and his plain-clothed shadow started up the steps as a limo stopped at the curb below. Peeking through his coffee cups, Wolf spotted Mia Wallace exiting the car finding herself immediately surrounded by dozens of reporters, camera crews and onlookers. He grinned as he continued his way up the staircase secure in the knowledge that all eyes were on the commotion commencing at the curb, reaching the entrance shortly thereafter.

Deliveryman, coffee and escort passed easily through security heading for the elevator. Five floors up they exited, made for a designated conference room where Wolf stripped off his outfit, straightened his tie and waited for the legal team to arrive, which they did shortly thereafter.

"Good morning Mr. Wolf," Wallace said. "I hope you spent a restful night." Wolf confirmed that he did and she continued. "If we manage to impanel a jury before lunch—an unlikely prospect—the judge will begin the trial after lunch. If jury selection goes past lunch, then we go to trial tomorrow."

"Sooner than later," Wolf quipped. He hated dragging anything out.

"Sooner if we get the right jurists; later if we don't," Wallace replied. "My guess is later, much later."

"Why would it be much later?" Wolf asked.

"Because you are a very high-profile defendant, Mr. Wolf." Wallace explained. "It will be near impossible to find even one jury candidate who has not heard of you and who does not have an opinion one way or another about you."

"Should we petition for a change of venue?" Wolf asked.

A droll grin played on her lips. "Can you think of any location in America you are not known?"

Wallace was right, of course. Wolf had encountered people talking about his books and exploits from Nome, Alaska to Key West, Florida. There was no city, town or hamlet where an impartial jury could be selected.

"We stand a better chance with a jury who knows all about Grayson Wolf to have doubts about your guilt," Wallace continued, "and a New York jury will be among the best informed about your history than one in Podunk, Iowa." An aide waived a hand. "Okay, let the games begin."

Flanked by his lawyer and several associates of her legal team, Wolf walked the Courtroom 5-B, a buzz erupting upon entering the chamber. It was a large room and Wolf noticed that every seat was filled. The circus had come to town and he was the star attraction.

The party came to rest at the defense table, the judge entering soon thereafter. After some preliminary remarks, the jury selection began with the court clerk speaking on a phone presumably requesting the first potential jurist. Soon a middle-aged woman appeared through a side door, taking the witness stand. Wallace began to ask her a series of questions designed to ensure, as much as possible, that the juror would decide the case based on evidence and without "passion or prejudice" and was free from any conflict of interest.

"Ms. Bass, have you or any close relative or friend been sexually molested or assaulted?

"No."

"Do you now, of have you ever, worked for a rape-crisis center or have a close relative or friend who does or has worked for a rape-crisis center?"

"No."

"Are you familiar with the defendant, Grayson Wolf?"

Ms. Bass shot a glance at Wolf. "I've read some of his books and talked about him with colleagues, of course. He's very famous."

"Do you and your colleagues agree with what Mr. Grayson writes in his books?"

A funny expression formed on Ms. Bass's face. "The employees tend to say good things about him; the management not so much."

A murmur arose in the court, the judge shooting the public in the gallery a stern look. The room became quiet under the man's glare.

Wallace asked Ms. Bass two more questions, selected her to be seated in the jury box, the prosecutor agreeing. Of the next two dozen potential jurors questioned, eight were accepted, nine were dismissed for cause—unsuitability mostly—the remaining five being peremptory challenged, rejected without a reason being given to the judge by either attorney.

Two hours had passed, the clock was creeping toward noon and the jury was still three short plus two alternates. Wolf understood the importance to his future of the jury selection process, but he chafed at the tedium; minutes felt more like hours. With thirty minutes remaining before the judge would call for lunch recess, Wolf was delighted when the three remaining jurors were selected with the two alternates following ten minutes later. Having impaneled the jury, the judge instructed all parties to return by one-thirty to begin the trial.

As the courtroom cleared, the prosecutor approached the defense table.

"The DA has instructed me to make a final offer to your client, Ms. Wallace," Korbin said. "Four years with probation in two. I'm am not happy with this deal but I'm not the boss. Frankly, I hope you turn it down."

Wallace peered at Wolf. "It's your decision, of course, but my advice is no deal."

Wolf nodded and gazed at Korbin. "Thank your boss for his offer, but no thank you."

"It'll be my pleasure I assure you, Mr. Wolf." Korbin smiled in a self-satisfied way. "This is going to be a short trial."

Wallace held the prosecutor's gaze. "Yes, it will."

As Korbin walked up the aisle to the exit, Wolf turned to his legal team and joked, "Maybe if we put off the trial for a day or two Korbin will offer me a nolo contendere plea in exchange for time served."

"You getting the impression the DA is a little nervous about the case against you?" Wallace replied. "He should be. Let's go; lunch is waiting for us in the conference room ... unless you rather brave the circus waiting for you outside and head for a nearby restaurant instead?"

A quiet lunch down the hall being far preferable to the crush of humanity parked on the steps and sidewalks waiting to ambush him, Wolf and his lawyers exited the courtroom pressing through a mob of reporters cluttering up the hallway firing questions and taking photos. Wallace kept saying "no comment ... no comment," the commotion ending a minute later when the door to the conference room shut behind them.

Unlike his earlier sensation of time passing slowly during the jury selection, the ninety-minute lunch break zipped quickly by and Wolf found himself once again sitting at the defense table listening to New York Assistant District Attorney Jonathan Korbin's opening statement to the jury.

".... show that the defendant, Grayson Wolf, after being asked repeatedly by Ms. Talbot to stop making sexual advances and leave, ignored her demands, sexually assaulting her several times throughout the night. The State will produce footage of the building's security camera showing Mr. Wolf entering the building with Ms. Talbot and the night manager who will corroborate the authenticity of the security recording. You will hear Ms. Talbot herself testify to this heinous act ... and the State will produce physical evidence in the form of explicit photographs taken that very night inside Ms. Talbot's home of the assault proving beyond a shadow of a doubt that Mr. Wolf sexually assaulted Ms. Talbot."

"Not good enough, counselor," Mia Wallace said, under her breath as Korbin finished and walked back to his table.

Wolf asked one of the associates what she meant about not being good enough. The lawyer explained that opening arguments are important because they allow an attorney the opportunity to present the case as a cohesive whole and not squander that opportunity by presenting just facts or summarizing what witnesses are going to say.

The explanation was cut short when the judge called upon Mia Wallace for her opening statement. She rose from her seat and faced the jury.

"Your Honor, ladies and gentleman of the jury," she said, her eyes sweeping the jurors, "for fifteen years, my client, Grayson Wolf, has been the scourge of corrupt lobbyists, presidents of corporations, law firms, college administrators and politicians. For his valiant efforts to expose criminal activities and corruption, Mr. Wolf has endured censure, harassment, verbal and physical assault, threats to his life and endless lawsuits. For fifteen years, Mr. Wolf has refused to buckle under this endless onslaught designed to silence him and failing to do so for fifteen years, the man who has done more than any single individual to expose corporate and political corruption, the man who has been deluged by threats against his life and livelihood, that same man, universally recognized as a paragon of truth and justice, who in his entire life has never been accused of even a hint of impropriety by any woman he has had a professional or intimate relationship with ... *that man* throws it all away to allegedly *rape* a woman?"

Wallace continued for another five minutes reviewing the prosecutor's evidence and its inherent weaknesses, addressing the dubious nature of the victim's claim, concluding her presentation, saying, "Grayson Wolf will take the stand and admit he spent the entire evening with Ms. Talbot, that she invited him up to her flat and invited him willingly into her bed ... The prosecution has stated that the testimony of its witnesses and the evidence it provides will prove beyond a shadow of a doubt that
Grayson Wolf committed the crime he is accused of. He is mistaken. What the evidence and testimony will show once brought to the full light of day for all to see will prove conclusively that Mr. Wolf is innocent of this crime."

Wallace returned to the defense table and the judge instructed the prosecutor to call his first witness. Korbin called the night manager who was sworn in by the Bailiff.

"Mr. Walczak you are the night manager of One Hampton?"

"Yes."

"How long have you worked at One Hampton?"

"Since 2006, when the building opened its doors."

"Were you working on the evening of March 31st of this year?"

"Yes."

"What time did you come on duty that evening?"

"Eleven p.m.," Walczak replied. "Like I have every night for eleven years."

"Did you see Ms. Talbot enter the lobby of the building the evening of March 31st?"

"Yes, I did."

"Was anyone with her?"

"Yes," Walczak said. "She came in with a man."

"Is the man who came with Ms. Talbot in this courtroom today?"

"Yes sir, he sure is."

"Please point to the man in this courtroom you saw accompanying Ms. Talbot entering the lobby of One Hampton on the evening of March 31st." Walczak pointed at Wolf. "Let the record show that the witness is pointing at the defendant, Grayson Wolf."

Wolf gazed calmly back at the witness, wondering if the man expected him to shrivel up under his accusing finger pointing dramatically at him. The associate to his left made a quiet comment about Korbin milking this for all its worth.

The prosecutor presented his first exhibit of evidence, security footage from the building's lobby. A large monitor adjacent to the judge's bench facing the jury and the gallery came to life. The security footage played for a brief moment, Korbin pausing on the images of Wolf and Talbot entering the lobby, date and time stamped on the lower edge of the screen.

"Mr. Walczak," Korbin began, "do you recognize these individuals?"

"Yes; that's Ms. Talbot on the left, and Mr. Wolf on the right."

"To the best of your knowledge," Korbin continued, "is this recording from the night of March 31st of this year?"

"Yes sir, it is," he said. "That's Mr. Wolf with Ms. Talbot and they came together that night."

"Thank you, Mr. Walczak," Korbin said. "No further questions."

Wallace stood up but remained behind the table.

"Mr. Walczak, how often have you seen Ms. Talbot enter the building through the lobby while on duty this year?"

The witness looked thoughtful for a short moment. "Couple dozen times at least."

"How often during those encounters was Ms. Talbot accompanied by a man?"

"Objection," Korbin said. "Relevance."

"Establishing a pattern of behavior," Wallace said, gazing at the judge.

"I'll allow it." The judge ruled. "You may answer the question, Mr. Walczak."

Walczak looked up at the ceiling, thinking. "Four, maybe five times?"

"To the best of your recollection," Wallace continued, "how did Ms. Talbot appear the times you saw her entering the lobby accompanied by a man? Smiling? Happy? Frowning? Frightened?"

"She always seemed happy to me," Walczak said. "She'd usually say hello to me as she passed by, smiling. Happy."

"On the evening in question when you saw her in the lobby with Mr. Wolf, how did she appear to you?"

Walczak shot a look at Maddie sitting at Korbin's table, then at Wolf.

"How did Ms. Talbot appear to you that evening when she entered the lobby with Mr. Wolf?" Wallace repeated.

"Really happy," he said. "They were both smiling and laughing as they walked to the elevators."

"Thank you, Mr. Walczak. One more question: would you please read the date and time stamped on the security footage?"

Walczak peered at the screen and said, "April the first, one-twenty a.m."

"April. Not March. Thank you, Mr. Walczak," Wallace said. "No further questions."

"Redirect, Your Honor," Korbin said, immediately. The judge nodded and Korbin said, "Mr. Walczak, were you on duty the evening of March 31st until seven a.m. the next morning, April the first?"

"Yes sir."

"Did you see Mr. Wolf enter the building with Ms. Talbot at or near 1:20 a.m. April the first, 2017?"

"Yes, I did."

"Thank you. No further questions."

Wallace asked the judge for permission to ask a clarifying question of Walczak, receiving an affirmative response.

"Mr. Walczak, how did you know that Mr. Wolf and Ms. Talbot entered the lobby that night at or near 1:20 a.m. April the first, 2017?" When he didn't respond, she continued. "You know the exact time for the same reason everyone in the court knows when Mr. Wolf and Ms. Talbot entered your lobby that night: because it is clearly imprinted on the security footage on the court monitor. Mr. Walczak, did Mr. Wolf and Ms. Talbot enter your lobby on the evening of March 31st or the early morning of April 1st?"

"I'm not sure, ma'am."

"Thank you, Mr. Walczak," Wallace said. "No further questions, Your Honor."

Having questioned hundreds of informants and individuals connected to a person he was investigating, Wolf recognized the error committed by Korbin and its importance to his case. By overlooking something that appeared insignificant, Korbin allowed Wallace to create a measure of doubt in the minds of the jurors concerning the integrity of his witness's testimony and perhaps even the competence of the prosecutor himself from the outset of the trial.

The next witness for the prosecution was a visual imaging expert who testified that the photographs Korbin has previously entered into evidence were not manipulated. When Wallace declined to cross-examine the expert, the judge shot her a questioning look to which she replied saying she reserved the right to recall him later, though Wolf knew Wallace had other plans for the photos after the State rested its case.

When the prosecutor called his star witness to the stand, Wolf understood why Korbin had warned Wallace earlier this would be a short trial. The entirety of the State's case rested on a night manager, security footage, the accuser's testimony and a handful of photographs. Wallace's cross-examination of One Hampton's night manager had already sowed doubt about the reliability of the prosecution's case from the outset and knowing her reputation, Wolf was feeling sorry for Maddie when the time came for his lawyer to cross-examine her.

Madeline Talbot was sworn in by the Bailiff and took a seat. She shot a glance at Wolf, he giving her a surreptitious smile, she holding her attacker's eyes longer than a terrified rape victim would dare.

Her testimony took up the better part of an hour, Korbin taking his time to allow Maddie to explain how she knew Wolf, leading her up to the night in question. Proceeding carefully, his questions gently guided her through the "horrible events" of that night, Maddie's testimony of the sexual attack becoming more explicit than Korbin had expected, judging from the man's alarmed expression. Enjoying the spectacle, Wolf was certain Maddie's explicit descriptions were an indirect way to communicate her intimate feelings to him in open court for everyone to hear but not understand.

Wallace leaned toward Wolf, a smile playing on her lips.

"Quite a testimony to your prowess." He stared at her, surprised she'd understood the hidden message within the words. She made a low snorting sound. "Don't worry, it's not obvious, though she ought not to be looking directly at you during the racier parts of her testimony."

"She's giving us a green light to go after her," Wolf said, feeling more confident about his decision to have Wallace press Maddie during cross-examination.

"And I will," she replied. Something caught her attention and she looked up. "Photographs time."

Korbin lifted a packet of papers, identified them as People's Exhibits two through thirteen, asking for and receiving permission to approach the witness. His assistant walked over to the jury foreman carrying copies of the photos and stood waiting for instructions. Korbin explained how he came to have these photos in his possession offering the theory that an unknown voyeur had installed hidden cameras in Talbot's home to spy on her and upon witnessing the assault sent the photographs.

Korbin handed Maddie the first exhibit. "Ms. Talbot, who is the man in photo entering your home with you?"

"Grayson Wolf."

Korbin nodded at his assistant who handed the photo to the foreman.

"Was this photo taken the night Mr. Wolf sexually assaulted you?"

"Yes, the morning of April first." Maddie confirmed. "It was the only night I have ever invited Mr. Wolf to my condo."

Korbin handed her two more photos, the first showing the pair talking to each other the second a close-up of Talbot's face exhibiting an expression of concern. He handed her a third photo.

"Would you tell the court what is occurring in this photo?"

"Mr. Wolf has me by the arm and walking me toward the bedroom."

The last four photos were the most incriminating, showing Wolf ostensibly grab Maddie's shoulder and begin to undress her, the next pushing her on the bed followed by one with him engaging in sexual intercourse and the last showing Maddie's face, her anguished expression clearly visible. Korbin's assistant doled out the photos to the foreman as his boss handed them to Maddie, the foreman passing the photos along to the jurors.

"I know this is painful and thank you for your courage to testify today," Korbin said. Looking over at Wallace he added, "Your witness."

"Ms. Wallace," the judge said, "it's approaching four 'o clock. I would imagine your cross-examination of the witness and Mr. Korbin's redirect will exceed an hour. We will adjourn for today and you can begin at nine tomorrow morning."

"Of course," Wallace said, standing up. "Thank you, Your Honor."

The judge stood up, Wolf along with everyone else following suit. Reflecting on the proceedings, were the jury to decide his innocence or guilt at this moment, Wolf knew he'd be sent up the river.

His eyes held Maddie's as she passed by. Unlike the last time he'd been this close to her, no heat of eager anticipation blazed in them today.

Chapter 21

Best Defense is...

The morning began with a bang when Wallace's first question insinuated that Maddie had falsely accused Wolf of rape.

"Objection!" Korbin cried, jumping up from his seat. "Inflammatory, not to mention insensitive."

"Sustained."

Wolf noted that Maddie never even flinched at Wallace's blatant accusation. People with integrity, unlike liars, tend not to react when hearing the truth spoken.

"Ms. Talbot," Wallace continued, "did Mr. Wolf call and ask you out to a date the evening of March 31?"

Maddie gave a good impression of feeling uncomfortable. "No. I called him."

"When was the last time you actually spoke with Mr. Wolf?"

"Over a year ago."

"Why did you call him?"

"I guess I was feeling lonely."

"Lonely?" Wallace said, her tone uncompromising. "Have you ever dated Mr. Wolf in the past?"

"No."

"No." Wallace repeated. "Why would you call a man you had never dated?"

Maddie shrugged. "Just a lark."

"According to your testimony earlier," Wallace said, pressing on, "you and Mr. Wolf went to dinner, walked around Manhattan talking and looking at sights followed by dancing at a popular nightclub, entering the lobby of your building twenty minutes after one a.m. Did Mr. Wolf ask you to invite him up to your home?"

Maddie did not respond.

"I'll ask you again, Ms. Talbot." Wallace's tone was icy. "Did Mr. Wolf ask you to invite him up to your home?"

"No."

"Thank you." Wallace paused. "You asked him up to your home and invited him to your bedroom."

"Objection," Korbin said. "Leading the witness."

"Sustained."

"Did you invite Mr. Wolf to accompany you upstairs to your home?"

"Yes."

"Did you invite Mr. Wolf to your bed for the purpose of engaging in sexual intercourse with him?"

"Objection."

"I'll allow it," the judge ruled.

Maddie's gaze flicked briefly at Wolf. "No."

Wolf had to squelch the urge to smile. Maddie was a lawyer and technically her response was not a lie: she hadn't verbally "invited" him to her bed; things just naturally moved in that direction.

"Why did you not report the assault to the police immediately after Mr. Wolf made you breakfast that morning and left?"

"Objection!" Korbin cried. "Inflammatory and argumentative."

"Sustained."

"Ms. Talbot," Wallace said, pressing on as though nothing happened, "did Mr. Wolf make you breakfast?"

"Mr. Wolf made breakfast." Maddie replied.

"And why did you not contact the police and report this heinous crime when it occurred?" Wallace challenged. "Why did you wait *two months* after the alleged incident to contact the police?"

"I was embarrassed," Maddie replied.

"Then two months later you're suddenly not embarrassed?"

"Objection. Argumentative."

"Sustained," the judge said. "Proceed with caution, counselor."

"Yes, Your Honor." Turning back to the witness, Wallace continued. "Did you install the cameras in your home?"

"No, I did not," Maddie said. "Some sick pervert broke into my home; I have no idea how long they've been there."

"Are you now, or have you ever been," Wallace began, "involved in a conspiracy to falsely accuse Mr. Wolf of a crime or actively to harm Mr. Wolf in any material manner?"

"Objection," Korbin said. "Ms. Talbot is not the one on trial here."

"Sustained."

Wallace pressed on. "Have you falsely accused Mr. Wolf of sexually assaulting you?"

"Objection!"

"Sustained." The judge ruled. "Ms. Wallace, I am warning you."

"Yes, Your Honor," She said, contritely. "No more questions of this witness at this time, Your Honor. I do reserve the right to recall Ms. Talbot."

"So noted," the judge replied.

Korbin redirected Maddie who re-affirmed that Wolf did sexually assault her and rested the State's case, surprising Wolf and his legal team who had expected the prosecutor to call the defendant to the stand. In consideration of the time, the judge adjourned the proceedings until one p.m. and the group retreated to the conference room for lunch and to prepare for the defense in the afternoon.

In light of Korbin declining to call Wolf to the stand, the lawyers were debating the merits of calling Wolf to testify on his behalf, Wallace leaning toward not having him testify.

"The State's entire case rests on he said, she said. By the time our visual media experts finish with Korbin's photographs, he might as well shred them because they'll reek worse than an open sewer in Bombay and the jury will hold their noses. If we still feel we need Mr. Wolf to testify, then we'll swear him in."

The debate was settled just as lunch arrived and the group dissolved. Having been out of touch for the past few days, Wolf called Diana for an update of events at Camp Liberty.

"Juan filed the civil suit against VPC and Dr. Wilson on behalf of Lee Sterling yesterday," she said. "The class action is waiting in the wings. Juan wants to have as many pieces assembled so that the filing will be a wake-up call on a national level. He calls it the lawsuit heard around the world. I love it. How are you doing? How's the trial?"

Wolf brought Diana up to speed and gave her a brief glimpse into what Wallace was planning for the defense beginning right after lunch. He heard the concern in her voice as she wondered about the outcome, Wolf assuring her that Mia Wallace is very confident that she'll destroy the prosecution's evidence and with it, their case against him.

"It takes only one juror to have enough doubt to hang the jury," Wolf said. "From what Wallace explained to me, most or all jurors will have more than a reasonable doubt about my guilt. Just too hinky and stinky and I trust the jury to see it, too."

"I hope you're right, Wolf," Dana replied, "though I'm not as confident as you are. You told me that Maddie would answer in a way that would throw doubt on her testimony, but from what you've said, she didn't seem to act like she was breaking under cross examination to me ... I really hope your attorney gets the job done, Wolf."

"She will..." The door opened and Wolf spotted a bike messenger enter. "Diana, I've gotta go. Don't worry, Wallace will rip Korbin's pictures to shreds. Call you after the trial..."

He terminated the call and came over to see what Wallace received.

"A flash drive," she said.

"Who sent it?" Wolf asked.

"No clue," she said. Looking at one of her associates she said, "Hand me an iPad." She inserted the drive and tapped her finger on the iPad several times, silently peering at the screen. "Holy cow..."

"What is it?" Several people said simultaneously.

Wallace pointed the iPad at the group assembled before her. Wolf watched the video with rising excitement.

"More like every holy cow in India," he quipped.

Wallace checked the time. "Thirty minutes ... whole new ballgame..."

Their thirty-minute strategy session ran five minutes past the start of the trial, the judge communicating his displeasure in no uncertain terms. Wallace apologized profusely, assuring the judge that this would not happen again, his puckered lips a grudging acceptance of her apology.

"Call your first witness."

Wallace called the first of two visual imaging experts. The man was sworn in and she proceeded.

"Dr. Samaras, you are founder and President of Imaging Impact, one of the leading visual media companies in New York," Wallace stated. "What exactly does your company do?"

Samaras spent the next two minutes explaining how his company employed digital imaging to create and design products for use in advertising, television, web design, movies and much more.

"Does your firm use photographs as part of their creations?" Wallace asked.

"Millions of them," Samaras said.

"Dr. Samaras, I imagine you are familiar with the phrase, a picture is worth a thousand words? Is that really true today in our digital environment?"

"I can't speak to that," he replied, "but I can tell you with absolute certainty that in our digital world an image can be designed, placed or selected to say *exactly* what we want it to say to the viewer."

Wallace handed Samaras a copy of a photos that had been placed into evidence. "Please look at the photo labeled Exhibit # 4." The photo appeared on the large monitor for the benefit of the jury. "What exactly does this photo say to you?"

Samaras peered at the photo. "It tells me the subject appears to be surprised; apprehensive perhaps."

"Thank you," Wallace said. "Based on your twenty-year's experience as an expert in visual imaging, does this one photograph show the subject feelings accurately, without any doubt? Without any other possibilities?"

Samaras issued a snort. "Of course not. A photograph represents a micro-second glimpse of the subject; nothing more, nothing less."

"Please look at the photo labeled Exhibit # 13. What does this image say to you?"

Samaras glanced briefly at Maddie's face. "It speaks of pain. But as I said, this photo like all photos are only micro-second glimpses. The photographer who took this shot will most certainly have dozens more like it because as anyone who has ever taken photos knows, you have to take lots of photos of a subject to get a few good ones and hundreds to get a handful of exceptional ones. This photo of the subject's face *appears* to suggest she is in pain. The one that was taken a second later might very well shout about the subject's happiness or rapture. One photograph, a dozen, or even a thousand, a complete story does not make. Imaging Impact is in the business of creating images that tell a story our clients want to communicate to their clients and customers."

"Would it be fair to say," Wallace continued, "that in today's digital manipulative environment, a picture can be worth a thousand lies?"

"Objection," Korbin said. "Leading the witness."

"I'll allow it," the judge ruled.

Samaras grinned. "Any image can be used to tell exactly what someone wants it to say."

"Thank you, Dr. Samaras," Wallace said. "Your witness..."

Korbin peered at his notes for a moment, then looked up. "Dr. Samaras, can the images in the photographs Ms. Wallace handed you be a truthful and accurate representation of what the subject is feeling?"

"Of course, but—"

"Thank you, doctor," Korbin interjected. "No further questions."

"Redirect, Your Honor," Wallace said. The judge nodded and she continued. "Dr. Samaras, can you say with even minimal certainty that the images in the photographs are a truthful and accurate representation of what the subject is feeling?"

"No," he replied. "A photograph is only a micro-second glimpse and one cannot and should not draw conclusions about what the subject feels or anything else about the subject. One can only take the picture at face value and nothing more."

"Thank you. No further questions."

Samaras returned to his seat and Wallace called her next witness, a university professor expert in the field of human sexuality. A smartly dressed woman was sworn in and took a seat. Wallace asked her to give the court pertinent background about her specialty and the applications of her research. She shot Wolf a curious glance.

"Thank you, Dr. Tomlinson," Wallace said. "Besides being a leading expert in the field of human sexuality, as part of your research over the years, you have complied a library of coital images, specifically faces leading up to, during and post orgasm."

"That is correct," Tomlinson confirmed. "Our department has worked with hundreds of couples."

"And you have brought with you a number of samples to enter into evidence today."

"Yes."

Wallace brought a flash drive to the bench. "If it pleases the court, I would like to enter this digital drive as Exhibit A for the defense, Your Honor."

The drive was marked by the clerk who handed it back to Wallace. She then handed a photo to Tomlinson, the image simultaneously appearing on the large monitor.

"Dr. Tomlinson," she began, "based upon your experience as a leading expert in the field of human sexuality, what emotion might the face in People's Exhibit #13 be displaying?"

"Orgasmic pleasure."

"Objection," Korbin said. "Speculative and immaterial."

"No more speculative and immaterial than the prosecution using a photo representing a micro-second's glimpse to claim pain and fear, Your Honor," Wallace shot back.

"Overruled."

"Dr. Tomlinson," Wallace continued, "Dr. Samaras, an expert in the field of digital imaging testified that images such as the one in your hand can be employed to communicate whatever message one wishes to project. The State claims the face shows pain and fear. You claim it shows orgasmic pleasure. Is there an objective way to help the jury become more informed about the emotion displayed in People's Exhibit #13?"

"I believe I can provide a wider perspective," she replied.

Wallace handed her the remote control. The face of Maddie changed to a university logo.

"The first series of facial video clips show women experiencing orgasm, each clip followed by a still image representing the summation of that woman's orgasmic experience," Tomlinson said.

She pressed a button and the first video played, a ten-second close-up of a woman in the throes of achieving sexual climax. After the video, a still image of the woman's face appeared.

"Going through the video frame by frame, my researchers collaboratively selected the one frame that best represented the orgasmic pinnacle of each woman," Tomlinson explained. "I'll now play the remaining samples...."

Seven more video clips followed, each with a still image. When it was done, all eight facial images captured at the height of orgasmic pleasure filled the screen.

"As you can see," Tomlinson continued, "every image of these women achieving sexual climax are similar: lips parted, eyelids partially or fully closed; highly erotic images of women at the moment of intense pleasure. One could almost feel the heat of passion radiating from the images."

Everyone in the court peered at the faces on the monitor. If it had been Wallace's goal to dispel the image of pain and fear from Maddie's face on People's Exhibit #13, she had failed spectacularly.

After a long moment, Wallace broke the silence. "Dr. Tomlinson, what else can you tell us about these series of videos and images?"

"All eight videos and subsequent still images are examples of pornography," she replied, her words striking listeners like cold water. "All these women are actors. The images of orgasmic climax—the facial expressions and all the rest—are fake. We have a hundred more videos along with extensive interviews of the actresses and actors, but these eight examples are sufficient, I would think."

"Your Honor," Wallace said, "I have copies of the accompanying interviews and would happily submit them as evidence if the prosecution wishes."

The judge glanced at Korbin.

"Not necessary, Your Honor."

Wallace turned back to her witness. "Dr. Tomlinson, you have another series of videos to share with us. If you would, please."

"Like the first series of videos, the following also show women's faces during climax."

She pressed a button and the videos played. This time the facial expressions were quite different from that of the sex actors. When the series was complete, eight facial images captured at the height of orgasmic pleasure glowed on the monitor.

"Dr. Tomlinson," Wallace asked, "you said that these photos best represent the orgasmic experience of each woman. Why do these facial images look the opposite of the women's faces in the first series of photos while in the throes of orgasmic passion?"

"Because these women did experience real, not fake, orgasms," Tomlinson said.

"How do you know that?"

Tomlinson went on to explain how both sexual partners were hooked up to monitors recording heart rate, temperature spike, muscle contraction, breathing. When prompted, she explained that her team conducted sessions and follow-up interviews with over two hundred couples. As before, Korbin declined the offer of Wallace to submit the written testimonies into evidence.

"Dr. Tomlinson," Wallace said, "these images of women experiencing the height of sexual release don't exactly look like someone enjoying the experience; just the opposite. In fact, a casual observer might easily conclude these women are experiencing pain and fear."

"Objection!" Korbin said.

"Sustained."

"Dr. Tomlinson," Wallace said, "based on over two hundred sessions with couples engaged in sexual intercourse and review of their facial expressions while in the throes of orgasm, to the best of your knowledge, Doctor, did any of these women whose images are shown on the monitor experiencing pain or fear before, during or post coital contact?"

"I am not familiar with any woman in our sessions expressing fear or pain pursuant to, during or after orgasm," Tomlinson confirmed.

"Yet each facial expression appears to suggest that these women are, in fact, experiencing pain and fear," Wallace insisted. "Why is that?"

"Because that is what women's facial expressions—and men's, too—look like when they are experiencing real orgasms and not performing in pornographic videos," Tomlinson said.

Wallace clicked the remote control and Maddie's face replaced the images of the eight women. "Dr. Tomlinson, looking at the expression on the woman's face on the monitor, what emotion besides the possibility of pain and fear might this woman be experiencing at the moment the camera captured her expression?"

"Assuming the photograph is genuine and the woman is not acting," Tomlinson said, "this image could easily have captured this woman as she approached or achieved sexual climax."

"Thank you, Dr. Tomlinson," Wallace said.

She clicked her remote and the screen filled with the previous eight women along with the photo of Maddie. All nine faces had similar expressions and Wallace made sure to point that out to the jury. She turned her witness over to Korbin who proceeded to ask questions designed to have Tomlinson say the photo of Maddie *could* be an expression of pain and fear, but she insisted that it was far more likely it was pleasure, not pain or fear. Korbin cut her off by insisting she only answer yes or no. Having nothing else with which to undermine Tomlinson's testimony, he retreated back to his desk.

Wallace called for her next witness. "I call Justin Bellamy to the stand."

Wolf had insisted Wallace subpoena Bellamy, explaining the high likelihood the man was behind this charade. He was also sure that this frontal assault against him was not just about payback for the way Wolf portrayed the scumbag as a scumbag in two of his novels, including Screw You, Suckers! and he had a plan for Wallace to implement.

"Mr. Bellamy," Wallace began, "you are the CEO of New World Hedge Fund?"

"Yes, I am. In the top three hedge funds, I'm proud to say." He shot Wolf a malevolent glance.

"Do you know Ms. Talbot?"

"Not personally."

"But you are familiar with her?"

"Familiar in that she's one of the lawyers representing my firm."

"In the past five years," Wallace continued, "you've had half dozen complaints of sexual harassment filed against you, is that correct?"

"It goes along with being successful these days apparently," he said. "Women trying to shake men down for money claiming 'sexual harassment' is the norm now."

"How about the three accusations of sexual assault over the last two years?"

Korbin stood up. "Mr. Bellamy is not on trial, Your Honor. Is Ms. Wallace going somewhere pertinent concerning her defense of her client?"

"Your Honor," Wallace said, "I assure the court that Mr. Bellamy's testimony is pertinent to the defense."

"I'll give you some latitude, counselor," the judge said. "Get to the point soon."

"Yes, Your Honor." Glancing at Bellamy, she continued. "Have you been accused of sexual assault by at least three women over the past two years?"

"Just misunderstandings; lovers' spats," he replied. "All the charges were withdrawn."

"Do you know Grayson Wolf?" Wallace said.

"The lowlife rapist writing lies about me and my company," he said.

"Have you publically said numerous times you would get even with Mr. Wolf?"

He made a dismissive face. "Just blowing off steam, is all."

"So, yes, you have threatened to get even with Mr. Wolf." Wallace said. "Would that threat include blackmailing a lawyer to make false accusations of rape against Mr. Wolf?"

"Objection!" Korbin shouted.

"Sustained," the judge said, shooting Wallace a castigating look. "I'm warning you, counselor."

"Yes, Your Honor," she replied. "No further questions at this time." She returned to the defense table and picked up a flash drive. "May we approach the bench, Your Honor?"

He waived both counselors to approach. Having muted his microphone, Wolf couldn't hear what was being said, but after a moment the judge called for a fifteen-minute recess, Wallace following the judge to his chambers. Korbin waved at Maddie to approach, the pair hustling after the jurists shortly disappearing behind the closing door. Though apprehensive about Maddie's fate, Wolf grinned knowing what was on that flash drive and hoping the judge would allow Wallace to procced as planned.

The trial resumed and his lawyer recalled Maddie to the stand. The way Wallace had smiled upon returning from the judge's chambers made him assume all was going according to plan ... unless Maddie failed to cooperate or didn't catch on to what she was really being asked to answer. If so, it would foil his gambit to seek justice in another important case.

Maddie was reminded she was still under oath and took the stand.

"Ms. Talbot," Wallace began, "are you being coerced to falsely accuse Mr. Wolf of sexually assaulting you back on March 31st?"

She glanced at Wolf and took a breath. "Yes."

A murmur arose in the courtroom. So far, so good.

"Do you know who is coercing you to falsely accuse Mr. Wolf of raping you?"

"No; it's a man on the telephone," she replied, looking increasingly relieved.

"Would you explain to the court how you are being coerced?"

"If I didn't do what the man told me," Maddie said, "he would bankrupt my family's company and ruin my parents and siblings; they all work for the firm."

"Exactly how did this man say he would bankrupt your parent's firm?"

Her eyes shifted to someone in the gallery. "He said his people would massively short-sell my parent's company's stock driving the value down to pennies. That would kill the company, put seventy employees out of work..."

As Maddie continued her explanation, Wolf stealthily texted Annika, CIR's Chief Financial Officer, giving her brief instructions to initiate counter measures. She confirmed the order and promised to get back him as soon as she had definitive answers. He terminated the communication just in time to hear the tail end of Wallace's next question. He crossed his fingers.

"...Mr. Bellamy ever pressured you to have sex with him?"

Maddie sat very still. She looked at Wolf.

"Yes."

Wolf worked to keep a neutral expression. This was it.

"Do you recall any specific dates when Mr. Bellamy pressured you to have sex?"

Wolf stared at Maddie, shouting December over and over again in his head. If there was such a thing as reading one's mind this was the time!

"I can't recall a specific date," she replied, slowly. "Last December, I think it was."

Wolf let out a hiss. She had remembered his conversation.

"During the Holidays?" Wallace suggested. "Earlier?"

"Earlier," she replied. "Sometime during the first week."

"The first week of December 2016." Wallace stated.

"Yes, the first week of last December."

There was a commotion in the Gallery and the judge rapped the gavel on his bench for order. Looking over his shoulder, Wolf spotted Bellamy standing and arguing with one of the officers guarding the entrance. Wallace recalled Bellamy to the stand and the man calmed down, rushing to the stand in a huff. Before Wallace could ask him a question, he complained loudly that Maddie was lying. The judge banged his gavel once more ordering him to get quiet.

"Ms. Talbot has testified in open court that you pressured her to have sex with you and—"

"The bitch is lying!"

"One more outburst," the judge growled, "and I will hold you in contempt of court and have you removed to spend the next three days in lockup. Do you understand?"

A furious looking Bellamy shut up and nodded.

"Mr. Bellamy," Wallace said, pressing the witness, "has every one of the dozen or so women who have accused you of sexual harassment or sexual assault lied, as you so often publically and loudly claimed?"

"That has nothing to do with the fact that, *that woman*," he pointed dramatically at Maddie, his face crimson, "is a liar! I've never even touched her!"

"You have never pressured Ms. Talbot to have sex with you back during the first week of December, 2017?" Wallace fired back.

"Hell no!" he cried. "I wasn't even in town…I was visiting my son at college! She a liar!"

"Thank you, Mr. Bellamy," Wallace said. "That will be all."

Anyone looking at Wolf that moment would see a man with a placid expression sitting calmly at the defense table. Appearances, however, can be deceiving. Internally, Wolf was mentally jumping excitedly up and down at the success of his plan and its expected outcome. If he were allowed, he would have rushed over to Maddie and kissed her!

As Bellamy stepped down from the stand, he pointed at Maddie, shouting, "You're fired! I'm going to sue you for every penny!"

The judge must have had enough of his outbursts and ordered the Bailiff to remove him from court, followed by the judge dismissing the jury, explaining that new evidence had come to light, which combined with Maddie's admission of falsely accusing him of rape, fully exonerated Grayson Wolf of the charges.

Korbin, the New York Assistant District Attorney had been right when he declared with so much confidence that this would be a short trial. From jury selection to dismissal of all charges within two days.

All's well that ends well. At least for Grayson Wolf.

But his quest for justice was far from over.

Chapter 22

Check...

No amount of assurance for success ever matches the reality of achieving the goal, especially when failure would in all likelihood be a death sentence. Though Wolf was reasonably certain that Maddie would have confessed rather than send him to prison, blackmail or no blackmail, he felt more relieved than he had realized as he walked out of the court with Maddie beside him.

Entering the conference room, Maddie placed a hand on Wolf's arm. "I am so sorry—"

"Hold that thought," he replied, tapping Annika's name on his phone. "We have only begun to fight." Wolf gave Annika a brief overview of the trial's outcome then asked about the progress pursuant to his texted request earlier, his face lighting up as he listened to her reply. "Fantastic. Tell our friends I owe them big time. Thanks; I'll call later."

He apologized to his legal team for having them wait and took a seat at the table. Maddie sat across from him, a remorseful expression clouding her usually sunny disposition. Gazing at her, Wolf marveled at how a touch of sadness revealed a rarely glimpsed facet of her beauty; he found it disturbingly enthralling. Her sudden smile must have caught him off guard because he felt himself blush. He grinned confidently back, hoping his own captivating smile (so he'd been told) would cover his embarrassment.

He thanked Wallace and her legal team for doing a magnificent job defending him and for agreeing to go along with his request to subpoena Bellamy.

"The results are better than I had hoped," Wolf said. To Maddie, he said, "I can't tell you how grateful I am to you for understanding what we were trying to do with Bellamy." He held up a hand stopping her from interrupting. "Before you say anything, I put you into the uncomfortable position of perjuring yourself with the Bellamy testimony. I've retained Ms. Wallace as your lawyer; anything you say in this room is covered under lawyer-client privilege."

Maddie slowly shook her head. "Do you know how crazy you sound? I wouldn't blame you if you never spoke to me again after what I put you through."

"Stop beating yourself up, Maddie," Wolf replied. "I've been in the cat and mouse business longer than most. The second the cops told me who brought charges against me, I knew you were being pressured or worse. Bellamy knew I was coming to New York and used you to set me up."

"Why me?" Maddie said, looking puzzled. "There's a hundred women Bellamy could have picked to do the deed."

"Because, my dear," Wolf said, "he surely knows I never hop into bed with some random woman and I'm sure Bellamy suspects you're were one of my informants. Why go for only one if you can crush two birds with one blow?"

"But why now if he suspected me?" she asked.

"Because of December 6, 2016," Wolf replied. "Because I'm thinking that papa bear and baby bear did a very nasty thing and this was a good way to stop not only the big bad wolf breathing down their necks, but the wolf's helper, too."

"Right," she said, nodding. "That rape case and suicide you're were investigating in Colorado."

"Which will now heat up significantly because of your perjury about Bellamy; which upon recollection I'm certain you must have been mistaken about," Wolf said, grinning mischievously. "Many people will thank you for remembering me talking about that case back in March and for catching on when you were being questioned on the stand."

"Assuming Mr. Bellamy is behind this scam," Wallace said, "how do you want us to proceed, Mr. Wolf?"

"He's not the only one who can knock two down with one blow," he replied. "If you'll indulge me..." He keyed a number in his phone, reached toward the polycom unit resting on the table and switched it on allowing everyone in the room to listen. He held a finger up to his lips indicating no one should speak. The phone rang several more times when a male voice answered. Everyone in the room recognized the man by the naturally grating tone of his voice.

"What the hell do you want, you miserable bastard!"

"To give you some important financial advice," Wolf said.

"Go to hell." Bellamy snarled.

"Better check after-hours trading first," Wolf replied, his tone taunting. "I hear New World Hedge Fund is dropping like a stone … go on, I'll wait…."

One of the associates keyed in the fund at the New York Stock Exchange's website and put NWF's data on the room's monitor for all to see. Large, colorful graph and data charts filled the monitor's screen, the point of interest being NWF's future's trading numbers glowing red, the negative percentage increasing steadily under the pressure of mounting sell orders.

"What the hell?" Bellamy shouted, sounding highly incredulous.

"Very soon, Mr. Bellamy," Wolf said, his tone threatening, "the massive computer managed stock market system will awake to protect its clients' investment in your company. When that happens, your stock and that of all your friends in NWF will shrivel into single digits … Listen very carefully: You are going to cancel your waiting sell orders on Madeline Talbot's father's company immediately and forget you've ever heard the name of Talbot. If you don't…well let's just say that currently NWF is down 5% representing a loss of about forty million. By my estimation you have about sixty seconds to act before you lose another forty million or far more if the computers kick in.   Tick-tock, Mr. Bellamy… Fifty-nine seconds and counting…"

There was a stretch of silence followed by Bellamy's voice.

"Okay, done." One could imagine the words spoken through clenched teeth.

"I'm putting you on hold…" Wolf texted a sell order to Annika, receiving confirmation. "Pressure off as agreed, Mr. Bellamy. Sorry about the," he looked at the monitor, "fifty plus mill loss of value when the market opens tomorrow morning. And Mr. Bellamy, I see anyone shorting Talbot Industries for more than one percent I'll take far more than fifty. Are we clear?"

"Yes."

"Nice doing business with you." Wolf terminated the call. "Can't wait to take a shower when I get back to the hotel."

"How did you manage to put that kind of financial pressure on his stock?" Maddie said, amazed.

"I have made powerful enemies," Wolf explained, "and many more powerful friends. Friends of the multi-millionaire and billionaire persuasion who very kindly helped me out. And made a few bucks doing it, too."

This announcement had everyone in the room staring at Wolf with what appeared to be admiration mixed with a healthy dose of respect for the reach of his influence. Even for someone as successful as Mia Wallace and her New York law firm, the prospect of one man being able to rally hundreds of millions of dollars within an hour to force the owner of the third largest hedge fund to back down was impressive; perhaps alarmingly so.

"On behalf of my family and their employees, who had no idea about the gun pointed at their heads," Maddie said, "and for me—thank you, Wolf."

"The least I can do for getting you fired," Wolf joked.

"I'll be fine," she replied. "Bellamy's company isn't my only client."

After another hour of tying up loose ends, everyone took a deep breath and ventured into the wild outdoors, applause and loud cheers marking Wolf's appearance at he exited the building. He shot his fans a big grin and waved as the group slowly made their way down the steps to cars waiting at the curb ready to whisk them away from the crush of reporters and onlookers. If Grayson Wolf wasn't famous enough before being on trial for rape, his complete exoneration and emerging conspiracy to frame him would shoot him to the top of the worldwide newsfeed for many days.

Peering out the dark-tinted window as the car rolled slowly past the huge crowd that had assembled upon hearing the news of his exoneration, Wolf realized that his old career was over regardless his personal desire. For years he had managed to keep a low profile: no photos on his book covers, successfully avoiding cameras, always conducting interviews via phone and avoiding any social scene like the plague. After this media blowout, it would be near impossible for him to effectively conduct the undercover activities needed to worm his way into target organizations and the people running them.

Wolf closed his eyes, his body relaxing into the comfortable car seat, unwinding from the recent drama. He was happy this ordeal was over and happier still at the knowledge that he was truly done being a muckraking novelist spy. He was also delighted at the thought of his financial portfolio receiving a million-dollar bump in value come the next morning courtesy of shorting Bellamy's company. And if things worked out the way Wolf was hoping, this little bump in the road was only a preview of bigger and badder things to follow for Justin Bellamy, scumbag extraordinaire.

Having completed his business in New York, Wolf flew back to his home in Virginia, this time chartering a private flight, which touched down at Dulles Washington airport shortly before the financial markets opened Wednesday morning. By the time the Uber dropped him off at the Patrick Henry Building, Wolf's short of New World Hedge Fund stock was sold and he was nearly $900,000 richer from the sale.

His first order of business after starting the coffeemaker was calling Colleen Silverstone. He tapped her name on his phone's call list.

"You do realize that it's only seven twenty here?" she said.

"And you do realize that I know you've been up for two hours?" Wolf shot back. He heard a snuffling sound.

"Congratulations on getting away with rape." She must have realized her joke was inappropriate because she quickly added, "Sorry. Dumb thing to say."

Wolf took her apology as a good sign, considering he was far from her favorite person and Colleen rarely apologized; mostly on account she was known not to do or say things she later had to apologize for. He decided the best course of action was to ignore the gaffe.

"Thanks to Maddie's help—"

"Excuse me," Colleen interjected, "did you just thank the woman who falsely accused you of rape?"

"Yes, I did," he replied. "Because of Maddie I've got Justin Bellamy testifying in open court he was visiting his son at Overland College the week of December 6." He stopped, waiting for that information to sink in.

"They both did it," Colleen said.

She was quick.

"My guess, too." Wolf agreed. "But suspicion a case does not make. We need to go back to the college and talk with everyone again; show Bellamy's picture around. Not just his, Kerry's too, with his father."

"We do, do we?" Colleen replied.

He could hear the smile in her tone. "And by 'we' I mean you and your peeps."

"And when may we expect you to come and join the greater we?" she retorted, the smile in her voice continuing.

"You keep talking like that, people might get the wrong idea about why you're so anxious to see me," Wolf teased. "I need to hang around the home front for a couple days to get caught up with everything, having been distracted by New York and all. I'm hoping to catch a flight Friday evening or Saturday morning."

"Good," she replied, "because this gig is off the books and there's only one peep working it: me."

"Right ... um, how's Kat?" he said. "Just checking to see if she's okay."

"She is," Colleen said. "You'll be happy to know that Kat has been seen eating lunch with one of my section managers; real down to earth guy. That's your doing...helping her to move forward." When Wolf didn't respond, she added, "You okay?"

"Absolutely. Happy to hear it," he said, though that wasn't entirely accurate. He liked Katherine and wouldn't have minded picking up where he'd left off, but Colleen was right. Kat was too vulnerable having lost her entire family in a tragic accident three years ago; the last thing she needed was to get romantically involved with Grayson Wolf, a man with many enemies, some of whom had already tried to kill him twice.

"Good," she replied. "I look forward to seeing you."

"It's nice to know I'm wanted," he teased. Her reply came in the form of a hiss followed by a click. He grinned, saying to no one in particular, "No retort ... progress, it is." Intoning the latter to sound like Yoda.

His phone made a low Yo sound. Wolf read RJ's text message, texting back that he'd be down in five. "No rest for the weary," he said, aloud and took a detour to the bathroom. Wolves have to attend to personal matters like all other living creatures sooner or later.

Entering the lobby of CIR, Wolf was greeted by loud applause and cheers. He executed several low bows, then made his way to the conference room grinning from ear to ear, arms raised above his head flashing a victory signal with both hands. Before entering the room, Wolf thanked the throng who had followed him for believing in his innocence, for their support and thoughtful emails and texts during his ordeal.

"Surprise ambush," Wolf said, to the grinning faces of CIR's Executive Board as he entered the conference room. "It is nice to know I'm wanted. Thanks."

"The only thing we did," Diana said, "was letting people know you were coming in. The rest was all them."

"I felt very welcomed," he replied. "It's great to be here, for sure."

"And we're happy you are," RJ said. "I know you thought you'd be acquitted, but from two hundred miles south, it didn't look all that certain to us."

"Diana told us you sounded way too cocky when she spoke with you." Brett added. "A good thing that video showed up when it did or you might be sitting in a cell right now."

"Even without that video," Wolf replied, "Mia Wallace and her experts shredded the prosecution's evidence and her cross of Maddie pushed her into a corner. I was ready to testify, too, if the video hadn't shown up. Wallace would have introduced the results of the polygraph I took which I passed with flying colors and in the end, it would come down to he said, she said. No jury would convict on such a weak, problematic case. But that video totally destroyed the State's case."

"Well we are all relieved it's over," Annika said. Heads around the table nodded in agreement. "Did the financial gambit do what you hoped?"

"In spades," Wolf replied, excitedly.

"What financial gambit?" Diana said, surprised.

Wolf explained his theory that his arrest for sexual assault was connected to his investigation in Colorado and that the arrest confirmed for him that Justin Bellamy was involved.

"With the help of Maddie on the witness stand and Annika's help contacting a passel of wealthy supporters and personal friends," he explained, "we were able to force Bellamy to stop threatening Maddie's family business and Maddie herself and make a tidy sum in the process, though that's just icing on the cake."

"I got some icing, too," Annika announced. "I put up a hundred-K shorting NWF and made ten percent in less than twenty hours when I sold the short this morning."

"You risked a hundred thousand dollars?" Brett said, looking incredulous. Gazing at Wolf, he added, "How much did you put up?"

"First off," Wolf said, "it's not that big of a risk. New World stock would have to jump significantly for us to lose money and New World isn't some tech startup susceptible to wild stock swings. Bellamy backed off because when his stock price was suddenly put under pressure by half billion dollars shorting his company, the price can and did drop fast. New World lost about fifty-million dollars and had our friends kept pushing, it's likely the robotraders would kick in and then the stock price could drop into the basement."

"Is that legal?" Diana asked. "Sounds like it could be considered insider trading."

"It's a gray area," Annika said. "Insider trading restricts a person who is privy to something happening in a company—a fantastic new product being launched, instance—and shares that with some friends so they can start buying that company's share before the company makes a public announcement of the product. What we did was put downward pressure on New World not because we got inside information pursuant to the company's business. We might get some FCC queries and we'll deal with that if it happens."

"And by 'deal with that'," Juan said, "Annika means we will have yet another opportunity to challenge the Constitutionality of insider trading, a concept rife with arbitrary language, arbitrary enforcement, not to mention the violation of freedom of speech and several other key issues. If the FCC goes after us, we will be ready."

"If there are no further questions for Wolf, I'd like to proceed with the business at hand," Diana said.

"Before you proceed," Wolf said, "unless you need me to be here, I plan to fly to Denver Friday or Saturday."

"So noted," Diana said, proceeding with the meeting.

Juan Mendez discussed Lee Sterling's upcoming civil case against Virginia Patriots College and the progress being made to assemble the class action suits against colleges nationwide. Teena Sanoe broke the news that the State Police had arrested and charged two former VPC students with the shooting of the trespassing insurgents at the Lawson Conference Center.

"Apparently the Red Fascists feel increasingly embolden, or desperate more likely, to use violence as a means to achieve their objectives even if it means harming their own supporters," Teena explained. "One more potent fact to add to your growing list of claims for your class-action against complicit university administrations, Juan."

Jewel King updated the group about the progress of the fall conference in Richmond, Brett Casings gave a report about the increasingly problematic state of computer security, informing all that he's talking with Colleen Silverstone's people about dramatically improving the security of CIR's electronic systems and security codes.

"I'd advise everyone to change passwords and security prompts to four or five random word chains," Bret said. "No more Monk!y2@u&me. Hackers have cracked these passwords in under three hours. Leading software security engineers say that a four-random word chain might take hackers 500 years to crack. I-am-not-joking. Do it today. Make sure the word chain is random."

RJ brought everyone up to speed about completion of various media campaigns with special emphasis on type and variety pursuant to the launch of Juan's class-action offensive, the meeting ending with Annika's financial report.

"I've established several new account portals in expectation of the possibility of a flood of settlement monies from the class action cases," she said. "The complexity of payouts and the like being as challenging as anything we've managed before. But like I always say, we should have such problems as billions of dollars blowing our way."

Diana adjourned the meeting, signaling Wolf to remain behind. She asked and received a more detailed account of his trial, shaking her head when he was finished.

"A hell of a risk you took partner," she said. "What if Maddie failed to pick up on what you hoped she would say, or worse, was involved? You might have gone to jail for a crime you didn't commit."

"I've been taking calculated risks my entire adult life, Diana." He flashed her a big smile, adding, "I hired you, didn't I?"

"And I might make you really sorry you did, you keep talking that way," she retorted. Her expression became more solemn.

"You're making light of it all, but we were worried about you, Wolf ... You're too nonchalant about what's lurking out there to hurt you."

"Thanks, I appreciate that, Diana," he said. "Even if Maddie were part of the conspiracy to get me and that video hadn't appeared when it did, Mia Wallace definitely destroyed the prosecution's case. I would have walked."

"You might have been set free, but you'd have that shadow of doubt following you for the rest of your life, Wolf." Diana sighed. "Enough of that depressing subject. How much longer do you think your Colorado venture will drag on?"

"Now that we have Bellamy's unintentional admission he was visiting his spawn in Colorado the week Sarah Lewis was raped, I think we'll have a resolution sooner than later," Wolf explained. "I'm planning to head out late Friday; is there anything you need me to do the next two days? Drop by the college and rile up the natives? Buzz the president's resident with my copter, perhaps?"

"No thank you," she said, laughing. "You are to stay far away from VPC. Stay home, relax and work on your Tara Mason novel ... Wolf, I'm really happy you're continuing to write and I'm looking forward to reading your new series."

Wolf heeded Diana's advice, retreating to his penthouse and spending the next two days making excellent progress writing *Bulldozed*, the second Mason novel. He was approaching the half-way mark, feeling delighted about his impromptu decision to delve into this writing project. He genuinely enjoyed writing straight fiction, exhilarated by how easily plots and characters popped nearly fully developed into his head and the words flowed forth chapter after chapter.

As he saved the document and got ready to leave for Denver that Friday evening, he gave serious consideration to spending the foreseeable future retreating into his study living a life of quiet reflection, writing a few dozen novels and let the world take care of itself.

The only problem with that saccharine thought was the rising excitement he felt as his flight made its way west.

Chapter 23

3-6-5

Wolf appeared bright and early Saturday morning at Silverstone Security and Investigative Services' main entrance after spending an uneventful night at a local hotel ready for action. Unlike his last two visits to the highly secure building, this time he was chosen by its security system's random selection to suffer all stages of security protocols: surrendering his weapon, removal of all loose items, belt and shoes, followed by the body X-ray scan, the Sniffer and a final electronic scan performed by live security personnel. Having successfully passed through the security gauntlet, he was escorted to Colleen's office.

"Good morning Wolf," Colleen said, looking up from her computer. "Coffee? Perhaps breakfast?"

"Morning to you; Coffee is always appreciated, thanks."

Touching her intercom, she called for a carafe of coffee and two mugs.

"Connor and his team believe they have narrowed the suspect pool of possible killers down to a handful of possibilities. All of them work for the prison," Colleen said.

"But?" Wolf said.

"Unfortunately, all have solid alibis," Colleen replied. "Alibis for killing James. Three of them, however were not working during the time you were attacked on the road leaving the prison and during our shootout in Creede."

"Any progress on Justin Bellamy now that we know he was here early last December?" Wolf asked.

"Connor and I haven't had a minute to spare for anything beyond company business," she replied. "I've squeezed some time from my calendar for us to go another round."

Wolf nodded. "Knowing Diana's crazy schedule, I do understand and I'm thankful for whatever time you can devote to this investigation … I know you declined to take payment, but I'm offering to compensate you and your people."

The coffee arrived, Colleen filling both mugs and handing Wolf one.

"A deal's a deal," she said, sipping her coffee. "One good turn does deserve another so you owe me. Much better than any monetary payment."

Wolf scrunched up his face. "Why do I have the feeling that your remuneration is going to cost me far more than monetary compensation?"

"And the really juicy part is that there's no statutes of limitations for when I make that Wolf call," she replied, looking very self-satisfied.

Wolf chose to ignore that disturbing comment. "What's on first today?"

"What's on third," she said, eyes glowing looking over her mug. "Our 'who' is Sergeant Hernandez of the Castle Rock constabulary who your generous donation to the police social fund has procured to be our police leverage."

Fifteen minutes later Wolf was in the passenger seat of Colleen's car on his way to pick up their police chaperon for what he hoped would be the final and decisive round of investigations leading to the truth behind Sarah's rape and James' murder. Only a week remained of Overland's spring semester and once classes ended, students would disperse across the country and beyond, effectively ending any chance to solve this case until September, if at all. Like Elvis's hit love song, it was now or never.

"No cowboy outfit today, I see," Hernandez said, giving Wolf the once-over.

"Don't want to excite the ladies too much," he retorted. "How've you been, Sergeant Hernandez. Looking none worse for the wear since last we talked."

"Been copacetic," he replied. "Heard the New York boys roughed you up a mite."

"Just a light toss, but a worthwhile detour as it turned out." Wolf updated the officer about Bellamy's testimony. "Thanks to the anonymous video, I'm fully exonerated and anxious to finish what I started."

"Looking forward to working with the dynamic duo," Hernandez said, grinning at them. "Happy to get outta the office and do some field work. I help crack this case it might get me a promotion to detective."

"I can't speak for Ms. Silverstone," Wolf said, "but I'll be most happy to give you and the Castle Rock police all the credit."

Hernandez shot a look at Colleen who gave him a clueless expression.

"I'm only the driver," she said, a sly grin playing on her lips. "Don't want to get in the way of men's work."

"My kind of woman," Hernandez said, ignoring her taunt. "As you requested, I got permission from the Captain to deliver the Rape Kit swabs and related evidence to Centennial Forensic Lab."

"Excellent," Colleen replied, looking satisfied. "Centennial is the best lab east of LA and west of Chicago. I've put a rush on it and if there's trace evidence to be found, they will find it ... thanks Carlos."

A large grin appeared on his face. "Always try to please the ladies ... especially the pretty ones ... who might also hurt me if I didn't do as asked."

"You have all the qualification for making a great detective," Colleen said, chuckling. "Let's begin with a visit to Karla Grisham. Considering the time, I imagine we'll interrupt her beauty sleep, but I like catching her off guard."

Which they did. The drowsy coed, clearly hung over from a late night of partying, gazed confusedly at the trio of resolute faces at her door. Even in her muddled state of mind, she still had enough awareness to decline entry into her dorm room, her effort to close the door foiled by Hernandez flashing his badge. She left her door wide open, shuffled to a seat and plopped into it.

"What do you want now?" Karla croaked.

"We'd like the truth about your involvement in the drugging and rape of Sarah Lewis for start," Hernandez said, his volume resulting in Karla grimacing in discomfort. "Then we'd like the names of your co-conspirators."

His stark demand had the effect of sobering her up, judging from the change in Karla's expression. She cleared her throat.

"I don't know what you're talking about and I'm not saying another word ... I will call my father, however; he's going to be very unhappy about you people coming here accusing me of stuff."

"Ms. Grisham," Hernandez said, his tone indicating he was undeterred by her threat of a US Senator coming down on his head, "please do call your papa. You can tell him that the semen retrieved from Ms. Lewis had DNA from several different individuals. Be sure to inform the Senator that Sergeant Hernandez of the Castle Rock police expects to make several arrests in the near future and that his daughter may very well be among them ... or you can tell me a name possibly connected to one of those strands of DNA. Your choice."

Karla blinked several times, her face turning a whiter shade of pale. Wolf shot a look at Colleen, her eyes communicating as much surprise as he felt about Hernandez's bluff. He looked back at Karla in expectation, wondering if she'd spill any useful information.

Karla cleared her throat once more. "I have no clue who raped Sarah. Now, unless you are going to arrest me, I want all of you to leave—now."

Not so muddled or cowed after all, Wolf surmised, though Karla did look glum, guessing it had little to do with her hang over. He knew he shouldn't feel pity for the spoiled, vindictive brat, but he had seen first-hand over the years the dissolution that in all likelihood awaited Karla, the thought dampening his disgust somewhat.

They turned to leave when Colleen asked to speak with Karla alone. The coed agreed and the men exited her suite.

"What do you think that's about?" Hernandez asked Wolf.

"Senator Grisham is Colleen's client; she's probably saying soothing words encouraging Karla to reveal whatever she knows."

"Wish her good luck with that," Hernandez replied. "That girl's twenty-one going on forty-one. From what I've heard about her and half the kids at this college, there's precious little they don't know about activities of the irresponsible kind. Don't think Colleen's going shake anything outta her."

Hernandez was right. Colleen appeared in the hall five minutes later looking resigned.

"They've circled the wagons, that's for certain," she said. "Tried to encourage her to talk to me about anything that might implicate her pursuant to Sarah and James or anything else that might come to bite her in the ass, but not a peep. I'm certain daddy told her to keep her mouth shut and that he'll handle it like he's done many times before, but she is rattled, that I know. Most likely about our investigation, but considering all of her extra-curricular activities, she could be worried about a dozen past discretions blowing back on her."

"Once again, bupkis," Wolf quipped. Investigating real crimes had turned out to be far more challenging—frustrating really—than ferreting greed, hypocrisy, double-dealings, back-stabbings and highly questionable actions of corporate, academic and political subjects he had hunted over the years.

"Not quite," Colleen replied. "She referred me to her second in command of the click, Lisa Shell. North Wing. Room 311; let's see if she's in."

Wolf shot her a skeptical look. "Referred?"

"Referred," she repeated. "Like in maybe she's pissed at her for something and it's her way of payback having us put heat on her."

The premier residences that housed the offspring of VIP's was a U-shaped complex. For security reasons the buildings were not connected by hallways and the trio exited Karla's building, crossed the courtyard and entered the North Wing. Hernandez showed his badge to security informing the officer behind the desk of their destination.

"Don't bother," the officer said. "Lisa never checked in."

"Any idea where she is?" Hernandez asked.

The guard issued a low snort. "Some guys' bed somewhere."

"Thanks."

"Bupkis strikes again," Wolf quipped, grinning. "Bet you a C-note Karla knew that."

"Forget Lisa for now," Hernandez said. "According to the case file, both James and Sarah reported having a vague recollection of being out that night somewhere in the town. When James confessed soon after his arrest the investigation was shelved. However, they did get lists from Sarah and James where they tended to hang out: favorite coffee shops, art galleries, book stores and social hot spots off campus they patronized most often."

"Let's roll," Colleen said. "We're burning day light."

And daylight the trio did burn indeed. It was tedious work, slogging through stores, pubs, social clubs, coffee shops and the occasional restaurant either went with a date. No one that might have seen or encountered James or Sarah—waiters, hostesses, bouncers, managers—had any recollection of seeing either one, though in fairness, the likelihood of doing so going back six months was a long-shot in any case.

"Jeezus," Wolf ejaculated, frustrated after leaving the thirteenth establishment with not one clue to move forward on. "Talk about déjà vu all over and over and over again!"

"Believe it or not," Hernandez said, laughing, "the large majority of crimes we investigate are pretty straight forward and solved in a day or two. This is unusual, though expected when mixing together a cold case, rich kids, powerful parents, sex, drugs and rock 'n roll."

"I'm beginning to appreciate why cops sometimes go rogue and kick ass," Wolf replied, feeling very much like kicking *someone's* ass if the opportunity presented itself. "I never knew how easy I had it tracking down social scumbags until today. This is physically painful."

"Want to quit?" Colleen said, her subtle smile clearly taunting him.

He shot her an evil glance, picked up a stone and hurled it at a metal trashcan. It made a satisfying bang.

"Feel better now?" she said, a smile spreading across her face.

Wolf ignored her. "What's next on the list?"

Hernandez checked the file. "We've got four more possibilities." He looked around the street, thinking. "3-6-5 is closest; couple blocks east."

"What's 3-6-5?" Wolf asked.

"Night club," Hernandez replied. "Not the typical dive; best of the best. Live music, decent food, dancing. The type of place you'd take a date to impress, not get smashed."

It was early afternoon, hours before the club would open. Hernandez took them around the rear, entering through a service door. When confronted by a worker, he flashed his badge and was directed to the manager.

"I remember hearing about that back last year. Sad story," the manager replied when Hernandez showed him photos of Sarah, James, Kerry and his father. "We've got tons of kids crowding in here every weekend and most weekdays; can't remember their faces from yesterday, let alone months back."

"Well, thank you anyway," Hernandez said. "We've got a few more places to check' maybe we'll get lucky."

"Wait," the manager said. "Why don't you check December's panel of pics before you go." He pointed at a far wall covered with photographs. "The 3-6-5 Club—as in 365 days a year—is so named and known for the thousands of photos from every month placed on our walls … follow me."

He raised the house lights and escorted the group over to a huge floor-to-ceiling panel titled December 2016 totally covered with photographs. They thanked the manager and made their way through the panel beginning by kneeling on the floor and slowly making their way up, eventually standing on chairs to study the top photos.

Wolf was just about to step off his chair when Colleen said, "I think that might be James."

Wolf leaned close, peering at a photo showing people dancing in the foreground and customer-filled booths behind them. He took out his phone and using the magnification app confirmed that it definitely looked like James.

"Who's the girl sitting with him?" Colleen asked.

Wolf focused his unit on the girl. She was sitting with her back to the camera and he could only see thin slice of her cheek. She had long, dark silky hair. He was sure he had seen that hair some weeks ago. He took several photos of the pic.

"Let's go," he said.

"Hello, Jennifer," Wolf said, when the co-ed opened her door.

"Um, hi, Mr. Wolf," she said, looking warily at Colleen and Hernandez. "Have you found out what happened to Sarah and James?"

"This is Detective Hernandez and Colleen Silverstone," he replied. "May we come in?"

"Yeah, sure. Come in." Jennifer said, opening the door and stepping back.

"You have lovely hair," Wolf said, looking appreciatively at her dark, straight strands flowing over her shoulders." She smiled wanly and thanked him. "Do you know that only two dozen Overland co-eds have hair length, color and texture similar to yours?"

He held the screen of his phone toward Jennifer. "And that one of those two-dozen women sat across from James Collins at the 3-6-5 Club on the night he was drugged and kidnapped? And that of the twenty-four long-haired, dark beauties none have a connection to James or Sarah—except one." He clicked on the close-up pic he took of the one on the club's wall. "You, Jennifer; Sarah's roommate and James's friend."

"That could be anyone," she retorted.

"Maybe," Wolf countered. "Fortunately, DNA is far more conclusive than a photo as the west's foremost forensic lab will confirm."

Jennifer's face became still and pale. She sat down.

"It was you who drugged James." Wolf asserted, taking advantage of her reaction. "It was you who had sex with him and later used the semen collected in his prophylactic to place inside Sarah to implicate him for her rape." Tears started to roll down her cheeks. "I was thinking about what Sarah and James did to make you angry enough to do something so vile, then I remembered our conversation here in this room back in March; your vehemence against Karla and her bitch click and Kerry Bellamy. Hating these rich brats for acting like they're better than everyone else, for hassling and denigrating the common folk, for ignoring everyone not in their click. Ignoring you. Rejecting you. Never allowing you to join them because you'd never be good enough; not even good enough for a night at their drunken sex parties."

The trickle of tears turned into a flood under Wolf's relentless description of her experience living with and absorbing the toxic emotional brew that she must have experienced year after year. Colleen handed her a box of tissue.

"You have one opportunity to tell us the story before officer Hernandez from Castle Rock arrests you and you go down for half-dozen crimes including kidnapping, accessory to rape and murder just to mention some of the top ones," Colleen said, piling on more pressure. "I was you, I'd give up your accomplices now before they hear of your arrest and run for cover behind their expensive lawyers. Don't cooperate and you'll wind up spending the rest of your life in prison while they get a slap on the wrist like they always do, walking away free and clear laughing all the way to their summer vacations in Paris, Rome or the Riviera."

337

There was a long stretch of silence, Jennifer's head hanging on her chest. She sighed loudly and swallowed audibly several times.

"It was supposed to be a joke," she said, finally. "Give James this drug to get him in the mood, have sex and hand over his rubber. I've always liked him, but he liked Sarah and this was my chance because she was just stringing him along, always doing her own thing, never caring what others thought or wanted ... They promised I'd be invited to their parties, but when James was arrested for rape they told me they'd say it was all me and I'd go to jail if I said anything..."

Listening to her story, Wolf wanted to feel pity, but the scope of Jennifer's crime, her betrayal of her friends to the wastrels she claimed to hate, was inexcusable. The coed had acted to destroy the good because they were the good and did so for the lowest of reasons: to be part of the crowd that rejected her for not being good enough to give the time of day to.

She gave names, dates and details, Hernandez recording her testimony. When done, he arrested her but did not walk her out of the dorm in cuffs in the hope that no one would suspect she had been arrested and tip off her co-conspirators. In the car, he made a call to the town's police station where he would hand Jennifer over to their safe keeping then go after Kerry.

Hernandez's badge continued to work its magic, the doors to the Lodge opening to admit the three investigators without challenge. Entering the lobby, Wolf opened his mouth to tell Hernandez the room number.

"211," the officer said, grinning at Wolf. "Angling for detective, remember?"

"And a good one you'll make," Wolf retorted, walking up the stairs and along the corridor.

Hernandez's insistent knocking was loud enough to wake anyone sleeping several rooms down the hall, but Kerry's door stayed shut. Even the threat of forcing the door brought forth no response.

"Not home," Colleen said.

"Now what?" Wolf asked.

"We go back to the college and conduct interrogations," Hernandez said. "We've got a dozen suspects; I start mentioning arrests for rape and murder, someone will talk."

They were on their way down when Wolf spotted a young man he recognized looking up at him from the common room. The student made a subtle jerk with his head then walked out of the room toward the rear of the building.

"Drive slowly," Wolf said, once back in the car. "Our mystery friend from last visit wants to join us again."

Colleen pulled out of the driveway and drove unhurriedly down the road. Seeing a figure appear from between foliage some distance ahead she slowed and picked him up, then drove on.

"Who's that?" the student said, looking at Hernandez.

"Detective Hernandez of the Castle Rock police," Wolf replied.

"Police…" The boy appeared to look pleased. "You gonna arrest Kerry and his crew, I hope?"

"Perhaps," Hernandez said. "You got anything to tell might help find him?"

"He didn't come back last night," the student replied. "He and his gang are probably hanging out at one of several crash pads where they get drunk and have orgies."

Wolf observed how Hernandez said nothing, gazing steadily at the boy waiting for him to keep talking. It's an effective technique, keeping one's mouth shut, so that another has lots of opportunity to spill his or her guts. He recalled that Colleen was an expert, too, having been subjected to her mute gaze several times over the past two months.

"I've never been to any," the boy continued, "but I've overheard them talk about it plenty and I can tell you the general area for two of their places."

Hernandez said he knew the area like the back of his hand, thanked the kid, then like previously, Colleen drove him to the commercial area of town and dropped him off. Hernandez directed Colleen to the first area where she drove slowly up and down half dozen narrow streets, their police escort explaining what he was looking for.

"Stop here," Hernandez said. "See that cluster of cars up ahead? Could be our boys. Wolf, you with me; Colleen, you block anyone trying to hightail it by car."

Wolf shot a glance at Colleen, wondering how she was reacting to Hernandez giving orders, but her expression, as usual, was blank. He supposed she agreed with the officer's directives, which made sense, of course.

Wolf followed Hernandez up to the front door, the officer knocking loudly. Momentarily the door opened, revealing a pretty face.

"May I help you?"

"Is Kerry Bellamy here?" Hernandez asked. Seeing her dubious expression, he rattled off a few more names. "Jeffrey Ostara, Morgan Williams, Seth Becker?"

"Sorry; never heard of them," she said. "In fact, no males here at all. Just five Overland alumni women planning our reunion."

"Sorry to bother you," Hernandez said, giving her a bright smile.

Fifteen minutes later scouting out the next neighborhood, Colleen was driving past a dead-end road when Wolf called a halt.

"Back up ... on the left, near the end of the road," he said. "Bunch of cars and the clutter in the yard is a dead giveaway; like the comic character Pigpen, Bellamy and company discard trash and spread disorder everywhere they go. Cleaning up after them is the hoi-polloi's job."

Hernandez snorted. "Good eye, Wolf. Colleen—"

"Block the road, got it," she quipped, cutting him off.

Wolf shot her droll look and said, "I like a woman who understands this job is men's work."

Hernandez laughed. "You must also like getting your ass kicked by women, too."

Looking over his shoulder as they started down the road, he saw Colleen draw a finger across her throat. He shot her his most confident, who's-afraid-of-Colleen-Silverstone grin and hurried after Hernandez. He could almost imagine her call after him about running but never succeeding to hide.

Hernandez banged on the door. After the second vigorous knock, he tried the door, finding it unlocked. He stepped away from the door and looked expectantly at Wolf.

"I think I heard someone say to come in," Wolf said, making a humorous expression. He stepped gingerly into a darkened living room. "Stinks like five-year-old stale beer..."

They made their way down a narrow hallway. Carefully opening the door on the right to what he assumed was a bedroom, Wolf peeked in. Disheveled bed but no occupants. Stepping back into the hall, he figured the door at the end would be a bathroom and made for the door on the left side.

Besides the sight of naked bodies, the pungent odor of stale beer, sweat and sex struck Wolf's senses as he stepped into the bedroom. He shot a questioning look at Hernandez who made a thoroughly disgusted face.

"The girl first," Hernandez said in a low tone, walking to the bed and throwing a cover over her nude form.

Peering at two boys strewn on the bed and one on an easy chair, Wolf figured he'd have to yell long and hard to get any to come out of their drunken and most likely, drugged stupor. He heard Hernandez say something and looked over at him.

"Call an ambulance," he said, looking closely at the young woman on the bed. He took out his phone and took photos.

Wolf called 911. He didn't know the address and put the operator on hold while he called Colleen to look for a street sign. Task accomplished, he also snapped a series of photos then proceeded to wake the three males, groans of discomfort issuing forth as they began to stir.

"Wake up and get dressed!" he ordered, tossing clothing at the naked boys.

The realization of strangers in the bedroom energized the boys who snatched the clothing tossed at them. One partially dressed boy made for the door, finding it blocked by an imposing six-foot-three, two hundred-plus pound man glaring at them.

"No one leaves this room." Hernandez growled. The sound of sirens filtered into the room. He pointed toward an adjacent corner. "Sit. I've got a few questions for you."

He corralled the boys into the corner, looming over the cowed trio. Wolf watched their eyes repeatedly glance at the comatose woman on the bed, expressions of worry clouding their faces.

EMTs entered the bedroom making a beeline to the woman. The good news was she had a pulse and was breathing. They carefully rolled her on her back, placed her on the gurney and wheeled her to the ambulance. Wolf heard Colleen's voice outside the bedroom, making an appearance shortly thereafter.

Seeing the partially dressed boys on the floor, she came over and stood next to Hernandez. Wolf crowded in behind her, careful not to make any physical contact after his "men's work" comment earlier. Never poke the momma bear.

"That girl dies," she said, her tone icy, "you boys are looking at many years of post-graduate studies at Centennial prison."

"That girl lives," Hernandez said, echoing her comment, "you boys will still participate in years of post-graduate studies at Centennial. Maybe none—for any that wish to talk."

"We under arrest?" the one sitting in the middle of the group said, looking up at them. "Lawyer."

"You must be Jeffrey Ostara," Colleen said, "Kerry Bellamy's right-hand lackey. Good luck with that lawyer; you'll need a passel of them ... how about you, Morgan?"

"Keep your mouth shut!" Ostara said.

"No one is being arrested—yet," Hernandez said. "Nothing you say can be used against you. The one who tells us what we want to know is the one the three of us here will put in a very good word to the prosecutor for."

"Keep your mouths shut!" Ostara repeated.

"Get up," Hernandez said, glaring at him. When he didn't move he jerked Ostara to his feet and took him out of the bedroom, shooting a look at Wolf and Colleen on the way out.

"You're Seth Becker," Colleen said, pointing at the one on the left. "Nod if you know who I am." Becker nodded once and she continued, "Then you know I do what I say I will do. Nine out of ten times the person telling someone to keep their mouth shut is the one who has the most to lose. So, you tell me, Seth. Are you going to tell me what I want to know before Morgan here does, or worse, before Jeff spills his guts to officer Hernandez sitting in the car outside and you both go down?"

They looked like a pair of cornered rats, their rattled expressions and darting glances reflecting the inner turmoil raging in their minds. Wolf could easily imagine wheels furiously spinning in their heads. Whatever they had been doing with the girl on the bed, he was sure they've been doing with other females for some years.

"Don't..." Morgan said, apparently thinking his friend was going to talk.

"Don't?" Becker spit, his head spinning to face Morgan. "I'm not going down for that bastard! I didn't drug her and I'm not going to jail for all this shit Jeff and Kerry and his bitches been doing."

"Shut the hell up!" Morgan shouted, taking a swing at him.

It never landed, blocked by Colleen's lightning-speed movement of her hand. In one continuous motion, she bent Morgan's arm behind him, forcing his body to twist and fall face-down on the floor with a satisfying thud. Satisfying to Wolf and Colleen, not Morgan, of course.

"Say another word and I will break your wrist, got it, sunshine?" Colleen hissed. "I'm going to help you up and we're going to join your pal in the car. Move…"

"Now that we can speak without interruptions," Wolf said. "Do you know where Kerry Bellamy is?"

"No idea," Becker said. "He and Lisa were here all day—well, until we all conked out; around three."

"Who drugged the girl?" Wolf asked.

"Kerry's usually the one with all the drugs, though she was already flying when she came to party," he replied.

"Your crew ever Rofi girls?" Wolf asked.

"Why would we bother with stupid stuff like that?" Becker snorted. "Our crew is like, super popular. Girls line up to party with us; we get drunk, have sex, drink and have more sex."

Wolf was not averse to romantic experiences while in college or since, having engaged in liaisons himself. What Becker was describing, however, was the polar opposite of romance, their sexual acts most closely resembling bodily waste removal. Wolf took out a photo from his pocket.

"Ever see this man with Kerry?"

"Yeah, that's Kerry's dad," Becker said. "Seen them together every so often."

"Did you see them together last December?"

"No … but I know he was here because Kerry talked about him coming and then he wasn't around for a few days. I assume he was with his dad."

"He ever talk about where he was or what he did with his father?" Wolf asked.

"No, but he seemed like, high for like a week afterward," Becker said. "We'd ask him about it, but he never said anything except they had a good time … this is about Sarah Lewis, isn't it?"

"Yes," Wolf confirmed. "Someone Rofi'd her, raped her and set up James Collins to take the fall. You got any ideas who might have done that?"

Becker shook his head. "It wasn't anyone from our gang; I'd have known because everybody brags about exploits with the girls."

"You have any ideas where Kerry is now?" Wolf said.

"Maybe back at the Lodge."

"Any other place they might hang out?"

"He likes to take girls to some remote place, mostly some motel," Becker said. "He never tells us where. Probably there with Lisa; that girl's a nympho."

"Okay," Wolf said. "Let's join the others."

"Are we getting arrested?"

"Not sure," Wolf said. "When that girl wakes and talks about being drugged by Jeff or someone in your crew, or Krishna forbid, dies, then all of you will face charges."

"If she was drugged," Becker said, looking worried, "then it's either Kerry or Lisa because they like to spice things up and play tricks on people."

"I'll remember that," Wolf said.

When Wolf stepped outside he saw Colleen and Hernandez talking by the car. Looking closer he noticed no one sitting in the car, surmising that Hernandez let Jeff and the other boy go.

"You're free to go for now." Hernandez said to the boy. "You are not to leave the area, however. Do you understand?"

Becker nodded and went on his way.

Wolf asked about the girl's condition, Hernandez telling him the EMTs stabilized her. "We won't know much more until she wakes up ... he give up Kerry's location?"

"He didn't know," Wolf said. "Kerry likes his privacy so he hits various motels to conduct carnal activities."

"I'll put a BOLO on him," Hernandez said. "He drives an Aston Martin; rare in these parts even for the rich kiddies. Drive me back to the station and I'll borrow a car to transport Jennifer back to Castle Rock. I want to interrogate her and get her testimony on record as soon as possible."

Colleen dropped the officer off at the local police station, promising to issue an arrest warrant for Kerry Bellamy and Lisa Shell once he had Jennifer's official testimony wrapped up. When Colleen asked him about getting a warrant to locate Kerry using his phone's GPS, he reminded her it was a weekend and short of a terrorist threat, judges were off duty until 9 a.m. Monday.

"By now his crew have apprised him of the fact we are looking for him," she said, after Hernandez exited the car. "By Monday, Kerry might be long gone, especially if he believes he'll be arrested."

"What are you going to do?" Wolf asked, as Colleen pressed a number on her phone.

"Have Connor find him," she replied. "I'm not waiting two days for a warrant."

Connor answered the phone on the second ring, his voice filling the cabin. Colleen explained what she needed, then placed him on hold. She made a second call, patching Connor back in. By the fourth ring, Kerry's voice was heard on the speaker.

"My lawyer told me to say nothing," Kerry retorted, when Colleen identified herself. "Unless you're calling to invite yourself to my little party, I'm going to hang up; I've got pleasant things waiting for me."

"While you're engaged in pleasant activities," Colleen replied, "you can think about what you and your father were doing the evening of December 6th with Sarah Lewis and James Collins." A soft hiss emanated from the speakers and after a moment of silence, Colleen continued. "I hear you like to spice things up and supply all kinds of goodies for your buddies. It's just a matter of time until forensics does a proper job with the DNA swabs taken from Sarah and James. After that, you, your father, Karla, Lisa and anyone else connected to Sarah Lewis and James Collins will be arrested and charged with a basketful of capital crimes."

"You are going to be one sorry bitch when my dad hears about this," Kerry sneered. "He's gonna fire you and he's gonna get lots of his friends to fire you, too."

"You've got it all wrong," Colleen retorted. "It's going to be your father that is going to be fired when the news of his arrest for rape, murder for hire along with a couple other charges hits the evening news. The hedge fund will crash and the money dry up, not that it will make much difference for twenty or thirty years. Well, I'll let you get back with Lisa and rack up as much fun as you can because the joy ride is coming to an end." She terminated the call and touched an icon on the screen. "Got him?"

"Plains View Motel," Conner said. "Inputting the location in your GPS as we speak."

"Excellent," Colleen said. "You're the best." She cut the call and touched the GPS icon on the car's monitor. "Eight miles. Let's go and say hello to the raping piece of shit."

"I've met the children of the various adults that I investigated and wrote about, of course," Wolf said, "but this is my first experience being submerged in the breeding ground from whence the adult scumbags emerged."

"Wasted lives," Colleen said. "Many of these kids from wealthy families are spoiled, lost little children with the deck stacked against them ever becoming fully functioning human beings. Some like Karla and Kerry become sociopaths, spreading their personal disease far and wide, ruining the lives of others for sport..." She shot a glance at Wolf. "Can't blame you for changing careers; stay too long in that business and it would drag even the most dedicated down into the dump."

"You're in a similar business, aren't you?" Wolf replied.

"I have my trials and tribulations, but I'm not up to my neck in the muck like you've been for going on twenty years," Colleen said. "Doing this job with you is rare for me. Most of my time is devoted to running the firm and I'm really good at doing that."

"You remind me very much of Diana Ruiz," Wolf said. "She's a dynamo driving CIR to ever greater success. But no matter if you're Grayson Wolf or Colleen Silverstone, the cost of doing what we do is the same; just different addresses and outer attire."

She shot him one of her rare brilliant smiles. "I've heard you have worn women's attire more than once."

"I've got impeccable taste and I look stunning in a dress," he quipped.

"I bet you do," she teased, making a right turn into a wide driveway leading to a motel trimmed in a western motif. "That's Kerry's Aston Martin. He's the only one at Overland driving one."

She pulled up to the silver sports car and stopped behind it, blocking any escape were Kerry to attempt a getaway. They exited the vehicle and walked toward the door, Colleen rapping loudly announcing herself. She didn't wait long before knocking louder. The door opened.

The sullen face of Kerry appeared, his eyes darting to Wolf then back to Colleen. "I've got nothing to say to you."

"Since my firm hasn't been officially fired by your father," Colleen replied, "I felt it my duty to drop by in person and inform you that the girl you and your friends drugged and engaged in sexual intercourse is in the hospital and might die."

"I don't know what you're—"

"Don't waste your breath, Kerry," she said, cutting him off. "Your crew gave you up. You were present at the scene and a full participant, and you supply the party drugs ... at the rate the crimes are piling up, you'll be lucky to get parole by the time you're fifty."

An ugly smirk formed on his face. "Maybe, but you're finished, bitch." He slammed the door.

"No good deed goes unpunished," Wolf quipped. "You gonna do a citizen's arrest?"

"Not while SSIS is still contracted to Bellamy's company," she replied, starting to walk back toward the car. "Not going to give him cause to sue me for millions, not to mention breeching my integrity in the eyes of other clients ... I'm calling Carlos and get him to arrest Kerry while we wait in the car. I'm not letting that creep out of my sight."

Colleen was approaching the driver's side door as Wolf opened the passenger side when he spotted a white sedan approaching from the far end of the parking lot. There was nothing unusual about that; it was late afternoon and traffic by guests was picking up. What caught Wolf's eye however, was the sedan's passenger side window sliding open as it drove up.

"Get down!" he screamed, as the sound of automatic fire erupted.

Chapter 24

...and Mate

Wolf's pistol was in his hand as he ducked behind the car and just as quickly popped back up, propelled by an incomprehensible rage to kill the sonofabitch who had managed to ambush him and Colleen again and again. Sprinting after the car, he fired in quick succession into the rear window and at the tires, the latter action causing the car to swerve and slam into a light pole, which came crashing down on the vehicle's roof.

Reaching the disabled car, he saw a figure behind the wheel, aimed and pulled the trigger, twice. No explosion of sound followed Wolf's repeated effort to kill the man, having emptied the pistol's magazine in his furious assault to stop him.

He was breathing heavily, sweat streaming down his head; his shirt soaked. Then he remembered: Colleen! He turned, expecting to see his worst fears confirmed, nearly knocking into the woman who had come up behind him.

"Good shooting," she said, matter-of-factly.

Gun in hand, Colleen moved cautiously toward the car, pointing her pistol directly at the occupant through the open passenger side window. She called Wolf to join her.

"I think he's out. Open the door and remove the gun lying on the floor while I cover you. Use a handkerchief if you have one or pick it up by its barrel, then place it on the roof." She waited until he completed the task. "Now put a fresh mag into your gun ... keep your pistol aimed at him while I place his automatic in my trunk and bring back some restraints ... if he wakes up and goes for a gun, try not to kill him."

"I'll do my best," Wolf replied. "Though I'm highly tempted to shoot the bastard whether he goes for a gun or not."

Colleen gave him a warning look and made for her car, returning a moment later carrying a handful of nylon ties. While Wolf covered her, she managed to open the driver side door, frisk the shooter for any additional weapons, pulled him out of the car, dragging him over to an adjacent street sign where she tied his arms around the pole.

"That's Tony Henson, one of the three unaccounted for employees of the Centennial the day you were ambushed on the road after leaving the prison," Colleen said, looking at the miscreant slumped at the base of the pole. She reached for her phone and first called for an ambulance, then for the state police. "Follow me…" Wolf accompanied her back to Kerry's motel room door. "You are going to make a citizen's arrest. Ready?"

She banged on the door and stood aside. Kerry cautiously opened the door. Wolf shoved it wide open.

"Hey…!"

"Collect your things," Wolf said. "I'm placing you under citizen's arrest." Seeing Lisa rushing up, he pointed at her, adding in a threatening manner, "Open your mouth and I'll arrest you, too. From what I heard about your exploits, I've got half dozen crimes to choose from."

The ambulance arrived, followed moments later by two Colorado State Police cars. Colleen instructed the medical attendees to patch up the now conscious shooter as best as they could while he was bound to a pole, then walked over to the police officers getting out of their cars. Wolf recognized one of the State Troopers, Captain Ken Jeffrey who he had met some weeks earlier.

"Nice to see you again, Ken," Colleen said.

"Heard you were involved in a shooting so I had to check things out myself," Jeffrey said.

"Actually, I never discharged my weapon," she replied. "That honor goes to my partner, Mr. Wolf."

Jeffrey glanced over at the wrecked, bullet-riddled car then gave Wolf an appraising glance. "Tell me what happened…"

Wolf provided a blow-by-blow account of the brief but violent encounter. When he was done, Jeffrey asked a few clarifying questions and the interview seemed over until the officer congratulated Wolf about "getting his man" and foiling yet another attempt on his life.

"He wasn't coming for me this time," Wolf said. He looked at Colleen standing next to the man. "He was trying to kill you. If he wanted to kill me, why not time the attack when I was fully exposed walking to the car instead of waiting until I was behind it giving me plenty of cover? He timed the attack when you were fully exposed. Kerry's words: you're finished. They tried to kill you, Colleen. That's what Kerry meant."

Her eyes shot over to Kerry sitting on the ground, leaning against the side of the building. She nodded.

"Payback for sticking your nose into my investigation," Wolf said.

"Ken," Colleen said, "the shooter's name is Tony Henson. He works in Centennial's IT center and colluded with Don Welling, a guard at the prison's surveillance center to kill James Collins. The man pulling the strings behind everything then instructed Tony to eliminate Welling. He's cleaning up loose ends and I'm sure Tony would have been next after completing his job killing me. You've got to keep him safe, Ken."

"You can count on that," Jeffrey said. "Who's the string puller?"

She took a quick glance around, then said in a low voice, "Justin Bellamy."

Jeffrey's eyebrows rose a notch. He shot a glance at Kerry Bellamy.

"The Lewis-Collins case back in December."

"We think it was a dad-son affair. Some of his pals and gals are involved, too." Colleen explained. "Carlos has a key player in custody ... Wolf has made a citizen arrest; could we transfer Kelly into your custody, too?"

"It'll be my pleasure," Jeffrey said, with obvious gratification. "That punk's been a pain in everyone's ass the past four years; the college being one huge pain for couple decades now. Wish I could shut the damn thing down."

"We're working on it." Wolf said it so matter-of-factly they both stared at him. "A project the Center is working on." He didn't elaborate further, mentally kicking himself for being careless.

Jeffrey promised to keep the prisoners safe and deliver them to Hernandez before the end of Monday. Satisfied that the miscreants were in good hands, Colleen collected Wolf and walked to her car. They peered thoughtfully at the bullets that had struck the windows and side of her car, but failed to penetrate the armored glass and side panels.

Colleen's gaze turned from the car to Wolf. "Thank you."

"Anytime." Wolf walked around the hood to the passenger side. "What's next, Ms. Silverstone?"

"Jeremy Bellamy."

Her expression was cool and her tone even, but he saw the fury in her eyes. Colleen made a phone call to someone called Chat in New York, instructing him to collect "the package" and unwrap it. Wolf assumed this Chat person was in New York having spotted the area code on the phone's screen when she tapped on the name.

Asking what that was all about, she shot him an enigmatic smile and drove on, saying only that Chat was going after "Bellamy's Connor".

Wolf made a sniffing sound. "Bellamy's Connor is his go-to guy who knows where all the bodies are buried. Just like your Connor who knows all about your what, where, who and why."

"I've got to remember you're not as dense as you look." She teased.

Wolf peered at her so long she barked, "What?"

"Thank you."

Colleen shot him a sidelong glance. "For what?"

"Tsk, tsk," Wolf mocked. "Not as dense as I look, remember? You had the video sent to the courthouse." Taking her silence as confirmation, he continued. "I think Connor's skills are superior to Bellamy's techie and he hacked into that guy's server, found and extracted the video. Considering our, er, relationship--"

"We're partners—temporary partners," Colleen interjected. "The number one rule of that relationship is that partners always have each other's' backs. Just like you had mine back at the motel."

"Right," Wolf said. "Thank you for having my back, temporary partner."

"Thank you for having mine, temporary partner."

"Thank you for being my temporary partner, temporary partner," Wolf snorted.

"You have no clue how annoying you can be, do you?" Colleen retorted, shaking her head, though he did spot a subtle twitch of her lips.

"I most certainly do," he quipped. "One of my most endearing features, I've been told."

This remark did earn him an audible snort from his temporary partner, but he felt it wise to quit while he was ahead.

"I'm looking forward to giving Sarah's and James's families the news once we get testimonies and confessions into the record," he said.

"Knowing the truth is important; allows families to move on," she replied.

"Even after muckraking all these years," Wolf said, "I'm still shocked at how far and low some people go believing they can get away it; that the rules don't apply to them because they're rich or powerful or well connected. All this pain, murder and mayhem because a pair of degenerates wanted the thrill of doping, raping and setting up an innocent for the crime."

"Jaded, bored, dissolute and stupid," Colleen said. "A combination guaranteed to sink anyone to the bottom of the human cesspool every time."

Wolf heartily agreed, convinced more than ever that his decision to end his immersion in that toxic environment after a decade and a half was a most rational and healthy one.

The trip back to Denver was largely a silent one, the temporary partners engaged in their own internal conversations. Wolf reflected upon the twists and turns that brought him to this point in time, Colleen assumingly contemplating whatever issues the head of the nation's leading investigative and security firm dealt with.

She dropped him off at his hotel in Aurora, promising to pick him up Monday morning to observe Hernandez interrogate the prisoners. Wolf was sorely tempted to ask her out to dinner, but decided at the last moment before he shut the car door that Colleen's emphasis on "temporary" would preclude accepting a date with her father's nemesis.

*   *   *   *

"I guess all's well that ends well," Wolf said, on the drive back from Castle Rock Monday afternoon.

"You sound disappointed," Colleen said.

Wolf certainly wasn't disappointed about the outcome of the interrogations at the Castle Rock police station. How could he be?

Jennifer Park confessed her part of the sordid affair, drugging James and having sex with him, handing the semen-filled prophylactic to Karla Grisham as part of an initiation into her group.

After intense negotiation between Karla's lawyer and District Attorney Sylvia Catelli, a deal was struck whereby Karla would testify against Kerry Bellamy and Lisa Shell in exchange for fifty hours of community service and sealed records of her involvement in the crime.

Besides targeting Sarah and dropping Rophenol into her drink and later driving an unconscious James to the abandoned house, Lisa's greatest offense was replacing Karla as Kerry's main squeeze, payback being as powerful a motive to give up Lisa as the prospect of jail time. Perhaps even more so, considering Karla Grisham's take-no-prisoners reputation.

Like falling dominoes, Lisa implicated Jeffrey Ostara, Kerry's second in command, as the one who intercepted a confused Sarah when she left the art exhibition she had attended, effectively kidnapping her. Jeff in turn confessed to delivering Sarah to Kerry, who was waiting for his special delivery at a caravan located in a secluded area and who had later transported an unconscious Sarah to the abandoned house where she woke up the following morning in the company of James Collins lying naked next to her on a mattress.

Pursuant to strong advice from his counsel, Kerry said nothing during interrogation. He just sat there, stone-faced, never making eye contact. Even the news that his friends had confessed and given him up didn't elicit a reaction.

Hearing about the deal Karla made, an outsider might very well be incensed at her receiving what was little more than a slap on the wrist—another rich kid getting off easy. That is until he or she learned the blockbuster news that Karla would testify against Kerry's father, spotting him waiting in the car that evening when she transferred the semen received from Jennifer to Kerry. With definitive proof that Justin Bellamy was with his son the night of the crime committed against Sarah and James, an arrest warrant was issued along with an extradition order for New York police to arrest and hold him until Colorado police picked him up.

The proverbial icing on the cake came shortly after lunch when Hernandez informed them of the news that Justin Bellamy's head of Information Services had walked into the office of the New

York City DA that morning to strike a deal. He testified Bellamy instructed him to hire Tony Henson as the point man to coordinate James's murder in Centennial State Prison, ordering the hit on Wolf investigating the rape, the hit on Wellington and finally the attempted murder of Colleen Silverstone. The IT head also confessed to pressuring Maddie Talbot to accuse Wolf of rape, placing the cameras in her condo and provide selected photos to the prosecution to ensure he'd be found guilty.

No, Wolf certainly wasn't disappointed. There will be trials; there will be convictions and his impromptu adventure in Colorado was nearly finished. The only task remaining was to visit James's and Sarah's families to tell them the good news in person, something he planned to do tomorrow.

What should be a moment of triumph and relief that this ongoing ordeal had come to a successful end, Wolf felt instead a vague sense of loss clouding his thoughts. He sighed.

"Your man in NYC, Chat, must be highly persuasive to convince Bobby Stevens to run to the DA and spill his guts," Wolf said, glancing at Colleen behind the wheel.

"You know Stevens?"

"Indirectly; I served him Manhattans on the rocks while tending bar during Blue Sky events, working on one of my novels."

Colleen shot him a droll look. "Worried I might press the passenger ejector button? You were working on Screw You, Suckers! featuring my dad."

"And Bellamy and half dozen more paragons of civil society." Wolf added.

She ignored his sarcasm, saying, "Chat's an excellent communicator of reality. He conveyed to Stevens the two options awaiting him: fall on his sword for his boss and reside in Ryker's for the next thirty-plus years or stick the sword into Bellamy's gut where it belongs in exchange for five years at the Federal Correctional Institution at Otisville, N.Y., considered the cushiest of the federal prisons."

"Nothing like the prospect of rubbing shoulders with killers for three decades to focus the mind," Wolf quipped.

"Knowing Bellamy, his army of lawyers will make sure he gets a cushy incarceration, too, along with half the years than the bastard deserves," Colleen said, her tone icy. "Unfortunately, his bad seed offspring will serve far less time too, if Centennial Forensics can't find any of Kerry's DNA in the Rape Kit samples."

"How much time if nothing shows up?" Wolf asked.

"Couple years; time served or even walk," she replied, disgusted.

"Walk? No way," Wolf said, incredulous at the idea that a jury would let a vile creature like Kerry off Scott free. "He planned the crime, committed rape, set up an innocent boy for the crime. And for sure he called his father knowing he'd call Henson to ambush you, or just as likely, called Henson himself. Kerry's the mirror image of his father: bad to the bone."

"As we speak the lawyers of all those perps are pressing down on Catelli to make deals in lieu of spending weeks and months prosecuting each and every prisoner," Colleen replied. "Even if the DA tells them all to buzz off, which she very well might, they'll all be out on bail by Wednesday and this will drag on for months. When it's over, some will get jail time, others time served or walk."

"You're making a solid argument for me to delay my retirement as national muckraker, Colleen," he said, feeling like smashing something; Kerry's face came to mind.

"Let it go," she replied. "You made the right decision. Better to walk away than be buried by it all … We're ten minutes from your hotel. Tell me about the new novels you're writing…"

Wolf shot her an inquisitive look. Is there nothing she doesn't know about what he's doing and where he's doing it?

"Colleen," he said, "you've had your people poking around in my life for some years now and must have a sizable dossier on me and my doings tucked away in that vault hidden in your inner sanctum. Why haven't you used whatever dirt and sleaze you found or sold it or allowed others to use it against me? I'm sure there are dozens of interested buyers looking for the juicy details of the big, bad Wolf."

Colleen kept her eyes on the road ahead, apparently ignoring his question as she had so many of his taunts, challenges and assertions throughout their two-month relationship. That is until he spotted a subtle twitch of her lips.

"Perhaps I'm not eager to start a war with the big, bad Wolf," she said. "I've seen you in action, remember?"

"Wolves are fierce fighters, especially if backed into a corner." He didn't intend for it to sound like a threat, but it must have sounded that way because she shot him a surprised look.

"Sorry, that didn't come out right," he said.

Nothing new about that, Wolf reflected. Feeling self-conscious and misspeaking while in Colleen's company had become a normal occurrence since his first visit.

They arrived at his hotel, Colleen stopping at the main entrance.

"I know the drill: *get out*," Wolf quipped.

Colleen shot him a droll glance, followed by a sincere laugh.

"It's scary how well you know me."

She laughed once more and drove off.

"Good bye, temporary partner," he said, standing alone on the sidewalk gazing after the departing vehicle, his sense of loss more acute than ever.

He stood there for a long moment lost in thought, musing about the last two months filled with whirlwind experiences, when he heard a pinging sound. He retrieved his phone and read the text message.

"Dinner at 7. Be ready."

At first, he thought it was a joke, but he had no intention of *not* being ready for a dinner date with his temporary partner. Better to be prepared and stood up than unprepared and wrong.

*　　　*　　　*　　　*

Five minutes before seven his phone dinged, the text informing him his dinner date was waiting for him in the lobby. He took a last look in the mirror, wishing he had a spiffier outfit for the occasion, sighed and made for the door.

Wolf didn't spot her when he entered the lobby. There was movement from his left and a woman rose from a seat and walked toward him.

"Wow," he said. It summarized Colleen perfectly.

She rewarded his compliment with a bright smile and sparkling eyes.

"Shall we?"

Wolf offered his arm and to his surprise she took it. Her car was waiting in the driveway and upon approaching it, handing him the keys, surprising him a second time.

"The GPS has our destination," she said, holding his hand as she lowered herself into the passenger seat. Seeing his questioning look, she added, "C Club."

It took him a second to recognize the reference. Centennial Country Club, commonly known as C Club by its fans and patrons.

"I must be someone special for my date to take me there."

"It's just dinner, Mr. special," she replied, grinning amiably at Wolf.

"But, I am special," he replied, giving her a humorous look.

"Yes, you are," she laughed, enouncing the words slowly as if speaking to a child.

"You are full of surprises," he said.

"Yes, I am," she replied, in the same, soothing tone as before. They both laughed.

The Centennial Country Club was nestled between the spurs of two mountains five miles west of Denver and though the sun had set an hour before, the sky was sufficiently bright to illuminate the valley, Wolf admiring the beauty of the setting. They were seated adjacent picture widows giving guests a panoramic view of the grounds and gardens. As beautiful as that view was, it did not compare to Wolf's dinner companion.

This date—*dinner* date—he reminded himself, was certainly most unexpected, though not inconsistent with the business Colleen was in, surprise being a highly effective means to throw a suspect or opponent off balance. Add a form-fitting dress, high heels, piercing intellect and abundant sensuality, she more than possessed all the elements required to detract or ensnare even the most impervious of males.

"What?" Wolf said, seeing her smile suddenly.

She lifted her glass and took a sip of wine. "What were you thinking about?"

Her tone and glint in her eyes suggested to Wolf that he was thinking about what would follow after dinner. Truth be told, he had been wondering where this evening would take him, though he squashed any possibility of it going somewhere sans clothing.

"Thinking how glad I am being here with you."

Colleen peered at him as though she was trying to ascertain some trick or falsehood in his simple reply. A smile returned upon her lips.

"Me too," she said. Wolf hoped she genuinely meant that. "Tell me about Tara Mason."

He gave her a summary of the character and plots of the first and several subsequent novels. When he finished, she asked about the chance of success in today's mystery story glut.

"Frankly, my dear, I don't give a damn about the novel's chance of success," he quipped, paraphrasing Rhett Butler from Gone with the Wind. "First and most important, I love to write the stories. That my publisher loves it, that I've got name recognition up the wazoo and that he's predicting a million-best seller, is all secondary."

"I'm looking forward to reading it when it's published," Colleen said.

"I'll send you a pre-sales proof." He didn't know why he said that.

She held his eyes. He could feel his pulse rising. Knowing her power of observation, he quickly continued or she'd spot, if she hadn't already, his growing arousal under her gaze.

"My publisher also suggested I consider writing adventure stories aimed at boys."

"Why for boys?" she asked.

"Have you seen the collection of fiction for boys?" he replied. "I'm an uncle of three young boys. The Adventures of Young Indian Jones and the Harry Potter series are among the best of contemporary stories around. The bulk published for young readers during the last two decades isn't fit for healthy young minds of either sex, though the girls have a larger selection of positive heroine-based novels from which to choose. The majority of male protagonists in stories mostly resemble eunuchs—emasculated wimps devoid of spirit, vision, courage, grit, goals and meaningful challenges to overcome: see Dick comfort his drug-addled single mom ... observe as Zeke joins the great collective, picking up trash, sorting it into politically correct receptacles!"

Colleen laughed. "I guess sometimes a good case can be made for burning books."

"Any ideas for male-oriented adventure stories?" he asked.

A sly expression formed on her face. "Dick decides his mother loves her drugs far more than him, that she'll never change, and leaves home. He runs into Zeke, convincing him there's more to life than picking up trash, and the pair hitchhike to Alaska where they pan for gold, strike it rich, invest in a drug-start up producing vaccinations to prevent people from becoming addicted to drugs."

Wolf nodded approvingly. "I think it has possibilities. How's it end?"

"The FDA refuses to approve the drug because it would deprive police departments significant income derived from the war on drugs. The boys move to India, manufacture millions of pills, make billions of dollars, most of which is used to raise a private army to defeat the hordes of assassins the drug lords around the world send to kill the boys and destroy their factory. But the boys successfully defeat the criminals thus saving millions of lives from death and ruin. The end."

"Love it," he replied. "You're a natural born storyteller." He held her gaze for a long moment. "Colleen—"

"Don't," she said, cutting him off. "It's just dinner."

"It's much more than just dinner," he countered, "and it's more than just a partnership, temporary or otherwise. I think of you as a friend and I hope you can come to see me as a friend one day, too. You're the most exceptional—unmarried—woman of my acquaintance and I've enjoyed getting to know you and working with you. Thank you for helping me, saving my butt and surprising me by asking me out on a date—*dinner* date."

She surprised him yet again when she reached over and placed her hand on his.

"Ditto."

*   *   *   *

Rolling down I-76 after visiting the Collins family in Ft. Morgan the following Tuesday, he was thinking about last night, the evening ending how he had expected: him driving back to his hotel and handing the car over to Colleen who drove herself home. Considering her totally unexpected dinner invitation it was not out of the realm of possibility that Colleen might have had other surprises in mind. Wolf knew this was nothing but wishful thinking, but pleasant enough to contemplate nonetheless as he drove to visit Sarah at Woodland Park.

The visit to the Collins's had gone as expected, James's sister Vicki feeling elated at the fact that James did not commit suicide, disgusted and angry at what Kerry and others had done, glad they would be punished for their crimes and relieved the ordeal of doubt was finally over. The meeting had been emotional one for all concerned, Wolf perhaps feeling the most relieved, having managed to uncover the truth behind James's death as he had promised he would.

His visit to Sarah and her parents was déjà vu; and though less overtly emotional, just as poignant. The news that Jenifer Park, Sarah's roommate and friend drugged James, had sex with him in a car, handed over his semen to Karla, left him alone in the car for another to drive him to that dump and set him up for her rape appeared to affect her deeply. After a long moment of reflection, she shook her head and issued a snort.

"I roomed with Jennifer for three years and I got to know her pretty well—or so I thought," Sarah said. "During our occasional heart-to-hearts, she'd confess feeling like an outsider growing up; always rejected by the 'in crowd', never invited to parties and events; I could tell it ate her up. She acted like a friend, but I sensed she was jealous of anyone who was really together; you know, clear sense of purpose, independent, didn't care what others thought. When she bitched about Kerry and other jerks like him—which was often—I always felt that was an act, too. I know for a fact she kept trying to hook up with him or his crew, but no dice. It was pathetic, really. She tried to hook up with James, but he liked me and wasn't interested. Had we'd been a couple, I would have needed to tell her to back off, but I wasn't into James. Jennifer was messed up, but I'd never suspected her doing anything that evil."

"Greed, love, envy, revenge," Wolf said. "All classic motives for stepping across the line. So is self-hatred. I'm very sorry you were caught up in Jennifer's malignant view of life, Sarah. I hope my news brings you a sense of closure."

"It does, Mr. Wolf. I don't know how to thank you for all you've done."

"The best way you can thank me is to move on with your life," he replied. "Don't allow circumstances to trap you in the past and what cannot be undone."

She nodded and sighed. "I'm not sure what to do next. I do know I'm not going back to Overland. I've been working in town part time, but that's just temporary."

"Sometimes the best way to leave the past behind is to leave," Wolf said. "Go find a job in another state or apply to another college far away." He could tell from Sarah's face she was conflicted. A strong believer in the adage that actions speak louder than words, he added, "Come to Virginia and work for CIR. We need smart, focused people; individuals who are creative, who take initiative. Someone just like you, Sarah."

"I... don't have a degree," she replied, surprised.

"Neither do I." Wolf confessed. "People assume I graduated, but I quit after my junior year. Had better things to do with my time. More to the point, we hire individuals, not degrees. Be honest, Sarah: of all the students at Overland you have more than a casual acquaintance with, how many would you hire to work for your company, if you had one, once they got their degree?"

A reluctant smile appeared. "Not too many."

"Would you hire yourself?" He challenged.

Her smile vanished, but she held his eyes. "Yes."

"Congratulations," Wolf said. He handed her a business card. "Expect a call from our human resource manager before the end of the day. Start gathering your things and begin saying your goodbyes; I'll expect you in Virginia by the weekend."

Sarah appeared dazed by the speed of this unexpected happening, but Wolf knew from experience that sometimes the best way to move one out of a rut was to grab them by the scruff and hustle them along a new path.

He grinned at her. "Any questions?"

Tears filled her eyes and she blinked several times. She hugged Wolf and kissed him on the cheek.

"Thank you, Mr. Wolf. I knew if anyone could find out what happened to James, it was you ... I don't have a clue what work I'll be doing at CIR, but I promise I won't disappoint you."

"I know you won't."

She insisted he stay for lunch, presenting Wolf with a tasty BLT club sandwich with slices of avocado and a chipotle sauce drizzled throughout. It was so delicious, he teased her, saying he might place her into CIR's kitchen where she could develop her talent for creating tasty sandwiches.

By two, Wolf was on the road to Colorado Springs with hours to kill before his flight back to Washington, DC later that evening. Normally he'd be rolling down the road well north of the speed limit, but this being perhaps his last visit to Colorado for the foreseeable future having completed his last task of the Lewis-Collins investigation, he was cruising along at a moderate pace, windows lowered, enjoying the view.

He thought about his plans once back in Tysons Corner, completing his second Tara Mason novel being top of his list. CIR business would occupy a big chunk of his time until recalling he had resigned from his leadership position. He'd still be involved, of course, but his role would be less hands-on and more consulting. He'd have much more time to do whatever he wanted. Now all he had to do was think about what he wanted.

Route 67 from Woodland Park to Colorado Springs is twenty miles of easy downhill driving with plenty of straight road, few tight curves and even less dangerous drop-offs. At the moment, he was driving through a section with more curves and checking his review mirror, he spotted a truck some distance back. The vehicle kept its distance, Wolf's figuring his speed suited the truck's driver, too.

Entering a straightened section of road some miles later, the truck sped up and moved into the oncoming lane to pass. Experiencing a flash of déjà vu, Wolf glanced at the vehicle just as it swerved toward him. Wolf hit the brakes and jerked the wheel to the right, the truck barely missing his front bumper and speed away.

"Oh, hell no!" Wolf cried, smashing his foot on the accelerator, the car roaring forward, tires loudly squealing in protest.

Within seconds, Wolf was upon the fleeing truck, its power and speed no match for his rented BMW sedan. He rammed the truck from behind, pressing down on the accelerator, pushing it to ever higher speed. The truck's brake lights glowed brightly as the driver attempted to slow down causing its rear wheels to lock up, the smell of burning rubber seeping into Wolf's car.

Coming to his senses, Wolf lifted his foot off the gas pedal and braked. As his bumper disengaged from the truck, the vehicle's rear end skidded right, then veered to the left as its driver assumingly attempted to correct for the skid. Wolf braked harder to put distance between himself and the truck as it veered off the roadway and down the embankment, enveloped in a cloud of dust, coming to a sudden halt when it struck a stand of young Aspen trees.

Wolf cut across the oncoming lane, stopped the car on the shoulder and got out, pistol in hand. He cautiously approached the truck, his weapon aimed at the cabin determined to lay down deadly fire at whomever had attempted to kill him a second time while driving. Reaching the truck, he spotted a figure through the window struggling to undue the seatbelt.

"Show me your hands!" Wolf shouted, opening the door. "Hands on the wheel or I will shoot you! Do it now!"

The driver's hands came up slowly and rested on top of the steering wheel.

"Get out—slowly," he ordered, backing away from the vehicle.

The driver stepped out and faced Wolf. It was then he saw it was woman, not a man as he had assumed, dressed as she was in overalls and a Denver Rockies baseball cap on her head. He did not recognize her.

"Who are you?" She stared silently at the ground. "You nearly killed me the first time when you ran me off the road and if you've been keeping up with the news, it's been a trying two months for me. I'm losing patience real fast and I'm going to ask you one more time. Fail to answer or jerk me around I will shoot you in the knee as a start." Wolf pointed the pistol toward a knee.

"You wouldn't dare!" she cried.

"One...two...."

"Alright! ... Sharon Clarkson."

"Clarkson..." Wolf said, looking thoughtful. "Clarkson, as in Mitch Clarkson, the former President of Overland College who embezzled a tidy sum during his term?" She peered at him with such hatred he couldn't help but adding, "Sorry for interrupting you and your hubby's plans to live it up on whatever tropical island you had intended to retire to with your ill-gotten gains."

"You can't prove that I ran you off the road then, or today for that matter," she sneered.

"Sorry to inform you, but high-end rentals have dashboard cameras, so I've got you on vehicular assault," Wolf replied. "And now that I recall, that's the same truck you used back in March when you ran me off the road a few miles west of our present location."

"You're lying just like your books are full of lies, you bastard," she ejaculated. "I wasn't driving a truck and you should have died ... I was you, I'd leave before the cops come by and I tell them you ran *me* off the road and that you threatened to shoot me for no reason."

"You are a piece of work, Ms. Clarkson," Wolf replied. "You and Mr. Clarkson make a perfect pair of bookends between which is stacked volumes filled with lies, theft, attempted murder and of course the whining and bitching about how your misfortunes are all someone else's fault ... well I have news for you: the police *are* on their way and when they get here I will hand over the recording I've made of our discussion ... now get on the ground with the rest of the vermin!"

She must have seen something in Wolf's expression because she lowered herself on the ground without protest. Peering at her, he reflected on the last five minutes, shocked to discover that he would have shot her without giving it a second thought had she produced a gun instead of placing her hands on the steering wheel of the truck.

Something had definitely changed. Or maybe it was always there, lying hidden like a coiled snake until getting stepped on once too often. One thing had become crystal clear to Grayson Wolf: though he had announced his retirement from hunting and exposing society's upper crust malefactors, he could never escape from the consequences of the path he had forged over the years.

He grinned, recalling Aristotle maxim, that one can choose to evade reality but not the consequences of reality. Not until this very moment had it occurred to him that the philosopher's admonition referred not only to those making poor or evil choices.

"Check your premises...one or more might be wrong," he said, laughing at being the butt of life's cosmic joke.

The End

Lone Wolf

ABOUT THE AUTHOR

They seek him here, they seek him there,
Desperately seeking Jack N Kolbe everywhere;

Words that flow from fingertips, so pure,
Provide fans near and far their desperate cure;

Heads shake, stomachs growl, noggins they do ache;
Warm days, hotter nights: there be no mistake.

Wishes granted, prose so rare, so deep,
Greedily consumed; no time for overrated sleep;

The fix is quick; require, it does, single fingertip,
Prose unfolding line and page of radiant manuscript.

Look they high, look they low,
None discerning where he does go;

Jack N Kolbe contentedly basking
In published afterglow.

Made in the USA
Columbia, SC
12 January 2018